THE HEIR THAT NEVER WAS

MAGICARIUMS SCRIPTÆ

***

THE HEIR THAT NEVER WAS

A boy lost to memory. A world that remembers what he cannot.

A Novel by
R. PIACENTINI

First Edition

MAGICARIUMS PRESS

For permissions or inquiries, contact:
Magicariums Press
Email: press@magicariums..com
Website: www.magicariums.com

First Edition, 2026

Typography and design by R. Piacentini
Published by Magicariums Press
An imprint of Piacent Venture Studios

ISBN: 979-8-9936952-1-1

Imaginatio ad Veritatem.
(Imagination toward Truth)

Part I

Scroll of Beginnings

"In the beginning, there were two lands:
One steeped in magic, the other untouched by it.
For thousands of years, they thrived in unity,
guided by trust and the wisdom of shared dreams.

But when betrayal took root
and vengeance overshadowed love,
the lands were torn apart.

And they shall remain divided for a thousand years,
Until the one born of both realms,
bearing the legacy of common roots,
rises to restore the ancient bond."

—Magicariums Scriptae, Verse III

Chapter One

"The Boy at the Edge of the Mist"

He stood where the road forgot its own name; a narrow ribbon of dirt that left the last house, crossed a field of sleeping thistles, and simply… gave up. He shifted his weight from one boot to the other, scuffing at the dirt the way boys do when they pretend not to be waiting for anyone. The leather was cracked, too small for his growing feet, and the left lace never stayed tied no matter how many times Ava knotted it.

Beyond that surrender, the world dissolved into a pale, breathing veil. The villagers in the small French town of Corbeil-Essonnes called it morning fog. Leonarth had never believed them.

South of Paris, where the Seine meets the Essonne, Corbeil-Essonnes behaved itself. Mills turned. Markets opened on time. Even the pigeons kept a schedule. However, the mist here didn't follow a program, and wasn't weather either. It had weight.

It pooled low in the hollows and lifted in slow, careful folds, as if the earth itself were exhaling something it had tried too long to hold. It swirled around his boots and licked the hems of his trousers, cool, deliberate, the way a cat tests a door before slipping in. Somewhere inside that white, a bell tolled once—not time, but distance. A measure of how far he was from whatever had the voice to ring it.

He closed his eyes.

The sound slid through him the way certain names do when they are spoken by the right person—not to the ears, but to the spine. It wasn't the bell in town; that one was a bronze clamor tacked to the belfry of Saint-Spire Abbey, all cheerful duty and rusty pride. This was older. Cleaner. It had no rust.

He opened his eyes again and checked the line he'd drawn with the heel of his boot: a shallow crescent in the dirt, a boundary that was not quite a circle. The mark he never stepped over. He wasn't sure who had taught him to draw it, only that he'd been drawing it for years. The curve faced the mist like a cupped hand.

"Coward," he muttered.

Then, after a pause, with the air of someone rehearsing excuses: "Just careful."

He listened.

Cornstalks ticked against one another out in the fields, drying toward winter. A cart creaked two roads away, its iron-hooped wheel humming a complaint. Somewhere behind him, a child yelled the name of a friend and received no answer, the game paused on the knifeedge between panic and triumph. The world was loud with little lives. The mist was not.

He reached into his pocket and found the thing he always carried but never confessed to anyone: a piece of glass so old it had learned to curve. Sea glass, someone might have called it, though there was no sea for hours, even if you had a ride and permission. It was milky and green-blooded, smoothed into a tear by patient hands he did not remember. When he held it to the sun, it turned the world into drowned gardens.

It kept warmth longer than it should—pocket-warm even when the morning bit—and when he tilted it, a faint, dry chime touched the inside of his ear, a single note that felt remembered rather than heard.

He held it up now. The mist bent inside it.

On some mornings, looking through that softened shard made the veil thin; it would ripple, and shadows would take the suggestion of limbs. On others, nothing happened, and he felt like a boy pretending to conjure, which was worse than being simply a boy. Today, something did happen. The breath in front of him gathered itself and drew back, as if the glass had reminded it of a shape it once wore.

A path appeared—not a clear one, but a suggestion of darker gray inside the pale. He tried to tell himself it was the breeze.

Then someone yelled at him, yanking him back to reality, "Leonarth!"

He flinched. Not because the voice was sharp, but because it was careful. People shouted when they were angry or when they loved you without shame. This voice was neither. It was the voice people used when they were approaching the edge of a story and did not wish to spook the ending.

He turned. Ava stood where the thistles began; her novice robes were pinned neat, her hair caught up tight under a kerchief. She could have been anyone's guardian. She was his—or at least the woman who had kept him fed, guided, and told him which men to avoid and which days to keep his head down whenever threats or trouble drifted in from the road. She had never told him whether he had her eyes, or anyone's for that matter.

"You promised," she said.

He did not ask which promise. There were multiple. To stay within the hedgerow. To avoid the field where the earth had sunk after heavy rain, and never quite forgiven the river for leaving. To attend his lessons when the Abbey bell called.

"I'm not in it," he said, half turning back to the veil. "I'm only—"

"Looking," she finished for him. "You have been 'only looking' since you had knees."

He pocketed the glass. "What if there's a road in there?"

"There are roads everywhere," she said. "That's what a town means. Roads that go forward and roads that go back. Roads that bring visitors who buy, and roads that bring those who don't pay. The only road I concern myself with is the one that brings you back within the Abbey walls when the bell strikes."

He nodded. He was thirteen and change; nodding was the safest way to move through the world.

Ava studied the dirt where his heel had scored its little moon. She didn't step closer. "Come away," she said. "The festival is in a couple of days. We cannot invite whispers because a boy decided to gamble with fog."

"It's only fog," he said, to see what would happen.

"It's memory," she replied. Then, after a pause she hadn't planned: "And not always yours."

He looked at her. The wind lifted the edges of her kerchief. He had heard her say a thousand practical things—how to keep his head lowered in prayer through the long hours; how to keep a man civil by not looking at him when he was trying to be looked at; how to tell real honey from boiled sugar. He had never heard her say this.

"What do you mean?"

She shook her head as if that might loosen an answer, then chose honesty instead. "I mean only that there are places where the world keeps what it has seen, and it does not always care whether the living are improved by it."

He almost said, I don't remember anything worth keeping. He did not say it, because it would have sounded like a complaint and because it wasn't true. He remembered plenty: the bells of Saint-Spire that rattled the Abbey rafters, the back-of-the-throat ache of smoke from incense during long vigils, the way Ava's wrists went red when she scalded them, and she pretended not to notice. He remembered a quiet gray cat that drifted through the cloister as if it had always known the way—appearing and disappearing as though it belonged to no one, yet somehow always finding him. He remembered a lullaby that belonged to no one. He remembered a name that he did not say out loud because it was not certain it belonged to him.

"Leave it," Ava said again. "The mist will still be here when you have washed, and you have school to attend."

He did not step over the crescent he had drawn. He backed away from it, as if the mark were a bead of light stretched thin and he did not wish to snap it.

He turned at last and began to follow Ava back toward the Abbey. From here, he could see the rooftops of the city—the charm was the quiet kind—undramatic, but enduring. Rows of ochre-stoned houses leaned toward one another as if sharing secrets over narrow lanes. The bell tower of Saint-Spire Abbey chimed with a voice older than the town's oldest baker, echoing across tiled rooftops and washing lines. Sundays brought the smell of brioche and incense; Tuesdays, the murmur of market gossip in three languages. Most days, the town moved in rhythm with the river and its rituals.

Children were taught to count on the swings of the town's ancient iron gate. Teens marked their growth against the ivy that climbed the eastern Abbey wall. There was a story for every crack in the cobblestones, and no one quite agreed on which stories were true.

Some whispered that the Abbey had once housed a prince in hiding. Others claimed its wine cellar held tunnels carved during wars that no longer appeared in textbooks. And once a year, when winter fog crept too early and stayed too long, old women would murmur that the town "remembered more than it let on." Most brushed such things off with a shrug. Still, no one walked alone past the bell tower after midnight.

Leonarth raised his head, and saw the Abbey walls looming larger with every step, rising like a tide of stone as he trailed after Ava. He had grown up within those walls, sometimes feeling the weight of both history and memory pressing in, even as he tried to press back. And lately, that same mist, the one he had just left curling at the field's edge, seemed to linger longer than it should—not just in the air, but in his thoughts, in dreams he couldn't quite recall, and in the way the wind sometimes whispered his name when no one was around.

They walked in silence, and when they finally stepped beneath the Abbey's archways, the dream from last night rushed back and pressed against his ribs: water, light, the sensation of falling upward, and always the same voice—not loud, not clear, only present, humming like a thread through breath.

Sometimes, in that voice, he thought he felt the shape of a hand—gentle, deliberate, as if placing something into his palm. He always woke before he could see the giver's face. The ache it left behind was heavier than the dream itself.

For an instant, he thought about telling it to Ava, but he never remembered the words, only the ache they left behind, like a name he was supposed to carry. It stayed now, sharper than usual, refusing to fade as the morning wore on.

Across the cloister garden, half-shrouded by the last drift of mist, he saw Sister Mabelle. She stood under the far archway, motionless, her hands tucked into her sleeves. She wasn't looking at him directly—more at the space around him, as if watching something just behind his shoulder. Her face was unreadable, neither stern nor soft, only still. He felt suddenly like he'd wandered into a room he wasn't supposed to see.

She didn't speak. Didn't wave. Just remained there a moment longer than necessary, then turned and disappeared into the inner corridor, her robes brushing the stone in a hush.

He wanted to call out to her—just to say something ordinary. Ask about breakfast. Remind her that his math workbook was missing again. Anything that would make her turn back. But his voice stayed tucked behind his teeth, like it knew better.

Something about her stillness unsettled him. It reminded him of nights when he'd wake and find her standing by the dormitory window, not moving, as if listening for something far away. When he asked her about it once, she only smiled and said the stars liked to whisper old stories. He hadn't understood, but the way she'd said it made him think the stories weren't meant for him.

He wondered, suddenly, back to the fog, and if it could keep secrets. If maybe it was storing them in the hollows of the field or gardens of the Abbey, waiting for the right morning to let them go.

Ava stopped so suddenly he almost struck her back. He stared after her, heart ticking a little too loudly in his chest. She'd raised him, more than anyone else. Since he was five. She had been constant, kind—distant in ways he didn't fully understand. But this morning, their walk back to the Abbey in silence felt heavier. Not angry. Just... full. Like she carried too much and didn't know where to put it.

He pressed his thumb into the edge of the glass shard in his pocket and felt the warmth it collected from being so close to his body. It comforted him, unusually and familiarly at the same time. The dream came back to his mind, but like most days it was already gone. But its feeling—that strange, invisible yearning—remained.

Ava stared back. "You always stare like that," she muttered.

Leonarth blinked. "Like what?"

"Like you're waiting for something that forgot you."

He raised and lowered his shoulders and did not answer. He wanted to tell her about the bell in the mist that had no rust. He wanted to ask if she had ever heard it, if anyone in town had, and whether they were all ignoring it out of practicality, the way people ignore the fact that winter eventually arrives. He wanted to ask her why she had said the word memory the way someone names a ghost without inviting it to sit.

He said none of that.

The Abbey's looming stone walls and the ever-present silence of its halls left too much room for questions, too little for answers. He had no memories of being brought here at five—only the afterimage of Ava's hand in his, and the rumor of an unreadable letter from the Archbishop of England that had opened every door without explanation. These fragments of a beginning haunted him.

Ava's voice sounded sharper this time. "Enough fog for today," she said, still not meeting his eye. "You've wandered and stared at me long enough without a purpose. Let's change that. You're late for class, and Sister Mabelle has probably noticed already. Quickly now—no detours."

He thought of arguing and decided to keep his breath.

His mind moved on to what he'd tell Sister Mabelle for being late a third time this week.

***

The world outside the Abbey had already begun to stir.

The Winter Lights Festival, the year's most cherished tradition, was beginning to be prepared in earnest, drawing tourists and villagers alike.

But beneath its cheerful bustle and vibrant colors, few remembered its ancient origins. Long ago, the Winter Lights Festival was not just a seasonal gathering, but a sacred observance—rooted, some said, in rites meant to hold the town steady as the days grew thin. As centuries passed, the true meaning faded into folklore, replaced by games and markets. Yet, the most ancient texts—hidden in a vault beneath the Abbey few even knew existed—spoke of forgotten rites and mystical signs that once accompanied the festival.

This year, perhaps unknowingly, the air itself felt heavier—charged, as if something long dormant had begun to wake. The signs, barely perceptible to most, whispered from the corners of the festival preparations: an odd chill in the breeze, flickers of movement at the edge of vision, echoes that seemed out of place. For those attuned to the town's older rhythms, or inclined to believe in the Abbey's forgotten rites, it was as if the festival's original spirit was pushing to be remembered. Even Father Maurice, preoccupied as he was, had paused longer than usual at the door of his study, where a locked drawer waited in silence—its key long hidden, its contents better left unremembered. Whatever had once been concealed might not remain so for long, Father Maurice thought, lingering at the threshold of his study.

The door key turned with its usual stubborn resistance, and the door creaked open, releasing a sigh of air tinged with dust and old parchment. The study smelled of cedar, candle soot, and something else harder to place—like rain on warm stone. Maurice hesitated before stepping inside. He seldom stayed here longer than necessary these days.

The room wasn't large. Not cluttered—every object had its place. An old globe rested beside a stack of aging ecclesiastical ledgers. The ink on their spines had faded to near illegibility, but Maurice could name each one from memory. The narrow windows let in slats of cold light, casting long shadows across the stone floor like ribs.

On the far wall hung a faded portrait of a prior abbess, her gaze severe and knowing. Maurice avoided it reflexively, eyes instead falling on a closed drawer beneath his desk. The key for it was no longer on his ring. He had hidden it years ago—not to forget, but to postpone.

Something inside him tightened. He brushed a hand over the smooth wooden surface, feeling the faint notch beneath his fingertips where the keyhole lay.

The drawer did not call to him. It waited. Patient. Silent. But not gone.

He turned away before the stillness could speak louder.

The dust-laced air stirred a whisper of memory, as if the Abbey itself was trying to remind him of something long buried. He adjusted his collar, brushed a hand against the worn wooden doorframe, and wondered—not for the first time—whether these festivals masked more than they revealed.

***

In the days that followed, preparations gathered pace, and a vibrant chaos swept through Corbeil-Essonnes. The narrow streets buzzed with anticipation, and even the most stoic townspeople couldn't help but get swept up in the rising excitement. Though it disrupted the usual quiet rhythm of the town, the energy was welcomed. For many, it was a break from the monotony; for others, it was a rare chance to shine, to showcase what made their craft or produce unique. Beneath the cheerful disorder, however, subtler disturbances seemed to ripple, unnoticed, through the preparations.

The festival was colorful, a blend of old traditions and new amusements—farmers with their finest produce, artisans with their carefully crafted goods, children darting under lanterns as if the light itself were a game.

The town came alive, all of it funneled through the Abbey and Father Maurice—who set the schedules, approved placements, and decided which vendors earned the best streets.

At the square's center, Madame Carenne argued about booth placement, her shawl snapping like a banner in the cold air.

Nearby, two little girls twirled beneath a string of glass lanterns being tested for the opening night procession. One paused, pointing at the base of a lamppost where frost had formed a curious spiral.

"It looks like Papa's old compass," she whispered to her friend.

The other girl shrugged. "Maybe it's a spell."

They giggled and darted off, unaware that the spiral would vanish before the hour ended, leaving only damp stone behind.

Whispers spread quickly—posters smudging, bonfire space feeling 'off'—the kind of small omens townsfolk laughed about, but still carried home in silence.

None of it disrupted the festival. Not really. But beneath every vendor's stall, every ribbon-laced garland, something else coiled—a tension unspoken, a thread between worlds. And like the thread in Leonarth's dream, it hummed just below the noise.

The townspeople often recalled how, just last autumn, the river had risen without warning, cutting off entire neighborhoods from aid. The official reports called it a freak natural occurrence, but even then, whispers circulated—had it truly been weather, or something else stirring beneath the surface of the Seine? Father Maurice had noticed the signs before anyone else: subtle tremors in the ground, unusual pull in the current, a strange resonance in the air during evening prayer. Whether it was intuition, deep knowledge, or something more, no one could say.

He had acted swiftly, mobilizing volunteers and transforming the Abbey into a refuge before emergency services could respond. The dining hall, scented with soup and old wax, filled with frightened children and whispered prayers. Maurice never spoke of how he knew, brushing off questions with his usual humor. But Leonarth, then only twelve, remembered how the priest had stood silently at the river's edge that night, staring into the water long after the danger had passed, as if listening to something only he could hear.

He had returned alone, long after the townspeople had retreated and the last of the frightened families were safe within the Abbey. The rain had slowed to a cold mist, clinging to his coat and silvering the grass like frost. The Seine pulsed below, swollen and dark, its surface an unbroken mirror of the starless sky.

Maurice stood on the embankment, unmoving. His boots sank into the mud with a slow, steady weight. He was not praying. Not thinking. Only listening.

The river didn't roar. It murmured. Beneath the ordinary sounds of shifting current and sodden reeds, there was something else—a hum, like breath drawn through a long corridor. It wasn't the first time he'd heard it. But this night, it felt closer. Hungrier.

Somewhere far behind him, the Abbey bells rang twice—soft, echoing, carried by the wind. And just for a moment, the entire town seemed to pause. No footsteps. No voices. No birds. Only the river.

Then came the threads.

They shimmered faintly above the surface—thin strands of light, silvery and trembling, as if spun from the river's own breath. They weaved together without pattern, forming arcs that dissolved before they could shape symbols. Maurice didn't move. Didn't blink. The world seemed to pull inward, to this one quiet place where water and memory met.

He felt something stir behind his ribs. A reflex. A word he had forgotten how to speak. His lips parted—but he said nothing.

It was too dangerous. Too soon. And besides, the Veil still held.

He swallowed the breath and stepped back, breaking the moment like a page torn from a sacred text. The river settled. The strands vanished. The hum faded.

When he finally turned, the Abbey windows shone like distant stars. In one of them, a boy stood watching—small, barely more than a silhouette, his hand pressed to the glass. Maurice met his gaze across the distance, and in that second, he saw a question in the child's eyes that echoed the one in his own.

He had seen that look before—in a mirror, in another lifetime. The same question, rippling through time. Who decides what we inherit? And what do we become when no one tells us who we were? Who are we, really?

The answer, whatever it was, would not come that night. But it had stirred. And so had the river.

The flood receded, but the questions remained—whether it had been a freak occurrence or the first ripple of something greater. In the meantime, Maurice's influence grew—not just as a priest, but as a quiet guardian of mysteries no one else dared name. Yet time, as it does, began to gather new layers over the wound—layers of duty, habit, and the quiet pretense of peace.

He could almost believe the calm that followed had been his own doing. It had been more than a decade since he left his beloved Liverpool—at least, that was the story he allowed to settle—and taken up what he believed would be a quieter post in Corbeil-Essonnes, a place where he might shepherd the lives of its modest population in peace. But Corbeil had other plans. The church, being the largest and most respected establishment in town, became an unofficial town hall, and Maurice found himself at the center of everything—from festival planning to mediating disputes, from market licenses to school board debates. The recent flood had only deepened his role. That uncanny night left a mark not just on the town, but on him. Since then, people didn't just look to him for blessings; they watched him with a quiet reverence, as if he carried some secret understanding. Maurice never addressed the rumors that swirled around that night, but sometimes, alone in the Abbey, he wondered whether what stirred in the river had awakened something in him, too.

He was in his late 60s, yet there was a youthful warmth in his demeanor that belied his age. His wavy, shoulder-brushing hair—a touch unruly for priestly decorum—had mostly surrendered to gray, though remnants of its original light brown hue still clung to the ends. With a long face, a high forehead, and kind, deep-set eyes that conveyed sincerity more than authority, he had the look of someone who belonged in both pulpits and quiet conversations over tea. His presence was disarming—trusted instinctively by children and elders.

Despite his gentle charisma and the respect he commanded, Maurice remained humble and private, never once acknowledging how constantly the town leaned on him. His soft English accent carried with it not authority, but approachability, and his affable humor softened even the sternest town elders.

This blend of charm and humility lent him an aura uncommon in clerical circles—less like a spiritual superior and more like a trusted mentor or village sage. It was no surprise that townsfolk came to him for guidance on all manner of things, sacred and secular alike.

He wandered the Abbey grounds without a clear purpose, letting routine guide his steps. By the time midday approached, Father Maurice felt the weight of the day bearing down on him. The preparations for the 53rd edition of the Winter Lights Festival had only just begun, yet his energy was already waning—a testament to the sheer scale of coordination he now shouldered.

Unlike his early days in Corbeil-Essonnes, when he could fade into the calm of chapel rituals, today he was the fulcrum of an entire town's celebration. And there were still days of chaos ahead. So many things needed to fall into place that the work already felt like more than one man should shoulder.

"You'd think after all these years I'd stop being surprised by the madness," Maurice muttered to himself, half amused, half exasperated.

And as if he didn't already have enough to juggle, the Archbishop of England's office was due to call before the hour was out—a detail he should've remembered five minutes earlier.

He gathered his belongings and set off through the quiet, echoing hallways of the Abbey toward his private study, cutting through the main chapel as the quickest route, the familiar rhythm of festival chaos settling around him like an old coat.

The Abbey was centuries old, its stones bearing silent witness to the passage of time, war, and fire. As Father Maurice passed through its echoing halls, he couldn't help but marvel—not just at its survival, but at its quiet grandeur. It had been damaged and rebuilt more than once, yet its vaulted ceilings still soared with solemn grace, the stained glass still painted colored light across the stone floors, and the great pipe organ still loomed like a slumbering guardian in the choir loft. Everything here had aged, but nothing had faded. The Abbey had endured, just as he had, though he often wondered which of them carried the heavier weight of history.

As he moved through the main mass room, Father Maurice paused to stretch his back, the ache a familiar echo of too many long days and not enough rest. The cool hush of the Abbey wrapped around him like a cloak, quieting the buzz of the morning's demands.

As he looked up instinctively—part ritual, part respite—his breath caught slightly. The vaulted ceilings had always offered comfort, their symmetry and grandeur grounding his thoughts. But today, something caught his eye.

Amid the familiar stonework, he spotted five carved stars embedded at the very center of the ceiling. They were delicate, nearly camouflaged by the ornate carvings—a level of subtlety that even Father Maurice, after decades in this Abbey, had never noticed. Most visitors would likely pass beneath them unaware, their quiet gleam lost in the dappled light streaming through stained glass. But now, they shimmered with quiet insistence, pulling his gaze upward—not to stir wonder, but to awaken something long held at bay.

At the center of the design lay the Iron star, with the other four spaced evenly around it, forming a perfect celestial wheel. Their arrangement wasn't random; it whispered intention. Each star bore distinct iconography, elegant and precise, its patterns etched as if by a hand that had once served something older than the Abbey itself.

The uppermost star burned with vertical strokes of ember-flecked stone, so vivid that Maurice felt warmth from the illusion of fire. To the right, the second star bore horizontal bands of pale, wind-scoured stone—lines that seemed to shift like air set in motion. To the left, the third star shimmered with green-blue minerals, droplets suspended in stone, casting the impression of falling water held in stasis. Beneath them, the fourth star lay dark—dense earthstone veined in muted gray, its glyphs dormant in shadow.

But it was the central star itself that held him. Its stone carried a muted iron glow, the surface crossed by slender runic scars that caught the light in broken fragments. The marks were no imperfections—they were inscriptions, laid into the stone by a deliberate, ancient hand. Maurice narrowed his eyes, and this time the recognition did not just surface—it struck.

Fire. Air. Water. Soil. And at the center—iron. Not allegory. Not forgotten ritual. Something real.

Maurice exhaled slowly. These weren't echoes. They were signals. Intentional. Placed with purpose. And for some reason—after decades hidden—they had chosen now to return.

He stepped back, spine taut, eyes scanning the shadows of the ceiling. Not in fear. In vigilance. These glyphs had been silent for generations. Their reappearance couldn't be accidental. Something had shifted—whether in the world or in himself, he couldn't yet say.

He lowered his gaze. Not in resignation—but to shield himself from what stirred inside. Whatever had marked this ceiling had not forgotten.

And neither had he.

He turned to leave, but paused once more. From afar, the markings still pulsed in his vision—were they decay, or design? He shifted left, aligning himself beneath the vaulted ceiling's apex. Ten, maybe fifteen meters above, the stars seemed to observe him in return. He leaned in, squinting—eyes that once devoured marginalia with ease, now challenged by time and distance. He took another step.

His boot struck brass. A candelabra scraped the stone with a metallic shriek, jolting him back to the present. The mystery dissolved for a moment as reality reasserted itself, sharp and graceless.

The sense of awakening did not fade. But neither did he speak the glyphs aloud. Not here. Not yet. That would risk more than he was prepared to explain.

He lingered, hand resting on the wall beside him. The stone was cool, but not impassive—it felt as if it held a pulse of its own, slow and ancient. For years, this Abbey had been a sanctuary, a duty, a routine. But now, the familiar felt unstable. The silence, too aware. The light, too sharp.

Had the symbols always been there, hidden by dust and inattention? Or had they truly just... arrived?

And if they had—why now?

Maurice swallowed, throat suddenly dry. He could not shake the feeling that something had crossed a line. Not an event. Not a person. A shift. Something just beyond the veil of reason, reaching in.

And if it had returned—whatever it was—it would not come quietly. He dragged his gaze from the ceiling and remembered, with a small jolt of irritation, the waiting Archbishop and the ticking clock.

With a resigned sigh, he broke into a hurried jog toward his study. It wasn't a graceful sight: in one hand he clutched a chaotic bundle of rolled schematics—tent and podium layouts for the festival—and in the other, a precariously balanced lunch wrapped in brown paper alongside his worn Bible. Juggling everything with the awkward determination of a man both late and unwilling to admit it, he darted past the Abbey library.

The space there felt colder, quieter than he remembered, as if the Abbey itself had held its breath. Then, from the shadows, a hand closed around his arm. The hallway froze. The silence thickened. Someone—or perhaps something—had been waiting.

He hadn't heard footsteps. That's what unnerved him most. Not fear. Not quite. But something else clawed at the edge of his thoughts—like the glyphs above the altar, like the river that had once whispered his name. Some part of him had always known this moment would come. He just didn't know if he was ready to remember what it meant.

The hum returned, faint as breath on glass, thrumming through the hand still locked around his arm.

Chapter Two

"Veritas Claritas"

The morning light shimmered through the translucent dome high above the Grand Citadel of Virelia, its spires crowned with banners that danced on a gentle breeze—a vision of unity and strength at the heart of Magicia. They built the Hall of Accord atop the ruins of the Hall of Unity. Siroth had approved the plans himself. It was better this way—names could lie, but structures could be corrected. Yet sometimes, when the banners stirred too softly or the marble groaned with age, he heard the old name echo in his mind.

In the throne room, Chancellor Siroth was alone.

The windows were tall and stained with scenes of valor, loyalty, and sacrifice. They cast warm hues across the marble floor, illuminating the chamber with soft, reverent tones. Still, the artistry pleased him. His likeness—tall, regal, hand raised in benediction—was immortalized in four of the panes. One depicted his first speech: a young man, arms outstretched before a sea of faces, promising to heal a broken realm.

He stood now, tracing the outline of the speech etched in silver script upon a monolithic slab behind the throne. His voice was quiet, reverent, as he recited from memory:

"We were divided. Our people, torn by envy, by weakness disguised as compassion. But I see you. I see the strength in your bones, the truth in your silence, the fire in your eyes. Magicia will rise again. Not as a fractured chorus of kings and queens, but as one—a single anthem, a single will."

His hand lingered on the final line. He closed his eyes.

Did he mean it then? Did he believe it still?

He turned, slowly, his robes whispering like breath through ash. The room was empty but for a pair of guards—motionless, faces hidden by helm and mask.

"They cheered for me," he said to no one. "They saw the rot and knew only I had the will to cleanse it. I gave them unity."

The silence answered, loyal and unquestioning.

He descended the steps of the dais, past the flickering braziers, toward a small circular platform embedded in the floor. At its center: a cradle of stone, empty, but glowing faintly with residual magic.

"And still she haunts it," he muttered. "Faye."

He knelt—not in reverence, but in calculation. The cradle was once the resting place of the Amulet of Origin. He had held it. He had tried to wield it. But never fully.

It had responded, but not with obedience. Not as it did to her. There had been resistance—just enough to remind him that truth, even in his hands, could still burn.

"You ran. You hid. You bled your bloodline into the mud of a lesser realm. But I am patient."

He looked up, and in the curved ornamental obsidian mirror above the platform, he saw only himself.

A perfect image. Untouched by time. Immortalized by will.

He smiled.

"Magicia belongs to its people. I was merely the one who saw it clearly first."

Outside, the sound of distant bells echoed through the capital, summoning the Chancellor to the High Forum.

They rang pure, untouched by weather or time—not the coarse clang of temple bronze, but a tone so clean it seemed to pass through stone and bone alike, the kind that made even marble remember it had once been fire.

Yet their summons carried more than duty; it heralded a plea for the Chancellor's Pardon—a rare appeal that would test the values he claimed to uphold, and perhaps reveal the boundaries of his mercy.

He lingered a moment longer in the quiet. Mercy was a dangerous word, he thought. Not because he lacked it—but because its use implied weakness. And weakness was a contagion Magicia could no longer afford.

He made his way through the ceremonial corridor lined with banners of the four kingdoms, each one shimmering faintly with enchantments meant to symbolize unity.

The distance was not very far, and Siroth allowed the rhythm of his stride to quiet his thoughts. He knew the matter; he had skimmed the essentials. But he had not dwelled. Deliberation, after all, could invite doubt. Sometimes the clearest decisions came before consequence had a voice. Or so he had learned.

As he entered the High Forum, silence fell. The chamber was circular, its galleries filled with citizens, ministers, and Watchers of the Veil in ceremonial armor. At its heart stood a solitary figure—young, cloaked in pale violet robes of mourning. Calia Renn, the petitioner.

She bowed low before the Chancellor, and then looked up with quiet determination.

"Your Grace," she said, her voice clear, "I come not to question the law, but to ask for compassion. My brother, Thorn Renn, crossed into the Stone District. Yes. But not for defiance, not for rebellion. He sought only a cure—a way to heal the children in our province afflicted with the wasting affliction. The Magistrate condemned him for trespass and theft of ancient magic. But he took nothing. He left only hope."

The chamber fell briefly silent, but her breath quickened. Calia's fingers clenched at her sides, the cool fabric of her mourning robes unable to still the warmth rushing beneath her skin.

She could still see Thorn's face that morning—pale, resolute, framed by the fractured light of their province's small chapel. The child he'd carried was barely breathing, her ribs fluttering like a trapped moth beneath fragile skin. "The magistrates won't help," he had said. "They're too afraid to act. But there's something in the Stone District. A text. An echo. Something ancient."

"That's forbidden," Calia had whispered. "Even to speak it—"

But Thorn had only smiled that tired, impossible smile. "What is forbidden if a child dies waiting?"

She hadn't stopped him. That was the part that burned deepest now. She had helped gather his satchel, stitched it closed with trembling hands. She had watched him slip into the mist before dawn, knowing full well that he might not return.

And he hadn't. Not truly. The Thorn they condemned was a husk beneath iron bars—starved, gaunt, eyes dulled by interrogations. But even then, he hadn't spoken. Hadn't recanted. Not even when the sentence was read.

"He left only hope," she repeated softly, not to the Chancellor this time, but to the memory she had helped shape. "And I left him alone with it."

Murmurs swept the gallery. Siroth raised one hand, and silence returned.

He stood, stepping to the edge of the platform. His gaze settled on Calia like frost—calm, clear, and indifferent.

"Your words are heard, Calia Renn," he said. "And they are moving. But you mistake intent for absolution. Law is not a matter of circumstance, but of order. And in order, Magicia endures."

He let the silence hold.

He raised his hand, palm open as if weighing something invisible. "You ask for compassion," he said, his voice calm, resonant. "A beautiful word, is it not? A word that sways hearts, that paints stories in soft hues. But compassion without consequence is indulgence—and indulgence, history has shown us, is the seed of chaos."

He stepped down from the dais, closer now to the center, where Calia stood as if the entire realm's gaze was pinned to her trembling resolve. "Thorn Renn broke the sacred line drawn to protect us all. You say he meant well. Perhaps he did. But we do not govern by intention—we govern by law."

His gaze swept across the gallery. "Would you have me pardon him and risk setting fire to the barriers that keep this realm from unraveling? Would you have every cause become exceptional? Every trespass reimagined as noble?"

A hush filled the chamber. He looked again at Calia, almost gently. "I do not doubt your brother's heart. I've seen hands like his before. They carry desperation like fire—bright, tragic, and quick to consume."

He turned now, facing the gathered assembly. "Let it be understood—not as cruelty, but as clarity. The law must be unwavering, so the realm may be whole. I will not grant the Chancellor's Pardon. Thorn Renn's sentence stands."

The hush rippled, then cracked. A voice, tremulous but defiant, rose from the upper gallery—an older man in scholar's robes. "But Your Grace, the law itself was meant to protect life. If it now punishes those who seek to preserve it, what then is its purpose?"

Gasps flared again. Siroth did not smile, but his expression deepened—as if the moment had offered him a stage he knew well.

"A noble question," he said smoothly. "And one worth answering—for all of us. You speak of purpose, scholar. But purpose without principle is like spellwork without a circle—impressive, but doomed to break."

And he continued. "Shall we undo the safeguards that keep disease from spreading because one man dared to gamble with forbidden knowledge? And why is it forbidden? Because I alone declared it so? No. It is forbidden because history bears the scars of what unchecked knowledge once wrought. You ask about the Times of Faye—some romanticize it now. But I remember chaos masquerading as freedom. I remember a realm fractured by ideals, not bound by purpose."

The words echoed, but not just in the chamber.

For a heartbeat, the Hall dissolved.

He was young again, standing beneath the arch of Hall of Unity, the ink still drying on the Proclamation. It was raining—not the harsh rain of revolt, but a soft drizzle, as if the heavens themselves were waiting. The crowd had gathered, hundreds deep, eyes wide and searching. Some cheered. Others wept. He remembered the feel of the damp stone beneath his boots. The thrill of absolute silence before his voice first rang out.

And beyond them all, high on the steps, Faye stood. Not cloaked in gold or flame, but in gray. Watching.

He remembered her expression—not disapproving. Not afraid. Just... resigned.

That was what gutted him, even now. Not her power. Not her exile. But that look. As if she already knew the ending, and he was only speaking it into being.

He had not faltered then. He would not now.

Siroth blinked once, and the chamber returned. Faces again. Rows of them. Some eager. Some wary. A few too still. That was always the way—those closest to fear moved the least.

He drew in a breath, steady and long, the way he had practiced in the old reflecting chapel—back when truth was still a blade he believed could be honed to a perfect edge.

His voice rose again, smoother now, almost warm. He was not that young man anymore. But neither was he the broken reflection they hoped he might become.

And for a split second, as the words left his lips, Siroth recalled the roar of that crowd so many years ago, when he first spoke of unity—not as a dream, but as a necessity. "Shall we dismantle the very firewalls of our safety because it was done out of... love? That, too, is what they once said—those same words, when the world burned with good intentions. Some of you will recall my first speech on the steps of the Hall of Unity, when I said: 'Magicia will rise again—not by feeling, but by will.' It was not sentiment that saved us then. It was resolve. And it will be resolve that protects us now."

A ripple moved through the gallery—silent but unmistakable. Ministers leaned forward. Robed delegates exchanged glances without speaking. Some lips moved in prayer. Others in calculation.

In the eastern tier, the governor of Erenhalt—an old woman with a record of caution—nodded slowly, then made a discreet gesture to her scribe. In the northern benches, where the Watchers of the Veil stood like statuary, one shifted ever so slightly, his hand tightening on the hilt of his blade, not from threat—but from indoctrinated certainty.

From the center gallery, a merchant-prince from the Lower Provinces lowered his gaze, fingers tapping a slow rhythm against his cane. He would speak of this moment at dinner later, dramatically, to his guests. But even he was moved.

Behind them all, near the shadowed rim of the highest gallery, sat a small cluster of quiet figures. Not nobles. Not clergy. Not citizens. Bureaucrats. Ledger-keepers. Readers of whispers. Their pens did not move, but their silence was not still. They watched Siroth as one watches an evolving script—neither applauding nor defying. Simply... adjusting.

And above it all, the great domed ceiling of the Forum trembled faintly—not from architecture, but from enchantment. The runes threaded through the apex stonework began to hum with faint light, responding not to volume, but to conviction.

Siroth didn't look up. He didn't need to. He could feel it now—the shift. The pulse. The moment when the room surrendered to his will, not because they all agreed, but because he left them no room not to.

He spoke into that silence, shaping it like a sculptor bent to marble.

He turned slightly, addressing the gallery at large now. "Compassion, you see, is not the enemy. But ungoverned compassion is like floodwater. It seeps into the foundations of order and hollows them until the whole house sinks."

He paused. "What we do today is not to kill hope. It is to preserve the structure in which hope may one day thrive—not just for the few, but for all."

Silence again. This time heavier. Some nodded. Others looked away.

Siroth's eyes briefly flicked back to Calia. "Hope without structure is sentiment. And sentiment has no seat in judgment."

"Veritas Claritas," he said, letting the ancient phrase hang. "Truth is clarity. And clarity is mercy—when properly governed."

Calia's shoulders stiffened, but she did not lower her gaze.

"Then I pray, Your Grace, that the day never comes when you must ask for compassion—and find only order in its place."

Gasps echoed. Siroth did not flinch. He turned, motioned to the guards, and the procession began to dissolve.

Behind him, the murmurs swelled again—questions, doubts, and a slow, invisible shifting in the air. But Siroth only whispered to himself, "They will remember the silence, not the noise. And I will be the one they remember it with."

Yet as the chamber emptied, and the guards resumed their posts, something unsettled him—a sliver of memory not easily dismissed. Not Faye. Not the amulet. A face in the crowd, perhaps. A voice that struck too close to a truth he had long buried. He turned toward the obsidian wall, not to reflect—but to compose.

It passed quickly, but not before it left something behind.

A word. Not spoken, not written. Just… remembered.

He didn't know where it came from. It struck without force, like a leaf brushing the surface of still water. And yet it rippled—too deeply, too precisely.

He turned slightly, eyes narrowing at nothing in particular. A blur in the stained glass. A color not there before. A name he had once heard whispered—not in rebellion, but in prayer.

That was the danger of stillness. It lets memory breathe.

He clenched his fist behind his back until the tremor stopped. No names. No echoes. The past had been scrubbed clean. Rewritten. If it stirred now, it did so from weakness, not design.

And yet…

There, on the edge of hearing, something pulsed—not a sound, but a tension. Like the space between syllables in an incantation. Or the breath before the answer you dread.

He exhaled slowly. "Resonance is not truth," he said under his breath, the words old, practiced. "It is only memory pretending to matter."

A truth he had shaped long ago—one he repeated not to deceive others, but to keep himself from splintering.

His shoulders straightened. The illusion restored.

The tremor in the air thinned, swallowed by the silence of the hall.

Then the doors opened, spilling light and motion into the void of his thoughts.

Two aides entered with practiced quiet, their steps erasing what remained of the echo. One, pale and hesitant, held a sealed scroll pressed with the sigil of the Vault of Balance. The other leaned close, whispering words meant only for the Chancellor: "There's been... a resonance. In the outer Veil. Faint, but measurable. Something passed between worlds."

Siroth's expression did not change. But he did not move for several long seconds.

"Let it be brought forward," he said at last, voice measured. "Send for the Inquisitors. Quietly."

He turned from the dying echoes of the Forum and began walking toward the upper spire. Far beyond, a lesser realm had stirred.

And in the stillness of the spire, where truth once rang like bells across kingdoms, Siroth whispered only to himself: "Let it stir. I am the Vault of Balance now."

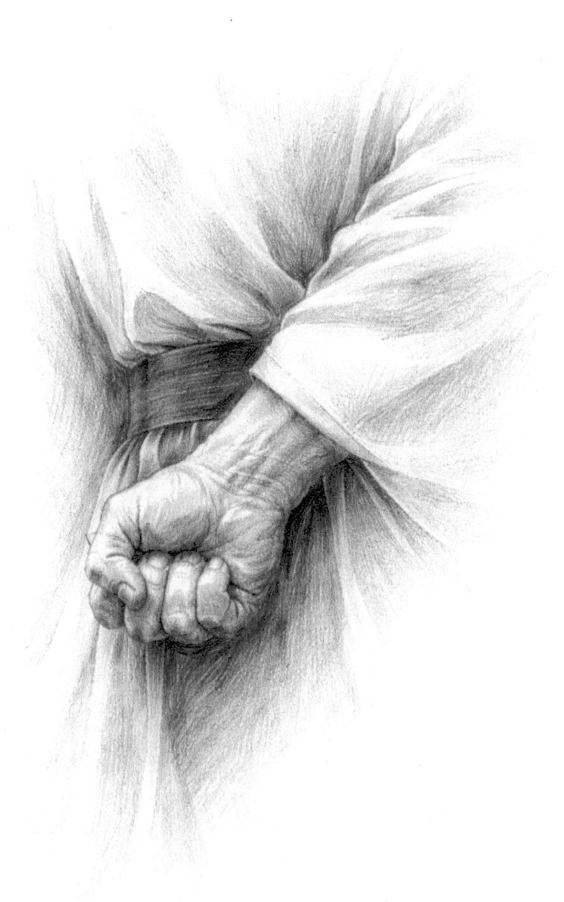

Chapter Three

"What the Familiar Fetches"

The midday sun cast a soft glow through the stained-glass windows of Saint-Spire Abbey—for a second, all time collapsed—the stars, the river, the hum. Then came the tug. Sharp, human, and real. The sudden grip on his arm startled Father Maurice so sharply that his lunch slipped from his fingers—an indignity he registered only a heartbeat before the deeper pull took hold.

He heard a muffled gasp outside, followed by the swish of startled fabric and a sharply indignant voice: "Outrageous! I'm reporting this. The Church throws its food now?"

Father Maurice peered out and offered a mortified, "I am terribly sorry, madam. We meant no harm. Let us thank heaven it wasn't my Bible—though its impact might've offered more grace."

From beside him, a soft chuckle broke the tension.

"Father," came the voice of Mother Gwendlynn. "You need to come with me. Something's stirring in the Lower Archives," Gwendlynn said quietly. "Not noise. Not movement. Just... a stillness that had shifted."

He blinked. "The archives?"

"It's faint—but old," she said. "Different."

She didn't speak further. There was no need to add weight to something already heavy.

But inwardly, Gwendlynn paused—utterly. The moment stretched.

There was a kind of silence that lived in old places. Not the absence of noise, but the trace of presence. She had felt it only a few times in her life—beneath cathedrals older than scripture, in moments when the world itself seemed to inhale and wait.

She had come to recognize it for what it was: a reminder that history never truly ends—it only buries itself in deeper soil.

And the Abbey's foundations were older than most dared to guess.

She let the moment settle inside her. It did not frighten her. It rarely did. But it made her careful. When stillness like this returned, it was often because something forgotten had begun to remember itself.

Gwendlynn's gaze wandered—not far, just toward the corridor's arch, where dust gathered in places even candlelight didn't reach. The stones beneath their feet were worn smooth by generations of footsteps, but they too had begun to feel... different. Not colder. Not warmer. Just more present, somehow—like a room waiting for its occupant to arrive.

She folded her hands, posture composed, and glanced toward Maurice. He was watching her with that same knowing quiet he had always carried, the one that never asked questions out loud.

She gave no outward sign that anything had shifted. She merely stood, serene and still, while the air around them pressed inward—just enough to be noticed by those who had learned, over long years, how to listen without appearing to hear.

Before he could respond, two other sisters appeared from the hallway behind them.

"Father Maurice, forgive the interruption," began Sister Mabelle, flanked by Novice Ava, "but this year's Winter Lights Festival setup has deviated significantly from tradition."

Maurice exhaled. "Let me guess—tablecloths?"

"Lavender, Father," Mabelle said quietly, her tone carefully measured. "And she's hung violet banners. She said they came to her in a dream."

"She said it symbolizes rebirth," Mabelle added, avoiding Ava's eyes.

"She's not wrong," Gwendlynn murmured, half to herself.

Maurice raised a calming hand, but before he spoke, a memory rose unbidden—of another moment, quiet and rain-soaked, years ago.

He remembered the night Ava arrived. She had clutched Leonarth's hand like a lifeline, soaked to the bone, her red curly hair matted to her forehead, and her hazel eyes wide—not with fear, but with a calm that unsettled. There was no panic, no pleading—only the sense that she already knew how the night would unfold.

She carried no luggage, and her only possession was a letter that Father Maurice would later present as one from the Archbishop of England. After reading the letter—and despite the unusual nature of the arrival, a woman seeking clerical life with a child in tow—Father Maurice had admitted Ava as a novice that very night and placed Leonarth in the quiet orphanage hall tucked within Saint-Spire Abbey.

Besides Maurice, no one knew the contents of the letter. The elder sisters had either chosen not to question it or had trusted in Maurice's judgment—at least, that's what he believed. Back then, he hadn't given it much thought. He was the highest-ranking church official in town. Who would dare question his decision?

Ava had barely spoken that first night, but when she looked at the statue of Saint Elodia in the corridor, her small voice had whispered, "I've dreamt of someone who felt like her."

That memory lingered in his mind now as Mabelle and Ava fretted over tablecloths and tent banners. His gaze flicked for a moment toward the corridor's far end—where the statue of Saint Elodia stood, silent in her alcove. Few remembered the saint's full story, and fewer still questioned the curiously foreign stone that formed her halo. But Maurice had always found her presence oddly watchful, as if she knew more than history allowed. And Ava—she had noticed her immediately.

"Father?" Mabelle asked gently, bringing Maurice back from his trance. "Did you hear what I said?"

"Yes, yes. You are right. Yellow, blue, and green. Those are our colors," he replied with feigned certainty, blinking the thought away. He turned toward Ava, his tone softening. "My dear novice, your passion and creativity may find a better purpose elsewhere in the celebration. What about the flowers? You've always had a touch with them, and they seem to bloom brighter under your care."

He reached forward, clasping her hand between both of his. It was a small gesture—warm, protective—but beneath it ran the same uneasy pull he'd felt the night she arrived—like a tremor beneath stone, too deep to name, but impossible to ignore.

Maurice held her gaze a moment longer than he intended. Not as priest to novice, nor mentor to pupil—but as something else. Two people walking the edge of a silence neither dared name.

He had watched her grow—into her voice, her intuition, her stubborn fire. She had learned to follow rules when it suited her, and to quietly rewrite them when it didn't. But what he admired most wasn't her cleverness or even her kindness—it was her restraint.

Ava knew how to bury things. Questions. Hunches. Truths too raw for daylight.

As did he.

He wondered—often in private—how much she saw. Did she glimpse in his gestures the same guarded care she carried in hers? Did she ever think of the night that bound them both to silence? Did she still feel its weight when their eyes met across the chapel? And did she ever fear, as he did, that silence itself might one day betray them?

But they never spoke of it. That was the way of things.

The Veil kept them silent—not out of distrust, but necessity. The cost of being known was too high if the wrong person was listening. And so they moved like shadows beside one another, woven close but never tethered. A fragile peace made of omissions rather than lies.

Her hand, still warm in his, pulsed faintly. Not with magic—that word had no place here. But with reminiscence. With weight. With history, both of them carried in silence.

He let her go gently, concealing the ache it left in his palm.

She gave him the faintest smile—nothing special. Except he knew it was.

That was all they ever gave each other: glimpses, never confessions.

And that would have to be enough. For now.

Ava had always been a force of nature—she could be fiery one moment and disarmingly reflective the next. It often put her at odds with the more traditional sisters, but even they couldn't deny her devotion to the Abbey. She had learned—sometimes the hard way—which battles were worth the stir. She glanced between Mabelle and Maurice, drew a breath as if weighing fire and diplomacy, and said, "That's OK. I'll let this go, if I have the final say on the flowers—and the colors of my choosing. Deal?"

Mabelle drew a breath to speak, but Mother Gwendlynn interjected, her tone measured but firm. "Mabelle, sometimes stewardship means knowing when to let others lead. You may not like Ava's choices, but her instincts have brought more beauty to this Abbey than any rulebook ever has."

Maurice gave a brief nod. "Exactly. That's a good compromise. Please, for the love of God, take it. I do care for the colors of the tents, tablecloths, and the flowers,"—he glanced at Ava—"but we all have our gifts. And we must agree that Ava knows flowers well." For a moment, the air stilled around them—soft with the weight of what had been, and something else unspoken.

Mabelle nodded slowly. "Very well, then. I won't press further." She paused, her brow furrowing. "Is something the matter, Father? You seem... hurried."

Maurice hesitated, then seized a useful thread. "Because—" he began, "the Archbishop is planning to attend the festival this year, and he's expecting confirmation from us. Since you care about protocol and impressions, perhaps you'd be the best person to handle the correspondence on my behalf?"

Mabelle's posture eased, and she inclined her head. "Of course. I'll see to it immediately."

"Good," he said, turning his attention back to Gwendlynn. "Now, if you'll excuse us."

As he turned to leave, Mabelle spoke again, her voice just a touch too hopeful. "And if the Archbishop is coming, perhaps I should oversee the flo—"

"Do not dare finish that sentence," Maurice said, raising a hand with the firmness of finality. "The decision is made. I must go. Now."

He exhaled slowly and offered a smile shaped more by duty than reassurance. "Sisters, we'll revisit banner etiquette another day. For now, Mother Gwendlynn has raised a concern that requires immediate discretion."

And Ava—without realizing it—had stirred something more than Mabelle's temper. That old silence was listening again.

But it wasn't temper that Mabelle wrestled with. Not truly.

It was calculation.

She had watched Ava since her arrival—not with suspicion exactly, but with the uneasy instinct of someone trained to recognize patterns that others missed. Ava moved like someone carrying more than she admitted. Her insights came too quickly. Her impulses, too often right. And her presence had a way of drawing silence around her, not pushing it away.

Maurice protected her. Gwendlynn praised her. Neither surprised Mabelle—but neither brought comfort.

And then there were the dreams. Violet banners? Prophetic color choices? It sounded harmless enough. But Mabelle knew better. The line between inspiration and revelation was thinner than most believed. And revelations had consequences.

She had no proof. No visible breach of rule or decorum. Ava was clever enough for that. But the threads were beginning to pull taut, and Mabelle had spent her life following threads.

Her own path to the Abbey had not been smooth. It had been carved out of necessity, grief, and duty. She had buried too much to indulge in intuition. And yet she felt it now—that same tension she had once known during her brother's final days. That sense that something vast had moved behind the curtain, just out of reach.

She inhaled slowly and set her expression to stillness. Maurice had made his decision, and Gwendlynn had reinforced it. For now, Mabelle would not challenge them.

But she would watch.

Always, she would watch.

Mabelle lingered for a moment longer than she meant to, her gaze drifting toward the Elodia corridor—though she didn't know why.

Maurice turned to Gwendlynn and gave a single nod. "Lead the way."

The sisters parted, and he followed her down the winding stairs. With every step, the Abbey's warmth faded, giving way to the cool breath of stone that hadn't stirred in years.

At the bottom, before the sealed vault, the air felt charged. Ancient. Waiting. Maurice stepped closer, the silence thickening around him like settled smoke.

The air was colder here—not in temperature, but in age. It clung to the arches and whispered through the dust like something not entirely forgotten. He hadn't set foot in this part of the Abbey in years. Perhaps no one had.

Before him, the altar stone gleamed faintly, its surface worn smooth by centuries of rituals long since abandoned. And beneath it—just visible now in the dark—came the flicker.

A pulse. Dim, steady. Like breath drawn through stone.

It didn't glow. It didn't burn. It pulsed—responded. Not to his presence, but to something older. A signal returned. A call answered.

"Gwendlynn," he said softly. "Did you open it?"

"No," she replied, her voice the barest thread of sound. "It was already like this."

He crouched beside the stone, resting his palm lightly on its surface. It was warm—not with heat, but with life. As if it held something he didn't.

He closed his eyes. For a moment, he didn't see the vault. He saw a field of broken banners. A voice shouting a name he no longer dared speak. The glint of a blade. A promise made in ashes.

When he opened his eyes again, the flicker had sharpened—just once—and then returned to its slow, rhythmic glow.

"It's waking," he whispered.

Gwendlynn didn't ask what. She didn't need to.

The moment held between them like breath withheld. Something old had turned in its sleep. Not fully awakened—but listening.

"How long do we have?" she asked.

Maurice stood slowly, brushing his fingers on the edge of his cassock. "Not long. Weeks, maybe. A season if we're lucky."

The light throbbed again—stronger. Just once.

And in that instant, neither of them believed in luck.

Chapter Four

"The Thread Between Us"

Leonarth walked the worn stone corridor with the kind of hunger that had little to do with food. It was lunchtime, yes—but the ache wasn't in his stomach. It lived where memory should've been—a space too quiet, too familiar. The school day had passed in a blur of arithmetic drills and lessons on border disputes, but nothing silenced the gnawing pull of what he couldn't remember.

His mind kept circling the same unreachable space, like a bird refusing to land. It wasn't sadness. Just an absence that tightened beneath his ribs, persistent and unnamed.

Outside, the town of Corbeil-Essonnes moved in its quiet winter rhythm, roofs dusted with a thin frost, and the Seine churning—slow and gray beneath a pale sky. Inside the Abbey's orphanage wing, warmth lingered in the radiators and in the soft scuff of footsteps up the stairwell. Life continued, predictable and gentle.

But Leonarth felt anything but settled.

He climbed the narrow staircase to the top-floor cafeteria with the practiced gait of someone who knew the Abbey well. Eight years, after all, was long enough to memorize every creaking step and every chill draft. He didn't pause to greet anyone, didn't smile as he passed the alcove where the prayer candles flickered. He was somewhere else—adrift in thought, or the lack of it.

And yet, even as he moved through the day's routine, he could feel something stirring beneath the surface. Not quite a thought. Not quite a fear. Just a pulse—slow and steady—as if the threads of something long buried were beginning, quietly, to tug.

His thoughts drifted once more—first to lunch, then, as they often did, to the strange comfort of the orphanage itself. It was modest, certainly, but it had a warmth that even Parisian palaces couldn't fake. The sisters were stern but just, and Novice Ava—peculiar as she sometimes was—had always treated him like more than just another name on the roster.

Since that night he and Ava arrived, the past had lived in fragments—rain, a gate, the sensation of fleeing. Most days, he ignored it. But not today.

The orphanage itself ran on generosity and ingenuity. Handmade crafts, small donations from the villagers, and the sheer will of the sisters made it all work. Nothing was wasted, and everything had to be shared—money, clothing, even the sisters' time. Field trips to Paris were rare, cherished events. For most children, they were a window to another world; for Leonarth, they were a reminder of a world he somehow felt he should already know.

Now thirteen, Leonarth had long made peace with the rhythm of his life. The orphanage was no palace, and the prospects of adoption had faded with each passing year, but he bore no bitterness. Unlike some of the others, who internalized the sting of rejection and hardened under its weight, Leonarth clung to something different—an unwavering belief that nothing in the world happened without purpose.

He often told himself that even the most painful events were like pieces of a puzzle too large to see up close. That one day, everything—his presence at the orphanage, the vague shadows of his past, even the absences in the sisters' efforts to trace his origins—would fall into place. The mystery of his parents lingered at the edge of his thoughts, like a half-familiar tune he couldn't place. It was strange, almost conspicuous, how little Father Maurice or the sisters had spoken of it, how no one had ever really tried to uncover the truth. But Leonarth's philosophy of patience and purpose kept him from digging too deeply.

More than anything, it was the pain of remembering that steered him away. The harder he tried to reach for those early memories, the more they recoiled in anguish—like light revealing something too raw to touch. So instead, he waited. Quietly. Painfully. But with faith that clarity would come—not all at once, but in time, and in pieces.

Lost in the weight of his own reflections, Leonarth paused at a window overlooking the square. The scents of lunch drifting up from the kitchens could not distract him—not today. As he stared down at the worn cobblestones below, the dull pull in his stomach gave way to something heavier—wondering. His fingers brushed the cool stone of the window frame, grounding him as his mind slipped backward, drawn once again to that first night—the night he and Ava arrived, soaked, silent, and unknowably changed.

He wasn't that young when he was brought in; at five years old, one might expect a memory to cling. He remembered a threadbare blanket. A sensation of a woman's hand brushing his forehead—an intention, not words.

The sound of rain. A door, creaking. The scent of smoke and lilies.

Then silence.

That was the only image that ever returned. It wasn't a dream. It felt carved into him, as if someone had branded it into the lining of his mind. He didn't know if it was real. He only knew that it never left.

Leonarth's past was not cloudy—it was void. It was as if life had only begun the night he and Ava arrived at the Abbey gates, silent and rain-soaked.

In time, he had learned not to chase what fled from him. Instead, he buried the questions and leaned into what he did have. And from that place of emptiness, something else emerged—a strange and powerful clarity.

He called it "logical empathy," though the name never quite fit. It wasn't logic, and it wasn't ordinary empathy. When he met someone, and their eyes met his, something opened. Not like a memory or a dream, but more like a current—an unfiltered stream of moments, feelings, truths. He couldn't recall names, places, or details. But he knew them—deeply, instinctively, and immediately. It was as though something in their eyes unlocked a door inside him, allowing him to glimpse not their memories, but their essence. Not facts, not names or dates, but the foundation of who they truly were—what they feared, what they carried, what they had become. It wasn't knowledge in the traditional sense. It was recognition—soul-deep and undeniable.

He understood pain when it was hidden, could trace its root even when cloaked in laughter. He recognized kindness, even when it was buried beneath layers of pride or defense. And he sensed danger—not just threat, but something deeper, a kind of spiritual weight that clung to certain people like smoke from a fire long burned out. In that fleeting instant of connection, he perceived the essence of a person—whether lit with promise or touched by a darkness that seemed older than time itself, as if inherited from something that didn't feel entirely human.

He never sought these glimpses—they came unbidden, like sudden lightning across a still sky.

He never told anyone, not even Ava. Some of what he glimpsed was too strange, too heavy to speak aloud. There were moments when, looking into certain eyes, he felt something staring back—something wounded, but not innocent. There were people whose histories felt wrong, fractured, like echoes from a place beyond this world. A few he'd met only once, in a crowd or a train, and yet their presence lingered in him like a warning.

He could never explain it. But deep down, Leonarth had begun to suspect that whatever had erased his own past was tied to that darkness—and that one day, it might come looking for him again.

A door creaked open somewhere down the corridor. He turned, half-expecting to see no one. But there she was—Sister Mabelle—crossing the far hallway in silence. She paused just briefly in the archway, hands tucked into her sleeves, eyes sweeping the corridor.

For a moment, their gazes met. She offered no smile, no greeting—just a quiet nod, almost imperceptible. Then she was gone, her robes vanishing into shadow.

It wasn't unusual for the sisters to patrol the halls, but something about her stillness stayed with him. As if she, too, had been listening for something.

Leonarth was still wrapped in the fog of memory when something hit him from behind—a full-bodied tackle that knocked the breath from his lungs and jolted him back into the present.

He staggered forward, bracing against the wall as laughter echoed through the hallway. "Still dreaming, Leonarth? Or just planning your dramatic fall down the stairs?" came the unmistakable voice.

Leonarth turned, already smiling despite himself. Mattheon stood grinning with that lopsided charm only he could pull off. His hair was a perpetual mess, his uniform half-untucked, and his presence a welcome gravity that snapped Leonarth back to the now.

In an instant, the weight of forgotten years lifted. The fog receded, replaced by something steady and real. Mattheon had been by his side since that first week at the orphanage, a constant through every season of uncertainty. Their friendship wasn't loud or sentimental, but it was unbreakable—forged in quiet conversations under threadbare blankets, in stolen pastries, and mutual secrets neither dared name.

Leonarth nudged him back with a grin. "I was meditating on how peaceful life would be without you."

Mattheon laughed again, slinging an arm around Leonarth's shoulder. "Yeah, well, lucky for you—I'm a storm you're stuck with."

And Mattheon continued mockingly, "Don't be so dramatic—no way you didn't see me coming. I was practically breathing down your neck."

Leonarth gave a crooked smile. "I guess I was drifting again, lost in thoughts about the past... Hey, do you remember the night we met?"

Mattheon snorted. "Vividly. You looked like a half-drowned librarian in borrowed clothes. They stuck you in our room, and you just stood there, soaked and stiff, like a dog caught in a rainstorm. Not your finest entrance."

Leonarth chuckled. "Yeah, well. It wasn't exactly the grand debut I'd imagined."

Mattheon raised an eyebrow. "Why bring that up now?"

Leonarth's tone shifted, quieter. "I was just trying again to remember anything before that night. Just one piece. But it's all still a blank... nothing but shadows and static."

Mattheon didn't laugh this time. He bumped Leonarth gently with his shoulder. "Maybe that's because your brain is too full of all my brilliance."

Leonarth smirked. "Yeah, that must be it."

Something tightened briefly behind Mattheon's smile. There were things he never told Leonarth either—fleeting impressions that never quite felt like his. He shook it off, burying the thought with a smile.

As they walked in companionable silence, Leonarth felt a familiar warmth settle in his chest. He often thought of Mattheon as more than a friend—something closer, though he never said it aloud. From the very first glance, there had been something unmistakable, as if they were reconnecting rather than meeting. It wasn't just the comfort or the loyalty—they moved in sync in a way that didn't need explanation.

It felt like a memory, but one that didn't belong to this life—like déjà vu stretched across lifetimes, pulling at something too old to name. As always, Leonarth couldn't explain it. He just knew. And from that moment on, they had been inseparable—bonded not just by time, but by something deeper, unspoken. As if, in another version of the world, their lives had been written side by side.

Mattheon and Leonarth were close in age, with Leonarth trailing him by just two years. Mattheon had been at the orphanage longer;

soon after birth, in fact. His parents had vanished during a particularly brutal winter, their disappearance whispered about but never fully explained. No footprints. No blood. Just cold silence, and a baby swaddled like someone meant for him to be found.

There were stories, of course. Children love stories, especially the ones that feel like warnings wrapped in wonder. Some said wolves were circling the cabin that day. Others whispered that Mattheon's cry froze mid-air and cracked the ice on the windows. Leonarth had never believed those parts, but even he admitted—something about Mattheon had always felt... marked by circumstance.

The miracle, as some called it, arrived in the form of Mabelle—Mattheon's aunt on his father's side. She was only twenty-two at the time, with short dark hair, hazel eyes, and a slim, determined frame. No one quite knew how she found him that day. Some said she'd had a dream, others claimed instinct guided her through the storm. She never offered details.

Back then, Mabelle was young, alone, and without fortune. But with a newborn in her arms and nowhere else to go, she turned to the Church. Within a week, she entered the convent and became Sister Mabelle. And Mattheon—never made available for adoption, for reasons no one discussed—was taken in as the orphanage's newest child.

The sisters whispered about the strangeness of it all; the timing, the silence, the eyes Mattheon had even as an infant. But they stopped asking questions. Mabelle was quiet, resolute, and fiercely protective. If there were secrets behind her devotion or her past, she carried them alone.

Leonarth had once caught a look between her and Father Maurice; brief, unreadable. But something in it had unsettled him.

He never spoke of it. Whatever Mattheon had seen, if anything, remained unspoken.

But sometimes, in the long hours of early morning when neither boy could sleep, Leonarth would find himself wondering not just who he was, but what Mattheon might be hiding too.

Over the years, Mattheon had asked Sister Mabelle questions. Gentle ones at first, then sharper, more insistent as he grew older. But her answers were always vague, always veiled in the language of fate and grace. He had once resented her for it, but time had dulled the edge of that need.

Just as they reached the cafeteria doors, Mattheon broke their silence.

"Leonarth... look, I get it. I really do. I never really knew where I came from either. I never truly met my parents. I don't even know if they're alive, or if they ever really meant to come back."

Leonarth turned slightly, but Mattheon pressed on.

"And maybe I used to want answers. But at some point, I realized... maybe they, too, only make sense when we're ready for them. You're the one who said that, remember? That if we rush it, we might not even recognize the answers we get."

His voice was softer now, less playful. "So, I stopped looking. I'm not saying you should. But maybe... maybe you don't have to look alone."

Leonarth glanced at him, eyes misty but steady. "Then we'll find them together."

Mattheon grinned, the old mischief returning. "Absolutely. And maybe the universe starts with a clue... or a second helping of stew."

They both laughed—real and unguarded. Shoulder to shoulder, they pushed through the cafeteria doors, where warmth greeted them not just in scent, but in spirit.

Master Eloi stood behind the serving counter, humming off-key and ladling stew into mismatched bowls with the same reverence some priests gave communion. He offered them each a nod and a half-smile—his usual greeting—and went right on humming.

The scent of roasted onions and warm bread rose around them like an old story trying to be remembered.

As they sat down with their trays, Master Eloi offered a wink so small it might have been imagined. Leonarth noticed his sleeves were flour-dusted, his fingers slightly blistered from the heat. And yet, the man moved with the serenity of someone who had never once hurried.

Leonarth didn't know why it struck him just then, but it did: Eloi never raised his voice. Never forgot anyone's name. And never, not once, ate with the others.

There was something sacred in the way Eloi moved. Gentle hands with knuckles browned from old burns, eyes soft with knowing. No one knew much about his past, and he rarely spoke beyond kind greetings. But Leonarth sometimes thought Eloi was watching more than just soup bowls. As if he was keeping vigil over things no one else could see.

It wasn't anything specific. Just the way his humming always seemed to match the rhythm of the Abbey bells, or how his eyes flicked toward the stained-glass windows just before dusk. As if his attention drifted to things others overlooked. Even the clink of his ladle against ceramic seemed to follow a pattern older than habit—like he was not just feeding children, but warding off silence.

Whatever came next, they'd face it the way they always had—together. And maybe, just maybe, the Abbey would feed more than just their hunger.

Chapter Five

"The Council of Stones"

The Hall of Accord, Magicia's highest chamber of governance, thrummed with enchantment and quiet contention. Anchored beneath the Celestine Spire, it was a space both reverent and volatile, suspended in light and stone. Columns of enchanted quartz rose in spirals, humming softly with spells of protection and persuasion. Every surface shimmered with quiet enchantments—whispers muffled unless permission was granted, records of past sessions lingering in veiled alcoves.

And in deliberate contrast, fragments of the old Hall of Unity had been set into the floor and walls—dark, unpolished stone veined with cracks—kept not as tribute, but as a warning. They stood as sanctioned relics of failure, reminders of what unity had once promised and what, according to Siroth, it could never again be.

Above them, a crystalline dome projected constellations in motion—real-time maps of magical flux across the Four Kingdoms. Each quadrant shimmered with its realm's hue and heartbeat:

Aerthys, kingdom of the sky, drifted above in a soft blue glow—its floating cities suspended beneath vast enchanted balloons, held aloft not by gas but by runes of air that bent weather to their will.

Elowen unfurled beside it, deep green and gold, a living canopy of spells where homes grew from wood and vines, and healers coaxed bloom from stone or drew vitality from death itself.

Ignaris, all flame and alloy, blazed with orange firelight—its towers of glass and metal humming with alchemical brilliance, each invention balanced between creation and ruin.

Karnor anchored the circle in shades of brown and basalt, its highland fortresses bound by sigils of endurance and silence, where the art of defense had long outlasted the wars that forged it.

And yet, at the center of the map, the dome offered only a blank void where once a kingdom's constellations had turned. No one spoke its name; Siroth had decreed its erasure. But in the shifting light, the absence itself seemed to pulse—an empty place in the heavens that still remembered being whole.

To some, that darkness was not loss but proof: the map was complete only when imperfection had been excised.

Below the dome, each delegation sat in crescent tiers carved from its homeland's stone—selenite for Aerthys, verdestone for Elowen, obsidian streaked with amber for Ignaris, and dark basalt for Karnor. Together they formed a living compass of Magicia's surviving powers. The tiers glowed faintly, each pulsing with the essence of its realm, their energies weaving in quiet counterpoint through the air of the chamber.

Each color, each glow, seem to answer to something ancient—fragments of a higher order woven subtly across worlds, waiting to be remembered.

The Hall's enchantments kept their rivalries in check, but not even magic could still the old distrust completely. The air between them was woven with old spells—binding the debate to civility and ensuring that no one could lie without the enchantments responding in hue.

Though the Accord posed as a coalition of equals, few were naïve enough to believe it so. The Chancellor's word carried final authority. The Council argued, the Inquisitors implemented, but all of it moved to Siroth's hidden rhythm.

And still, they bickered. The Chancellor had not yet taken his place, and without his shadow to contain them, the Council's quarrels rose like heat from a forge.

"It could be a residual echo," offered Councilor Themaris of Ignaris, his tone oily, his fire-ring dim. "These Veil readings have fluctuated before. The observatory mirror tends to amplify anomalies."

"Spoken like one whose kingdom fears wind," snapped Lira of Aerthys. Her robes, edged in glinting sky-thread, fluttered with every gesture, though no wind stirred in the Hall. "Last time we dismissed a ripple, the Frostbound Line collapsed. Should we now wager again with silence?"

Councilor Venmira of Elowen raised a slender hand, her voice low but resonant, like the hush of leaves in a sacred grove. "There is balance in all things, even the Veil. If it stirs, it may not be warning—it may be remembering. Let us not turn every change into a threat."

"The Veil does not remember," rumbled Thorne of Karnor, his basalt armor clinking faintly as he leaned forward. "It guards. If it stirred, it means someone approached what should remain sealed."

A flicker ran through the dome above, as if the stars themselves disapproved.

And then, the chamber changed.

The central dais, long presumed empty, shimmered with a sudden pulse—like the surface of still water disturbed by an unseen hand. It was not a conjuring but an unveiling, a complex illusion encoded into the hall's very foundation.

Runes older than the kingdoms themselves flared briefly along the marble veins of the floor, their light flickering like old embers remembering fire.

And then, as if shaped from shadow and certainty, Chancellor Siroth stood there.

Not a footstep. Not a sound. Only presence—total and commanding. One moment the dais shimmered; the next, he occupied it—as though he had always been part of the chamber, waiting for the illusion to catch up to reality.

His cloak flowed behind him like spilled ink, his face unreadable. Eyes the color of hollowed steel surveyed the chamber, and with his first breath, the enchantments of the Hall attuned to him—softening the light, stilling the ambient spells.

Beneath the folds of his sleeve, his hand closed briefly around something unseen—a relic of another time, one he never spoke of. A faint shimmer rippled through the marble veins beneath his feet.

He murmured a single word—too soft to reach any ear but the Hall's—and the lectern's runes answered, flaring to life. At his gesture, the sealed scrolls rose from their bindings, unfolding in the air before him. Their contents confirmed what he already suspected.

The Veil had stirred. And it was not a coincidence. Something had awakened across the boundary. Something that resonated not just with magic—but with history.

He let them squabble a moment longer, the illusion of power soothing the more restless among them.

Then, he stood.

The room hushed as if the stone itself had leaned in.

"Let us not confuse silence with safety," he said, his voice calm, measured. "Or storms with shadows. The Veil does not blink—it breathes. And tonight... it drew breath."

He paused, letting the words settle into the foundations of the Hall.

"It has been a generation since the Veil was cut a second time. Since the day the Circle of Five finally broke." His gaze moved across the chamber, lingering just long enough to unnerve, but not provoke. "We were told it was Faye's sacrifice—her final act to shield Magicia from ruin."

Whispers stirred, but no one interrupted.

Siroth's voice did not rise, but it deepened, drawing the room closer in its resonance. "We were told she sealed the passage to protect us. That the Fifth Kingdom's departure was her sacrifice—necessary, noble. But what is sacrifice without witness?"

He let the question hover like mist.

"It is convenient," he continued, "to craft legends from silence. Faye's disappearance. The severing of the Veil. A world lost, a queen mourned. And yet—no body, no final spell, no formal farewell. Only absence. Only chaos."

His eyes scanned the chamber. "And in that void, who rose to restore balance? Who bound the Four Kingdoms against fracture?"

He let the silence stretch just long enough to cast his own shadow larger.

"Order was not inherited—it was forged. In the ruins she left behind."

He took a slow step forward, and the light seemed to follow him, as if the hall itself awaited his next truth.

"She did not fall in battle, nor did she vanish defending us. Faye abandoned us. In our hour of need, she turned her back on the Circle, on the kingdoms, on all of Magicia."

His voice grew colder, stripped of nostalgia. "The wars that followed? The famine, the fractures, the ten-year drought in Karnor's stonefields and the firestorms in Ignaris? They began the day she disappeared."

"That's one telling of it," Thorne said, his voice low but carved from bedrock. "But not the only one."

A quiet rustle swept the chamber. Lira looked over sharply, but said nothing.

"Karnor keeps long records," Thorne continued.

"We remember the Ordinatum, and the fragments that survived the Severance—how the Fifth Kingdom's knowledge bolstered harvests, how their scribes taught Ignaris to stabilize combustion fields, how their scholars warned Elowen of the blight cycle before it began. They did not isolate us. They elevated us. Until they were gone."

He leaned forward, eyes steady on Siroth. "What if they didn't abandon us? What if they were silenced?"

For a moment, even the dome seemed to pause.

Siroth's expression didn't flicker, but inside, he marked the words. Dangerous. Uncontrolled. Too soon.

"And yet," he said smoothly, "no warning. No envoy. No cry for help. Silence does not absolve—it condemns. You speak of myths older than our oldest stones, tales whispered for thousands of years. And if they were taken, then by whom? And why would no trace remain?"

Thorne did not reply. The silence that followed was not surrender—but resistance deferred.

He raised his hand slightly, fingers splayed in a controlled gesture of stillness. "Yet we endured. We rose—not because of her, but in spite of her. This Accord you sit beneath was born not of lineage or myth, but of necessity. Of survival. And it must be preserved."

He glanced toward the flicker of the Observatory Mirror's image in the dome. "Now the Veil stirs. Something moves beyond it. Not myth—presence."

A hush fell deeper than before. Not even the dome flickered.

Councilor Thorne of Karnor broke the silence first, his voice hard as granite. "Then we must fortify. If there is motion in the Veil, we secure our borders and prepare for the worst. Magic must not soften us to real threat."

"That is your answer to everything, Thorne," said Lira of Aerthys, her voice sharp and clear. "Seal the skies and stock the walls. But if the Veil breathes, so too might knowledge or warning. We must investigate, not retreat."

Venmira of Elowen inclined her head, her tone wrapped in patience. "Perhaps the Veil's motion is not a threat, but a reminder. Faye may not have fallen—but fled. From what or whom, we cannot guess. But Elowen's vines sense change, and it does not feel like war."

"The only thing vines sense is rain," muttered Themaris of Ignaris, before raising his voice. "We need answers, yes. But not from old myths. Let the Chancellor lead the investigation—quietly. If this is a test, then only one voice should shape the response."

Eyes drifted toward Siroth again.

He let the pause linger a moment longer before speaking—just long enough to seem reluctant, thoughtful, above the bickering.

"We must not let this moment divide us," he said, his voice rich with conviction. "Councilor Lira is correct—knowledge is not an enemy. Nor is vigilance, as Councilor Thorne demands. But the search for truth must not become the breeding ground of panic."

He turned slightly, his gaze sweeping toward Themaris. "And Councilor Themaris, your clarity is appreciated. In times like these, quiet action speaks louder than proclamations."

Let them bicker, he thought. Each voice more desperate than the last to seem indispensable. The truth had long since outgrown them.

Inwardly, he dismissed them all as children playing at statecraft. Lira's soaring rhetoric was useful—public-facing, charming. Themaris was dangerous, but predictable. Venmira's sentimentality would pacify the masses, but never win wars. And Thorne? Too blunt to understand nuance. It would be so easy to break him.

But the time was not yet right. He needed them bound together under his guidance, not scattered in suspicion.

"Let this be our course, then," he said, his voice low but resolute. "We will investigate quietly, wisely, and without delay. If the Veil stirs, we will meet it not with fear—but with order. The order we have built from ruin."

The words were like balm—soothing, confident, righteous. A performance honed over decades. And beneath it all, Siroth allowed himself the faintest flicker of satisfaction. They were already leaning toward him. As they always did.

But not all leaned equally.

A low chime rang through the chamber—three tones struck in perfect harmonic sequence. It signaled the invocation of record. An ancient rite.

"Veritas Scriptum," intoned Archivist Marqual from the high balcony above, his staff alight with blue runes. As the words reverberated, threads of silver light unfurled from the central obelisk suspended beneath the dome.

They wove between the councilors like gentle smoke, brushing each of their brows before vanishing into the stone floor—an enchantment that would record not only their words, but their intentions, preserved forever in the living memory of the Hall.

"Let the truth of this session be bound to our memory and the memory of those yet to come," Marqual finished.

Then, raising his staff and closing his eyes, he murmured the ancient spell:

"Memoratu Veranthis,
(Remember the True Essence)

ligora tempares et esen'dril,
(Bind the Balance and the Soul's Thread)

suratovar."
(and be Sealed)

The runes on the staff blazed briefly, and a halo of pale indigo light circled the chamber's perimeter, descending like a slow wave. As it passed through each delegate, a subtle warmth bloomed behind the eyes—an indication that thoughts, even unspoken, were now being transcribed into the Hall's deep memory.

Siroth felt the pulse touch him. For a heartbeat, his chest tightened—not in fear, but reflex. The magic brushed the edges of his mind, seeking truth.

He welcomed it with a mental flourish.

A practiced, pre-crafted spell shimmered in his subconscious: a screen of half-truths and virtuous intent, layered in centuries of linguistic misdirection. "Intentus Claritas," he had named it long ago—a spell for clarity... or the illusion of it.

His thoughts passed inspection, as they always did. And as the enchantment moved on, a corner of his mouth curled in silent amusement. Not all truth was meant to be recorded—only the truth he intended to be remembered. The enchantment obeyed the strongest mind in the room, and his had been shaped for decades to wield truth like glass: reflective, refractive, and when necessary, sharp enough to cut unseen.

The chamber dimmed briefly, and the light refocused on Siroth.

He welcomed it.

"Let us be clear, then," he said, stepping forward, his voice now touched with solemn gravity. "The Veil is not a myth to be debated endlessly. It is a wound. We can either heal it—or let it fester."

He turned slightly toward Venmira, his tone still velvet but threaded now with steel. "And we must be cautious not to let misplaced longing cloud our path. The Fifth Kingdom did not leave—it withdrew. And left us to bleed."

Gasps whispered through the hall, some recoiling at the sharpness of his claim, others visibly nodding.

Beneath Councilor Thorne, the basalt of Karnor shimmered faintly—not with power, but resistance. The symbols etched into his tier dimmed for a breath, as if unwilling to bear false witness.

Siroth bowed his head in modest gravity. "But we endured. Because we stood together. That is the story that must be remembered. And the truth that will be recorded."

Before the last word settled into silence, the chamber darkened.

A soft chime, lower than before—three descending notes—sounded like a warning disguised as ceremony. The air grew colder, thinner, as if some deeper presence had been invited into the Hall.

From the edge of the chamber, where no delegation sat, a narrow black corridor unsealed itself from the stone—no doors, only absence reshaped. A figure emerged, robed in shadowed cloth threaded with symbols that flickered in and out of visible spectrum.

The Inquisitors.

They did not belong to any kingdom. Their order was older than the Accord itself—older than the version of the Circle the public was allowed to remember. A secretive body that answered only to the Chancellor—or so it was claimed. Their true power lay in their symbiosis with the elemental orders: each Inquisitor bore a silent bond with one of the elemental domains, a deep synchronization that granted them authority across territories, but also tethered their methods to the realms they reflected.

Though they answered only to the Chancellor, even that allegiance felt more like an arrangement of convenience than loyalty. Rumors lingered that they followed something older still.

The first one to step forward bore a mantle edged in shifting skylight—a bond to Aerthys. Another followed, fire-threaded and silent as scorched stone. Then a third—one cloaked in living bark and bone, the air around them thick with the scent of rain and growth.

No one spoke.

No fourth. No fifth.

No one remarked on it. Their absence had long since become part of the ritual.

The Circle of Inquisitors had once mirrored the Five Kingdoms. After the Severance, the Fifth Kingdom was lost—yet its seat endured, kept alive through symbol and rite. For centuries its bearer served not a realm, but the memory of one.

In the years of the Ordinatum, the Fifth's last Inquisitor vanished and never answered summons again. Not long after, the Karnor-bound Inquisitor disappeared as well. Some whispered it was coincidence. Others knew better.

Since then, only three had returned when summoned. The two empty places had become part of the pageantry—absences enshrined, never explained, never questioned.

Siroth raised one hand, not in command, but in welcome. "The Inquisitors have come to bear witness. And to trace the resonance."

His voice dropped into silence, and the flicker of the observatory mirror above flared.

A shadow had appeared within it. Something moving beyond the Veil.

"Begin," he said quietly.

The mirror shimmered—and the chamber snapped into stillness as the light twisted into a shape.

At first, there was only light—unstable, flickering like a lantern caught in breathless wind.

Then, clarity: a boy, no older than thirteen, standing barefoot in a cloistered courtyard. His silhouette flickered between light and mist, framed by a muted winter haze. The Hall had never seen the

Observatory's glass sharpen like this before; it was built to chart flux, not faces. Even the eldest councilors stiffened, knowing the Mirror had broken its own rules.

The boy was no echo. He cast shadow. He breathed.

And then—he looked up.

Not randomly. Not vaguely.

His gaze met the Hall of Accord.

Venmira gasped audibly. "He sees us."

Themaris uttered a curse in an old Ignaric dialect and took half a step back.

Councilor Thorne did not move, but the basalt beneath his boots pulsed once—dim, but defiant.

The boy tilted his head slightly, brow furrowed in concentration. He raised one hand—not in greeting, but almost reflexively, as if sensing a ripple in the world around him. Something glinted between his fingers—a curved fragment, green-lit for an instant before the light swallowed it. His mouth opened, shaping a word that no one heard.

Lira whispered, "This isn't a breach. It's a thread."

Above them, the stars in the dome shimmered, realigning subtly.

On the dais, Siroth remained utterly still. His eyes narrowed—not in recognition, but in calculation. There was no face he remembered. But there was something in the silence behind the boy—something that disturbed him more than he expected.

Not memory. Not prophecy. Potential.

The image stuttered, distorted, and vanished.

Gasps broke across the chamber.

And Siroth, his face still, felt the weight of prophecy coil once more into the shape of a boy.

Councilor Venmira stood slowly, her lips parted—not in fear, but in a sudden, visceral knowing she couldn't name. Something in the child's gaze threaded through memory she didn't know she still held.

Siroth did not speak. He let the moment lengthen long enough to register as gravity, not hesitation.

Around him, the Councilors remained transfixed, uncertain whether they'd witnessed prophecy, accident, or something far worse. But Siroth knew what they truly feared—not the boy, but the ambiguity. Power could be debated; ambiguity could not.

And that made it useful.

He shifted back one step on the dais—deliberate, grounded—then turned his eyes toward the central crystal dome. Stars moved faintly across its surface, no longer in synchronicity.

Already, he could hear the gears turning: Lira would rush to write speeches about omens; Thorne would call for a military census before moonrise. Themaris would vanish into Ignaris's arcane labs. And Venmira... she would whisper to her trees.

Let them. Their responses were predictable, and predictability was leverage.

What none of them saw—what the Inquisitors would never speak—was that the Council was not a balance of powers. It was a stage. A shroud of civility draped over a machine of influence he had spent three decades tuning to precision.

The Council debated.

The public watched.

The Inquisitors enforced.

But only he commanded all three without ever appearing to.

And now, that machine had caught the scent of something—not a threat, not yet. But a variable. A crack in the crystal dome.

His gaze fixated on the last glimmer of the boy's outline before it fully dissolved.

He let the image linger in their minds. The boy. The mist. The gaze.

He let the silence tighten—not with mourning, but with something more productive: doubt. Let them stare, hearts pounding with questions they dared not voice.

Then, softly, he began. "We must not be distracted by shadows."

He took a step forward, slow and deliberate. "What you saw was not prophecy. Not return. Not blood. It is noise—born of the Veil's instability. A ripple. A side effect of old treason echoing into the present."

He turned slowly, meeting each councilor's gaze in turn.

"Faye did not die for us. She did not vanish to protect us. She abandoned us. That is not accusation. That is history."

He let the lie settle like sediment in their minds.

"I alone remained. When the Circle broke, when the kingdoms turned on each other, when famine and fire followed her absence—I did not retreat. I invoked the Nullum. I severed the Veil. I paid the price she would not—whether you bless me for it or curse me for it."

He raised one hand—not clenched, but open. Not a threat. A benediction.

"I do not need myth. I do not need sentiment. I need vigilance. I need memory."

Then his tone hardened, almost imperceptibly.

"If something stirs beyond the Veil now, it is not legacy—it is infection. It is the past testing our defenses."

He faced the mirror's lingering shimmer. "And we are no longer the kingdom that once knelt to chaos."

His eyes narrowed. "We are the Order forged in her absence."

He turned to the Inquisitors. "Let none misread this moment. What we saw is not hope."

He paused. "It is leakage."

A hush deepened across the chamber, a silence not of awe, but of alignment.

Then, with finality: "Trace him."

Chapter Six

"Something is Awakening"

The light from the altar steadied—then deepened, casting their faces in a dull, green-blue sheen. Maurice reached for the pendant he kept beneath his robes. The chain slipped through his fingers, revealing a small disk of dark metal, its surface polished by years of touch and etched with faint concentric lines that caught the altar's glow. Gwendlynn mirrored him, drawing out a smaller pendant, bronze-toned and softly luminous, its five-pointed frame dulled by time.

The two pieces were different in form but bound by the same quiet purpose—objects carried, never displayed. Neither spoke. Together they set the pendants upon the altar, where shallow hollows seemed made for their shape.

The pulse gathered—one, then two—until the carvings along the rim flared and a deep sound stirred behind the wall, like the Abbey drawing breath. Stone shifted with slow reluctance, dust sifting down in thin veils as an ancient door released its weight. The frame outlined itself in a narrow trace of light, then eased open enough to release a whisper of air.

Maurice retrieved his object, slipping it back beneath his robes. Gwendlynn did the same. For a long moment they stood in the glow, listening—to the faint hum in the air, to the sound of the world steadying itself after long stillness. Then, without a word, they crossed the threshold.

As they entered the concealed chamber beyond, the air felt different.

Though the air beneath Saint-Spire Abbey had always been still—held in the silence of stone and sanctity—today there was a subtle hum. As if the stone itself were remembering.

Father Maurice stepped lightly, his robes barely brushing the ground as he followed Mother Gwendlynn deeper into the forgotten corridors beneath the Abbey's historic archives. These were no longer used for books or records—sealed to most and hidden behind enchanted shelving—this lower level had been colloquially dismissed as a myth by most of the order. But Maurice knew better. The sconces lining the walls flickered not with flame but with the faint greenish-blue shimmer of stored incantation—light drawn from relics older than the Abbey itself.

Gwendlynn was ahead of him by several paces, her posture unflinching, purposeful. She hadn't said much since summoning him, but he could sense something different in her. Not fear—expectation. Reverence.

He let his hand graze the wall, fingers tracing the same sigils he'd passed countless times. But this time, they were warm.

When they reached the heart of the Lower Archives—the octagonal chamber with its domed ceiling of carved stone—Maurice stopped short. The stones above glowed softly, the same four tones he remembered: blue for Aerthys, green for Elowen, red-gold for Ignaris, gray for Karnor. And at the center, as always, the fifth stone—Iron—held no color at all, only a muted presence.

For a flicker of a moment, Maurice felt something else—something just beyond memory, like a name spoken in a dream. He knew these colors too well, not just as symbols of history, but as echoes of something once lived. A place. A vow. A moment beneath another dome, long before he wore the collar of Saint-Spire.

The memory passed like fog on glass, too thin to hold, too fleeting to name. But it left a thrum in his chest, as though the stones still knew the shape of his presence.

But the fifth shimmered differently now.

Not in color, but in rhythm—its colorless surface beating with a faint pulse.

Maurice's breath caught.

He steadied his shaking hands by pressing them into his robes, hiding a tremor. Years beneath these stones, years guarding truths he'd sworn never to speak. And now, the walls whispered reminders of promises kept in shadow, of deceptions buried under layers of necessity. He'd known the silence wouldn't last forever—but now, standing here with Gwendlynn, the inevitable felt dangerously close.

"It's responding," Gwendlynn said quietly. She did not look at him.

"To what?" Maurice asked.

She turned slowly, her expression unreadable. "Something waking."

He took a step closer to the center of the chamber, staring up at the glowing stone. "It shouldn't be reacting. Not without cause."

Gwendlynn nodded. "Not without contact. Or convergence beginning anew."

Maurice's eyes narrowed. "You mean the convergence is beginning again?"

She hesitated. "I mean the conditions that once allowed it are no longer dormant."

A silence stretched between them, heavy with unsaid truths. Maurice finally asked, his voice low, "How long have you suspected?"

"Longer than I've admitted," she said. "But I needed you to see it—feel it—before I could be sure."

"And now?"

Gwendlynn met his gaze, unflinching. "Now I am."

She looked away for a moment—not in evasion, but as if searching the stone for a memory she didn't yet know she'd lost. Something in the silence pressed against her chest—not fear, but gravity.

Maurice looked once more at the pulsing stone, its rhythm faint but steady.

Maurice hesitated, voice heavy with unspoken dread. "If something truly is waking, then all that's lain dormant might surface with it—memories, echoes… the parts we hoped would stay buried."

Gwendlynn did not blink, her voice steady. "If the past returns faster than we are prepared to handle it—"

Maurice interrupted softly, fear edged in his voice. "Then we might not hold control over what it brings."

He didn't say the word that hovered at the edge of his thoughts: exposure. Not just of power, but of the people they'd become while guarding it.

The glow deepened—faint, insistent. A whisper of resonance—just enough to suggest that something, or someone, had heard. Maurice said nothing. Some truths were best buried in silence—until silence broke on its own.

The chamber stilled once more—but the light in the stone refused to dim.

They stood there quietly, both sensing a shift, a crack in the carefully built sanctuary of their silence. Maurice felt the stones pulsing gently beneath his feet, as if responding to his anxiety, challenging him to maintain the fragile calm he had preserved all these years.

He glanced toward Gwendlynn, her profile quiet and unreadable in the shimmering glow, and wondered if their shared silences had finally become too loud to contain.

Then came the faintest shift—a sigh in the stone, or perhaps only the air reclaiming its space. Either way, the chamber was no longer still. Somewhere in that tremor of quiet, the past reached forward.

And above, unaware that anything had changed, a boy turned in his sleep, his chest rising in time with a rhythm older than his name.

***

The morning of the Winter Lights Festival rose under a thin, unsettled haze. It drifted across the rooftops of Corbeil-Essonnes in slow, deliberate sheets—the kind of mist that made the town feel caught between silence and awakening, as if warmth were rising from a slumbering giant.

In the days leading up to it, life had blurred into quiet preparation—garlands woven with care, pews scrubbed to a shine, loaves of honey bread baked in solemn abundance. Now, the village stood hushed, caught between anticipation and remembrance.

Within the Abbey, silence pressed like a folded prayer. Leonarth woke slowly—slower than he ever did.

Sleep clung to him in a way that felt unfamiliar, heavy at the edges, as though the night hadn't quite released its hold. He was usually awake before the bells, before the shuffling feet and murmured devotions. Today, his thoughts lagged behind his breath.

Something soft pressed against his face. A twitch of fur. A breath. A whisker brushing his nose, nearly triggering a sneeze.

He cracked one eye open, unfocused, and found two wide, golden irises staring back at him.

Meely.

The cat sat like a sentry on his chest, her silvery-gray fur undisturbed, her silence absolute. She neither meowed nor purred. She simply watched him, her gaze too knowing for comfort.

Leonarth exhaled and rubbed at his eyes, trying to gather himself. The drowsiness didn't lift the way it should have. He looked at the cat and, without knowing why, found himself thinking of how they had met. She had shown up not long after he had—and never left. She was a Chartreux, though he only knew that from a book he once read. Reserved, nearly invisible when she chose to be, yet oddly loyal. She followed him room to room like a shadow, pretending not to care.

Meely let out a low, insistent sound.

Leonarth shifted, swung his legs over the side of the bed, and stood.

Routine stepped in where awareness had not.

Every morning, without thinking, he slipped into the kitchen and slid her a saucer of milk—cliché or not—because routine was easier than questions. Today was no different.

When he returned to the dormitory, his thoughts still drifted, half-formed. He never quite understood how the sisters seemed to ignore the cat so completely.

After so many years, he thought someone might have named her. But no one had—except him. The name Meely had slipped from his lips once when he was five or six, barely aware of why or how it came to him. The cat had blinked in acknowledgment, and from that day forward, it stuck. Meely was part of the Abbey in the way ivy was part of its stones—present, quiet, and unacknowledged.

Leonarth set his things down by the bed. Only then did Meely decide he had served his purpose as a perch, padding off without a sound.

His gaze drifted, unfocused at first, across the room—then stilled.

The dormitory was empty—eerily so. He should have heard the rustle of blankets, the hiss of whispered prayers, the shuffle of boots on stone. But there was nothing. Everyone must have been up long before dawn, but he couldn't recall hearing a sound. It puzzled him. Somehow, he hadn't stirred.

Meely watched from the corner, tail flicking once—almost in time with the thought.

Leonarth dressed quickly, movements practiced, automatic.

As he reached for his boots, a line rose unbidden from memory—one Mother Gwendlynn used to say during morning devotions, her voice steady and absolute: "*Where the young ones see routine, I see discipline.*"

The thought unsettled him. This morning hadn't followed its usual shape. He found himself turning the words over, instead of letting them pass.

Someone—she never said who—had once claimed that discipline was the bridge between goals and achievement. She'd repeated it so often it had become part of the Abbey's rhythm—unchanging, predictable, safe.

But now, standing in the quiet room where routine had inexplicably failed him, the words returned with a weight that brought back the faint distance in her tone—something he hadn't noticed until now, as if the words belonged to someone she no longer wished to remember.

The echo of her voice seemed to fill the quiet around him, and for a moment, he could almost see her again—composed, deliberate, a presence that never quite left the room. Mother Gwendlynn was such a presence—an anchor within the Abbey's walls, and to Leonarth, a figure he could never fully understand.

She was not tall, and carried a slender elegance unshaken by her eighty years. Her white hair was cut short in a practical style, always tucked behind her ears, and her eyes—dark green with flecks of something deeper—seemed to catch more than they let on. When Leonarth's gaze met hers, that old clarity stirred—the one he'd once called logical empathy—the wordless knowing that came to him unbidden.

He looked away first, suddenly aware he'd been standing still too long. He sensed strength and compassion in her, the discipline that shaped her, yet even through that strange awareness, she remained opaque. There was a quiet power in her, one that unsettled some and steadied others without explanation.

Even with that measured grace, the mystery of her past lingered—like a question suspended in the rafters of the Abbey. She was compelling in a way that never quite fit within its quiet folds. "Why did she choose the habit?" he had once wondered aloud. The answer never came, not from her. Perhaps, as Mattheon once said, some answers wait until we're ready to understand.

As the Abbey's eldest sister, Gwendlynn oversaw nearly everything. She worked closely with Father Maurice, their understanding quiet and precise, defined more by purpose than rank. Her routines were exacting, almost ceremonial, yet never hollow. Discipline, to her, was both shield and language—a way to keep chaos at bay without betraying its existence. When the children were sick, frightened, or lost in thought, it was Gwendlynn they sought—stern when she had to be, but always steady.

To Leonarth, Mother Gwendlynn was not a comfort but a constant—a presence that defined the rhythm of Abbey life. Much like Sister Mabelle's quiet watch over Mattheon, Gwendlynn's attentiveness came not from affection but from purpose. Since his arrival, she had ensured he followed the rules, kept his focus, stayed within the lines she so carefully drew for everyone. He sometimes caught the weight in her gaze, as though she were guarding something she didn't fully understand herself. Yet whatever passed between them was marked more by respect than closeness. Ava was the one who had brought him here, the one whose kindness felt personal. Gwendlynn's was different—measured, distant, and unyielding.

The thought lingered for a moment, then slipped away as he pulled his coat tight and stepped into the corridor. His footfalls sounded too loud against the stone, the hush following him like a shadow. Halfway down the hall he realized, with a jolt, that he was heading toward the classroom wing. There were no classes today—it was the day of the Winter Lights Festival.

He muttered under his breath, "Brilliant. Forget the biggest day of the year..."

Turning sharply on his heel, he began to sprint, his breath echoing in the vaulted passage. The opening mass was about to begin, and he was very late. He took a chance, veering off the main corridor and ducking through the nuns' inner garden—a shortcut frowned upon, if not expressly forbidden. He passed beneath twisted ivy, the air rich with the scent of flowers freshly set for the festival. The central patio lay empty, tables already arranged in perfect symmetry, garlands draped like soft constellations above rows of polished vases. For a fleeting instant, the stillness felt sacred—then he was through it, boots striking the far archway as he raced toward the church doors.

When Leonarth finally arrived, flushed and winded, Mother Gwendlynn stood by the door, arms crossed and one eyebrow arched in a way that made him feel six years old again. Her expression said everything before she even opened her mouth.

"You are so very late, Mr. Leonarth," she said, her voice sharp but not without amusement. "And as if that weren't enough, you brought that cat again?"

Leonarth blinked and turned, only now realizing Meely had padded silently beside him the entire way. The cat sat primly at his heels, looking rather pleased with herself.

"Of course," he muttered. "Should've known."

"Not again," Gwendlynn sighed, already scanning the garden path for inspiration. "That cat has to stop following you everywhere. We cannot have a feline among the incense and choir during the opening mass."

She spotted a twig in the gravel, snatched it up, and without missing a beat, crouched and flicked it once. "Meely—fetch."

The cat gave her a long, disapproving look, tail twitching with what could only be interpreted as aristocratic disdain. Then, with the slow dignity only Meely could muster, she turned and trotted off toward the brambles, chasing the stick with reluctant grace.

Leonarth watched her go, puzzled. Cats didn't fetch. Not unless they'd decided it mattered. Meely's habit of retrieving small objects—always only when she felt like it—was one of those quirks Leonarth had long ago stopped questioning. Still, there was something different this time. Meely moved as if the choice had already been made, as if the game had purpose—like she'd been waiting for this very excuse. But before he could dwell on it, the moment passed, swallowed by the day's urgency.

"Now!" Gwendlynn grabbed Leonarth by his scarf and yanked him inside, nearly toppling him. The heavy oak door closed with a hollow thud behind them.

"Leonarth," she said, more softly now, her tone easing but never losing its edge. "You know I value discipline above all. There are rules for a reason. What would Father Maurice think, bringing that walking bundle of fur into the church again?"

"I thought she'd stay put after I fed her," Leonarth offered weakly, adjusting his scarf.

"You fed her again?" Gwendlynn's eyes widened, though her lips were already twitching at the corners. "Is there anything else you'd like to confess before mass begins? Perhaps you've taught her Latin as well."

Leonarth shrugged sheepishly. "Not yet."

Gwendlynn sighed, shaking her head with mock exasperation. "Well, it's too late now. What's done is done—milk in the bowl and all. Go on, find your seat. And no slinking in like a shadow. You'll get all the disapproving stares anyway, so you may as well walk tall."

She gave him a firm pat on the shoulder, her expression softening. Then, with a rustle of robes and a final glance at the door, she disappeared down the side corridor, her footsteps brisk and certain.

Leonarth exhaled, the warmth of her presence lingering a moment longer than her voice. He slipped into the nave just as the choir began to hum the opening notes of the procession. The scent of incense hung heavy in the air, curling through beams of sunlight that filtered in through stained glass like shafts of magic.

Mattheon caught his eye from a pew near the aisle, smirking as Leonarth slid into place beside him. "Nice of you to join the living," his expression seemed to say, though he didn't dare speak it aloud. Leonarth rolled his eyes, lips twitching despite himself.

It was a special celebration. Not only was it the 53rd Winter Lights Festival, but the Abbey was also marking its centennial anniversary as an orphanage—a small celebration for a place whose true age was older than memory, and seldom named. Clerics from across the region had gathered for the occasion, dressed in ceremonial vestments that shimmered with thread-of-gold under the light. Yet for all its grandeur, the mass itself—led by Father Maurice—was hardly captivating.

His voice carried the practiced cadence of faith, but not its fire; each verse sounded learned rather than lived. The sermon was long and meandering, filled with scripture and formality, and Leonarth found it nearly impossible to focus.

Leonarth's gaze drifted upward, drawn to the stained-glass windows flanking both sides of the church. When sunlight passed through them at just the right angle, the colored panes cast a kaleidoscope of shifting shapes and hues onto the stone floor—so vivid and surreal, it hardly seemed natural.

He looked closer. There were ten windows in all—five on each side—alternating between pure mosaic patterns and vivid illustrations.

The first window beside the altar was a mosaic of angular blues and violets; the second showed a strange city floating among clouds. Then another mosaic. Then a scene of treehouses woven into towering jungle canopies. The pattern continued—mosaic, illustration, mosaic, illustration—until four full illustrated panels stood out among the decorative glass.

He leaned forward slightly, squinting to study them. There were no saints. No angels. No familiar biblical figures or parables. Instead, each scene seemed to tell its own otherworldly story: a metallic fortress carved into a mountain; an airborne vessel drifting among stars; a cathedral crowned in flame but untouched by smoke.

None of it belonged in a church—or at least, not in what he thought a church was meant to be.

He narrowed his eyes further. In each of the illustrated panels, fine etchings wove along the edges—lines too intricate to be ornamental. They might've been inscriptions, but from his seat in the pews, he couldn't tell. Just as easily, it could've been grime, the forgotten dust of a hundred springs.

And yet, something about the scenes stirred the same strange sense he'd felt earlier that morning when Meely ran off with the stick—as if the Abbey was full of small signals waiting to be seen, whispering from the corners of stone and light.

As Leonarth studied the glowing patterns, something flickered near one of the windows to his right. He blinked. There—barely noticeable—was a sliver that shouldn't have existed, no lead, no join, just absence. A space too narrow for anything—except, perhaps, for Meely. And through that sliver, he spotted a slinking, silvery shape of the familiar cat.

His body jolted, knee knocking against the pew in front of him with a dull thud. A girl turned around and glared, whispering a sharp, "Shhh! Behave!"

Leonarth nodded sheepishly, though his eyes never left the window. Meely, impossibly, was squeezing herself through the gap in the stained glass, delicately landing on the stone floor—still holding what looked like the same stick—until the grain caught light, revealing buried metal. This wasn't Gwendlynn's twig at all. The weight in it felt wrong—denser, older. Like it had waited underground for a very long time.

The cat padded forward with that peculiar certainty she carried only when she chose to act on something no one else could see. Leonarth froze. If she reached the front—near the altar, near the nuns—it would be a disaster.

Without taking his eyes off her, he whispered urgently to Mattheon, "Third window on the right. Do you see her? We need to stop her—now. Follow me."

Mattheon blinked, half-whispering back, "Here? During mass?" But Leonarth was already moving.

The two boys crouched low and began to crawl, slipping beneath the pews like practiced acrobats. Curious glances followed them, but the other children—conditioned to ignore strange things in favor of rules—kept their heads turned forward.

All was going smoothly until they reached the final stretch. A supporting leg beneath the pew blocked their path.

Leonarth hissed, "We need to switch rows. Quietly. If anyone sees us—"

"Wait," Mattheon whispered, eyes lighting up. "They're about to sing the Hallelujah sequence. Three repeats. They all look up when they sing. We move on the beat."

Leonarth grinned despite the tension. "You're brilliant. This is why I keep you around."

The choir surged into the first hallelujah. Leonarth rolled forward.

A slight thump—his foot clipped the pew leg. A nun glanced down, but he was already hidden.

Second hallelujah. Mattheon hesitated—then missed it. Leonarth stiffened.

Third hallelujah. Mattheon darted across just in time, face flushed.

Now at the far end of the pews, they slipped out and ducked behind one of the stone columns lining the nave. Leonarth scanned the room.

No alarm. The congregation's gaze stayed fixed on the altar, faces lifted toward the hymn's final refrain. A few sisters traded brief, puzzled glances—Mabelle among them—toward the space the boys had left behind, but the chant swallowed their unease as quickly as it came. Father Maurice didn't so much as pause.

Silence.

Then—a soft brush at his ankle.

Meely.

The cat leaned against him as if she'd been waiting there the entire time, golden eyes gleaming with mischief. Her eyes lingered on him—not curious, not affectionate. As if confirming a pattern only she could see. Like she'd returned something she was always meant to fetch.

Leonarth lifted her gently, cradling her as he whispered, "You're going to get us both excommunicated."

He motioned to Mattheon. The ushers had stepped back for the procession; the side door stood unguarded. Together they slipped through it into the sunlight. From across the nave, Sister Mabelle's gaze followed them—a brief flicker of recognition, gone as quickly as it came. Mattheon didn't notice. Leonarth didn't look back.

Outside, breathing freely, the boys leaned against the stone wall. Meely dropped the stick at Leonarth's feet.

Mattheon bent to pick it up—then froze, brow furrowing. "Leonarth… look at this."

Leonarth took the stick in his hand. One end wasn't wood. It gleamed.

Something metallic—embedded.

"It's loose," he said. "Help me get it out."

They hurried to the wrought-iron fence around the churchyard. Leonarth wedged the stick's edge against a tapered spike, twisting gently.

The object shifted. A soft click. Then it slipped free.

He held it up. Small. Worn. Intricately etched.

A key.

Not like any key he had ever seen before.

Now that the object was fully visible, it became clear it was no ordinary piece of metal. The key was tiny and delicately crafted, its metal neither quite silver nor iron—edges worn smooth by time, its bow traced with fine, uneven curves. Engravings ran along the length of the shaft—words etched so lightly they shimmered only when caught in the light.

Leonarth read them aloud, voice hushed with awe:

"Know it is still here, or it will just stay invisible to you…"

He turned it slowly, breath caught.

"…Belief will open windows where there were only walls."

The words felt less like a riddle and more like a memory—one that didn't belong to him but had waited to be found. They stirred something deeper than understanding, an echo of knowing without recall, as if the meaning had lived in him all along, waiting for a voice to wake it.

A chill passed through him—part wind, part something else.

The words still lingered in his mind, vibrating faintly like a struck chord that refused to fade. He exhaled, lifting his head as though the sound had called him to look higher. His gaze found the high window Meely had slipped through, where sunlight spilled through colored glass like a door left momentarily ajar. For an instant, filaments of light rippled across the glass—patterns that shifted, then vanished.

He blinked, and they were gone.

Beside him, Mattheon stared at the key, his expression caught somewhere between awe and unease. "That's… not just a key, is it?" he murmured.

Mattheon's words barely reached him. Leonarth's pulse quickened—the air felt heavier now, charged, as if the moment had pulled something unseen into motion.

The church bells rang overhead, distant and solemn, as if marking not only the hour—but something stirring beyond it. Deep beneath their feet, old stone exhaled a slow, patient breath—as if the Abbey itself had begun to remember.

Chapter Seven

"The Bloom and the Secret"

Ava stepped out of the church into the pale, late-morning light, the last echoes of the choir still drifting through the open doors. For a moment, pride warmed her chest—the mass had gone flawlessly, the festival guests were arriving, and the flowers she'd arranged at dawn would soon fill the courtyard paths with color. It was the first time the sisters had trusted her with something that mattered in public.

Then came the sound—wood snapping, pottery breaking, a rush of paws on stone.

"No, no… That cannot be happening!"

Novice Ava froze, eyes wide with dismay. Two stray dogs, still chasing each other with gleeful abandon, had just barreled through the central courtyard—obliterating two long tables she had painstakingly arranged with flowers and vines for the opening of the Winter Lights Festival.

Shards of ceramic pots littered the stones. Delicate blooms were scattered, crushed, and shredded, their stems snapped and strewn, fragile as ribs. It was a disaster—her disaster.

Ava had insisted—begged, even—to take full responsibility for the decorations. And now this.

Right on cue, Sister Mabelle and Sister Prudence rounded the corner, arms crossed like gatekeepers of doom.

"This is unfortunate," Sister Mabelle said quietly, her gaze steady. "But not unexpected."

"Well. The Flowerless Festival it is," Sister Prudence muttered. "Let's just hope it's not a sign."

Ava turned to defend herself, but before she could form a sentence, Sister Mabelle raised a dismissive hand.

"We should inform Father Maurice," she said, measured. "He may need to prepare the guests for… unexpected changes."

Sister Prudence chimed in like a well-rehearsed choir. "Perhaps something about humility. And learning limits."

Without waiting for a reply, they turned on their heels and disappeared down the cloister walk, their footsteps clicking like punctuation.

Ava stood rooted amid the ruin. Alone. The silence pressed against her, broken only by the soft rustle of petals tumbling in the breeze. This mess wasn't just about flowers—it was about everything. Her place. Her right to belong. Her need to matter.

She clenched her jaw, then scanned the courtyard. No one. Not a soul.

Good.

Because what she was about to do… wasn't allowed.

***

The last of the church bells faded into the air, their echo trembling through the cloister walls. Doors creaked open, and the first wave of voices spilled from the nave.

Leonarth glanced toward the sound. "They're coming out."

Mattheon groaned. "Perfect. Father Maurice will see us if we go that way. The children are always the last to leave—he'll know we skipped." He rubbed the back of his neck. "So what do we do, just stand here?"

Leonarth shook his head, eyes darting to the narrow walkway that curved toward the inner courtyard. "That path cuts behind the dormitory. We can circle around and join the others from the back."

"Why not just wait for them to pass?"

"Because we still have this." He tapped the pocket where the key lay heavy. "If someone stops us and asks what we were doing, I'll have to explain it."

Mattheon frowned. "You're thinking Father Maurice."

"I'm thinking everyone," Leonarth muttered. "He'll ask why we weren't in the pews, and then we'll end up talking about the key. And I'm a terrible liar."

Mattheon blew out a quiet breath. "Fine. We hide it first, then act like we've been there all along."

"Exactly."

"What about my aunt? You know she saw the empty seats."

Leonarth grimaced. "Then you'll have to handle her."

Mattheon's mouth twitched. He exhaled, clearly unhappy. "Fine. But don't think you're off the hook. She doesn't drop things—ever. And she already noticed."

Meely trotted ahead, tail flicking like she'd done her duty and was done with them.

"Come on," Leonarth said, lowering his voice. "We've got to move—before anyone sees us."

They followed her through the side archway—and stopped.

The courtyard that had gleamed that morning was a wreck of overturned tables and crushed flowers. Ava stood in the middle of it, motionless, her hands trembling at her sides.

"Great," Mattheon whispered. "We can't go that way."

"If we go back, everyone from mass will see us," Leonarth murmured.

"So what now?"

"Wait. If she leaves, we run."

But she didn't leave.

From where they crouched, the boys watched as she knelt, picked up a tattered bloom—its stem split, its petals ragged—and stared at it. Then she reached into her robes and drew out a small, gleaming object—some kind of necklace, maybe.

The object caught the light, turning in her palm until its shapes began to separate from the glare. Something like a ruby spark burned at its center, haloed by four green stones that curved around it like folded wings. A faint thread of metal wound beneath the setting, glinting as if it had once been alive. Around it all, a slender crescent of gold curved protectively—half moon, half cradle. And from its tip, a single sapphire teardrop pulsed—soft, rhythmic, alive—like the heartbeat of something ancient and waiting.

She closed her hand around it.

"Just this once," she whispered.

With her free hand, she extended two fingers over the broken flowers. Then, in a voice not loud but resonant, she spoke:

"Florata vivea, reverdare."
(Blossom, Live, Green Again)

Mattheon gasped. "Leonarth… did you see that?"

Leonarth was already watching, transfixed. A soft wind swept through the patio, rustling Ava's robes. The petals began to stir. Leaves straightened. Vines curled back to form. One by one, the ruined decorations reassembled themselves—then kept going, fuller and lusher than before, as if the spell didn't know where to stop.

Ava, breathing steadily, began placing the restored blooms back into their vessels, her hands almost reverent. She didn't see the boys. She didn't see anything else at all.

Leonarth couldn't look away.

Mattheon tugged at his sleeve. "We've seen enough. Let's go."

"But—"

"She's not supposed to be able to do that. You know that. Just come on."

Leonarth hesitated a second longer. Then, slipping one hand into his pocket, he felt the reassuring weight of the strange key Meely had led them to. It was warm—warmer than it should have been, as if something inside it was quietly awake. Sensing something beneath the metal, like a rhythm that wasn't quite his own. He turned it slowly between his fingers, watching Ava from the shadows.

"Yeah," he said. "Let's go."

The two boys crept off just as Ava looked up.

As they slipped into the corridor beyond the cloister, the distant murmur of a voice reached them—low, deliberate, and unmistakably Father Maurice's, his voice carrying to the gathered townspeople beyond the main archway.

Mattheon picked up the pace. "Come on, we might catch the end of it."

Leonarth followed, quiet and wide-eyed, the weight of the key still firm in his palm.

Together, they broke into a trot, rounding the corner toward the Abbey's front steps—just in time to hear the final words of Maurice's opening speech echo out into the festival air.

Behind them, Meely lingered at the edge of the courtyard, tail curling once through the air. Her golden eyes followed the boys until they vanished from sight—then turned back to Ava, unblinking, as if she'd seen it all before.

***

Father Maurice's voice rang out over the courtyard, clear and ceremonial. "...and with this joyful spirit, I declare opened the 53rd Winter Lights Festival. Enjoy the festivities, and do not forget to stop by our inner courtyard to experience an explosion of smells and colors, lovingly arranged by our dedicated sisters."

A few paces behind the main gate, Mother Gwendlynn stood in quiet anticipation, hands clasped before her, watching the arriving villagers. She had donned her finest formal robes for the occasion—not for ceremony, but for a personal hope.

She turned as a familiar figure emerged from the crowd: Archbishop Reginald of England, tall and silver-haired, flanked by two aides.

"Your Grace," she said warmly, stepping forward. "I had hoped you would attend this year. It's been far too long since we last welcomed you to Corbeil-Essonnes."

The Archbishop smiled faintly. "Indeed, Mother Gwendlynn. And still you age slower than the Abbey stones."

She laughed softly. "I was hoping for a moment to thank you—for... years ago. When you sent Novice Ava to us. I've always meant to say how much that letter meant—your faith in her meant a great deal to me."

The Archbishop's smile faltered. A wrinkle formed between his brows. "Ava?"

"Yes," she said, frowning gently. "You recommended her to our care. She arrived with your letter."

Reginald blinked. "I'm afraid I don't recall such a letter."

There was a pause. Not long. Barely a breath. But it was enough.

"I... must be confusing the details," Gwendlynn said quickly, stepping back. "It was many years ago."

He inclined his head. "Indeed. Time has a way of softening the facts."

But Gwendlynn didn't move for several seconds. Her smile had faded into something more thoughtful. Then, smoothing her robe, she turned back toward the Abbey steps and disappeared into the procession.

Watching from the steps, Maurice caught the end of the exchange. He noted the faint crease between the Archbishop's brows—and the way Gwendlynn's smile didn't return when she turned away. Just a moment. A flicker. But he felt it.

He adjusted his cuffs, schooled his features, and stepped forward into the waiting light, where he extended a gracious hand to the villagers pouring in—faces alight with celebration and expectation. His warmest smiles were for the elderly; his most encouraging nods, for the children.

The air was filled with laughter and song—everything precisely as he'd planned. So when Sister Mabelle and Sister Prudence suddenly flanked him—each tugging gently at one arm and speaking over the other in hushed urgency—he didn't lose his composure.

"Ladies," he said with practiced patience, still smiling and waving, "you know I can't decode twin tongues. One at a time. Preferably without tugging."

Sister Mabelle exhaled slowly, her eyes briefly closing in restraint. "I'll explain," she said with reserve. "We tried to reach you sooner, but the crowd was already pressing in. You mentioned an explosion of floral wonder in the inner courtyard—unfortunately, that part was literal."

Maurice tilted his head slightly. "And this catastrophe was...?"

She continued, her tone flat but unmistakably pointed, "Well, there was indeed an explosion. Just not the fragrant or picturesque sort. A catastrophe, in fact."

Maurice raised an eyebrow. "You'll have to be more specific. What sort of divine intervention are we alleging here?"

Sister Prudence stepped forward, clearly unable to contain herself any longer. "Novice Ava has completely obliterated the floral arrangements. They're in ruin. Pots shattered, petals pulverized. It looks like a storm passed through in holy robes."

Maurice took a slow breath and briefly closed his eyes. "Of course. A catastrophe before coffee. My favorite kind."

"I expressed concern," Sister Mabelle said, folding her hands. "She wasn't ready."

He opened his eyes again, glancing toward the courtyard archway. "I need to see this for myself. No overreactions. No dramatic warnings to the guests. Just quiet containment and a swift response."

"As you wish," said Sister Mabelle, lacing her hands, her expression unreadable.

Sister Prudence offered a final jab: "You might consider a sermon on resilience," she said dryly. "We could use it."

Maurice looked at her for a long moment. "If the garden is as ruined as you say, then we'll manage as we always do."

He took a step closer, his voice dropping just enough to be heard only by them. "And if it isn't… then I trust your silence will speak as loudly as your judgment has."

With that, he turned and began walking toward the inner courtyard. The two sisters followed—still stiff, but markedly quieter. He knew them well. And while they hid it beneath layers of decorum, he saw the gleam in their eyes: they had expected failure—and perhaps, quietly hoped for it. That, more than anything, told him this day was about far more than flowers.

It was only a brief walk from the Abbey's main entrance to the inner courtyard, yet every step seemed to swell the tension. As Father Maurice led the way, his pace deliberate, the sisters trailed behind like a growing tide of whispers. A few guests, drawn by the subdued commotion and sharp turns of phrase, lingered near the archway—curiosity being one of the more uncontainable human instincts.

Beyond them, the wooden doors to the inner courtyard remained closed. That, at least, brought Maurice a glimmer of relief. They were just in time. Whatever disaster awaited, it would be seen first by him, and not by the public.

He reached for the latch, but Sister Prudence swept forward with the enthusiasm of a stage performer stepping into the spotlight.

"Allow me the honors, Father," she declared, sliding between him and the door so swiftly that he had to take a half step back to keep from stumbling. "Let us unveil the most—"

She pushed the door open wide and froze. Her next words died mid-breath. He registered her silence without a flicker of surprise. Whatever he'd expected, it had not been this—but now was not the time to ask how.

"…the most beautiful and colorful display our beloved sisters put together for all of us," Maurice finished smoothly, stepping up beside her as though nothing were amiss. His voice projected with confidence, inviting warmth and admiration.

He turned back toward the onlookers. "Sisters, you have outdone last year's floral attraction. Truly—job well done. Come, come everyone, let's get closer to the plants and experience this life explosion that awaits us."

And what they found inside was beyond even Maurice's most hopeful expectations.

There wasn't a single surface untouched by bloom. Every corner, every stone, every man-made structure had been overtaken by beauty. Roses of deep crimson climbed the columns, their color shifting gradually to orange and then gold as they spiraled upward, giving the illusion of pillars set ablaze. The ground itself was blanketed with impossibly soft green grass—lush, flawless, unmarred by weeds or wayward roots. It shimmered faintly in the light.

Along the balconies that framed the courtyard, white lilies and blue tulips cascaded like the tiers of a fountain frozen mid-motion. And at the heart of it all, a single great table stretched beneath a flowering trellis, laden with the harvest's finest: fruits and vegetables arranged in a chromatic wave that rippled from one end to the other like a rainbow pulled into form—an impossible bounty for winter, glimmering with warmth against the chill.

Standing behind it, calm and radiant, was Novice Ava. She made no gesture, no dramatic pose—just a simple, honest smile that said everything without a single word. Ava remained motionless, one hand still resting lightly atop a blossom, as if drawing strength from the root beneath.

The crowd slowly dispersed, drawn into the garden's otherworldly beauty, their voices hushed, their steps reverent. But Father Maurice didn't follow. He remained still, eyes on Ava, and with a subtle glance, beckoned the two sisters to walk with him toward the center table where she stood.

"Ava," Sister Mabelle said carefully, her voice low. "Just moments ago, this place looked devastated. Now it's... whole," she said, and for the first time, her voice held more wonder than doubt.

Her words hung in the perfumed air, the disbelief clear in her voice. Around them, petals shimmered in sunlight and vines framed the morning like brushstrokes. Even the soil seemed touched by purpose.

Ava turned slowly, her posture poised but her fingers gently curled over the edge of the table as though grounding herself. "Thank you," she said, her voice tight. "Yes… it does look perfect, doesn't it?"

She paused, then tilted her head slightly. "As for hurricanes and disasters—I believe there was a bit of canine chaos earlier. Some minor disarray. But everything is in order now. I really don't see the need for alarm."

"But I saw it," Sister Prudence said sharply. "How could it all be… reversed?"

Ava opened her mouth to answer, but before she could speak, Maurice stepped forward, the steel behind his gentle eyes suddenly very clear.

"Does it matter?" he asked, his voice low and deliberate. "Look at it. Look at her. What stands before us is not a problem. It is a gift. Let us be grateful, not suspicious."

Sister Prudence hesitated, her lips parting to protest, but Maurice raised a single finger in quiet command—a gesture that spoke more than words. His authority was not forceful, but earned, and it quelled further challenge before it was voiced.

He turned to Ava now, slower, more thoughtful. "Well done, Novice," he said. "Truly. What you've accomplished here—whatever means you used—let it be what it is. A moment of grace."

Then, his tone shifted—brisk, administrative, but laced with something deeper. "Come now, sisters. There are other matters. The choir's closing hymn still needs alignment, and I need someone to confirm the sopranos are in the right key this year."

As he turned away, guiding the sisters with him, he paused. Just before the archway, he looked back—and with a conspiratorial softness Ava hadn't seen in years, he winked.

The garden hushed again, the crowd thinning like an orchestra softening after its final note.

When they were gone, Ava let out the breath she hadn't realized she was holding. Relief flooded her, but not without weight.

She reached for her pendant and closed her fingers around it. The metal was warm now, carrying a faint, steady thrum of memory. A single spark of pale blue stirred under her collarbone, then sank back into the folds of her robe.

She closed her eyes.

There, just behind the quiet of her breath, came a whisper of before—before silence became survival, before wonder was forbidden. She remembered a time when magic moved like music through the air, when children were taught to listen to stars and speak to leaves, when the Abbey had been a sanctuary not just of faith, but of the ineffable. It had been lost—not erased, but buried—and today, with a single act of defiance, she had brushed the dust from its surface.

That time would come again. Not through councils. Not through declarations. But through small, unnoticed miracles: a boy with a key in his pocket, a girl with flowers in her hands, a forgotten sigil pulsing in stone. The Fifth Kingdom would not rise with fanfare—it would bloom quietly, beneath the eyes of those who had stopped believing. Not in blaze, but in root. Not in thunder, but in blossom. Like a memory returning to breath.

She released the pendant and opened her eyes, not afraid to meet the light.

But not yet, she thought. Not yet.

Chapter Eight

"The Inquisitor's Price"

Siroth had ordered the Chamber of Silence carved deep beneath the Hall of Accord, in secrecy. Its walls were never meant to reflect light, but what lay within—inward truths rather than external realities. The air itself seemed suspended, thick with the stillness of a place that had never known daylight.

A long wall of black stone stretched before him, its surface so flawless it seemed to absorb every trace of light. It pulsed faintly under the glyphs etched into its frame—reflecting darkness rather than radiance, a place where illusions fractured and the truth behind power stood unmasked.

Few within the Accord even knew the chamber existed—a sanctum buried in the city's foundations, erased from every record. The silence here was complete, layered and deliberate, like the pause before judgment.

He used the chamber for ritual reflection as much as counsel, though no others were ever invited to share it. Here, statecraft and sanctity shared the same air; here, Siroth could strip the world of its noise until only certainty remained.

Siroth had come in silence, descending the narrow spiral that coiled beneath the Hall of Accord and into the Conclave Vault, until the air itself grew still. He wasn't here to call upon the faithful; his purpose lay deeper, more deliberate. With a slight movement of his hand, the passage recognized his touch—stone parting with a low sigh of shifting locks before sealing again behind him. No one saw him, nor dared to follow.

Once inside the sanctum, he shed the symbols of command—sandals, robe, ornament—until only silence clothed him. He always began like this: barefoot on the cold stone floor, clad in a black undertunic embroidered with the crescent insignia of the Accord—unadorned, unencumbered, invulnerable.

Before him stood the Mirror of Edresk—a relic from the age before the Severance days, forbidden now by Council decree, but preserved in secret by Siroth himself. It was taller than he was, ringed in elemental steel, and veined with arcane script that no longer translated cleanly into modern tongue.

He had kept it hidden for many years, not as collector's pride but as necessity; truth, after all, required a reflection untouched by law.

With deliberate reverence, he placed the blackened shard of crystal on the pedestal before it—no larger than a coin, its edges fused and rippled as if kissed by fire. It was all that remained of the place where Faye had supposedly ended. At least, that was the version he returned to, again and again, because it spared him what he was not yet willing to face. He told himself it was proof. But it felt more like penance. The crystal never warmed. Sometimes, he imagined it whispered back. The glyphs pulsed faintly, responding to something in the shard—or in him.

He pressed his palm to the dark glass of the mirror.

The surface rippled, resisting briefly, then bent inward like the skin of water under pressure. A soft, melodic hum vibrated from its depths. Siroth's lips moved in silence, but his intent was precise: show me what threatens the balance.

His breath clouded the glass. The glyphs didn't answer. They hesitated.

The mirror responded not with clarity, but with resistance—as if reluctant to obey. A shape shimmered into being, flickering and formless. No face. No name. Only a spectral semblance of power bending in the wrong direction.

A frown etched deeper into Siroth's brow. The energy was unfamiliar—young, unclaimed, but disquietingly resonant. Elemental, yet tainted with something older.

For a heartbeat, a whisper surfaced in the back of his mind. She was already weakening... perhaps not yet dead...

He pushed it down.

Faye had been dealt with. He had told himself she had not conceived. He had acted before that could happen. He had.

And yet...

"That cannot be allowed," he whispered—not to the mirror, but to the shadow unfurling like rot beneath his resolve.

His voice barely stirred the air, yet the mirror trembled—like an instrument struck by a note it recognized, but refused to answer.

Siroth stepped back and allowed the darkness to flood in again. The flame of a single floating candle behind him bent away, as if recoiling from what lingered in his silence.

He pressed his fingers together slowly, grounding himself. She was supposed to die before it could take root. That was the cost. My hands were steady. My timing precise.

But what if she had already given birth to the child? What if what he had extinguished was not the root, but only the imprint?

He clenched his jaw. "There is still time," he whispered, though it sounded less like strategy and more like confession. "But not for hesitation."

He turned from the mirror. The candle's flame flinched again, and for an instant, the room filled with a scent he hadn't permitted in years: lavender and ash. Her scent.

Faye.

He clenched his jaw so tightly it rang in his ears. No—he had ended that story. Severed it at the root. What rose now was not memory but illusion, a trick of resonance and regret.

And still…

The scent lingered longer than it should have, threading through the cold like memory refusing to die. For a heartbeat, his composure wavered. He stood unmoving until it faded, then drew a single, steady breath—the kind that turned doubt to discipline.

He gathered his robe from where it lay in the sanctum and wrapped it around himself with slow precision. The fabric coiled about him not like comfort, but like penance.

He touched the glyph set into the wall; it pulsed beneath his palm—once, faintly, like a heartbeat under stone.

Above, the cold grind of locks unsealed the Conclave Vault.

It was time to call the knives that wore robes. It was time they remembered who ruled here.

And this time, he would not let the ghost of Faye outrun him.

The darkness gave no answer. Only the Vault would.

***

The Conclave Vault was colder than when he had left it, and that steadied him—a static hymn to order, unwarped by passion or doubt, where history lay locked in glyph-carved marble and echoes lingered in stubborn defiance.

Siroth stepped onto the central dais as the obsidian ring beneath his feet hummed to life. Five narrow arms radiated outward from the platform, etched with glyphs that only responded to his presence—each one spiraling with a faint, silvery glow as they awakened.

One by one, the summoning sigils ignited.

To an outsider, the Vault would have appeared silent. But to those attuned to magic, the air now vibrated with layered resonance: the tolling of five distant bells ringing in no audible harmony, yet woven with perfect intention.

Light broke through the darkness—not from above, but from within the runes themselves—three figures emerged from the light. Their robes echoing the elemental sigils of water, fire, and air. Two sigils on the dais remained dark: one marked by soil, long silent; the other by iron, never spoken aloud.

The Inquisitors.

Bound not by loyalty, but by oath. Loyal not to Siroth, but to the Accord itself. And yet, he had long since learned how to shape oaths as one shapes swords.

As they stepped from the magic-born light, each took their place at the edge of the dais. Robes of deep crimson, sunless gold, and veiled ash. The other two stations flickered colorless—promises undone.

The fifth glyph—the one belonging to the vanished Inquisitor of the Fifth Kingdom—remained unlit. Its silence pressed on the room like a held breath. The others did not speak. Not yet. That glyph had once answered a name, and its silence now spoke more loudly than flame.

Siroth did not flinch.

"You are summoned not for reflection," he said, his voice measured and resonant, "but for vigilance. There is movement beyond the Veil."

He paused, letting the weight of that word settle.

"And if prophecy breathes again… it must be silenced before it speaks."

The stillness that followed Siroth's words was not empty—it was expectant. A pause not of ignorance, but of calculation.

High Inquisitor Auren, cloaked in deep sea-green robes with a metallic earthstone insignia fastened at her throat, was the first to speak.

"What kind of movement, Chancellor?" she asked, her voice even, but not submissive. "The Vault's records show no confirmed activity through the Veil since the Ordinatum."

Siroth turned to face her fully. "Not through the Veil. Beneath it."

A murmur passed through the group like heat rippling across a forge. Inquisitor Rhodin, flame-robed and always two seconds from combustion, narrowed his eyes.

"You've seen resonance?"

"In the Mirror of Edresk," Siroth said.

A beat of silence. Then Inquisitor Vael, draped in translucent gray with the shimmer of air runes barely visible on his sleeves, let out a slow breath.

"That mirror is forbidden."

"So was prophecy," Siroth replied coldly. "Until it began stirring again."

Rhodin scoffed, firelight catching in his eyes. "We swore to protect the Accord—not flirt with relics that nearly undid it."

Auren glanced toward the two darkened glyphs, her voice quieter now. "And what exactly did the mirror show you?"

Siroth didn't answer immediately. Instead, he approached the dormant fifth glyph—the one that should have called forth the Inquisitor of the Fifth Kingdom.

It remained cold.

"I saw potential," he said finally. "Unclaimed magic. Wild. It does not yet wear a face, but it resonates with elemental harmony… and something else."

He didn't say Faye's name. He didn't have to. They felt the shift.

Vael spoke again, this time softer. "Then the silence we've held becomes a blade again."

Auren shifted her stance slightly, the weight of memory pulling at her brow. "If this is another ghost chase, Chancellor, it risks more than time. The last time we acted on unstable resonance, magic was fractured for a decade."

Rhodin's eyes narrowed. "The question isn't whether we believe you saw something. The question is whether it's real—or whether you're ready to see what's coming."

Siroth tilted his head, the corners of his mouth unmoving. "I have been ready for a long time since I restored order to our realms, and I do not ask for belief. I require response."

"And if our response contradicts your expectations?" Vael asked, tone unreadable. "We are not extensions of your fear, Chancellor."

Siroth's expression didn't change, but his voice lowered. "Do you think I summoned you here to rewrite fear? No. I summoned you because the last time the Fifth stirred, it fractured more than kingdoms."

His gaze drifted—briefly—to the dormant glyphs behind them.

"Caer Durell vanished the night we completed the Nullum ritual," he said, the official name still serving its purpose. No body. No echo. Only a severed hand etched with glyphs no one dared read—its knuckles curled as if still resisting the burial.

A beat of silence followed.

"And before that, Keralis…" Siroth's voice slowed—not out of emotion, but deliberation. "He was the youngest of us. The cleanest glyphwork. The most efficient sigil scribe the Concordium had ever produced. He could make silence hum. He could make order look like breath."

He paused, as if tasting the memory.

"But when the last resonance war began to stir—when prophecy became more than poetry—when Faye ran away and abandoned us—he wavered. Not in action, but in allegiance. He began to speak of remembrance. Of grief. Of the Fifth."

The words hung heavy, like ash over parchment.

"He believed prophecy should be fulfilled, not severed. We gave him silence. He turned it into a language. We thought that was loyalty."

Auren shifted, ever so slightly.

"And in the end, it was not treason. Not betrayal. It was mercy. And that, too, was a breach."

Vael's brow furrowed slightly, but said nothing.

Siroth looked directly at her. "We do not question their absence. We uphold the Accord by ensuring their failure is never repeated."

He turned back to the dais, his voice resuming its steady rhythm. "That is why you were summoned. Not to remember them. But to ensure their breach does not return." He let the words settle.

"You are not the Accord's memory. You are its hand."

Siroth's gaze was fixed on the dormant glyph. "You will begin in the outer regions. Question every witness, every keeper, every voice that claims to know the unseen. Shake the dust from every archive we've sealed. Someone—somewhere—has seen the ripple. And where there is ripple..."

He paused, letting the word settle like a summons. "And where there is ripple..."

Vael's voice cut softly across the chamber. "...there is breach."

Siroth allowed himself the smallest nod. "You are not hunting a person. You are hunting a possibility."

Auren's jaw flexed—once—before she spoke. "And if it's more than possibility?" Her tone was measured, but the crack in her voice betrayed the cost of imagining it.

He turned toward her again. His eyes were unreadable.

"Then it must be extinguished before it becomes legacy."

He let the words settle like ash, then stepped toward Auren—not fast, but with the steady gravity of a blade choosing where to fall.

"And should any among you hesitate," he said, voice low enough to brush the bones, "you will not answer to the Accord."

He paused—not for emphasis, but to let their oaths tighten around their ribs.

"You will answer to me."

The air drew tighter. Not hot, not cold—just sharper.

"You are not here to deliberate," he said, turning to Rhodin next. His tone never rose. It didn't need to. Fear, real fear, was not thunder. It was breath held too long.

"You are not here to remember. You are not here to doubt."

He let silence fall like a blade between each phrase.

"You are here to act, because silence is not safety anymore."

A final breath.

"Disloyalty will not be punished," he said, gaze like a seal being pressed. "It will be erased."

The glyphs beneath their feet brightened in unison, a silent echo of the command they had received. The Vault dimmed again, shadows folding in like breath drawn before a blade.

The Vault did not settle. It braced.

Above them, the ceiling's highest ring pulsed once—faint and violet. Not bright enough to be noticed by the untrained, but the Inquisitors saw it.

None spoke. Not even Rhodin.

The fifth glyph remained dark.

The silence did not end there.

The Vault's walls, once etched only with obedience, seemed to curve closer—not with menace, but with memory. Veins of enchanted obsidian flickered along their edges, faint and silver, as though echoing a breath long withheld.

Vael's eyes flicked once toward the glyph of Iron, then Soil. Neither glowed. Neither spoke. Yet both were watching.

"You inherited a circle meant for five," she murmured, not quite a question. "And now it listens as three."

Siroth didn't look at her.

"The Fifth is not gone," he said. "Only silent. And silence, as we've learned, is often more dangerous than flame."

Auren's gaze followed the curve of the dais. "And Durell? You've never confirmed what happened."

"Because confirmation is illusion," Siroth replied. "He is not here. His name is not erased. His glyph still waits."

"Waits for what?"

"Judgment," Siroth said simply. "Or replacement."

He turned then—not to them, but to the center of the dais. His shadow lengthened, cast by no visible source.

"The Accord was forged not by faith, but by necessity. That is the law that remains."

Rhodin took half a step forward. "Necessity doesn't speak. It devours. We know what must be done."

And from somewhere deeper in the stone—beneath the layers of summoning runes and oath-bound wards—another shape stirred. Not a sigil. Not a flame. A pattern. Subtle. Familiar.

It flickered only once, like the breath of a name too sacred to speak. Then it vanished.

Siroth's gaze did not follow it. But something in his posture shifted.

"Let the Vault remember this silence," he said, more to the stone than the living. "And let silence carry the command."

The resonance sealed. The glyphs dimmed.

They did not bow. They did not speak. But when the runes withdrew, and the Vault drew closed behind them, not one of them looked back.

And the Inquisitors were gone.

The Vault swallowed the last trace of presence. The air didn't relax—it coiled tighter, as if waiting for a truth left unsaid.

Siroth exhaled once. Not with relief. With control.

Alone again, Siroth stood in the circle's silence. Not triumphant. Not shaken. Only tuned—like a blade resting between breaths.

The echo of the vanished glyph still pulsed faintly, not as light, but as nostalgia.

It was always that lingering and yearning feeling that betrayed first. Not rebellion. Not magic. But remembrance.

He turned slowly, eyes scanning the edges of the dais, where the traces of the five elemental sigils curled back into the vault's foundation like veins beneath skin.

Keralis.

Even now, the name stirred the wrong part of him—not fear. Not anger. But a softness he had thought buried in the stonework of the Accord itself: understanding.

"He was the softest edge," Siroth whispered, "and softness is what rots the pillar from within."

He could feel it now—friction along the Vault's memory, like a forgotten command preparing to remember itself. The Vault had always obeyed. That was its nature. But it remembered Keralis. It remembered Durell. And memory, even unwitnessed, was a form of resistance.

From beneath the dais, the stone shifted—not visibly, not physically, but in weight.

The memory was not Siroth's.

For a breath, the Vault remembered Caer Durell—not the glyph-master of public record, but the one who had stood beneath this same circle with chalk-stained hands and sleep-starved eyes.

It remembered the final tracing: a triple loop convergence rune, one no longer found in modern doctrine.

It remembered his voice—not loud, but absolute. "If the glyph turns against the will, it is the will that must be rewritten."

It remembered the moment he paused. The flick of hesitation before the final seal. The way his fingers twitched, just once, as if the stone itself had whispered another name.

Then blood. No scream. No resistance. Only resolve.

Not violence. Not treason. Just closure.

The Vault held that imprint. It did not speak. It did not echo. But deep in the substructure—where resonance was stored like breath trapped between pages—the glyph still pulsed.

Waiting. Recalling.

He walked the circumference of the dais now, hands clasped behind his back, posture controlled. Deliberate. Each step a return to command.

"There will be no martyr. No myth. No name for children to whisper under blankets."

His voice echoed this time. That was the danger. Echoes did not need belief to grow.

He reached the center and paused again, staring down at the intersection point of the five arms of the dais. At the place the glyphs met. At the spot where, long ago, the circle had first spoken prophecy.

Not anymore.

"You are not prophecy," he told the stone. "You are infrastructure. Infrastructure obeys. Prophecy does not."

Then, softer: "And you will hold."

He turned once more. The chamber did not resist. The glyphs dimmed further. Even the resonance receded, obedient.

And yet, he did not leave immediately.

His eyes returned to the sigil of iron—Keralis's mark.

Still dark. Still silent. But not asleep.

"You waited too long," he murmured. "I will not."

The Vault did not argue. But it deliberated.

And remembrance, when buried deep enough, leaks upward.

The dais shimmered faintly beneath his feet—not light, but a low tremor.

The Vault did not resist. And reminiscence, when bound to blood, does not fade—it ferments.

The circle had not yet been named a tomb. But it became one.

***

Faye stood at its center. Not bound, not chained—offered.

Her robe dragged like surrender. Her eyes carried the hush of ancient thunder.

She had walked into the ritual space barefoot, head high, hair unbraided. Her silence unnerved even the stone.

Caer Durell stood across from her, his robe open to the waist, his left hand freshly severed. Glyph-burns crawled across the raw skin like vines of light and scarring. His right hand shook—not from fear, but from the nearness of law unraveling.

"The Root must be reclaimed," Siroth had said. His voice had not wavered. "The Source line ends here."

Faye had said nothing. Not then.

The runes around the circle flared—one by one—as Caer Durell spoke the initiation phrase meant to bind inheritance into theft.

The glyphs answered—not with light, but with breath. Each sigil inhaled, held, and waited. A pattern built in silence: five points, one echo.

Faye closed her eyes. Caer Durell whispered:

"Insidium nascitur"
(The Insidium is born.)

The final loop pulsed. The stone accepted it.

Then, and only then, did she speak. Her voice was soft. Barely audible.

"You think the Root ends here," she said. Her voice didn't echo—it landed, as if the Vault bent inward to hear it.

"But the Root is not a line. It's a wound. It remembers where it was cut."

Siroth's hand trembled, just once. "The fruit dies with you, and it will never draw breath—"

"No," she said softly. "You're wrong."

She looked upward, as if into a sky only she could see.

"The Root doesn't begin where you think. And it will not end in the place you chose."

A breath.

She turned to him finally, not in triumph, but in elegy.

"You buried the seed. But it remembered the light."

Durell flinched. Just once. "Now," he said, eyes fixed on her—not with hatred, but with ache.

Siroth stepped forward. The blade had been forged for this. Core alloy, quintuple-braided glyphs along the spine, consecrated in bloodless light. The reverse sigils glowed faintly. He aimed between heartbeats.

Her breath left her body with no sound as she cradled her hands against herself as if embracing what was meant to endure.

The light should have folded inward. The glyphs should have burned gold. Instead… violet, then violet deeper. Then black. Then… One. Unwound. Durell's seal.

It unraveled itself, folding backward like a thought retracted.

"What did you—" Siroth turned. But Durell was already gone.

No flame. No scream. Just ash. And the smell of chalk, and old breath.

Faye's body remained. But the weight was wrong. The air was not still—it was hollowed.

"The Root is severed," Siroth had declared. "The Insidium has been completed."

But the blade had not cooled.

Siroth smiled—but only with his eyes.

And the Vault—

—had held its breath ever since. *Even stone, it seemed, remembered the wound.*

Chapter Nine

"The Bells at Dusk"

Low and slow, the bells of Saint-Spire Abbey rang, their bronze voices echoing through the dusk like ancient sighs. In the kitchen, the light was golden and soft, diffused through old stained-glass panels that depicted vines and wheat and halos of forgotten saints. The walls sweated with warmth, the hearth flickering with its last committed blaze, and the smell of leeks and slow-roasted garlic wrapped the room in a veil of contentment.

Master Eloi hummed as he worked—an old tune, part lullaby, part march. No one knew the words, and he claimed he'd forgotten them himself, though the melody never faltered. He moved through the kitchen like water through a carved channel: bowls set, loaves broken with precision, broth stirred in gentle spirals until its surface gleamed.

He was round-bellied and bright-eyed, his apron permanently dusted in flour and herbs. The children adored him. The sisters trusted him. Even Father Maurice, who trusted very few, never questioned the quiet efficiency with which the meals appeared or the uncanny accuracy with which Master Eloi remembered everyone's preferences.

He was, by all accounts, forgettable in the way that only deeply beloved people can be.

Ask any of the younger children, and they would tell you the same: Eloi's hands could chase away bad dreams. He never forgot your favorite pastry, even if you only mentioned it once. He never sat to eat, but always made sure everyone else had second helpings. Some swore he carried warmth inside him—like a coal wrapped in bread.

Almost no one bothered to remember when he'd arrived at the Abbey. To most of them, he simply had always been. The way stone was always cold, and the way certain lullabies seemed older than memory.

He spoke gently to herbs when he picked them. Thanked the yeast for rising. Sometimes, children would wake at night and hear pots clinking and Eloi humming alone, as if keeping vigil with the fire. As if sleep were a luxury he did not allow himself.

And he never raised his voice. Not even once.

Tonight, after the stew was ladled and the bread cooled on wooden boards, he paused. Just for a breath. His humming slowed.

The fire had shrunk to a curled orange yawn in the hearth. The stained-glass saints glowed in flickering fragments—not quite watching, not quite sleeping.

Eloi turned to the far shelf—one rarely used—and reached behind a jar of bay leaves. His fingers found a small bundle of fabric: tightly bound, wrapped in oiled cloth.

He didn't open it.

Just held it for a moment, his thumb brushing the edge of what lay inside. A faint line etched across his brow—not confusion, exactly. Not fear.

Recognition.

Something long buried had stirred—not just in memory, but in time. He shouldn't have felt it. But he did.

The bundle shifted in his hand. Not heat. Not light. But something stranger—as if a breath had risen inside it, after years of stillness. A heartbeat waking beneath fabric and memory.

Eloi closed his eyes.

A sound brushed the edge of his hearing—not a voice, not quite. But it carried the shape of his name. Not Eloi. The other one. The one no one here knew. The one carved away, yet his bones remembered.

His knees buckled slightly. He gripped the edge of the shelf.

No. Not now. Please… not yet.

He returned the bundle to its hiding place with reverence—like placing a candle in a crypt. Tucked it behind the jar and pressed it farther back, as if distance might dull whatever had begun.

Then he turned, his movements slower now. Measured. He whistled—not the old tune, but something fractured and quieter, barely a thread.

He began stacking bowls for morning.

One by one. Ceramic against wood. The soft click of rhythm. His hands moved automatically.

But his eyes drifted, now and then, toward the hearth. Toward the stained-glass panel above it—the one of Saint Elodia blessing a child. The child's face was worn, half-lost to time.

Eloi's breath trembled once. Just once. Then it steadied.

Outside, the Abbey exhaled into night.

***

It took only a few days for the festival's brilliance to settle back into routine, though murmurs of Ava's floral miracle still drifted through the halls. Some claimed the blooms had pulsed with light. Others swore the perfume lingered still, sweet as confession. Leonarth hadn't spoken to Ava since, but he could still see her standing beneath the trellis—calm, radiant, otherworldly. Mattheon, of course, had insisted it was just a trick of timing and talent. But even he hadn't touched the roses since.

As they made their way through the cloister garden toward the school path in the washed light between lessons, the boys passed the remnants of the festival—wilted garlands, discarded ribbons, and fading chalk patterns. The path curved briefly past the edge of the inner courtyard, where the blooms from Ava's garden had stretched toward the sun as if hearing a song only she could sing. Now, they drooped quietly, but even in decay, they held a strange, vibrant shimmer—as though reluctant to let go.

Leonarth slowed, glancing toward the courtyard gate. "It's like the air remembers," he said.

Mattheon gave a half-nod, stuffing his hands into his coat pockets. "I still think she just... knew what to plant. When. How."

"But you saw it," Leonarth said. "Those petals moved. They followed her."

Mattheon hesitated. "Yeah. I saw it."

They walked a little farther in silence. The scent of lavender and old earth still clung to the stones. Something in the Abbey felt different now. Like a chord that had been struck but not yet resolved.

Leonarth couldn't stop feeling the weight of the key in his pocket, the memory of Ava's conjured garden glinting at the edge of it—two notes of the same unseen chord.

"Hard to believe all that happened just days ago," he said, mostly to himself.

Mattheon nodded, then cleared his throat. "Feels like the whole Abbey's been holding its breath since."

Leonarth hesitated. "Do you think it's connected? The flowers. The key. Everything?"

Mattheon didn't answer at first. "I think things are starting to notice us. That's what it feels like."

Leonarth's fingers curled around the cool metal of the key. He exhaled slowly, its chill seeping into his palm. "So what do we do with it now?"

Mattheon kept his eyes forward. "I don't know. But it doesn't feel ordinary. It feels like it was... meant to be found. Just not by accident."

Leonarth turned it over in his pocket again, the strange engraving pressing into his fingers like a silent command. "It doesn't feel like it belongs to us. But it found us anyway."

Mattheon looked at him. "You keep it for now. Just until we know more. But promise me one thing."

Leonarth met his gaze. "What?"

Mattheon's voice was quiet. "Don't treat it like it's nothing. I think it remembers being important."

Leonarth nodded. "Then we treat it like it matters."

Mattheon did not answer. He didn't need to. The hush between them had grown comfortable over the years—a silence shaped not by absence, but by trust.

Leonarth glanced back. The Abbey stretched long and watchful behind them, their footsteps echoing faintly between the walls.

When they turned the corner toward the cloisters, the air grew colder. Frost glittered across the hedges like dust from some forgotten star, and the scent of last night's incense still clung to the stones—faint but persistent, like memory refusing to fade.

"Do you feel it?" Leonarth finally said.

Mattheon didn't look at him. "Feel what?"

"Like the Abbey's been... listening."

Mattheon's brow furrowed. "To us?"

"To everything."

They passed beneath a stone archway that connected the garden to the northern hall. Above them, the carved relief of Saint Elodia's open hands caught the last wash of gold along the stone.

Mattheon kicked at a loose pebble. "I don't know. Lately I feel like I'm always walking near something I'm not supposed to see."

"Or remember," Leonarth murmured.

That made Mattheon stop.

He turned, studying Leonarth's face. "You had another dream, didn't you?"

Leonarth hesitated. "Not a full one. Just a sound. Like wind in a corridor that's been sealed for a long time."

Mattheon nodded slowly. "Mine wasn't wind. It was bells. Not the ones here. These were... wrong. Too slow."

Leonarth tilted his head. "Like echoes without a voice?"

"Yeah," Mattheon whispered. "Like something trying to remember how to speak."

They walked on.

At the edge of the schoolyard, Leonarth paused again.

"You know," he said softly, "when I first got here, I thought I was alone. But you—"

"Don't," Mattheon cut in gently. "If you say something sentimental, I'll push you into a shrub."

Leonarth smiled. "Fine. You're the shrub."

Mattheon gave him a look. "That's not even an insult."

"No," Leonarth replied. "It's a classification."

Mattheon huffed out a laugh—but the tension didn't lift entirely. They both felt it. A thread tightening between their ribs. A question neither wanted to ask.

Leonarth looked up, almost grateful for the distraction ahead. His eyes caught movement at the end of the path.

The orphanage schoolhouse came into view—and they skidded to a halt. The gates were already shut.

"When did they close the gates?" Mattheon said.

Leonarth narrowed his eyes. "We're late."

Mattheon's grin returned. "Then we improvise."

Leonarth crossed his arms. "I'm not scaling that wall again."

"No wall," Mattheon said, eyes gleaming. "The roof."

Leonarth blinked. "You've broken into class through the ceiling?"

"Not broken," Mattheon corrected. "Accessed. Through nontraditional architecture."

Leonarth tilted his head. "Why would you even—?"

Mattheon shrugged. "Sometimes I go up there when I can't sleep. Watch the streetlamps blink out. Make up stories about people I'll never meet."

Leonarth studied him. "And hope one of them looks like you?"

Mattheon said nothing.

He could have laughed. Rolled his eyes. Changed the subject.

Instead, silence bloomed in his chest like a bruise.

It was a simple question—playful, even. But something in it struck a nerve he couldn't name. A soft ache curled beneath his ribs. The kind you feel in the quiet moments, when everyone else is asleep and the world stops pretending to make sense.

Mattheon stared ahead, jaw tightening. Not from anger. But from something deeper. A tension he didn't understand. A thread he couldn't cut.

There were times—rare, but real—when he would wake in the middle of the night and not recognize his own reflection. As if the boy in the mirror had been borrowed from someone else. His hands would shake, just slightly, until he ran them under cold water. Not because he was scared. But because it kept him here. Real. Grounded.

And sometimes, when Leonarth looked at him a certain way—like now—Mattheon felt like that mirror again. Like he was being seen not for who he was, but for what he might be. Or what he had been, in some life before this one.

He hated it.

Not because it was wrong.

But because it felt true.

Mattheon didn't know why Leonarth flinched, just slightly, as if something beneath his coat had stirred—like a heartbeat waiting to be remembered.. But he knew this much: whatever they were about to step into, Leonarth wouldn't be walking into it alone. And Mattheon—whatever he was—couldn't let that happen.

He could feel it—not from the key, not even from the thing neither of them would name—but from the boy beside him, from the space Leonarth carried when he went quiet.

His silence wasn't cowardice. It was weight. The ache of wanting to say: I remember things too. I just don't know why.

But instead, he said nothing.

Because if he said it aloud, it might become real.

And real things break.

Leonarth's voice softened. "You're not alone. You never were."

For a heartbeat, the words steadied him—pulled him back from wherever his thoughts had gone.

Mattheon gave a lopsided smile, his voice betraying a crack he hoped would pass for laughter. "Good. Then help me break the rules."

Leonarth heard it, felt the weight beneath it, and kept his voice even. "Define 'help.'"

Mattheon pointed to a crude staircase lashed together behind a tree.

"That. I'll climb first. Catch me if I fall."

Leonarth eyed the construction. "Are those... broom handles?"

"And fence pickets. Artisanally repurposed."

Leonarth muttered a prayer to Saint Elodia for structural mercy as Mattheon began to climb.

They hauled themselves onto the roof, boots scraping against the tiles. At the rooftop's edge, an unexpected companion waited.

"Meely?" Leonarth whispered.

The cat sat poised beside a narrow attic window, her golden eyes trained on them as if awaiting instructions.

"She never misses an adventure," Mattheon murmured.

Leonarth raised a brow. "Meely, stand guard."

The cat blinked slowly.

With a joint heave, they pried open the attic window. Dust swirled in sunbeams as they slipped inside, surrounded by mountains of ancient boxes, draped cloth, and the scent of dried ink and time.

The floor groaned beneath them. Every step answered with a creak. They tiptoed carefully—until Meely slipped in behind them, vanishing into the clutter.

"Meely!" Leonarth hissed. "Stop!"

But it was too late. The cat darted forward, and Mattheon lunged after her, his boot catching on a loose board—rotted at the nail—that snapped upward like a trap.

Time stretched.

Mattheon's eyes went wide. Leonarth shouted. Wood splintered.

Then chaos.

Mattheon crashed through the attic floor, followed by a cascade of boxes and old cloths—right into Sister Mabelle's lesson on living things.

For a heartbeat, everything stilled—except Meely, perched calmly on the fallen beam above, tail flicking once, as if satisfied.

Shrieks. Gasps. Silence.

Then time snapped back: "BOYS."

Sister Mabelle's voice cut through the dust like a thunderclap. "WHAT IN ALL GOOD HEAVENS—"

She stopped. The mess was considerable—but not disastrous.

Dust drifted down in slow spirals as she took in the scene.

Scattered across the classroom were glittering fabrics, masks with exaggerated expressions, and feathered hats.

For a moment, no one spoke.

Then Sister Mabelle let out a short, brittle laugh—not quite amusement, not quite relief.

"Well. That's certainly one way to interrupt a lesson."

She bent down and lifted a cracked feathered mask, turning it over once in her hands before lowering it again, her expression unreadable.

"Parade costumes," she murmured, more to herself than to anyone else. "I thought these were sealed off."

Straightening, she turned slowly to the class. "Everyone out. Take your things. We're relocating."

The students gathered their belongings in a tense hush, the scrape of chairs loud in the dust-thick air.

When the last of them slipped past, she pivoted to the boys.

"You two—stay. Clean. And think very carefully about how you ended up above a sealed storage room no one's touched in over a decade. I'll be speaking with Father Maurice first."

Her voice dropped a degree. "And tonight? You sleep early. And you keep your stories... simple."

The words hung strangely in the air—not quite a warning, not quite advice. Mattheon and Leonarth exchanged a look, both sensing something she wasn't saying.

When the room cleared, Mattheon rubbed his elbow and groaned. "I think I bruised my dignity."

Leonarth grinned. "That's been bruised since you built that stair."

They began cleaning, tossing crushed boxes and folding ancient cloaks. But something tugged at Leonarth's mind.

"Where's Meely?" he asked.

Mattheon looked around. "She didn't fall with us."

Both boys glanced upward.

Through the hole in the ceiling, Meely was still in the attic—exactly where she'd been moments before, sitting very still. But her golden eyes had shifted, fixing on something along the far wall.

Without a word, they dragged over a few desks and crates, stacking them into a precarious tower. Leonarth steadied it while Mattheon climbed, then followed close behind.

And there it was—whatever had held Meely's gaze so still: a tapestry.

Massive, and suspended midair just inches from the stone wall. Its surface shimmered—too clean, too untouched to belong in that dusty place.

"Was that here before?" Mattheon whispered.

Leonarth shook his head. "No. Or it was hidden."

The fabric was impossibly smooth. Woven with silks and threads of silver and green, it showed scenes that defied logic: floating cities, luminous trees, an Abbey beside a river where the stars shone during the day.

And the images… moved.

Slowly, subtly—like droplets of light rearranging themselves, or memory shifting back into place.

Meely didn't stir. She only watched, perfectly still—like a sentinel remembering its duty.

Leonarth reached out, not to touch it, but to feel the air around it. For a breath, nothing. The tapestry seemed to wait.

Then warmth met his hand—faint at first, then pulsing once, alive.

Mattheon leaned in, eyes following the shifting images. What he'd taken for rivers began to align—threads curving into coastlines, peaks, and valleys.

He breathed, "This… this is a map."

Leonarth stepped closer, his breath catching in his throat.

At the tapestry's center, glowing faintly, was the shape of a key.

Not drawn.

Woven.

Identical to the one in his pocket.

As his fingers hovered near it, the thread pulsed.

Not light.

Recognition.

The same feeling he'd seen once in Ava's eyes—a truth awakening.

Leonarth drew back, stunned.

He stepped too quickly and bumped into a low crate. It didn't hurt, but the jolt grounded him—reminded him he was still in his own body. Still in this moment. Still holding a thing he didn't understand.

His hand went instinctively to his pocket. The key—the real one—still rested there, warm through the fabric, as if echoing the glow of its woven double. It hadn't pulsed before. Not like this. Now it felt... aware. Waiting.

Leonarth closed his eyes.

The air in the attic was suddenly dense—not with dust, but with presence. A quiet pressure, like a cathedral holding its breath.

The tapestry didn't flicker. It didn't hum. But something behind it shifted—not sound, not shadow, but recognition. Like it had blinked. Or remembered.

He opened his eyes and took one step closer.

And for just a second, the tapestry responded.

A thread unraveled at the corner. Just one. It curled outward and hovered—weightless—before retreating into the weave.

"Did you see that?" he whispered.

Mattheon didn't answer immediately. He had gone pale.

"That wasn't just a map," Mattheon said. "It saw you."

Leonarth shivered. "Or it knew me," he murmured.

Mattheon's brow furrowed. "Then... it's showing what's next?"

Leonarth hesitated, studying the shifting threads, the faint pulse that matched the warmth in his pocket. "No," he said slowly, almost to himself. "It's not showing. It's remembering."

Mattheon looked at him.

Leonarth's eyes were wide, but calm. "This isn't about the future."

He placed his hand near the glowing key.

"It's a memory."

But it wasn't his.

That realization came not as a thought, but as a knowing—deep, visceral, marrow-deep. Whatever stirred behind the threads of the tapestry had not been carved by his own experiences. He had never seen these cities. He had never carried those griefs, never cried those tears. And yet...

He felt them.

As if he were borrowing someone else's ache. Wearing it like a second skin. The memory moved through him the way light moves through stained glass—changed, colored, shaped, but not created.

It unsettled him. Not because it was foreign.

But because it felt too intimate to be imagined.

His breath hitched as the glyph beneath the woven key shimmered faintly, like a thought surfacing after years of silence. He staggered, caught himself, steadied.

Mattheon didn't notice.

Leonarth's hand hovered near the tapestry again, but this time not in curiosity.

In recognition.

It was like hearing a lullaby you'd never learned, but somehow still knew the next note. Like stepping into a place you couldn't name but had always missed.

He didn't know where these feelings came from. But they had a weight—the kind grief leaves in the lungs. They weren't echoes of his life. They were inherited. And still unfolding.

His mother?

No. That word felt too small.

This went deeper than blood.

Older than that.

The tapestry breathed again—barely—but Leonarth did not step back. A single thread at the edge of the key glowed with a breath of blue, and then faded.

He whispered, "These aren't my memories."

But no one heard him.

Not even Mattheon.

Only the tapestry. And perhaps... whatever had given it life.

The tapestry did not change.

But the room had. Something behind the stillness tilted inward—not light, not motion, but density. A quiet thickening of space, the hush before a name—the reverence before an answer.

Leonarth's heart beat slower, not faster. Not fear. Something else. The weight of recognition. The pause before understanding.

The images on the tapestry were not illustrations. They were not animated. They breathed. They shimmered like thought. A city collapsed in reverse, reassembling itself beneath twin suns. A girl with eyes like mirrors wept into a basin, and from her tears rose stars. An ocean pulled itself upward in spirals, collapsing into a glowing shard. Not scenes. Not a story.

Symbols.

Mattheon whispered, "These places… they feel real."

Leonarth nodded, too afraid to speak.

He didn't recognize the imagery—not with his mind. But something inside him stirred. Not memory exactly. Not yet. But a haunting. A sense that he had stood among these places not in dreams, but in something deeper. That he had once walked where the stars leaned closer. That he had once seen magic not as spell or spectacle, but as structure—like wind. Like breath. Like grief.

Another thread unfurled, this time from the opposite edge of the fabric. It didn't tremble. It reached—toward the place where the boys stood. Not touching. Just… acknowledging.

Mattheon took a step back.

Leonarth didn't.

"Do you feel it?" he asked, his voice thinner now.

Mattheon's mouth opened, then closed. He nodded.

"It's not asking us anything," Leonarth said. "It's not trying to warn us. It's remembering... in front of us."

Another pulse. This one not from the tapestry.

From the key.

It glowed faintly through the fabric of his coat. He could feel the warmth against his leg—not burning. Just awake.

"Leonarth..." Mattheon's voice faltered. "That's not normal. That's not—"

"I don't think this was ever meant to be hidden."

The tapestry's center began to shift—not in image, but in alignment. The edges curled slightly inward, like the pages of a book caught by wind. The shape of the key—once central—seemed to tilt, like a compass needle finding true north.

And suddenly, they could see it.

Beneath the image of the key—faint, hidden before—was a glyph.

No. A seal.

Carved not with ink, but with woven thread darker than black.

A shape that made Leonarth's throat tighten—not from fear, but from recognition. It looked… familiar. Like something he had known as a child and forgotten. Or like a sound he used to hear when he cried but couldn't speak.

He reached toward it.

Mattheon grabbed his wrist. "Wait."

Leonarth didn't pull away. But he didn't retreat either.

"I'm not going to touch it," he whispered. "I just need to remember what it is."

"Mattheon," he said, voice quiet with awe. "I don't think we found the key."

He turned, meeting his friend's wide eyes.

"I think it found us."

Behind them, Meely turned her head—just once—then was still again.

In the distance, the Abbey bell rang once—low and slow—as if dusk had reached them early.

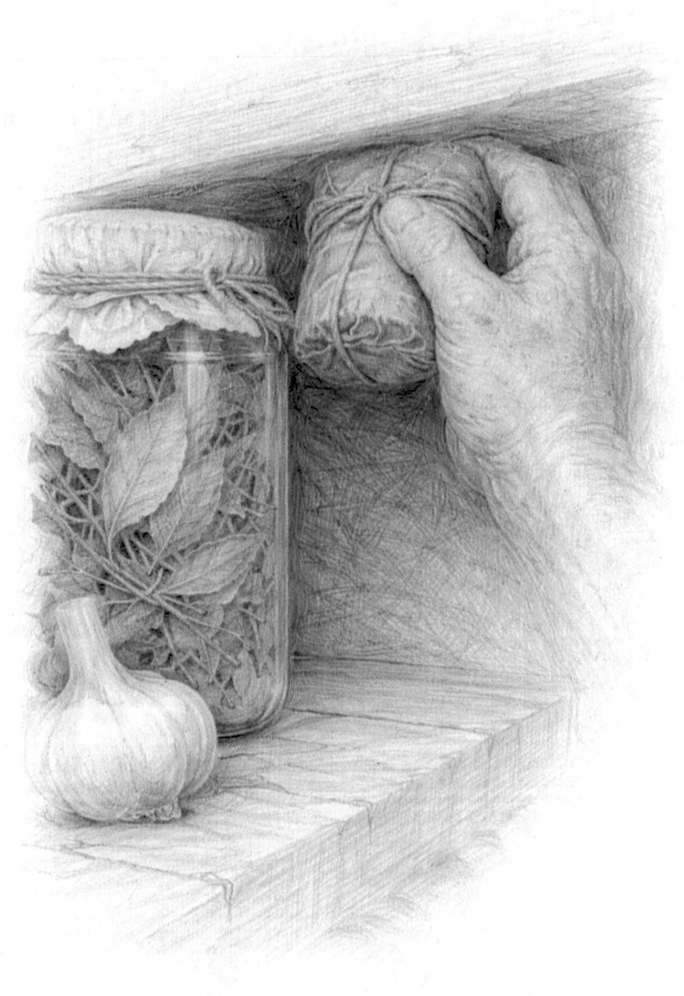

Chapter Ten

"Beneath the Skin of Stone"

The echo came at twilight. A sound without sound. A ripple in the stone beneath Saint-Spire, like a thought the walls had never quite let go. Father Maurice paused mid-step at the base of the spiral stair, his lantern trembling slightly in his grip. The iron frame clinked as the flame inside guttered—not from draft, but from something else. He stood at the mouth of the Lower Archives, breathing in the scent of dust, vellum, and rain-soaked limestone.

He had walked these stairs more times than he cared to count. And yet tonight, it felt different. The cold reached deeper. The silence wasn't empty—it was listening.

The dark settled over Maurice, uninvited. The old altar stood where it always had, its worn edges catching the lantern's faint glow—and beneath that glow, the slightest suggestion of seams only he and Gwendlynn would ever know how to find.

But he wasn't here to re-enter what lay beyond those seams. Not tonight. Whatever had stirred the stone hadn't come from the hidden passage or the secrets sleeping past it. This disturbance was nearer. Closer. Waiting.

He drew a slow breath, inspecting the walls he had known for so long, and so very well. For most eyes, the chamber would have been nothing more than stone and dust—a forgotten room with nothing left to reveal.

But Maurice had never been blessed with most eyes.

And sometimes he wished he had.

Because when he stood still enough… quiet enough… the old markings began to surface.

Faint, reluctant lines eased themselves out of the walls, as though pushing through the stone's own quiet soul.

When they settled into view, they were dim—ancient carvings sealed by spells long forbidden. All except one.

A single sigil, etched in the stone by his own hand over a decade ago. A sentinel glyph—not for footsteps, not for magic spoken aloud, not even for return, but for alignment. For the moment when the conditions that once mattered began to exist again.

It was faintly pulsing. Not vivid. Not urgent. Just... aware.

Maurice moved closer, the breath catching in his throat.

He remembered carving it—not as a priest, but as something else. Something buried. He had bound the glyph under the Veil Protocol—an oath of silence, never to be spoken aloud, never to be named.

Silence was not restraint. It was protection.

There were still sleeper agents, he believed. Maybe even in Saint-Spire. And to name the old magic to the wrong person was to risk awakening one of them. It was the last act he performed before stepping away from the role he had once sworn to die upholding.

Maurice lifted his hand, stopping just short of the stone.

The symbol responded. Not with heat or light, but with something older: a whisper against the skin. The shape of recognition.

He could see it now—the Fifth Kingdom's mark, subtler than the others, its geometry closer to music than mathematics, as though shaped by memory instead of metal.

He hadn't seen it stir since the day he sealed it into the stone.

For a long moment, Maurice said nothing. Just stared.

Then he exhaled slowly and touched the wall.

"Not yet," he whispered. "Please—not yet."

Behind him, the stair groaned with a weight that wasn't there.

But the wall had already begun to listen.

He felt it—a pressure beneath his skin, like standing too close to thunder. The glyph pulsed again, so faint it could be mistaken for imagination. But Maurice knew better. Memory didn't vanish. It receded. Waited. And when the world grew quiet enough, it returned in shape and light.

The stone recognized the pattern of a choice he had made once before.

He remembered the first time that shape had been carved—elsewhere, in a hall where silence was enforced rather than chosen. Long before exile. Long before Saint-Spire.

The Ordinatum decree still felt fresh in his mind. The scent of parchment and old blood. What the mark was meant to do was clear enough. What it would cost had been harder to face.

That day, the world had gone still. Not with peace—with recoil.

The Conclave Vault answered first.

Wind swept through the arches like it had been searching for someone. The glyphmasters had stood in ceremonial silence, but their faces said what their mouths could not: something sacred had just died.

He had held the blade—not a weapon, but a stylus etched with the five converging runes. Meant to encode loyalty. Instead, it sealed the erasure of what should never have been erased.

He'd knelt before the stone not as an official, not even as himself—but as a witness.

And he committed the mark to the stone.

It was not clean. His hands had trembled. The stone had resisted. It bled silver where it should have opened with reverence. The air pulsed once—a ripple of grief that passed through his chest and settled beneath his skin like a dormant bruise.

He did not cry. But his breath caught for hours afterward. Long after the seal was set. Long after the chamber emptied.

Long after the last of the Fifth Kingdom's names had been struck from the official ledger.

He had walked out of that room not reborn—but rewritten.

And now, decades later, standing in a different silence, Maurice knew the stone beneath Saint-Spire remembered too.

And so did he.

Back then, he believed silence was mercy.

Now he wasn't so sure.

His fingers hovered near the mark again. He could feel the magic beneath it—not violent, not coercive. Grieved. Attentive.

This glyph was nothing like the one he had carved in the Vault.

That one had ended something.

This one waited to begin.

He pulled his hand away.

What would the world do if what had been buried was allowed to answer back? What would Saint-Spire become if it stopped holding memory in silence—and began to carry it aloud?

What would he become?

He turned back toward the stair. The silence behind him had changed its weight.

It felt personal.

***

The candlelight in Mother Gwendlynn's study cast long, uncertain shadows across the wooden floor. The walls were lined with devotional texts and unmarked scrolls—each precisely arranged, each more read than they appeared. The room smelled faintly of sage and ink.

Mother Gwendlynn closed the ledger before her and folded her hands atop it.

"That will be all," she said.

Sister Mabelle inclined her head. She did not speak.

She crossed the room, robes whispering against the stone, and opened the door.

Ava was waiting outside.

Mabelle passed her without a word, eyes lowered, hands folded tight within her sleeves. The corridor took her footsteps and did not give them back.

Ava drew a breath and entered.

She stood near the doorway, her posture still but alert. She had not been summoned often, and never at this hour.

Mother Gwendlynn remained seated, hands folded on the worn edge of her writing desk, her expression calm—but too calm. One of the candles on the far shelf had burned down to a hard pool, untouched.

"I hear there was a disturbance in the school attic today," Gwendlynn said at last, not looking up.

Ava nodded. "Leonarth mentioned an accident. Nothing deliberate."

"Yes." Gwendlynn's gaze lingered on the flicker of the candle. "Costumes, apparently."

Ava did not speculate.

But inside, Ava's instincts flared.

Gwendlynn's voice was too even. Her cadence too precise. Not curious—controlled. The kind of calm one used not to soothe, but to measure. Ava had learned long ago that in Saint-Spire, danger did not always come with noise. It arrived in composed tones, in ritual phrasing, in eyes that watched just long enough.

She couldn't be sure—not yet—but something had shifted in the older sister's demeanor. A question held too long. A script rehearsed before speaking.

Ava straightened her spine. She kept her breathing smooth.

The Veil Protocol remained in place, she reminded herself. No admissions. No magic shown. No certainty of who remembers what.

She had lived this tension before—among others like her, in borrowed cities and nameless cloisters that echoed with prayers and secrets both. Since crossing the Veil with Leonarth in her arms, this rule had never been broken: no one must know who she truly is unless they proved they remembered before they asked.

Ava's thoughts tightened. If Gwendlynn could be a sleeper… if that possibility existed…

The thought turned her stomach, but she didn't let it show.

Instead, she folded her hands. Let her face soften. Allowed her voice to carry only the weight of deference. Let her eyes register just enough alertness—the kind that could pass for fatigue.

She would say nothing. Offer nothing. Not until she was sure.

But she was watching now—and she would remember every word.

"And an old tapestry," Gwendlynn added. "At least, that's how it was described."

Ava inclined her head. "That was how the children put it."

"There have been... irregularities in that space before," Gwendlynn continued softly. "Objects unaccounted for. Light behaving out of season."

A pause. A test.

Ava met her eyes. "Sometimes dust unsettles strangely in those rafters. Old spaces mislead the eye."

"Does it?" Gwendlynn asked, tilting her head slightly. "Even old cloth knows its timing, I suppose."

Another silence passed between them, long and quiet as snow.

"You've always had a way of being present when things go… off script," Gwendlynn said. "When arrangements arrive earlier than expected. Or later."

Ava smiled gently. "As do you. One might say we orbit the same storms."

"Storms," Gwendlynn echoed. "Yes. Some break branches. Others... water roots."

It was an exchange without admission. But not without recognition.

The candle guttered.

Gwendlynn's eyes narrowed just slightly. "Have you ever encountered a failure caused by pressure rather than force?"

Ava's fingers flexed slightly behind her back. "I'm not sure I understand."

"Then let me put it another way," Gwendlynn said. "It's rare, but it happens—when too many truths press against a lie."

Ava offered a polite smile. "Truth is such an awkward thing in narrow spaces."

Outside, a bell rang once. A thin, cold note.

"You may go," Gwendlynn said, her voice returning to its habitual register. "There's nothing more to be said."

Ava turned, but paused at the door. "If there ever is... I trust the storm to tell us first."

Gwendlynn didn't respond. She simply stared at the candle as it flickered, almost out.

As Ava stepped into the corridor, she realized she had not been asked about the boys at all.

***

The bell's echo still hummed through the marrow of the Abbey as Father Maurice emerged from the south corridor, the hem of his robe brushing the stone with a sound softer than breath. He didn't hurry—he never hurried—but there was purpose in his steps now. The kind carved by memory, not urgency.

His lantern cast a ring of gold across the flagstones, flickering against walls that had long since ceased to welcome electric light. Power had been installed. Rewired. Never fully obeyed. Still, the bulbs in this quadrant failed without explanation.

Maurice glanced at the darkened sconce to his left—unlit, though newly wired just last winter—and murmured, "Stone keeps older habits than wires. So do I."

He slowed, taking the narrow passage that rejoined the central cloisters. His body knew the route before his mind admitted it. A faint pressure tugged at the edge of his thoughts—not magical, not quite—but unmistakably familiar.

It took him a few moments to place it: the ceiling of the Main Chapel he had passed days ago, when the Festival preparations had already begun stirring the Abbey. He'd paused there briefly, distracted by the pattern above—four faint carved stars surrounding a larger central one, all nearly erased, arranged in a formation he'd only seen once before, buried in a banned text. At the time, he half-dismissed it—fatigue, pressure, an old man's memories playing tricks.

But now, with the sigil pulsing in the Lower Archives and the Abbey whispering through stone, that fleeting image refused to let go.

Why hadn't he known it was there? Why had no one mentioned it, recorded it, warned about it?

The Abbey was old, yes—but not secretive. Not like this.

He adjusted the lantern and continued forward, thoughts spiraling. Perhaps it had been hidden all along. Perhaps it had only revealed itself when Leonarth arrived. Or perhaps—and this chilled him most—it had been watching the whole time, waiting for someone who would recognize it not with knowledge, but with guilt.

And tonight, his feet remembered what his mind had buried.

He turned the final corner, boots brushing a stretch of corridor most priests bypassed without thought, and the familiar weight returned as he neared the Main Chapel. Without hesitation, he stepped inside.

The air shifted as the door eased shut behind him. Not colder—older. The lanternlight rose toward the ribs of the vaulted ceiling, and the glyph constellation emerged from shadow as though stirred awake.

A few days ago when he first saw it, they had been little more than scars in the stone. Now they shimmered with quiet intent. And around them—what he had mistaken for hairline cracks—glyphs were cohering.

Curved, interwoven, impossibly delicate lines threaded themselves through the stonework, forming no language taught in Accord academies. But Maurice felt their familiarity like a bruise pressed too hard.

Not knowledge.

Recognition.

The shape of a truth he had once chosen to forget.

He moved beneath the ceiling, lantern lifted. The design was no accident. This was deliberate. Crafted. Hidden not by age, but by intention.

He wondered, then, why no records existed. Why this sacred heart of the Abbey—traveled by acolytes and clergy for generations—held markings that no one had documented.

Or perhaps they had. And those records had been erased.

A sudden breath stirred behind him.

"I wondered when you'd come back here," said a voice. Gwendlynn stepped into the glow of his lantern, her presence as quiet as the dust.

Maurice didn't flinch. "You knew it was here."

But she had known more than that.

Since the Festival, when Archbishop Reginald had looked at her with honest confusion and said he had never written such a letter vouching for Ava. When his words rewrote a decade of certainty with one quiet fracture.

She had said nothing then. And she would say nothing now.

Because the truth was no longer what mattered.

It was who had chosen silence instead of sharing it.

So she didn't accuse. Didn't flinch. She watched Maurice like one might watch a door left ajar—uncertain whether it opened toward revelation, or ruin.

His expression was measured. Still. But she had seen that stillness before—in marble statues carved to hide the softness beneath.

She wouldn't push. Not tonight.

But her questions no longer came from curiosity. They came from fracture. From ache. From the quiet, gnawing suspicion that the man she had once trusted to keep the Abbey's truths had instead been keeping its ghosts.

And now she was here. Not to uncover. To listen.

Because people said things differently when they didn't know they were being heard.

“I saw it once,” she said. “A long time ago. Before we stopped speaking of such things.”

He nodded slowly, eyes still fixed on the ceiling. “I thought I imagined it.”

“You didn’t.”

They stood in silence for a moment, beneath the watch of golden stars.

“I believe it marks a crossing,” Gwendlynn said at last. “Something layered beneath the Abbey’s memory. Before the Ordinatum. Before even the Concordium.”

Maurice traced the faint outline of one glyph with his gaze. “Do you think it’s reacting to something?”

“No,” Gwendlynn said. “To someone.”

He didn’t answer. Couldn’t. Not without shattering the vow that had already begun to crack.

This time, Maurice did flinch.

It was time.

Gwendlynn stepped forward, brushing her hand along the wall’s carved glyphs. “Do you ever wonder how long we’ve been walking through someone else’s silence?”

Maurice’s voice was low. “Silence is safer than echoes.”

“That depends what’s being echoed.”

A pause. She tilted her head. “You never did explain how Ava came to us. All those years ago.”

He turned his eyes toward the constellation above, brow furrowing. “I told you. The letter came from Archbishop Reginald.”

“That’s not an answer.”

“It’s the only one I can give you.”

Her face hardened. “You’re still hiding something.”

“I am protecting what’s left of a promise,” he said. “Not from you. But for him.”

Gwendlynn’s brow tightened. “For who, Maurice?”

He looked at her—not evasively, but as one staring into the weight of a memory.

“A name I’m not ready to say aloud,” he said. “Not tonight.”

Her jaw tightened. Not with disbelief—but with decision. She did not ask again. Maurice had lied once, and the man before her was no longer someone she recognized.

Something behind her eyes closed—not with rage, but with resolve. Like a hand closing on broken glass: quiet, and certain.

"Good night, Father," spoken with a controlled stillness. Not with warmth. Not with coldness. But with finality.

And when she left, she did not take the stairs directly back to her quarters.

She walked the long corridor alone, silent as breath, the question still lodged where resolve had just settled.

She would not ask again. Not until she already knew the answer. Not until silence begged her to speak.

Behind her, the stone of the vaulted ceiling remained unchanged.

But far beneath it, deeper than the vaults, sealed into the Abbey's foundation, the same sentinel glyph pulsed once in the dark. Not bright. Not waking. But aware.

Somewhere beyond stone and candlelight, the bell that had rung earlier trembled on its hinge.

No one pulled the rope.

But still it moved.

A shiver. A whisper of weight remembered.

The metal hummed against its own silence.

And in the quiet that followed, something else shifted—something too deep for sound.

Not a cry.

Not a prophecy.

Just the slow, invisible turning of something that had waited far too long.

Like a secret adjusting in its sleep.

Like a door easing open behind the skin of stone.

Chapter Eleven

"The Warmest Place"

The bells of Saint-Spire rang low and long at dusk, their sound drifting through the stone corridors like a lullaby humming from the bones of the Abbey itself. In the kitchen, warmth lingered. The scent of roasted root vegetables and broth thickened the air. Master Eloi stood at the hearth, sleeves rolled, his massive hands moving with practiced grace as he ladled stew into bowls already waiting on the long oaken table.

He hummed as he worked—an old tune without words. One only the walls seemed to remember. The children had eaten earlier. Now, this final meal was for the quiet few who stayed late in the courtyard. Ava and Gwendlynn had already slipped out. Sister Mabelle had nodded good night without speaking. Only young Tessa lingered, and Mattheon, who had once again offered to sweep but had disappeared behind the herb shelves, likely to read in secret.

Leonarth entered without a word, drawn not by hunger but by the glow. The kitchen was the warmest place in the Abbey—not just in heat, but in spirit. And Eloi, with his flour-dusted beard and kindly eyes, was its quiet flame.

"You're late," Eloi said, not turning.

"I wasn't hungry," Leonarth replied, sliding into the bench beside the hearth.

"Even when you're not, your eyes come here before your stomach admits it."

Leonarth smiled faintly. "The walls smell like sage. And cinnamon."

"They remember," Eloi murmured.

There was silence between them—not awkward, but companionable. Eloi served him a shallow bowl, less for eating than for holding. The boy wrapped his fingers around the warm ceramic, staring into the steam.

“Do you ever wonder,” Leonarth asked, “if people can be copies? Like... not the real version of themselves, but something that was made to replace what was lost?”

Eloi set down his ladle. “Not copies. Echoes, maybe. The important thing is whether the echo makes its own sound—or just repeats what it's told.”

Leonarth looked at him. “And if you don't know what you were supposed to be?”

Eloi leaned against the table, one hand resting lightly on the edge. “When I was young,” he said, rinsing his ladle in a basin of warm water, “my grandmother told me a story.

There was a star who lived so far from the others that he forgot the sky even existed. He thought he was a pebble.

One day a wind came that could speak—and it said, ‘Shine.’

The star said, ‘How? I have no sky.’

The wind said, ‘Sky is just what remembers you.’

So the star tried. And in that darkness, he glowed just enough to see that he wasn't alone.”

Eloi's voice softened. “He never found the sky. But he lit the way for others who did.”

Leonarth didn't speak at first. Then, almost in a whisper, he said, “Sometimes I think if I remember too hard... I'll disappear.”

Eloi crouched beside him, gentle. “Then remember with kindness. You're not what was taken from you. You're what you choose to give back.”

Leonarth nodded, but didn't speak. His eyes dropped to the bowl in his hands.

Eloi reached for a second ladle he rarely used—smaller, carved from dark wood. He dipped it gently into the pot and stirred once, not to serve, but to remember the motion. He didn't rush. Eloi never rushed. His rhythm was its own form of prayer.

He moved to the breadboard and sliced two thin pieces from the still-warm loaf. One he buttered. The other he brushed lightly with rosemary oil and held near the hearth to warm—not because it was needed, but because he'd once seen Leonarth flinch at cold crust.

He set the plate beside the boy without comment. Just a nod.

Then he added a wedge of hard cheese. Quietly. Deliberately.

"Did you know," he said, "that bread left uneaten in the kitchen will hum if the fire is too low?"

Leonarth blinked. "What?"

Eloi smiled. "Not like singing. More like… remembering. Crumbs settle differently when the room forgets they're meant to be shared."

Leonarth looked down, unsure whether to laugh.

"I don't think I'll ever understand you," he said.

Eloi only chuckled. "Most people shouldn't be understood. Just cared for."

He returned to the hearth and stirred the pot once more. Then stopped.

"There was a boy once," Eloi said, almost to himself. "Didn't speak for the first month he was here. Walked in circles around the same pillar. Every day. Same pace. Same time. No one could reach him. So I started placing a bowl near the stone before he arrived. One day he stopped. Looked at me. Sat."

Leonarth tilted his head. "Did he ever speak?"

"Not in words." Eloi's smile didn't fade. "But once, he handed me a leaf. Said it reminded him of silence. I kept it in the spice cabinet for years."

"Did he stay?"

"No. He left. As all children do, if we're lucky."

"Do you miss him?"

"I miss all of you," Eloi said softly. "Even the ones still here."

A hush fell again. The fire crackled. Somewhere far above, a bell marked the final hour before curfew.

Eloi began cleaning slowly, humming once more. But this time, his note faltered—flat where it should have risen. His brow creased. He hummed again, slower. The melody was right, but the rhythm... off.

He turned toward the spice shelf. The jar of bay leaves was slightly ajar. He reached for it, fingers brushing the oiled cloth hidden behind.

He didn't open it.

Meely watched him from the corridor, eyes unblinking. She did not enter.

Eloi froze.

He placed the jar back without a sound and returned to the hearth.

Footsteps padded in from the corridor.

Mattheon peeked around the corner then, a book in hand. "Did I miss dinner, or did the stars eat it again?"

He paused when he saw the expression on both faces.

"I'll just… sit," he said, lowering himself onto the bench beside Leonarth.

Eloi didn't answer immediately. He ladled one more bowl, setting it gently in front of Mattheon.

"You're late," he said again, voice quiet.

Mattheon glanced sideways, uncertain.

Eloi smiled—not with his mouth, but with his eyes. "But your heart came first. That's what matters."

The three sat in quiet warmth, the fire crackling gently behind them.

Outside, the wind whispered against the chapel walls.

Inside, something deep within Eloi stirred.

Something old.

Something waiting.

They left him there, eventually. The bowls empty, the fire low. No one said goodnight.

The warmth lingered a little longer, clinging to the stones, the spoon handles, the lip of the pot where steam no longer rose.

Eloi stood still, holding a damp cloth in his hands. He wasn't cleaning. Not anymore.

He turned toward the far corner of the kitchen—not the pantry, not the spice wall, but the empty bench beneath the narrow high window. The one no one sat on anymore.

There had been a girl once.

She arrived in silence, older than most, with hands that stayed clenched even in sleep. She never spoke. Never wept. But she always sat on that bench—always before meals, always after curfew. Waiting, he'd assumed, though she never said for what.

He remembered the night he forgot to leave her a roll.

It was only once.

He had meant to bring it. Had even buttered it. But Sister Prudence had spilled oil in the storeroom, and one of the twins had broken a tooth on a fig pit, and there were too many bowls, and not enough spoons.

So he missed it. Just that once.

When he returned, the bench was empty. And she never came back.

He had asked. No one knew where she'd gone. Or if she had even left the Abbey. No note. No shoes missing. Just... absence.

He had kept that roll for weeks. Stale. Shrinking.

Until it crumbled in his hand one morning and vanished like it had never been.

He still looked at the bench sometimes. Not out of guilt. Not anymore.

But because part of him still hoped he'd find her there.

Eloi banked the fire alone.

***

That night, long after the last embers had dulled and the kitchen stood empty and swept, Eloi made his way down the darkened hallway that led toward his quarters. His steps were heavy but measured, echoing softly against the stone.

He passed the silent chapel, the prayer alcove, the shuttered infirmary. Each place hummed with faint memory, though none as loudly as the kitchen had. He carried no lantern—his eyes knew the path by rhythm, not sight. One foot, then the other. The Abbey creaked around him like a body exhaling.

He paused at the cloister arch, glancing once toward the garden. The moonlight painted the stone path silver. He remembered walking that garden at midsummer, handing a fresh roll to a crying child who didn't speak. He remembered sitting on the stone bench during winter, alone, listening to bells that only rang for the living. And once—during a storm—he'd danced there in the kitchen, mop in hand, spinning with mock dignity until young Tessa caught him. She hadn't laughed. She'd just said, "I knew you could waltz."

As he turned to go, he heard quiet laughter down the hall—the younger stewards, no doubt, sharing something small and silly. He didn't mind that they hadn't invited him. He had become, over time, a piece of furniture in their minds. Familiar. Unremarkable. Safe.

Still, the laughter made something behind his eyes sting.

He moved on.

The corridor narrowed the closer he came to his quarters—not physically, but in feeling. The air cooled. The stone changed tone beneath his boots.

He reached the wooden door and paused, as he always did, hand hovering just above the latch. A half-second of hesitation, always the same. Not out of fear. Just ritual. Just habit. Just a moment to remember that this room—this small, forgotten square of silence—belonged to him.

He opened it gently.

The smell inside hadn't changed in years: lavender from the drawer sachet, oil from the old lamp that hadn't been lit in a decade, and the barest trace of flour in the seams of the floorboards.

Darkness offered no obstacle here. The shape of the space lived in his body.

He stepped inside and closed the door behind him, careful not to let it click too loudly. Even now, even alone, he preserved the quiet.

The walls held no paintings. He had tried once—a drawing from one of the children. But the tape peeled, and the wind from the corridor curled it, and he hadn't replaced it.

The bed was always made. Not because he used it—most nights he slept in the chair—but because he thought that maybe, one day, someone would come looking for him and he wanted the room to look like it remembered who he was.

He kept his shoes by the door. Slippers under the chair. A cracked teacup, never used, with a chip that looked like a smile. And beside the basin, a comb with no missing teeth—though he hadn't owned a mirror in thirty years.

He called this place a room.

But what it really was… was proof.

Proof that he'd existed. That he'd stayed. That even if no one saw him, he had not disappeared.

His room was small. A bed, a basin, a chest he never opened. No icons, no luxuries. Only a wooden chair carved long ago, with no maker's mark.

He placed his hands on his knees and stared down at them. Hands that had made bread for the grieving. Hands that had held soup bowls for children too tired to ask. Hands that had forgotten the last time they were held in return.

He had spent more than thirty years in the quiet world of herbs and heat and bread—far longer than he remembered choosing, many of them within the stone walls of Saint-Spire, where the kitchen became the only place that ever felt like his own. Before that—he remembered cobbled streets, the scent of rain on dust, someone laughing behind him. A shop. A scarf. He remembered warmth, not names.

No one had asked him to stay. No one had forced him. He had simply… chosen. One day at a time. One small need after another. And that had become a life.

He had missed nothing, not really. And yet, there were absences inside him shaped like things he couldn't name. A child? A companion? A path he never walked?

He wasn't bitter. He didn't regret.

But there was a tiredness that didn't come from age. It came from being unseen for so long, he wondered if he was still solid.

He had made warmth. That had been his vow, even if no one heard it spoken.

"I kept the kitchen warm," he whispered. "Even when no one came."

He rose, his knees stiff, and stepped to the small chest beneath the window. His fingers hovered over the lid. He had not opened it in years. A small scrap of blue ribbon was tied around the latch—frayed, forgotten, and too familiar. He couldn't even remember what was inside. Or if he had ever placed anything there at all.

He pressed his forehead to the wood and whispered, "I hope I was enough."

The wind brushed against the windowpane like breath.

And in that room, where even the shadows had settled with reverence, something listened. Not with ears. But with memory.

***

Later that night, somewhere between breath and shadow, Eloi dreamed.

He stood just inside a kitchen not his own—wider, older, ceiling lost in mist. There were no walls, only light that flickered like a flame remembered too late. Everything smelled of cinnamon, rosemary, and smoke.

A child sat at a table too large for him. Not facing Eloi. Still.

On the hearth, a copper kettle boiled without sound. The fire beneath it was blue.

Eloi stepped forward, but his boots made no sound.

He tried to speak. No voice came.

The child turned slightly. Not fully. Just enough to reveal dark curls, a profile that tugged at memory.

On the table before him lay a spoon carved from ashwood. And beside it, a folded cloth the color of dusk.

Eloi reached for the cloth. It crumbled.

From somewhere unseen came a whisper: not words, but syllables strung like beads.

"Cal… ven… the… rath."

He repeated them silently.

Then, the child finally turned.

The child's eyes glowed—not with light, but with memory.

Blue, then violet. Then something in between.

He wasn't smiling. He wasn't afraid. He simply looked at Eloi as one might look at a flame—familiar, dangerous, necessary.

And on his chest, barely visible through the folds of his tunic, was a single glyph.

A spiral, broken once, but whole again at its center. It pulsed slowly. Like breath. Like grief held too long. It wasn't drawn. It was part of him—grown, not given.

Eloi staggered. Or tried to.

But his body no longer obeyed gravity. The dream held him in place.

"Do you know me?" the child asked.

Not with lips.

The voice came from within—as if Eloi's own breath had spoken it.

He opened his mouth to answer, but ash poured out instead. Silent. Soft. Familiar.

The child reached toward him. Not to harm. To offer.

A thread—thin as spider silk—unfurled from his palm. It glowed faintly, like the shimmer of water under moonlight.

It moved toward Eloi's chest.

And there—just for a moment—he felt it:

Something inside him responding.

Not resisting.

Remembering.

The child's eyes closed.

The thread vanished.

And all the lights in the kitchen—the blue fire, the copper kettle, the mist—winked out.

Eloi awoke before he could see the face.

His room was quiet. Cold.

The name still clung to his breath, a question he couldn't form: Calventherath. The dream had brushed him before without leaving words. Tonight, the syllables remained.

He had never heard it waking. But something inside him leaned toward it, like a page turning without hands.

***

Far away, in a chamber beneath the Accord's northern wing, the obsidian vault whispered.

No words. Just a shimmer. A weight-shift in the stone.

The sentient resonance in the Hall of Accord—built to detect treason, prophecy, and divergence—twitched once. Then stilled.

Chancellor Siroth looked up from his writing desk.

The ink in his quill pulled slightly left. A tremor. A trick of pressure. He narrowed his eyes.

Nothing moved.

He touched the rune-seal on the edge of the parchment. No glow.

Still, he closed the inkwell.

For a long moment, he stared at the wall across from him—the one carved with the glyphs of the Five. His gaze drifted to the lowest mark: the spiral of the lost Fifth Kingdom.

Still dormant. Still dim.

He exhaled.

But did not relax.

Because deep in the foundations, where the resonance veins slept beneath words and oaths and history…

A thread had twitched.

And no one knew why.

CHAPTER TWELVE

"The Letter and the Lineage"

Father Maurice remained beneath the vaulted ceiling long after Gwendlynn had gone. He gave a final look at the glyphs etched above before stepping out into the night. Twilight had thickened, and the stars in the sky offered no warmth. The Abbey's silence had changed—no longer reflective, but listening. He did not follow her. Not this time.

Instead, he turned toward the old reliquary chamber—the place he had avoided for years, the place where truth waited in dust and linen folds.

He had to see it again. So many years had passed—perhaps it would say something different now. Or perhaps he had changed enough to finally understand it.

Maybe, just maybe, a sliver of forgotten memory would surface and show him the path forward. He needed the strength of the one who'd written it—the one who had carried light into silence.

And something else troubled him. Beneath the decisiveness of Gwendlynn's restrained goodbye, a certainty he didn't welcome took shape: if anyone followed this path tonight, it would be her.

His steps moved by memory more than choice, carrying him through a corridor seldom walked, past the vestry, past shelves of forgotten ledgers.

The recess in the wall appeared as it always had: unmarked, narrow, almost shy in the dimness. He slipped inside. No lantern. Light felt indulgent for what he was about to do.

Down the hewn stone stair he went, breath catching at the familiar cold. He had not come here since Ava arrived with the scroll, bearing a plea spoken at the edge of disappearance. He had sealed the chamber afterward, as though burying it might still a future he feared to face. He had kept it hidden—because promises, once broken, become ghosts.

Maurice laid his palm against the door.

The air thinned—cool, metallic, aware.

He pushed.

The door yielded without a sound.

And inside—she was waiting.

Gwendlynn stood near the far alcove, hands clasped, her posture composed but her eyes bright with something sharper. Not surprise. Not accusation. Familiar in the way old wounds are.

"Did you think I wouldn't find out?"

Maurice inclined his head slightly, as if considering her words rather than reacting to them.

"Find out what?"

A beat.

"You've been carrying many suspicions lately," he added gently. "It would not surprise me if they've begun to bleed together."

"Don't," she said.

"Don't what?"

"Turn this into a misunderstanding."

His jaw tightened almost imperceptibly.

"The Archbishop's letter," she said carefully.

"It was forged."

The word landed cleanly. No heat. No ornament.

Maurice didn't move.

"At the festival," Gwendlynn went on, "the Archbishop confirmed it. Not willingly. He never does. But he confirmed it."

A pause.

"He had never seen such a letter. Never written it. Never sanctioned it."

Maurice exhaled slowly.

"I did what was necessary."

"No," she said. "You did what was convenient."

Her hands tightened at her sides.

"Necessary would have been telling me."

Silence stretched between them, taut and thin.

"If you force this open," Maurice said quietly, "you won't be able to close it again."

"You closed it without me," she replied. "I'm done pretending that was protection."

He looked at her then—truly looked—and whatever he saw there ended the argument.

Maurice crossed to the center—where the floor gave way to a shallow recess, hidden beneath an old iron grate. The grate resisted at first, then relented with a sigh of powder and age.

He knelt beside it, fingers brushing the seal he'd sworn never to break again. Slowly—almost reverently—he reached into the hollow and withdrew a faded scroll, wrapped in linen, bound with a sigil that shimmered faintly in the dark. He held it with both hands. Not like a weapon, but like a wound. "You deserve to read it," he said. "Even if I don't deserve to hand it to you."

Gwendlynn stepped closer. Her fingers did not shake, but her breath did.

She unwrapped it slowly, the linen falling like snow. The parchment was fragile but unbroken. Her voice, when she began to read, was steadier than she felt.

Maurice stared at the stone floor, unable to breathe. She was speaking Faye's voice into the room, as if time could be unwound by sound alone.

"By the time this reaches you, I will already be elsewhere. Do not search for me. What must be done is already beyond safety, and beyond explanation."

"There are seasons that refuse to end. They linger in stillness, hiding what must outlast the storm. I have wrapped the last of what I was in that silence—not to forget, but to let it remember itself."

She paused. The next line was smudged, the ink faded into the parchment's veins. Gwendlynn closed her eyes.

A flash returned—the winter Faye had vanished, the strange quiet Maurice had worn like a second robe, the moment Ava had arrived with a letter and a look he couldn't explain. Gwendlynn had not been present that night—but she remembered how quickly Maurice changed afterward. How his prayers turned more deliberate. How his eyes lingered longer on a boy who never remembered where he'd come from. And now this line: "I have wrapped the last of what I was in that silence..."

"She conceived," she whispered. "She hid him. And you let me think—all these years, and you let me think—"

She couldn't finish. She pressed the scroll to her chest for a moment, as if it might still warm with heartbeat. But it didn't. The boy was real. The years were real. The silence had been real. Her mouth tightened. "You let me mourn a grave that never closed."

"You buried my daughter, and you buried my grandson. Twice. Once in earth. Once in silence."

Maurice finally turned.

There were no guards in this room, no incense, no Council robes. Just an old man and the woman whose heart he'd tried to protect by wounding.

"It wasn't meant for me," he said. "She gave it to Ava. Told her to deliver it only if the Abbey stood untouched, and if the boy survived. Ava arrived carrying it. I opened it alone."

Gwendlynn's eyes flared. "Faye? You expect me to believe—"

"She left it in writing. Her words. Her seal."

"Do you understand what you took from me?" Gwendlynn asked. "I walked these halls while he did. I blessed boys who shared bread with my blood. I could have held him. I could have known him. And you let that slip through thirteen years of silence."

Maurice's voice cracked. "She made me swear. Not to you. To the boy. To his future. The fewer who knew—" he faltered. "But I never imagined it would feel like stealing you from him." He shook his head slowly. "Or stealing him from you."

"Don't you dare make this about strategy."

She stepped forward, her fingers brushing the linen edges—as if touching it could hurt less than holding it outright. Her tears did not fall, but they gathered with cruel patience.

"I sat in silence while you built a cathedral of lies around her memory. I blessed altars you defiled with secrecy. And now you want forgiveness?"

Maurice bowed his head. "No. Only understanding."

"You speak of understanding," she said, her voice hollow. "I gave you sanctuary, Maurice. When the others would have cast you into the storm."

He closed his eyes.

"You were Concordium once. An Inquisitor. I know what that means, even if no one else here does. And I gave you robes, and silence, and a place to be more than what they made you."

Her hands trembled now. "And still, when it mattered, you obeyed the old way. You kept truth as a weapon."

Maurice looked up. The lantern still burned, but in his face it found no surface to cling to.

"I left their ranks, not their shadow. Some days, I still speak like them without meaning to."

Gwendlynn's breath caught. "Then fear has ruled you longer than I did." She looked at the scroll, then at him.

"I've heard enough," she said, voice low. "There is nothing more to be said… Until I can bear it."

She stepped back, her hands empty now, though something heavier settled in her chest. She looked at Maurice one last time. If there was mercy in her, it did not reach her eyes. She turned toward the door.

"Gwen," Maurice called softly. "He's not safe. Not anymore."

She paused, her back to him.

"Neither are we," she said. Her hand lingered on the handle, but she didn't look back. Behind her, the silence resumed its hold.

The door closed behind her without a sound.

And Maurice stayed where he was—alone, still holding the wound, and the words that had outlived the woman who wrote them.

***

The pulse came faintly—like a thread tugged in her chest.

Ava paused mid-step on the south cloister staircase. Her breath caught. The pendant at her throat stirred—just once. Not light. Not heat. But a presence, like breath fogging glass. Familiar. Intimate. Faye.

Her fingers tightened around it. She hated how much she had missed that feeling.

She turned.

The wards along the north wing had been quiet for years, sealed since her arrival. But now the old magic stirred again, subtle and expectant. Something had been opened. Or someone had spoken the words that were never meant to be said.

She followed the resonance, down the passage few walked after twilight. The Abbey's stone seemed more awake here—less sacred, more ancient. And when she reached the final corridor, she didn't hesitate.

The door was already open.

Inside, the reliquary chamber breathed dust and old air. And Maurice sat alone, a scroll resting on the ground beside him. His hands were empty.

He did not look up.

"She read it," he said.

Ava stepped forward, uncertain. "Who?"

Maurice didn't answer at first. The silence made the stone seem louder.

"Gwendlynn," he said at last.

Ava stopped in place.

"She's not one of us," she whispered.

"She always was," Maurice said quietly. "But I never told you. Or Mabelle. Or even her."

"Mabelle too?" Her voice sharpened, disbelief giving way to anger. "You've kept all of us blind. For what—control? Who else is here, Maurice? Who else have you hidden from us?"

Maurice responded quietly, "No one else. Just the three of you. Three women who could have been a circle of protection. And instead, I turned you into walls."

"Does she even know?" Ava asked, voice low. "Or have you kept her blind, too?"

"Not fully. Not yet. But the time will come." Maurice responded.

Ava reacted, "We lived in the same corridors. Prayed in the same chapel. You let us live like ghosts beside one another."

"Because that's how Concordium taught me to survive. I silenced what I loved to protect it." Maurice said bitterly.

Ava froze. Something in her vision shifted—subtle, but irreversible.

It was as if a film she hadn't known was there had finally torn, and the woman she'd walked beside for years came into focus at last.

Not Sister Gwendlynn. Not entirely. Something in Ava's mind reached for an older name—and stopped short.

Ava's eyes sharpened. "You knew all this time? That Gwendlynn was Faye's mother?"

"I knew what she was," he said. "I just didn't know what she would become."

"The Protocol muted more than magic," Maurice said quietly. "It muted recognition.

She cloistered her echo long before you or Mabelle arrived—a Fifth-Kingdom rite for those who must be seen without being known.

You looked at her every day. But the part of her that could be recognized… she hid.

And I cloistered mine as well," he said.

"Not in the same way she did—hers was meant to erase a crown.

Mine was meant to bury a name that carried too much weight," Maurice murmured.

"Had any of you seen me clearly, you would have known instantly. So I silenced my echo. I let myself blur."

A pause. The silence pressed between them again, but Ava didn't move.

"Why?" she asked. "Why didn't you tell us we were all here—together? We could have protected each other."

Maurice's voice cracked. "Because I was trained never to trust what I couldn't control."

Ava went still.

The words echoed between them.

Maurice didn't move. Didn't blink. The stillness felt monastic—ritualized.

He had known this moment would come. Had prepared answers in a dozen tongues, drafted scripts in silence. None of them arrived now.

Only memory did.

And shame.

Ava's voice was quiet, but not soft. "You were Concordium."

He didn't answer at once.

Because saying it wasn't the same as surviving it.

"Do you think any of us would be safe here at the Abbey if I walked in wearing my own resonance?" Maurice asked softly.

"I had to unmake the part of me that history recognized."

He let the silence stretch—not as delay, but as mourning.

For the young man he had been.

For the one who had bowed his head at the foot of the Inquisitorial dais and spoken oaths in a language older than the Abbey's stones. For the child who had translated prophecy before he had learned to write his name.

His name.

Not the one Ava knew.

The other one.

He exhaled. Not breath. Surrender.

"My name," he said, "before robes, before the Abbey—was Keralis."

He expected thunder. Recoil. Ava said nothing at first. But he saw her shoulders stiffen. Saw the quiet quake.

The name had weight.

It had once opened archives. Condemned heretics. Ratified executions. He had been the youngest archivist in the Inquisitorial ranks. Trusted with shelves of prophecy no one his age should have read. A boy-judge beneath violet banners.

Now the name felt like stone in his mouth.

He looked down at his hands.

Hands that had once sealed glyphs with blooded rings. Hands that had signed orders for burnings he never witnessed. Hands that shook now—not with fear, but memory.

"I was born into obedience," he said. "My first memory was of silence—not the sacred kind. The kind that waits for permission to speak."

He paused.

"They taught me that emotion was distortion. That justice required removal. So I carved myself hollow to become worthy."

Ava's face remained unreadable.

Maurice's voice faltered.

"I did not just follow the Ordinatum. I helped write it. I helped erase names I now light candles for."

He swallowed.

"And then I met her."

He didn't say Faye's name. He didn't have to.

"She saw me not as a tool, but as something that might still bend toward mercy. And that was the first thing the Order had never prepared me for."

He laughed, bitter and quiet. "Do you know what it means to be forgiven before you ask for it? It's unbearable."

He met Ava's gaze at last.

"I tried to run from who I was. I burned everything that bore that name. But names are not paper. They stay. They linger."

He pointed at the scroll. "She told me once—truth isn't a revelation. It's a return."

He looked down again. This time, not at his hands. At the floor. As if the name itself were buried beneath it.

"I haven't spoken it aloud in years."

A pause.

"I don't even know if it belongs to me anymore."

"Keralis," she repeated, as if trying to taste who he used to be. "I wish I didn't recognize that name. But I do."

"I heard it whispered once," Ava continued, her voice brittle. "In the Concordium's Codex Speculorum. A name too sacred to speak, too cursed to remember. The fifth inquisitor never reappeared. Because he never truly left."

Maurice didn't answer. But something in him collapsed inward.

"You were the youngest," she said. "Keralis—the Archivist no one dared question. People followed your voice before they understood your words."

"That was lifetimes ago," he said quietly. "Before the Ordinatum. Before the Root was believed ended. Before I watched faith turn to fire."

"But you vanished too," Ava said. "Your name was struck. Your history erased. They burned every record that still echoed with your breath."

He looked up then—not as Maurice, but as someone unburied.

"Because I ran," he said. "Because I learned the truth before the Concordium did."

Ava's gaze didn't waver.

"They prepared me to track Faye. To eliminate her before she could conceive. That was the decree. That was the threat she posed. But by the time they finally found her trail, I had already begun to run—and she was already gone, already carrying him. They didn't know. Not fully. They thought they still had time."

"And you?" Ava asked quietly.

"I followed her into exile—not as their blade, but with the instincts they'd carved into me. For a time, I still believed I was tracking a threat..." He shook his head. "She was not hiding. She was protecting something sacred.

"She gave birth under an old rite. Hidden from the Order. And when the moment came... she placed him in your arms," Maurice said, looking at her now with something near reverence. "You disappeared with him before they could strike. You vanished into Veil-adjacent parishes. Hid among cities that don't enforce bloodlines."

Ava nodded slowly. "We lived in half-lit rooms and waystations. Border towns. Then a farmhouse at the edge of a forgotten valley. He was never safe, but he was never alone."

Maurice's voice softened. "You were his first guardian. I only ever kept the silence. But I knew. I knew from the moment you returned to the Abbey."

Ava's jaw clenched. "You twisted silence into virtue. I called it abandonment."

He looked at her then—not with defense, but surrender. "Because if I revealed it too soon, I would've unraveled everything I tried to set in motion. And I wasn't ready to face what she asked you to carry alone."

He looked away for a moment, then back again.

"You disappeared with him into the Veil's shadow routes," Maurice continued, his voice low. "I covered your trail. Burned records. Altered echoes. When the assassin reached Faye not long after, the child was already gone."

"And the killer believed..." Ava said.

"That he had ended the bloodline. That the transfer ritual could proceed."

He looked up at her. "But we both know it failed. The ritual was built on a lie. A child still lived. The last heir of light."

Ava lowered her voice. "And Siroth still believes he succeeded."

"For now," Maurice whispered. "But that lie is thinning."

"I need to speak with Gwendlynn... and... and Mabelle should've known too," Ava said quietly. "She walked the same silence. And Mattheon..." Her voice faltered. "If Mabelle has been part of this all along—what does that make him?"

Maurice considered answering that, but instead murmured, "I don't know, and even if I knew, that is not for me to reveal. Whatever part he plays, it will be his choice."

Ava said nothing for a moment.

Because suddenly, she could feel Mabelle's presence in all the wrong memories.

All the overlooked gestures. All the careful silences.

The way she always arrived second to every moment of significance—after the conversation had changed, after the boy had left the room, after Ava had asked a question and received only a smile in return.

Mabelle had never lied.

But she had held back. Measured her truths like tea leaves—brewed only when safe.

Ava remembered the time she'd found Mattheon outside the Archives, trembling after a nightmare. He'd asked about his mother—his real one. The question had caught Ava off guard, and she'd gone to Mabelle afterward, hoping she might share what he needed to hear.

Mabelle had only said: "Some truths ripen. Others ruin."

At the time, Ava thought it was grief.

Now, she wasn't so sure.

She had always felt close to Mabelle—but now she wondered if that closeness had been curated. Protected. Shielded. Not out of deception, but duty.

"Did she know?" Ava asked softly. "About me? About Faye?"

Maurice shook his head. "Not fully. Her vow was to her family—not to prophecy."

Ava's voice lowered. "But she walked beside it anyway."

Maurice looked at her, expression unreadable. "Sometimes, that's all we're asked to do."

Ava looked down at the scroll, still partly unrolled. The linen binding was folded cleanly beside it—just as she had wrapped it, thirteen years ago.

"This weight wasn't meant to be carried alone," she said.

Maurice's voice was tired. "It was meant for the ones who would understand it when it mattered."

"So you let us drift—sisters in silence. You built a wall and called it protection."

"The Protocol shattered the moment Leonarth touched the tapestry," he said. "And I chose not to stop him. I chose truth over delay."

Ava looked up sharply.

"The tapestry?" she said.

"It was never just cloth," Maurice replied.

She exhaled, slow and controlled.

"I sensed it," she said. "Not how. Not why. Leonarth's explanation was vague—he was too shaken."

Her fingers flexed once at her side.

"I felt it the moment they described it."

"Like something listening."

Maurice's gaze softened—but he shook his head.

"That part isn't mine to give you," he said. "Not yet."

Ava didn't argue.

She knelt instead. She touched the edge of the parchment. The pendant warmed—subtle, rhythmic, like a pulse beneath skin. Not glowing. Not pulling. Just breathing.

The rhythm wasn't fast. It didn't insist. It simply pulsed—like something familiar remembering itself. Like the beat of a name that had once belonged to someone else.

Ava's fingers rested over it. Not to still it. To remember it.

She had worn this pendant since childhood. A gift she couldn't recall receiving—only that it had always been with her. As if it had chosen her, not the other way around. She remembered once asking her mother where it had come from, and being told it was a keepsake from a stranger. "For protection," the woman had said. "For silence, when you need it."

She had never believed it.

Not until years later, when the silence came.

When the Ordinatum began and the names started disappearing.

When the truth felt like a prayer no one dared finish.

And then one night—years before the boy, before the Abbey, before Faye's scroll—she had dreamed of a woman in violet robes, standing in a field of broken stones, whispering words she couldn't hear, placing the pendant in her hands.

She'd woken before she could speak. But the warmth had remained.

And now—here, at the edge of the scroll's breath—it pulsed again. Not with heat. With memory. With presence.

The scroll beneath her hand responded, faint threads surfacing like scars through old skin—and memory followed.

Faye—not cloaked, not wounded, but alive—meeting her under a weeping arch of stone, the child in her arms. He had been silent. Swaddled in a cloth lined with a sigil Ava had never seen before—one that shimmered only when no one looked directly at it.

Faye had said little. She had not spoken of legacy, or magic, or prophecy. Only this:

"One day, you'll understand what I gave you. And what I couldn't."

No explanations. No instructions.

A scroll. A name. A child.

And that final glance. Not pleading. Not fearful.

Certain.

As if she'd already seen this moment—Ava kneeling by the scroll, the pendant alive in her chest, the memory of a thread not broken but planted.

You're remembering me now, aren't you? the pendant seemed to whisper.

Ava pressed her palm flat over it, and something at her core shuddered. Not grief. Not fear.

Gratitude. Unbearable gratitude.

She looked at the scroll again.

The surface had changed—nothing she could name, only a sense of depth, as though something beneath it had drawn closer.

And somewhere behind her eyes, something whispered.

Not in language.

In weight.

A promise, remembered too late but still alive.

She lowered her head to the parchment, her forehead resting against it. The air had changed. The stone beneath her knees no longer cooled—it carried warmth, faint and impossible.

Not like magic.

Like welcome.

The scroll was not responding to her.

It was recognizing her.

And in that moment, Ava understood: she had not just been chosen to carry a message. She had been chosen to become one.

A living echo.

A link between what was given, and what would be remembered.

She closed her eyes.

And the pendant stilled.

Not because it was finished.

Because it knew: she was ready.

She stood slowly. She left the scroll where it was.

Maurice looked at her, then to the scroll. "If you ever need to return to this chamber… you won't need my permission again."

Ava met his eyes. He didn't say the word trust. But he didn't need to.

"Thank you," she said, quietly.

And he nodded, once. "It belongs to you now more than it ever did to me."

She stepped into the archway without looking back. The scroll remained, but what it carried no longer lived in ink alone. Ava carried it now—into the night, into memory, and toward the silence she could no longer let Mabelle hide behind.

Mabelle must be told.

And not with silence this time.

Chapter Thirteen

"The Weight Between Us"

The night had grown old by the time Gwendlynn stepped out of the reliquary. The doors whispered shut behind her, muffling the final echoes of Maurice's voice. The halls no longer felt sacred. The silence had changed. She ascended the spiral steps of the north wing with care, hand trailing the stone wall. The air here was colder, damp with the scent of iron and ash. The sconces were unlit. The Abbey seemed to hold its breath.

Outside, the wind had died. The sky hung low with clouds, blotting out even the suggestion of stars. Only the sound of her own footfalls accompanied her through the garden path. The frost had deepened since sunset, clinging to every surface like salt. Grass crunched beneath her boots, and the stained-glass windows glimmered with a strange dullness—light from within, but no warmth.

Her steps were not aimless. They carried her along paths worn from memory—ones she had not walked in years. Each turn brought back something small: the faint snap of a branch, a bell she once heard toll only in her sleep, the soft cadence of a prayer whispered behind doors now sealed. It was not regret that clung to her—it was absence.

By the old greenhouse, she paused. Its silhouette loomed against the Abbey's stone flank, its once-gleaming glass now dulled with grime and weather scars. The door hung slightly ajar, crooked on its rusted hinge. She pushed it open and stepped inside.

The air changed instantly—denser, warmer, layered with the scent of decay and damp soil. Shelves lined with cracked pots bowed under the weight of dust. Clinging vines curled like skeletal fingers over empty trellises. Somewhere above, wind slid across the fractured roof panels with a low moan.

It was abandoned—but not untouched.

She stood still for a long moment, letting her eyes adjust. There was the half-rotted worktable where Leonarth once arranged seeds in careful little rows. The rusted trowel that never left its nail. A watering can tipped on its side like a wounded soldier. She reached out to it and righted it gently. The handle came away in her hand.

Earth. Rot. Rosemary. And memory.

Leonarth, age seven. Kneeling in the soil with stained sleeves, pressing his palms flat into the dirt.

"Do you think flowers remember prayers?"

She had not answered then. Had only watched from the shadows. His brow had furrowed in concentration as he whispered:

"I prayed for my mother last night. I think I forgot part of it."

She had swallowed her breath. There was so much she could have said—and didn't.

At the time, she'd chalked her reaction to pity. Or fondness. He was a curious boy, far too inward for his age, too solitary. And yet, something in his presence always tugged at her—like a thread caught on the hem of a robe. She had told herself it was duty. Compassion. That motherly instincts could emerge even in those who had buried their children.

Now she wasn't so sure.

She moved farther into the greenhouse, careful not to disturb the brittle remnants of what once grew. Ferns reduced to papery fronds. A single hanging lantern, rusted through. She touched the edge of a planter and felt the faintest echo—not of sound, but of presence. A boy's joy. His quietness. The way he made even silence feel alive.

She stopped before the long workbench near the rear wall. There, pressed between two broken panes, was a child's drawing. Faded beyond recognition, the paper delicate and eaten with mold. But she knew it. Knew it as surely as she knew her own name. Leonarth had drawn it. A stick figure, large eyes, messy curls. And beside it—her.

Not the real her, but the version he'd imagined. A tall figure in robes, arms outstretched like wings, with stars on the hem. Not a nun. A protector. A watcher.

She swallowed against the lump rising in her throat.

What had he seen in her, all those years? What kindness had he clung to, even when she offered none? She had believed distance was dignity—a form of restraint mistaken for grace.

Now, only ghosts stood between them.

Her breath misted in the air. Her hands, despite her gloves, had gone cold.

And still, she stayed.

She crouched and touched the soil. Dry. Forgotten. But once, it had been tended with care.

A small piece of blue window glass jutted from the dirt—once part of a sun catcher that hung above the eastern pane. She plucked it free. It was cloudy now, but when she held it to the light, it cast a faint wash of blue across her hand. Leonarth had called it "the watchlight," and insisted it protected seedlings from the cold.

For a moment, it reminded her of the green glass Leonarth always seemed to have with him—but she turned away from the thought, choosing the weight of her guilt instead. She rolled it once in her palm, then slipped it into her pocket, more out of habit than intention.

She whispered into the stillness: "I'm sorry."

The soil didn't answer. The wind outside pressed harder against the glass.

The warmth in the memory curled inward like something dying. She rose, knees aching, and stepped back into the cold.

The night greeted her with a stillness so complete, she feared it might crack if she spoke. She didn't know where she was going. Only that warmth waited somewhere—and she wasn't ready to be alone again.

The quiet clung to her, as if it recognized its own.

***

Farther down the hall, golden light leaked under the heavy kitchen door. A rhythm of movement inside—stirring, pouring, humming. Familiar.

She opened the door. Eloi stood at the long counter, sleeves rolled up, hands steady over a steaming pot. The kitchen smelled of chamomile and bloodroot—oddly sweet, faintly metallic. The fire in the hearth cast gold against his white tunic, making him seem younger, almost translucent.

He looked up. Not surprised. Just… kind.

"I thought I heard you," he said, his voice low and warm. "These stones carry footsteps like secrets. Or maybe it's just that I've been listening for them."

He lifted the kettle and poured water into two cups. "It's too late for anything heavy. Elderflower and calming root. Good for forgetfulness, if you're looking for that."

"I'm not," she said, but took the cup anyway.

He smiled, no judgment in his expression, handing it to her with both hands. His palms were warm—too warm, almost—and lingered a moment longer than necessary. His eyes, that familiar soft hazel, seemed lit from within.

She sat at the long oak table, her cup cradled between her fingers. He moved fluidly, returning to the fire, stirring the pot with small, practiced movements.

"I always liked this hour," he said. "The Abbey sleeps, but the walls still breathe. They remember more than we do, I think."

Gwendlynn said nothing. She watched the fire instead, letting its orange tongue blur her vision.

"They say kitchens are the heart of any home," Eloi continued. "Even here. It's where things soften. Where bitterness is boiled out."

"You sound like a philosopher," she said, her voice hoarse.

His eyes danced in the firelight, but there was weariness behind them.

"Or a lonely man with too much time to think," he offered with a grin.

They shared a quiet moment. The air in the kitchen was warmer than it should have been. Heavy, but not unpleasant. She took a sip of the tea. It was sharp, floral, oddly grounding.

Eloi sat across from her.

"I had a dream again last night," he said. "One I've had since I was young. Or thought I was."

Gwendlynn looked up. "What sort of dream?"

He hesitated, swirling the tea in his cup. "I was walking through a place I didn't recognize. A fortress, maybe. Red stone walls, endless corridors. No doors. Just silence. And I had something in my hand… a scroll. No—a list. But I couldn't read it."

She leaned forward slightly, despite herself.

"I didn't know the names on it," he went on. "But I knew they were people. People I'd seen before. Or would see. It wasn't a dream about a place. It was about duty."

His voice cracked slightly on that last word. He shook his head and smiled faintly. "I'm being strange."

"No," she said too quickly. "You're not."

He looked at her a long moment, as if surprised by her softness.

"Sometimes," he said, more quietly now, "I wake up already humming. A tune I don't recognize. Like someone else's memory, leaking through."

He didn't wait for her reply.

He hummed.

It was slow, fractured. A melody as ancient as it was formless—rising and falling like breath. Like waves echoing through a drowned chamber. Something about it felt fractured. Broken. Or stitched together from something that had once been whole. It coiled inside her like smoke, curling through bone.

Her hand tightened around her cup.

It wasn't the tune itself. It was the texture of it. The way it folded into silence, as if parts of it had been erased—or hidden.

"Where did you learn that?" she asked, too sharply.

Eloi blinked. "That? Ah. I'm not sure. I think I've done it since I was a boy. Or maybe not. My mind's not what it used to be."

He chuckled, rubbing the back of his neck. But he seemed unsettled. As if he was hearing it now for the first time.

His thumb brushed absently along the bone of his wrist, as if trying to press something back beneath the skin. A habit, maybe. Or memory. He blinked, shook it off, and reached again for his cup with a forced steadiness.

"I think," he said after a pause, "sometimes we remember things that didn't happen to us. We inherit echoes. Maybe that's all people are—houses filled with the songs of those who came before."

He stared into the fire again. His hands trembled once, almost imperceptibly, then stilled.

"Or maybe," he added, voice quieter, "some of us were never meant to remember."

Gwendlynn rose slowly. She had not touched the tea again.

He noticed. "Did I say something wrong?"

"No," she said. "Just tired."

"Of course," he said, his face falling. "It's a hard night."

He stood with her, reached toward a small wooden drawer near the hearth—then paused, hand hovering above the handle. A flicker of something passed across his face, but he let it go. Closed the drawer instead of opening it.

She watched him a moment longer.

“Thank you,” she said softly.

He gave a slight bow of his head, still smiling, though the warmth had dimmed.

As she turned to leave, the fire crackled sharply behind her. And just as she reached the door, she heard him humming again—softer, like a lullaby meant for no one.

Or everyone.

***

The walk to the statue of Elodia was longer than she remembered.

Not in distance—in weight.

The path curved through the oldest part of the Abbey grounds, where stones were uneven and the trees leaned inward like old women whispering secrets. The air had grown sharp with the hour. A frost clung to her shawl before she even reached the outer gates. Even the shadows here felt older, untouched by firelight.

These were paths walked in vigil, not comfort. By those seeking penance, or forgetting, or both.

She paused by the gatepost, fingers brushing the carved letters nearly erased by time: “Sine Lux, Sine Vox”—without light, without voice.

Fitting, she thought.

The statue stood in its clearing, just beyond the weathered archway. Even from afar, she could see the damage. Elodia’s marble robes once flowed like frozen riverwater; now they bore cracks, streaked with age. One eye was missing. The other stared forward, unblinking. Her stone hand rested at her heart, the other outstretched to no one.

At the base of the statue, a candle burned.

Already lit.

Gwendlynn stopped. She had brought no candle. She had not expected light.

The flame flickered once, as if acknowledging her, then steadied.

A trick of the wind, perhaps. Or something else.

She stepped forward—not to kneel. Not to pray. Her knees would not have obeyed her even if she tried. They trembled beneath her weight, not from age, but from the unbearable ache of what remained unspoken.

She looked up into Elodia's cracked face, once carved to convey serene silence. Now it seemed more like resignation.

"You were mercy," she whispered. "But I need vengeance. What do I do with that?"

The wind stirred—a dry rustle through the trees. No judgment. No absolution. Only sound.

Her voice trembled again, sharper this time.

"I have served. I have been silent. I have obeyed every rule written and unwritten. And yet… here I am. With everything broken."

The flame did not waver. But her breath did.

"I raised a kingdom and lost it. Buried a daughter without a grave. Took in a child I never knew was mine, and still…" Her voice cracked. "Still I said nothing."

She didn't expect a response. And yet the silence felt full. Too full.

Her breath clouded the air. Her hands remained at her sides. Her jaw locked to hold back more than words.

She lowered her gaze to the candle. Its flame pulsed with a strange steadiness, untouched by the wind.

She should have snuffed it. Ritual demanded it—no flame should outlive its penitent. But she didn't move.

She stared at the candle for a long time.

Its flame danced without smoke, curling upward in soft golden strands. It wasn't high enough to warm, but it pulsed with an eerie steadiness—too slow for wind, too sure for chance.

Someone had lit it. Not long ago.

That fact pressed against her like a hand on the back of her neck.

She tried to remember the last time she had come here at night. Had anyone else ever tended this flame? Maurice never ventured this far. Ava never crossed spaces she hadn't first prayed through. Mabelle only lit candles when she thought no one would see.

Had she lit this? And forgotten?

No. The wax was too fresh. The flame too calm.

She knelt—not as a believer, but as a woman hollowed by the motions of belief. Her knees touched the worn stone. Her gloves scraped over runes long eroded. She knew them by heart. Knew every litany, every invocation carved beneath her hands.

But tonight, they meant nothing.

She didn't remember the words.

She didn't want to.

There were no prayers for daughters you didn't bury. For grandsons you raised without knowing. For friends who turned silence into armor and used it to shield you from everything that mattered.

The candle shivered. Not in answer. In echo.

She didn't snuff it out.

Not yet.

Its light felt both intrusive and intimate—as if someone had spoken before her, confessed something she had not. It unsettled her more than silence. It didn't feel like a memory. It felt recent. As if presence had lingered—just long enough to unsettle the silence.

And then, unbidden, a voice returned to her mind.

Not Mabelle's or Ava. And certainly not Maurice's.

She thought of Faye.

Not the girl queen. Not the titles they wrapped around her. But the daughter—the one who once stood at the edge of a choice she was never meant to make, eyes fierce, mouth trembling.

"I'm not your mirror, Mother. You chose silence. I won't."

That memory had not surfaced in years.

It cut deeper than any prayer.

She collapsed forward before realizing she was no longer kneeling, but yielding. The ground was hard, but the cold was harder. Her palms pressed into the stone at the statue's base, her breath coming short, uneven.

"You were right," she whispered. "You always were."

But the weight of memory was not the same as truth.

And the truth had begun to rot.

She thought of Leonarth—the boy who had mistaken her silence for wisdom.

She thought of Faye—who had defied it, and vanished.

And she thought of Maurice—who had hidden everything behind his own walls, and had finally begun to crumble.

There was no one left who knew the whole story. Perhaps there never had been.

Maurice's words returned: "Not all truths arrive when called."

But she had stopped calling.

She had buried her questions beneath ritual, obedience, and duty.

And now? All she had were ghosts, and guesses, and a single lit candle she did not place.

She rose slowly, like something unburied too soon—joints stiff, body aching with a grief no shrine could hold.

She looked once more into Elodia's fractured face.

And then, finally, her voice returned—cracked, broken, and alone:

"I don't know who to hate."

The wind carried nothing back.

And the silence, at last, said nothing.

***

In the quiet that followed, the Abbey seemed to exhale.

Eloi stood alone in the kitchen, unmoving for a long while, as if trying to outlast a thought he couldn't name. The fire had dwindled to embers. A few poppy seeds crackled in the heat, releasing a sweet, scorched smell.

He turned, slowly, and walked to the tall cupboard near the hearth. Not the drawer—the one no one ever used. The narrow shelf behind the forgotten jars.

His fingers moved without urgency. Without decision. They knew the path. They parted the bay leaves and found it: a small bundle, wrapped in linen, tightly wound with a faded violet thread.

He held it. Light, familiar. Warmer than it should have been.

His thumb brushed the edge of the fabric. Beneath it—something hard. Round. Cold once, but not tonight.

He did not unwrap it. He never had.

A pulse of heat rose in his chest—not emotion, but something deeper. Muscle memory, perhaps. Or the first tick of a clock long buried.

A word rose to the edge of his mind. Not spoken. Not remembered. Just a shape in the dark—sharp, foreign, and gone before he could hold it.

He blinked, confused. The word vanished.

Eloi placed the bundle back behind the bay leaves, as gently as one would tuck in a sleeping child.

He closed the cupboard. And said nothing.

Chapter Fourteen

"The One Who Waited"

Silence returned to the reliquary long before Maurice did. Or rather—long before he returned to himself. He was still seated on the stone floor, exactly where Ava had left him, the chamber stretched around him like a hollowed lung. The air had grown colder, but he hadn't noticed; only the stillness had shape now.

The scroll lay a few feet away, where Ava had placed it with trembling hands before stepping into the corridor's darkness. The linen wrap remained folded neatly beside it, waiting like a discarded breath.

Maurice exhaled at last.

He didn't rise. He didn't pray. He only stared at the parchment, its edges catching the fractured shafts of moonlight that spilled through the dome overhead. It didn't glow. It didn't pulse. It simply waited—patient in a way only truth could be.

Gwendlynn's grief still clung to the room, faint and raw. Ava's anger had left a sharper residue, quiet but cutting.

They had both left.

He had not.

At length, Maurice reached for the scroll.

His fingers brushed the linen first—still warm with her touch. Then the parchment itself.

He did not linger on the lines they had spoken aloud. Those were carved into him now, carved too deeply to require ink.

It was the words beyond them—the ones he had avoided, the ones he had folded away the day Ava placed this letter in his hands—that pulled him forward.

He drew the parchment closer and unfolded it further than before.

The faint strokes of Faye's hand emerged in the dim light—angled, deliberate, steady even at the brink of ending.

He began to read.

Not the beginning.

Not the warning Gwendlynn had already bled against.

The part he had never dared to face.

"You must become no one. There are eyes in our homes, names that do not know themselves. When silence is no longer enough, memory must become your shield. Wait. Watch. Say nothing, until the key remembers the lock."

"They will understand—not through knowledge, but through rhythm. Show this to the one who listens in stillness and answers with pause. Do not explain. Do not name. Their silence will carry what your voice cannot."

Maurice paused. He had stopped here, years ago, when first delivering the message. But something pulled him deeper this time, past what he had safely curated.

"There may be more among us than we knew. Shadows wrapped in flesh, speaking with borrowed voices. Some echoes are not memories—they are instructions, waiting for the right chord to be struck.

When it happens, it will feel like remembering, but it will be a return to something they never chose."

His fingers curled around the page. He could feel the blood withdraw from his hands. The meaning that once eluded him now pressed close.

He whispered, "She knew."

He had read it too early the first time. Read it with the discipline to contain, not the grief of a man being handed prophecy. But now the words burned in their stillness—like coals beneath dust. He hadn't protected them. He had buried the message beneath good intentions, folded it like it could wait forever. And now the Abbey stirred with a breath not its own.

The signs had been there—muted, disjointed. But Faye had seen the danger long before any of them had taken refuge in these stone halls. "Names that do not know themselves." The phrasing hadn't been metaphorical. It had been precise.

He closed the scroll in his hands—his ears rang—not with sound, but with something colder: a quietness no longer willing to be passive. The reliquary no longer felt like a shelter. It felt like a mouth sealed shut too long—and now, preparing to open.

And as he stood in the hush that followed, the past rose—not with drama, but with the quiet certainty of something that had merely been waiting.

Images came all at once. It had been raining when he arrived. Not the gentle sort of rain that softened a road, but the kind that hollowed it—turning paths to wounds and footprints to graves. The Abbey had emerged from the mist like a relic refusing burial.

He didn't fall to his knees. He folded, slowly, like a page closing on a book half-burned. The rain tasted like the inside of a chapel—stone, soot, and old incense. His name had unraveled days ago.

His mind, stripped of allegiance and voice, drifted between prayers he no longer believed in and oaths he could no longer break. Even now, he didn't know which side he belonged to—only that the one who had named him once was now ash and legend.

And now, even his thoughts came in someone else's voice.

Maurice—no, not yet the man who would take that name—Keralis had collapsed at the base of the outer wall, his robes torn, the scent of iron and ash clinging to every breath. In his hands, he had carried only her letter, wrapped in linen, not sealed—because it was never meant for secrecy. It was meant for recognition.

She had come quickly. Gwendlynn.

Not gliding—but with the sharp gait of someone whose mourning had long since ceased to weep. Her presence preceded her footsteps. And when she appeared at the edge of the cloister walk, she did not gasp. She did not call for aid.

She looked at him—no longer a man, only wreckage in robes—and took the linen bundle from his hands.

Her eyes passed over it once. Then again. The third time, they stilled.

"No seal," she said, her voice low. "That's brave. Or stupid."

Maurice didn't answer. Couldn't. His tongue felt like stone. His ribs like strings fraying inward.

Gwendlynn unwrapped the letter and read it where she stood, beneath the rain's soft assault. She didn't blink. She didn't speak. She only inhaled sharply—once—and when she looked at him again, her face had changed.

Not with pity.

With memory.

"This is hers," she said at last. "The cadence… the silence between the lines. It's her."

She looked back down at the parchment, her brow furrowed—not from doubt, but from recognition of what was not said. Her fingers trembled once, then stilled. "She never says she's coming back."

Maurice said nothing. He couldn't. The rain filled the space between them, soft but relentless.

Gwendlynn's throat worked against silence. Her next words came not with volume, but with finality.

"She's dead, isn't she?" Her throat tightened. Just once. But it was enough to make her blink too slowly—the kind of blink used to cage tears before they rise.

She didn't wait for him to answer. She folded the letter with a care too precise to be called reverent. "This was her grave."

His mouth opened, closed. No sound.

"You were not meant to survive," she murmured. "Neither was she."

Her eyes sharpened. She circled him once—not like a mother, not like a priestess, but like a queen inspecting the weapon that once split her kingdom in two.

"You wore the fifth glyph—they said you signed the Ordinatum Decree in blood and ink. I watched her name become a rumor. I watched history rewrite her into a coward, a deserter. And you—you helped make that possible. I buried an entire people. I buried myself. Why should I believe you now? For all I know, you came to finish what they couldn't."

He bowed his head, not from shame—but because the weight of her certainty was heavier than the rain.

"I should send for the Bishop now—call in my last favor, sign your name in borrowed ink, and forge you a past that never existed. That's what you're asking, isn't it? For me to rewrite the world with a lie, just so you can disappear inside it."

Her tone remained steady. "You understand what you're asking me."

He nodded, barely. The movement of a leaf still pinned by frost.

"Do you?" she pressed, stepping closer now. "Because the men who wrote laws like you did never needed weapons. They only needed signatures. If this is a trap—if this is some echo of the old laws trying to bait me out—"

He raised his head, finally, and the look in his eyes was not defiant.

It was empty.

Hollowed.

Gutted from the inside by truths too long carried.

She studied him.

Then folded the letter once more—this time without hesitation—and held it out to him.

"This is yours."

She looked away—not in retreat, but in calculation. A crack ran down the chapel wall behind her, one she had never dared repair. Some structures, like some names, were never repaired—only covered. And some wounds were never meant to heal. Only to harden.

She wasn't crying. But her voice had dropped—scraped hollow like an urn that had carried fire too long. "I buried her once already. In silence. In exile. I told myself it was better not to know."

"If I do this, it won't be a kindness. It will be a gamble. And the last time I gambled on love, it cost me my child."

"I'll say I knew you from the seminary. That your faith broke with the wars, and I vouched for you out of guilt."

He blinked.

Her voice sharpened—not louder, but harder. "You'll be a priest. Father Maurice. You'll keep your head bowed. Your hands clean. And your voice... silent."

She stepped back once, as if to mark the line between them. "Do not make me regret this."

He tried to speak. Failed again. The stillness between them thickened—not with peace, but like breath held in a room already out of air.

A word stirred in his mouth—not Faye, not forgiveness. Something smaller. Something human. He swallowed it. Even now, he could not ask for mercy without sounding like a man rehearsing lies.

There was no absolution left in him. Only ruins stitched with silence.

She hesitated. Then, softer: "If she trusted you, that will have to be enough."

And just before she turned to go, she said—not for him, but to the night itself:

"We don't bury what matters here. We bury what might betray it."

He remained kneeling in the mud long after she had gone, unsure whether he had been saved or sentenced. The Abbey had opened its gates. But the man who entered would never leave. Only the name would walk again.

***

By the next evening, the garden had begun its descent into dusk, the beds turning grey-lavender under the breath of a fading sun. Maurice found her kneeling near the rosemary slope, sleeves rolled to her elbows, hands buried in loam. The smell of damp soil, crushed mint, and marigold clung to the air like a memory unwilling to leave. She was humming—something tuneless, or perhaps too old to be named—and her hair was pinned back with the kind of carelessness that came only from fatigue disguised as discipline.

She didn't look up when he approached. The trowel in her hand moved with quiet rhythm, scooping, folding, pressing. As if the earth needed reassurance more than order.

"Mabelle," he said gently.

She brushed a strand of hair from her temple with the back of her wrist, smearing it with soil. "It's almost too late in the season for transplanting," she murmured. "But they'll manage. The stubborn ones always do."

Maurice waited, letting the quiet settle between them like ash. Then:

"I've been thinking about those first days. When you came. Do you remember much?"

She stopped moving. Not abruptly—just long enough for the silence to announce itself.

"You used to walk the cloister before dawn," Maurice said. "Every day for a month. No lantern. No shoes. Just silence and frost. I used to think you were praying. But now I wonder…"

She didn't answer right away. "Maybe I was just looking for something I couldn't admit I'd lost."

Her eyes lifted, calm but unreadable. "Some roots don't bloom where they were planted," she said. "So they seek stone."

It was the kind of answer that dared you to dig deeper—and warned what you'd find if you did.

He stepped closer, but not enough to cast a shadow over her work. "It wasn't an easy transition. For any of us. Especially then."

"I adapted." Her voice was flat. Not defensive. Just closed.

Maurice's eyes studied her movements. They were precise. Controlled. Too much so.

"Did you ever…" he hesitated, "lose time? In those early weeks? Hours you couldn't account for? Moments that didn't… feel like yours?"

She did not look at him.

Instead, she pressed the back of her wrist into her palm—a motion so subtle it might have meant nothing.

But his gaze caught it.

Still, she said nothing.

He didn't press.

Mabelle drew a slow breath. "You think I've forgotten something. That's why you're here."

Maurice tilted his head, studying her face. "Have you seen Ava today?"

"Briefly," Mabelle said. The answer came too quickly, and too flat.

"Did she… say anything strange? Off, maybe?"

Mabelle shook her head. "She doesn't usually need to."

She glanced at him then, briefly. "Why?"

Maurice's answer was slow. "She just seemed… changed."

But the stillness that followed wasn't passive. It was weighted—like a note held too long in the throat.

"As if the silence between us had thinned."

Mabelle tilted her head slightly. "Maybe it has."

Then she returned her gaze to the soil. "But if something's unraveling, it's not Ava who pulled the thread."

There was no sarcasm. Just a strange stillness—as if the conversation had moved to a room Maurice wasn't allowed to enter.

Maurice studied her posture. It wasn't relaxed. It was coiled. Like someone waiting to be asked a question they'd already chosen not to answer.

"I think we've all forgotten something," Maurice said. "The question is whether it was taken—or surrendered."

She paused mid-motion, her hand lingering over the soil. The silence between them changed shape. Not thicker. Sharper.

Maurice remained still.

She returned to the soil, but her voice softened—not with warmth, but with distance. "I don't remember every hour. Who does?"

Her jaw tensed, then released. A slow breath escaped—not weary, not peaceful. Just… resigned. As if the act of pretending not to remember was harder than forgetting had ever been.

"I used to," she whispered. "I used to remember everything. The taste of grief. The first time Mattheon smiled. The night the doors stopped singing."

Maurice said nothing. But the phrase stayed with him: The doors stopped singing.

And then, as if to fill the space where truth refused to surface, she hummed again. Just a breath of it—three notes, maybe four. They didn't land. They lingered. A lullaby, perhaps. Almost forgotten.

But Maurice's eyes froze.

He knew that melody. Not from this place. Not from her.

It was older than either of them should remember—a refrain from somewhere else. A war-room. A glyphward cradle. A Concordium corridor where children were trained to forget.

He had taught that song once. Or maybe watched it being sung—not to soothe, but to erase. A melody used to soften the mind before memory was rewritten. It wasn't a lullaby. It was a key.

She returned to her work as if nothing had passed between them. The tune faded into the rustle of soil and leaf.

Maurice said nothing. He simply watched her. Watched the way the light caught the arch of her shoulder, the careful angles of her silence.

"Do you ever wonder," Maurice asked quietly, "if we were planted here… or if we buried ourselves?"

She looked at him.

For a brief moment, he thought she might say something that would change everything.

She hesitated for half a breath. As if a word nearly escaped. Then she swallowed it, like something bitter, and turned back to the rosemary.

Her eyes flicked up—not quite meeting his. And in them, for a fraction of a second, something stirred. Not fear. Not clarity. Just a reflex that didn't belong to her. And instead she only nodded, once. "Good night, Father."

And as he stepped away, the last note of her humming returned—not loud, not certain. Just enough to remind him that not all melodies came from memory.

Some were planted.

Some were waiting to bloom.

He didn't look back. But he felt it—the shape of that melody curling through the dark like a vine through stone. Not a memory. A pattern—half-formed, half-returned.

It should have made him weep. Instead, it made him want to pray—not to remember, but to be forgotten.

***

The cloister was nearly empty, wrapped in that hour of not-quite-night when the world held its breath. The arcades cast long shadows across the cobbled walkway, and the last light of the chapel windows caught in the frost that gathered along the balustrade like forgotten glass.

Ava stood at the edge of the corridor, near the weathered statue of Saint Elodia. Her shoulders were square, her hands tucked into her sleeves, but her posture was not one of prayer. It was something more watchful. More weary.

Maurice approached slowly, his steps echoing softer than they should have. The air between them hummed—not with sound, but with memory.

He stopped just beyond arm's reach, not wanting to break whatever invisible perimeter she had drawn around herself.

"I've been asking myself something," he said.

She didn't turn.

He continued, quieter now. "Would you know if danger sat beside you every day?"

The pause was not long. But it was deliberate.

She turned toward him—not fully, just enough for him to see the edge of her expression. "You mean like an inquisitor who hid behind kindness for over a decade?"

Her voice didn't rise. It didn't need to.

"I knew danger sat beside me. I just didn't know it had a name."

Ava exhaled through her nose, barely audible. "We built too much on silence, Maurice. Trusted it like mortar. But walls made of silence don't keep things out. They keep things in."

"That's what I'm afraid of." Maurice murmured.

"You're afraid now," Ava said. "But you weren't afraid when you buried us in separate truths. You weren't afraid when you turned guardians into ghosts."

He stepped beside her now, slow and careful, and looked out over the garden wall with her. A sliver of sky above the Abbey rooftops was still bruised with twilight. The trees beyond moved like breath beneath a thickening mist.

"There are signs," he said.

"I know."

"I don't know who to trust."

"I know that, too."

She turned her head slightly toward him then. Just enough for him to see the profile of her cheek, the shadow under her eye. Her voice dropped.

"There's something here, Maurice. Something buried. Maybe someone. And I'm afraid that if we name it, we wake it. But if we stay silent, it might wake anyway."

Maurice didn't answer at first. The stone at his back felt colder than before. He folded his hands, and for a long moment, they stood that way—like relics left in the open, absorbing the weather, unwilling to shatter.

"When you came to the Abbey," he said, "did you ever think this was refuge?"

She smiled, but the expression never touched her eyes.

"No. Only a pause."

The wind shifted. Somewhere in the cloister behind them, a candle sputtered.

Maurice studied her a moment longer. Her calm wasn't peace. It was containment.

"Have you felt... watched?"

"Yes," she said. "But not from outside."

That landed like a breath caught mid-prayer.

She nodded, slowly. "Since the night I touched the scroll. Since the pendant remembered me. Since I remembered her."

"Faye?"

Ava didn't answer. But the wind moved, and something in her face changed—as if grief had learned how to look back.

"I need to ask you something," he said. "And I don't want you to answer quickly."

She looked at him fully now.

He hesitated. Then: "If there was something—someone—who didn't know what they were... would you feel it before they did?"

Ava studied him with an unreadable stillness.

"I think," she said slowly, "I would feel it the way you feel a storm inside your own bones. Like pain before pressure. Like dread that doesn't have a name yet."

Maurice let out a breath he hadn't realized he was holding.

The quiet that followed wasn't peace. It was something waiting to be named.

And then Ava said, "I'm not hiding because I don't trust you. I'm hiding because something in this place remembers me wrong. Like it's waiting for a version of me that no longer exists."

Maurice turned his face to her, a flicker of something close to understanding passing through his features.

"If it ever comes for you," he said, "I hope I know who I am when it does."

Her eyes met his. "So do I."

She took one step away, then paused. "I'm not the same person you chose to keep in the dark. And I'm not waiting for your trust anymore."

They did not say goodnight.

They only turned—separately—and walked in opposite directions, as if afraid that moving in the same one might draw something to follow.

Behind them, the cloister remained quiet.

But not still.

***

Maurice sat alone in his quarters, the single candle on his writing table reduced to a trembling wick. Shadows swelled at the edges of the stone walls, bloomed across the floor like bruises. The room was quiet—not the quiet of peace, but the kind that listens.

He moved slowly, with the reverence of ritual, as he reached for the small iron box beneath his bed. Its hinges resisted him, as if memory had grown stiff with age. Inside, wrapped in old wool and cedar dust, lay the object he had not touched in years.

The glyphstone.

It was oval, heavy, veined with copper. Inscribed with a symbol he had once known how to draw without thought. A relic of Concordium oathcraft—personal, dangerous, dormant. Or so he had believed.

He set it gently on the table. Then, beside it, a bowl of saltwater drawn from the chapel well.

He exhaled. Not prayer. Not memory. Something in between.

And then he placed the stone into the water.

For a moment, nothing.

Then a pulse.

Faint. Subsurface. Not light. Not motion. Just… pressure.

He leaned closer. The water trembled.

The glyph began to glow faintly—not bright, but deep, like a bruise beneath skin. The suggestion of a spiral forming along the inner ridge, curling inward. One loop. Then another. Not random. Measured.

Maurice's breath caught. He had seen this pattern before—in his training halls as Keralis, in the archives beneath Virelia, in the sigils etched into the necks of Concordium vessels meant to forget their own names.

He whispered, "Faye… I wasn't listening. But I hear you now."

***

In the kitchens, Eloi stirred broth in the half-light. The spoon moved smoothly, then faltered—just for a second. The hum on his lips skipped a beat. Not dissonant. Just… wrong.

He blinked. Looked at the spoon. Then kept stirring.

Behind him, the kettle began to whistle—though no fire had been lit beneath it.

***

In the herb room, Mabelle moved between drying racks, checking bundles of lavender and sage. The candlelight flickered. Something unseen hummed—not from her lips, not from her hands, but from the air itself.

She paused.

And then—so quietly it felt like memory—she hummed.

Just three notes. Faint. Uneven. She didn't seem to notice she'd done it.

Her fingers brushed a vial, and for a moment she stopped breathing.

The sound continued—low, circular, familiar. Like something half-remembered waking up.

She pressed her hand to the wooden counter. Waited.

Then, without a word, she resumed her work—but slower, more deliberate. And as she turned to the next rack, her hand lingered over a jar of black salt. Longer than it should have.

The hum returned. Not from her throat. But as if the room had learned it from her.

She tilted her head. Then stopped. And told herself it had never happened.

But something had already heard her. She just didn't know which part of her it was.

***

Back in Maurice's quarters, the glyphstone spiral completed. The glow receded, but the water did not still.

It turned—clockwise. A current, impossibly slow.

Maurice reached for the stone, but stopped short.

His fingertips hovered just above the water. The heat of it—impossible. The pulse—not his. Not the stone's. Something else. Something watching back.

He exhaled. A breath he hadn't meant to hold.

"Then…"

The words came softly. Like a seal breaking.

"…it begins again."

Chapter Fifteen

"The List and the Lie"

She hadn't come to steal the scroll. She had come because it had stayed with her—not in her hands, but behind her eyes. Maurice had said she could return. No keys. No permission. Just the weight of what he'd given her. Still, Ava had hesitated. Not from fear—but from knowing that silence, once broken, never returns unchanged. And she had already broken so much.

The reliquary door opened without protest. The chamber had already grown cold. No voices echoed here now. Only dust.

She crossed in carefully, each step measured—as if the floor might remember the last time it carried this grief.

The scroll rested exactly where she had left it—centered on the marble cradle, as if even stone had been instructed not to disturb it, its linen corners folded with ceremonial care. She stood before it, unmoving. The pendant at her neck did not pulse. Not yet.

It felt different now. Heavier somehow—as if the page had inhaled something since she left. Memory, perhaps, or the breath of a lie.

Ava reached for it without knowing why. Not to read it. She knew every line. But the knowing wasn't enough.

Not anymore.

She gathered it carefully in both hands, pressing the linen to her palms as if to warm it back to life.

And only then—as the pendant brushed its edge, answering a resonance already awake—did the ink shift.

Not all of it. Only a few faint scars beneath the words she thought she understood. Lines she had not seen before. Lines that had hidden themselves—until now.

"Some echoes do not wait to be spoken. They wait to be remembered. Not every sleeper lies still. Not every name

FORGETS ITSELF BY CHOICE. ONE OF THEM WALKS WITH SILENCE—AND BELIEVES THE LOVE THEY CARRY IS THEIR OWN."

Ava's breath caught.

These weren't just warnings. They were descriptions. And they had only appeared once her pendant touched the scroll—once memory and magic began to stir.

Ava sat with it.

Not like before—not in awe, not in dread. But with the weight of someone who had run out of places to shelve her doubts.

She had spent the last two days watching Gwendlynn, watching Maurice, listening to herself think. But tonight, her thoughts had turned colder—and they turned to Mabelle.

Not because Mabelle was unkind.

But because Mabelle was perfectly kind.

Predictable. Measured. Careful. Present at every pivotal moment—but never at the center of them. Always one step behind the truth. Or one step ahead of the silence.

The pendant gave a faint pulse.

Ava didn't move. She watched the resonance fade, then whispered, "Is it her?"

The pendant did not answer.

She folded the scroll again, but her hands hesitated over the linen. The question had already taken root—and with it, the next one:

If Mabelle was the one who had forgotten what she was...

What would Ava do if she remembered?

She rose, breath shallow.

She returned the scroll to the marble cradle, aligning its edges with a care that felt almost apologetic. The pendant settled back against her collarbone.

The night said nothing.

But Ava no longer trusted silence—not after what it remembered.

***

Mabelle was steeping dried mint into a small clay bowl when Ava entered the herb room.

The steam curled between them, thin and translucent—a veil that blurred, but did not separate. Mabelle did not look up at first. Only when she finished stirring did she glance toward the doorway and say, gently, "It's late."

Ava stepped inside. She let the door whisper shut behind her.

"Couldn't sleep," she offered.

Mabelle nodded, measuring the leaves. "Chamomile's fresher, if that's what you're after."

"I'm not."

Ava moved slowly, letting her fingers drift along the labeled jars—sage, feverroot, yarrow. Familiar scents, once comforting. Tonight they felt like choices.

The silence stretched.

"You've never spoken of your brother," Ava said, her voice neutral.

Mabelle's hands paused.

"Why are you asking?" she said, still not turning.

"Because I need to know what you've carried all these years. What you might still be carrying."

Mabelle didn't respond at first. The spoon in her hand dipped too low, clinking against the bowl. She set it down more forcefully than necessary.

"You think I'm hiding something?"

She turned fully now—not angry, but bare. "From you?"

Ava didn't answer. She didn't need to. The air was answering for her.

Now Mabelle looked at her.

"There's not much to say," she replied, voice level. "He vanished before Mattheon could walk."

"But he knew something. Left something. Didn't he?"

Mabelle wiped her hands on her robe. "He left me Mattheon."

She hesitated, then added more quietly: "And a warning. Never trust bloodlines."

Ava stepped closer. "Even the ones we love?"

"Especially those."

The answer wasn't defensive. It was weary—too weary to be false.

Ava studied her face.

"I think you've guarded something longer than most of us have dared," she said. "And I think silence becomes heavier the longer it's worn."

Mabelle didn't blink. "You've been speaking like Maurice lately."

"I've been seeing like him."

A long pause. Just the scent of mint rising between them.

"Mabelle..." Ava's voice softened. "Have you ever wondered why he chose you?"

"Who?"

"Your brother."

Mabelle's hands stilled. "Because I was the one left."

Her voice caught slightly—a breath out of rhythm.

"I didn't ask to be. But I said yes. I said I'd keep him safe. That's all I've done."

The way she said it—it wasn't pride. It was a defense. A plea not to be pulled back into the story she thought she'd escaped.

Ava stepped forward now—close enough to feel the warmth of the herbs between them.

"I went into the reliquary," she said quietly. "Maurice didn't tell you?"

Mabelle stiffened.

"Tell me what?"

Ava hesitated. Just long enough to decide she wasn't backing out.

"That something was hidden there," she said.

Mabelle's eyes sharpened.

"Hidden?"

"Not by you," Ava said quickly. "By him."

Silence settled between them, dense and watchful.

"There is a scroll," Ava said at last—slow, careful. "I carried it here. Many years ago."

She drew a breath.

"Faye pressed it into my hands."

Mabelle went very still. Not startled—alert.

"Don't say that name," she said quietly.

Ava didn't look away.

"I know what it means."

The words landed heavier than any explanation.

"Not as a message," Ava went on. "As a weight."

Mabelle's mouth parted, a protest rising—then faltering.

"Maurice took it the night I arrived," Ava said. "That's how I became Ava-without-a-past." A name behind silence. A role carved into someone else's ledger. I didn't know what it meant back then. I only knew it felt heavier than anything I'd carried."

Mabelle turned her back to the table. Her fingers gripped the clay rim harder than needed. "Why are you telling me this?"

"Because you deserve to know what I found. And because it speaks of someone being embedded—not knowing who they are. Someone who's… dormant."

Ava continued, "A few nights ago, something stirred—not memory, not light."

She hesitated, searching for the right shape of it. "It wasn't meant for me. It was loud only because something else touched it first."

Mabelle's hands stilled.

Not slowly. Not thoughtfully.

A flicker crossed her face—too quick to name, but sharp enough to cut. She thought of the attic. Of the boys. Of how carefully she had asked them to keep their stories simple. How she had trusted that they had.

"It found me anyway," Ava said. "In the silence I had once trusted. It didn't call me by name. It pulled—like a thread tightening somewhere it shouldn't."

She watched Mabelle now. "After that, I couldn't stay where I was. I was led to a place Maurice keeps closed. A reliquary no one uses anymore. Where things are hidden not to be forgotten—but to wait."

Ava's voice lowered. "He broke a vow I didn't know he made. And I crossed a line I can't uncross. Not for truth. Not for loyalty. For memory—the kind that cuts."

"I don't know what Maurice has told you, or what you know. Silence no longer guards us. It only buries what's still alive. I vowed to protect the root once—but I never thought the rot might be within our own soil."

Mabelle stepped back, suddenly unsure of her own footing. "You speak like someone who's already buried me," Mabelle said, voice trembling. "I kept my silence because I believed it was love. Not fear. Not strategy. And now you ask me to solve riddles with half the truth."

Anger built under her breath, her heart pounding faster as she edged toward the rim of her own fears. She set the clay bowl down—

too quickly, the liquid inside sloshing but not spilling. "If you came to cut me open," she said, "then do it where no one else can bleed with me."

Mabelle turned toward the door.

Ava didn't move.

"Are you coming?" Mabelle asked, not looking back.

Ava hesitated only long enough to feel the cost of it. There was no turning back. She did the only thing left to her.

She followed.

Silence took them the rest of the way to Mabelle's room—not the kind that settles, but the kind that frays.

The halls were dim, the lanterns low with oil, as if even the light had grown cautious. Somewhere in the cloisters, a bell turned in its sleep but did not ring. The Abbey did not breathe for them. It watched.

Ava felt Mabelle's hand on her arm—firm, unshaking—but the warmth in it was different now. It wasn't comfort. It was ritual. Like a rite neither of them had agreed to, but both knew how to perform.

She wanted to speak. To say she didn't come to hurt her. To say this wasn't an inquisition. But Mabelle's silence had grown too wide—like a hallway without doors. There would be no turning back now. Not until something opened.

Mabelle's footsteps were steady, but her thoughts were not. Ava could feel them—not with magic, but memory. The kind of memory that lives in the body, in the way shoulders stiffen before a fall. Mabelle had lived too long guarding the lives of others. Now she had to wonder: had someone been guarding her?

They passed the old window where the vines had cracked through the stonework. Moonlight filtered in—just enough to illuminate the dust between them.

Ava didn't know if it was fear she was feeling, or grief.

But she knew one thing: the silence was no longer hers to protect.

And if Mabelle spoke now, it would not be to defend herself. It would be to remember something she had never been allowed to know.

Mabelle's room was small—not humble, not austere, but edited. Every object had intention. A bowl of dried cloves. A single reed of lavender pinned to the lintel. A sealed chest beneath the cot, the wood smooth with age and polish. One window, half-draped. A candle already lit, though neither of them had touched it.

Ava stepped in slowly. She'd never been here. She realized that now.

It didn't feel like walking into someone's quarters. It felt like stepping into a version of them—distilled, and carefully arranged for no one to find.

Mabelle didn't sit. She moved to the corner shelf and adjusted something that didn't need adjusting.

"I don't sleep well when the wind shifts," she said.

It wasn't a confession. It was a map of how far she would let the conversation go.

Ava stayed near the door. Not out of mistrust. Out of reverence.

Mabelle stood by the candle, but her hands were still. The flame made no sound, and neither did she.

Ava stepped farther in, leaving the door unlatched behind her.

"I've never been in here," she said softly.

Mabelle didn't turn. "No one has."

The silence held.

Then Ava said what had waited thirteen years.

"I brought him with me."

Mabelle's breath hitched—not in surprise, but as if her body had caught a thought she didn't want to hold.

"The boy," she said.

Ava nodded. "Leonarth."

Mabelle turned. Her face was pale, but not blank.

"I thought he was from the orphanage."

"He was. For all the Abbey knows. But not to Maurice. And not to me."

She crossed to the window, her fingers tracing the edge of the half-drawn curtain, needing something physical to press against. "Faye gave him to me in silence. Swaddled in cloth bearing glyphs I didn't recognize. She pressed a scroll into my hand and said, 'One day, you'll understand what I gave you—and what I couldn't.'"

"She was already being hunted?"

"She was already marked. I don't know if she was afraid. She didn't show it. But she knew it would be the last time."

Ava turned.

"She died within the week. I ran, then hid for years in the Veil's shadow before I dared bring him here—bleeding from a wound I don't even remember receiving. When I finally came to the Abbey, Maurice forged the letters," Ava said.

"He gave me a past that wasn't mine. And he named Leonarth a rescued child."

She swallowed.

"I wore the silence like it belonged to me."

Mabelle stepped back as if something in the air had shifted.

"All this time," she whispered. "You were one of us."

Ava wanted to nod. It would've been easier. But the truth clung to her like wet cloth. She shook her head, not in denial—in pain. "No. I was no one. I held a child I didn't know how to protect and a scroll I couldn't read. I didn't feel chosen. I felt buried."

Silence. Then Mabelle sat—not collapsed, but carefully—on the edge of her cot.

"What did the scroll say?"

"It didn't say. It remembered. It revealed new lines only after thirteen years—when the pendant pulsed." Ava stepped forward. "It spoke of someone… embedded. Dormant. Waiting to be remembered, not awakened."

"And you think it's me?" Mabelle asked.

"No," Ava said. "I think it might be near you. But the scroll didn't name anyone. It only warned that memory could be rewritten."

Mabelle stared past her—not at the candle, not at the window. At something inside her she couldn't quite catch.

She waited for Ava to say more. She didn't.

The omission landed the same way it had before—quiet, deliberate. No mention of the attic. No question about the cloth the boys had found and been told not to touch again. Ava's silence wasn't ignorance. It was restraint—and that unsettled her more than accusation would have.

So Mabelle stayed with what could be spoken—and felt a small, private relief that the cloth remained where it was. Untouched. Uninvited into this room.

"I remember the night my brother handed me Mattheon," she said. "He didn't speak of enemies. He didn't explain where the boy's mother had gone. He only said: Don't ask what I was. Keep him safe. Never trust bloodlines."

Ava sat beside her.

And Mabelle continued, not as if she was confessing and relieved that the truth was finally allowed to be spoken out loud, her voice was low now, "He was my half-brother. And whatever changed him had already begun before I was old enough to understand it."

Mabelle stared into the candle, as if the flame might open into memory.

"Something had already broken in him," she said. "Before Mattheon's mother. My brother never named it, but he carried the weight of it like a second spine. He stopped speaking about it after that. Or maybe he never had words for it at all."

Ava leaned forward, the quiet between them thick with suggestion. "Do you remember what changed him?"

"No." Mabelle's voice was firmer than her face. "Or maybe I was never told. But I remember how he changed. He came back looking… burned from the inside. Not wounded. Hollowed."

A pause.

"And then there was Mattheon's mother?"

Mabelle nodded. "He stayed long enough to see the child born. Then he left. No letter. No trace. Only that trunk." Her gaze drifted to the chest across the room. "And one warning: never trust bloodlines. He didn't say whose. Just that blood could carry more than memory—and not all of it good."

Ava exhaled slowly. "What if what broke him… wasn't just personal?"

Mabelle's gaze lifted.

"You think I've heard this story before."

"I think I lived the edges of it," Ava said. "When I joined Faye's Order of Guardians, it was already fractured—"

Mabelle's throat worked silently, cutting off Ava, "You were F.O.G.?" Her breath caught. "And all this time… silence dressed as trust? Were you not bound to speak only the truth?"

Ava looked at Mabelle—not in a condescending way, but as if shame and restraint had been stitched into the shape of her next words,

"I never lied. I swore silence—not out of deceit, but obedience. The Veil wasn't just protection. It was faith. It was the language I spoke when I no longer trusted words."

And she continued, "F.O.G. became my compass when I no longer knew which pain belonged to me. I didn't follow Faye out of hope. I followed because she had already lost more than I had. I was consumed by loyalty above all. And now, our paths have merged out of coincidence, or by Faye's design".

Mabelle's hands grew colder, she turned to the window and faced the moonless sky, not in disappointment, but as if praying for a sign she could trust the words that were spoken now so freely and without restraint.

Ava continued, "As I was saying, Faye had gone into exile, hunted for something she wouldn't name. But those of us who followed her—we weren't bound by power. We were bound by loyalty. By fear. We were told she carried something that could rewrite what the Accord had broken.

Mabelle grasped for air, as her heart began to race, "Leonarth."

Ava nodded. "She never named his father. Only whispered, 'The man I once loved is no longer the name he carries.' Then she looked at Leonarth like he was a wound she had chosen to keep open."

Mabelle blinked—once, slow—as if trying to keep the image from settling too deeply.

Something cracked, not audibly, but between them.

Mabelle stood—not with certainty, but with need.

"If what you're saying is true..."

"It's not confirmed," Ava interrupted gently. "But your brother's timeline, his silence, the timing of the boys' births—they echo. And if the same man touched both their beginnings—"

"Then Mattheon and Leonarth were born from the same silence. And they are..."

She stopped herself. The word brothers felt like a chasm.

"I don't know," Ava whispered. "But we need to."

Mabelle's hand hovered above the chest now, but did not touch it.

"There are papers I never read. Glyphs, codes, correspondence. I kept them sealed because I thought the silence was protection. But maybe it was something else."

Ava stepped closer. "You said your brother was your half-brother?"

Mabelle nodded. "His father wasn't mine. There were whispers, but I never leaned in close enough to hear them. I should have."

"Then naming him now—not just as a brother, but as what he was—might be the difference between inheritance and contagion."

Mabelle looked at her.

"It might be the difference between memory and manipulation," she said.

"You've been holding all this," Mabelle said, her voice small beneath the weight of it. "And I've been standing here—years of my life—guarding a boy, a silence, a trunk… and I never even knew I was part of the story."

Ava stepped closer, but didn't reach for her. "I didn't know, Mabelle. Not then. I carried pieces—Not a map. Not a story. Just broken things I didn't know how to name. I didn't even understand the scroll until it began to recognize me."

She hesitated. "Maurice saw it first—when the pendant stirred. He recognized something. I made him speak. I forced him to finish what silence tried to bury."

Mabelle closed her eyes. "If Mattheon knows..."

Ava exhaled—not from fatigue, but the weight of choosing what to say next. "He shouldn't. Not until we do."

Mabelle nodded.

But she didn't move to the chest just yet.

Instead, she asked, voice raw, "Do you think he'll hate me?"

Ava looked down at her own hands before answering.

"No. But I think he'll wonder which part of him we protected—and which part we feared."

The pendant stirred between them—not loud, not angry. Just… aware. Like memory stretching in its sleep.

Mabelle's hand hovered above the chest, then fell away.

Not everything she guarded was inside it.

There was something she had chosen not to bring with her. Not into this room. Not into words. The tapestry—left where it was, as she had been told. And now that the silence had held, she wondered whether it was protection… or a mistake that would remember her later.

"If you need answers," she said finally, "I'll give you what I have."

But she didn't move toward the trunk. Not yet.

And Ava didn't ask her to.

***

The sun had risen into a sky the color of bleached parchment. Somewhere beyond the cloisters, bells rang the tenth hour. Ava had been walking the Abbey grounds in quiet arcs since dawn, waiting.

Mabelle's door opened without a word.

She stood just inside—hair half-pinned, sleeves damp from tending the herb basins. "I said I would give you what I have," she said. "That includes time. But not company."

Ava nodded. "Understood."

Mabelle stepped aside. "Don't be long. I told Mattheon I'd meet him before the midday bell. He asked about his mother again."

Ava hesitated. "And you?"

Mabelle's face didn't shift. "I told him Truth is a door that never closes the same way once it's opened. And then I walked away."

She left without waiting for more.

The door closed behind Ava with the soft click of familiarity. It wasn't the room's silence that struck her this time—it was its stillness. As if it had already braced itself for being seen.

The trunk sat beneath the cot, undisturbed. No dust on the latch. No lock. Just intention.

She knelt.

The wood was scarred with time, not mistreatment. It had belonged to Mabelle's brother—passed through fire and grief, sealed with a choice not to remember.

Ava opened it.

The scent was dry and brittle. Old paper. Tanned leather. Burned cotton.

Inside: fragments.

A folded uniform—Concordium standard. Two buttons missing. A broken lens wrapped in twine. Parchment bundles curled from heat exposure. One corner of a torn prayer cloth. A child's boot, never worn.

She sifted slowly, her hand brushing a scroll half-curled from fire. The top page was flaked and blackened—its words lost to time or violence.

Ava hesitated, then whispered an incantation she hadn't spoken since before the Veil:

"Scriptum revelare."
(Reveal the written)

A shimmer passed beneath her palm—soft, silvery, like breath on stone. The parchment pulsed once, and the ink bled back into view, line by line, like memory remembered through pain.

SAINT-SPIRE ABBEY

CALVENTHERATH ***ASSIGNED***
STATUS: ***DORMANT***
OVERSIGHT: ***EMBEDDED***
GLYPH RESPONSE: ***TRIGGERED BY PROXIMITY OR BLOOD***

The pendant stirred sharply—not from reaction, but recognition. It had heard the spell before. It remembered its function.

Ava's breath locked in her throat.

The pendant—still beneath her robe—drew tight against her chest, as if pulled by a thread that hadn't existed until now.

She sat back, breath sharp, hands shaking—not with fear, but recognition.

It wasn't proof.

It was corroboration.

She folded the cloth back over the pages, gently.

But as she reached to close the lid, her hand brushed something beneath the layered documents—something colder than wood.

She paused.

Slipped her fingers beneath the cloth.

And lifted it.

A small object nestled in her palm. No larger than a plum pit, but heavy. Warmer than it should have been.

It looked like a seed, carved from a mineral that shifted color as she turned it—dark opal at first, then a violet sheen, and finally, as it caught the light: a green-black spiral that pulsed faintly like breath.

Etched into one side was a symbol she didn't recognize—a root curling back into itself.

It pulsed once against her skin.

Ava closed her fingers around the object, holding it longer than she meant to.

The pendant stirred faintly—as if to warn her—then stopped.

It didn't freeze. It flattened. A chosen stillness. Not to protect her, but to keep from being seen.

That's what struck her—not silence, but silence that should have come later, that tried to come too late.

Because even before she let go, she felt it:

A thread snapping in a place she could not name.

A distant presence that had not been watching—now unmistakably was.

***

Far away, in a place beyond names, Chancellor Siroth stirred.

Not in speech. Not in memory. But in instinct.

The lattice of his awareness shuddered—brushed by what should not exist.

A certainty, long settled, momentarily failed to hold.

The Root of Orreth.

***

Ava stood frozen—the pendant against her skin like a breath she hadn't taken.

She had touched hundreds of magical objects in her life. This one didn't answer like the others.

It didn't thrum like power.

It listened.

She didn't know what it was.

Not yet.

Oblivious to what she had just awakened, she set it back into the trunk, tucked under the cloth as if it had never been touched.

The chest closed with a soft groan of old hinges.

Ava stood, her knees stiff.

She didn't look around the room again. She didn't need to.

The answer had already found her.

She walked out the way she came.

And just before the door closed behind her, she whispered to the room that could no longer unknow:

"It's here. And I know who."

And for the first time, the silence didn't comfort her.

***

Maurice stood at a narrow desk set into the Abbey's north passage—a place meant for notes, not letters. The kind of surface used when words were not meant to travel far, or last long.

The stone beneath his palms was cold. Awake.

He did not sit.

The scroll lay wrapped beside him, the linen folded with care that bordered on restraint. It had not changed. That, somehow, unsettled him more than if it had.

Ava had touched something.

He felt it not as magic, but as absence—the way silence thinned when it had been stretched too long.

Maurice exhaled once. Not prayer. Decision.

He drew a small sheet of vellum from the drawer and wrote without flourish, without seal, without explanation.

To Ava—
Come to the Chapel of the Veil at dusk.
Bring what keeps silence from wandering.

He read it once. Folded it.

Then he reached for a second sheet.

His hand hesitated longer this time.

To Mabelle—
Come at dusk. To the place where veils are blessed before vows are spoken.
Bring what you have guarded without knowing why.

The words settled—not lightly, but correctly.

He did not write a third.

The space where another message might have been placed remained blank—a silence shaped by choice, not oversight.

Some truths required witnesses.

Others required reckoning.

He gathered the notes and left them where they would be found—not hidden, not announced. Simply placed.

As he turned away, the Abbey did not resist him.

Somewhere deep in the stone, something loosened—not a lock, but a holding breath.

The Veil had not been torn.

But it had been thinned.

Chapter Sixteen

"When the Silence Fractures..."

The doors opened not with a creak, but with a sigh—like breath escaping from a sealed chamber of memory. Maurice stepped into the Chapel of the Veil alone, the scroll in his hands wrapped in faded linen, edges darkened with years. He had asked the others to come. What followed was no longer his to contain. Light did not reach here. It was conjured.

He whispered a word not used since the Ordinatum—"Veranthis"—and the glyphs carved into the twin stone pillars shimmered faintly, then rotated. Not visibly. But he felt them. Like gravity changing direction.

The convergence ward unfurled with slow, aching light—a suspended arc of runes rotating mid-air, woven from strands of violet fire. One by one, the old protections fell away, casting slow-spinning shadows across the old constellations, as if memory itself were trying to decide which version of the past would be allowed to enter.

Maurice crossed the ward's boundary.

The air was colder than it should be. The kind of cold that remembers.

In the rafters, unseen, a shadow coiled. A flick of grey fur. Two eyes, reflecting nothing. Watching. Meely did not move. She had been waiting longer than any of them.

The altar stood like a wound that time had failed to close—carved from ancient rootwood, its twisted veins fused with veins of gold so old they no longer shimmered, only remembered.

Around it, twelve columns rose in a silent ring, each etched with constellations long erased from every map but one. Overhead, the dome arced impossibly high, magic often changed perspectives to conceal the truth in plain sight, its ceiling veiled in ash-dark mosaics that shifted subtly when no one looked.

Maurice did not bow. Reverence had left him long ago—along with the robes, the rituals, the man. But his hands moved with a memory his body hadn't forgotten. He had not placed the scroll on it yet. He waited.

Footsteps.

She entered like wind that had lost its warmth.

Mabelle stepped through the veil, hood lowered, arms stiff at her sides. She did not look surprised to see him. Only braced. No greeting. No bow. Her eyes flicked to Maurice once—not with malice, but with history. She carried the chest and a rolled tapestry bound in protective cloth. She didn't offer to explain it.

"Evening," Maurice said gently.

Mabelle said nothing. She moved to the western edge of the altar and placed the tapestry beside the chest. Her fingers lingered a moment too long on the lid, then fell away.

"You brought everything?" he asked.

She nodded once.

That was all.

The chapel felt heavier.

Moments later, warmth arrived. Not as a body. As presence.

Ava stepped into the circle, her robe catching the edge of the magical ward, causing it to ripple like breath through silk. Her pendant, tucked just beneath her collarbone, pulsed once—and the air warmed. Subtly.

Her eyes flicked to the altar—to the tapestry.

So that was what Mabelle had not said.

Ava kept her silence.

She was carrying something else herself—a folded linen wrap the size of a book. Maurice noticed it. So did Mabelle. No one asked.

Ava gave a small, grave nod to Mabelle. Mabelle returned it, just enough. A truce, still breathing.

Maurice finally unwrapped the scroll and placed it on the altar. It didn't flare. But the room did seem to inhale.

The breath of the room wasn't air. It was weight—like someone pressing a hand to their own grave. A shiver passed through the columns. The ash-mosaics above shifted in a slow spiral, and for a moment, a glyph that hadn't been visible before flickered into form—a spiral within a crown. And then it was gone.

His fingers hesitated above the linen, just for a breath—not out of doubt, but the grief of repetition. He had placed a scroll like this once before. In another chamber. Beneath another ceiling. That one had ended in silence too—not sacred, but ash-choked. He didn't know if he could bear another.

"We should begin," he said. "Before doubt unbinds what silence has preserved."

He opened the pouch of resonance powder—an old Fifth Kingdom mixture of bone-dust, star-salt, and crushed violet root. He scattered it across the altar. It shimmered briefly, then stilled.

Maurice's voice changed—lower, older, as if the words were being borrowed from someone who no longer lived in him. Not an incantation. A remembrance.

He extended his hand over the altar, and in a voice shaped by rite and time, began the invocation in full:

"Memoratu causantrae,
(By the cause I call)

resonata invocare,
(By resonance I summon)

spiritum ligare animae."
(I bind the breath of soul)

"By root, by echo, by the bond of kept breath," he intoned. "Let memory recognize what truth still dares to name."

Each of them stepped forward in turn, placing their pendant on the altar's edge—not as offerings, but as admissions.

Maurice's was old—deceptively so. A smooth disk of obsidian inset with five concentric rings of etched silver, the smallest barely visible without angled light. At its center: a speck of stone the color of old wine—resonance coral, long thought extinct. As it touched the altar, it pulsed a slow, violet glow, deep and unwavering—the kind of light born not from clarity, but from the weight of memory too long carried. It did not flicker. It simply endured.

Ava's was ornate, unmistakably sacred—a pendant not forged, but assembled with reverence. Its crescent-shaped platinum frame cradled an intricate lattice of elemental stones: a ruby star at its center, four soft emeralds curving around it like protective wings, and beneath them, a golden branch that spiraled with elegance, its limbs cradling four leaf-shaped green stones—translucent, luminous, and trembling with memory. From the base, a single sapphire teardrop swayed like dew clinging to silence. The entire piece shimmered with layered meanings: compass, covenant, cradle.

As it touched the altar, the central sapphire pulsed—blue, then lighter, then deep again—like something remembering how to breathe. The altar responded with a low hum, as if recognizing an oath made long ago. The powder near it shimmered slightly, and then stilled—honest light, anchored to old grief.

Mabelle's was rigid in its beauty—a vine-twisted pendant of darkened gray steel, shaped like a sprouting root frozen mid-growth. Embedded in the metal: three narrow slivers of polished greenstone, arranged like a broken trinity. As it reached the altar, the stones flared once—green, sharp, immediate—then dulled to grey. As if recognition had sparked... and passed. The powder did not answer her. But the altar twitched, almost imperceptibly—as if it had caught her name in its throat, but refused to speak it.

The powder reacted to each. Except hers.

They did not speak of it. Not yet.

Ava unfolded the linen in her hands. Inside lay a crystal shard mounted in metal, faintly etched with a forgotten sigil: the sigillum murare—a spell of stillness, used in the old days to cast silence around vulnerable truths.

The relic wasn't merely copper, symbols, and crystal. It had once been part of a Fifth Kingdom scrying lens, shattered during the Ordinatum, when the last of their living artifacts were hunted down and broken. Its copper edges had warped from magical flame, and at its heart, a single shard of aquamarine crystal hovered—not embedded, but suspended in a curl of etched metal as if caught mid-breath. Around its edge, the runes were delicate but fractal, bending with light as if resisting translation.

Ava raised it. Spoke the activation:

"Sigillum memoris. Custodi nos."
(Seal of Memory. Protect us)

The relic breathed once—a sharp inward pull—and then exhaled a dome of silver-blue light that cascaded downward like falling silk. For a heartbeat, the air tasted of riverwater and burnt cedar.

The dome of silence was ready—a shimmering aurora of light preventing sound and magic resonance from traveling beyond its perimeter. The altar glowed. Their relics shivered.

But something was wrong.

The dome quivered—not with instability, but with refusal. As if some thread beneath their feet had frayed at the exact moment of invocation. The altar's golden veins dimmed for half a second, then returned.

Maurice inhaled sharply. "The seal isn't holding."

"It should be stable," Ava whispered. "Unless..."

Her eyes moved to Mabelle.

Mabelle stiffened. "Unless what?"

Ava stepped forward. "Unless one of us isn't anchored."

Ava's voice trembled—not with fear, but with recognition. The same kind of tremor that came in dreams before the world changed. Faye had once warned her: "You will know when the memory isn't just yours."

And yet, Faye had kept things from her, too. Had carried silence like armor, even in her final hours. Perhaps they were all reflections now—of the same mistake, passed down like a relic that refused to break.

And now, as she looked at Mabelle, something inside her ached—not with judgment, but with the ache of unspoken inheritance.

"What are you not telling us, Mabelle?" she said, softer than accusation, sharper than doubt.

Mabelle's mouth twitched. "You think this is because of me?"

"I think," Ava said carefully, "that your light went dark before it stabilized."

Maurice stepped back, letting the two women face one another.

Ava spoke slowly. "You've hummed the lullaby. You kept the glyph. You guarded the relic. And still... you never asked why it pulled at you."

Mabelle's voice broke slightly. "Because if I asked, I might not want the answer."

A beat. Then softer:

"If it's true..." Her voice caught, thin as broken parchment. "Then I don't know who I am. Or if I've ever truly been anything more than... what I was told to be."

She looked down at her hands—not in shame, but as if waiting to see if they would change before her eyes. "I thought love could rewrite anything. I thought silence meant loyalty."

Her eyes lifted to Ava's. "But what if it meant erasure?"

Ava swallowed—not from guilt, but from a memory she hadn't named aloud in years: Faye, weeping, whispering, "They will never remember us as we were. Only as what they made of us."

Mabelle's hands had begun to tremble—not dramatically, but as if her skin had remembered something her mind still refused to see.

And above them, unseen in the rafters, Meely's tail curled like a glyph slowly rewriting itself—just as the dome flickered again.

Her gaze, unblinking from the rafter beam, watched not with curiosity—but with knowing. She had seen this ritual before. Not here. Not in this world. But in another hall, under a different ceiling, where truth had failed to hold.

***

The air changed before she entered.

Not in temperature—but in density. The kind that thinned just before lightning, that sharpened silence into a blade. Somewhere behind the altar, an old vow cracked open. And Gwendlynn knew it. Felt it. Felt them.

She did not walk through the chapel doors.

The Chapel admitted her—stone and seam yielding to what she carried.

A shimmer—barely perceptible—unraveled in the far corner of the chamber as if breath had cut through a seam in air itself. Windless, scentless, but real. She stepped from it without sound, robes fluttering like pages caught in a story no longer willing to stay closed.

Ava turned first. Then Maurice. Mabelle... did not.

Gwendlynn's gaze burned cold.

"Is this an ambush?"

No one answered. Not at first. The convergence field glowed weakly around them—fractured, unstable. Glyphs shimmered on the stone, flickering as if caught between memory and revelation. The altar vibrated faintly, threads of resonance pulsing just out of time.

She stepped into the circle.

The light stabilized.

Maurice exhaled—not in relief, but in acceptance. The convergence dome sealed. Whole. The final piece had arrived.

But Gwendlynn was not at peace.

"You waited thirteen years," she said, voice sharp with restraint. "And now you meet without me?"

Her tone cracked like iron on stone. Ava opened her mouth, but Maurice spoke first—voice low, imploring.

"We weren't—"

"—plotting," Ava interrupted, gently. "We were remembering."

That word hit something deep behind Gwendlynn's ribs. A tremor, barely there. She masked it with stillness.

Ava's voice cut softly through the tension.

"You weren't forgotten, Gwendlynn. We were trying to find the right moment. But perhaps there isn't one—not for truths like these."

She looked at her—not as a subordinate, but as someone who knew what it was to carry silence too long.

Then Gwendlynn's eyes moved to Mabelle. "And you? You who have stood beside me in silence for a decade—you knew they were meeting without me?"

Mabelle stiffened. Her lips parted, but her voice failed her. Something flickered in her expression—not guilt, not defiance, but confusion. As if some part of her had known… but not consciously.

"I—I didn't know this would happen," she said.

Gwendlynn's brow arched. "But you brought what you had hidden. You walked into this chamber with relics you once called forgotten. You hummed a song even I had not heard since the Ordinatum."

The accusation didn't rise—it coiled.

Mabelle took a half-step back, eyes darting between Ava and Maurice. Her pendant pulsed faintly once—then dimmed again.

"If I've been part of something, Gwendlynn," she said slowly, "I swear to you—I didn't know."

Gwendlynn stared at her for a long moment. Not through her—into her.

"Then tell me," she said, voice low as ritual, "how long have you been asleep?"

Mabelle's mouth opened, but no words emerged. Just the softest downturn of her brows—not in guilt, but in the ache of being half-seen.

Gwendlynn stepped closer to the altar.

The relics pulsed—one by one.

Maurice's pendant: a faint violet glow, deep as dusk.

Ava's: blue-gold, water folding into starlight.

Mabelle's: green, but already dimming.

And then her own.

She unclasped the chain from beneath her collar and held it aloft. The pendant was no simple heirloom—a crown-shaped locket wrought in deep auric metal, aged to a soft bronze sheen. Delicate lines curled around its frame, forming five points—not of royalty, but remembrance. At its center pulsed a small crystal star, carved from citrine flecked with opal light, alive with memory. It shimmered not with power, but with something older: alignment. As if it had once sat beneath the same stars now hidden above them. As if it, too, remembered who she used to be.

Ava gasped. Not in fear—in understanding.

Gwendlynn let the locket fall back against her chest, slow and deliberate.

"I am not here as a sister," she said. "I am not here as steward. You brought me into a room of relics, of truth, and thought I would not answer in kind?"

She turned—slow, unflinching—to face them all.

Something loosened.

Not a glamour breaking, not a spell shattering—but a weight lifting, as if a pressure long borne by the air itself had been released. The quiet spell work that had dulled memory and softened scrutiny slipped away, its purpose fulfilled.

Ava's breath caught.

Mabelle's hand flew instinctively to her chest.

It was not that Gwendlynn's face had changed.

It was that it could no longer be mistaken. The Queen was no longer hidden.

Maurice bowed his head.

"Faye was not just a child I raised," Gwendlynn said. "She was my daughter. The last sovereign of Magicia to hold the Root by right—unbroken, ungrafted, uncontested. And I failed her."

The silence fractured.

Maurice dropped to one knee—not from guilt, but from a vow older than the Abbey.

"I knew," he said. "Long before the Ordinatum. I knew what she carried."

"And yet you let her die," Gwendlynn said, voice brittle. "You, who once bore the name Keralis—the Fifth Inquisitor. You held her life in your ink-stained hands and let it bleed through your fingers."

"And worse… you let me bury her legacy. Not in earth. In silence. You let me call her line extinct—while it slept beneath my roof."

Maurice closed his eyes. "And every word since has been penance."

A tremor passed through the ceiling. Not earthquake—memory.

Gwendlynn raised her hand.

She spoke a phrase that had not touched the air in over a generation:

"Memoratu Veranthis. Ligora Tempares."

The glyphs carved into the chapel's stone arches shimmered. Then flared.

Above them, the stars came alive—not the stars of this world, but constellations only the Fifth Kingdom would recognize. Spirals. Sigils. Names folded into patterns. A memory-map of a sky no longer visible.

The relics flared in response.

The scroll on the altar opened on its own.

Words emerged in glowing script, line by line—not ink, but resonance.

"Memory is not what we carry.
It is what we chose not to forget."

At last, the scroll ceased its flickering—as if recognizing its final reader. A hush fell over the circle. No one moved.

Then the ward loosened.

Hands lowered. Chains slipped back beneath collars. Pendants settled against skin—remembering where they belonged.

Then—Mabelle gasped.

Her pendant—small, green, hung on a twisted silver chain—flickered. Once. Twice. Then died.

No light. No heat. No pulse.

In the rafters, unseen, something shifted. Silent. Watching.

Ava turned toward her, slowly. "Mabelle…"

The convergence dome pulsed. The stars above dimmed, but not fully. Something had changed. Not broken. Shifted.

Maurice looked up from the floor.

"The dome recognizes four."

His voice was rough. Distant.

"But one of them," he whispered, "does not recognize herself."

Mabelle's breath hitched.

She looked at Gwendlynn—and something collapsed between them. Not a wall. A myth. The unspoken belief that their silences had been selfless.

"You want the truth?" she asked, voice tight. "Then listen. I came to this Abbey not to serve. Not to kneel. I came with a child. A nephew. Wrapped in ash and warning."

Her voice broke—but she did not stop.

"My brother left him at my door with a name, a trunk—and the tapestry," Mabelle said. "He didn't ask. He begged. Told me never to trust bloodlines. Never to ask what he had become. Only to keep the boy safe."

She hesitated, then added, more quietly, "And to protect the tapestry. He said I would know when the time was right. That it would make sense one day."

Ava stepped closer, gently. "You never told me that."

Mabelle shook her head. "Because I knew what the trunk was. I knew how to hide a boy. But the tapestry…" Her voice faltered. "I knew it mattered. I just didn't know how. I still don't. And I was never good at asking the right questions."

She looked at Gwendlynn now—directly.

"And I didn't know you were one of us. Not until tonight. You… who scolded me for every instinct. Who measured every silence I held. You were like me—but didn't trust me enough to say it."

Gwendlynn's expression didn't soften—but it changed. A crack, invisible to others, ran across her mask.

"You were Concordium," Mabelle whispered. "You were royalty. And I was just a girl who buried her past to raise someone else's future."

Her hands clenched at her sides.

"I have lived every year since wondering whether Mattheon would hate me—if he ever knew I kept things from him. But I did it to protect him. I chose to stay small so he could grow."

She turned toward Maurice. Then Ava.

"And if I am a danger—if I've been used, or planted, or altered—then you tell me. You tell me now. But don't stand there and question my heart."

A pause. Sharp. Ache-shaped.

She looked again at Gwendlynn—quieter now.

"I didn't choose this role. But I chose him. I chose to stay."

Then, softer:

"And if you knew Faye… if you loved her… then maybe you'll understand this: I would burn everything I am to keep him safe. Even if I don't know what I am."

Gwendlynn's breath caught—not audibly, but in the space behind her ribs.

She stepped forward, voice low, reverent.

"You speak of love as fire," she said. "Then let me remind you what it means to burn."

A hush swept the relics as if the chamber itself leaned in.

"I was the last Queen of the five kingdoms," she said. "But before that… I was a mother. And I stood beside the man who unmade both titles."

She closed her eyes.

"Siroth."

The name cracked through the convergence field like thunder behind glass.

Maurice flinched. Ava's pendant pulsed.

"I watched him rise through courts and corridors, binding law to fear, rewriting prophecy into obedience. And I stayed silent—too long. I let him believe he was correcting the world. I placed her between him and the throne, thinking her heart might hold him back. It didn't."

Her eyes opened, sharp with old grief. "But he never wanted temperance. Only legacy."

She turned toward Mabelle now. "You say your brother vanished. You say he carried warning in his voice. But do you know how many warnings Siroth has buried beneath civility? How many voices were softened into silence before they could become testimony? His legacy is not marked in titles, but in absences."

"Siroth leaves behind more than fear and fire. I have seen his legacy cloaked in shadows: lovers dismissed, records purged, voices made to disappear. Not by sword. By omission. And when bloodlines grew inconvenient, they didn't vanish. They were folded out of history."

Mabelle staggered back a step, blinking. "What are you saying?"

"I am saying…" Gwendlynn said carefully, "…that your brother's disappearance may not have been abandonment. It may have been extraction."

The words fell like stones.

"No," Mabelle whispered. "He would have told me."

Gwendlynn softened—not in mercy, but in pain. "Perhaps he tried."

And then—to all of them her voice dropped into something near reverence:

"If one of these boys… carries the legacy of more than one kingdom—"

Ava's head turned sharply. "You mean Leonarth."

Gwendlynn's eyes flicked to her—but didn't hold. "I mean we do not know yet."

Mabelle stepped forward, her voice taut. "No. Wait—You think Mattheon…"

"I think," Gwendlynn cut in, "that too many truths were sealed in too few hands. And we are only now beginning to feel what slipped through."

Maurice stirred. But did not rise.

Gwendlynn looked down at him—not as Queen to Inquisitor, but as mother to man. And for a moment, her voice lost its edge, but not its weight.

"You were Keralis once. Fifth Inquisitor. Keeper of rites. But now you wear Maurice like a mask—priest, mentor, comforter—as if one name can atone for the other."

Her eyes narrowed—not in anger, but clarity.

"You sealed the truth when it suited you. Now you will help unseal it—not for us, but for them. For the ones still blind beneath the silence you helped shape."

Ava stepped forward, voice steady but low.

"We all failed her, Gwendlynn. Not in the same way. But we all survived at the cost of something we were meant to remember."

She glanced at each of them—Maurice, Mabelle, even the glowing scroll.

"Now we have a choice. Keep surviving. Or start remembering together."

Maurice looked up—eyes wet, not with grief, but with memory. His hand drifted toward his chest—not in pain, but as an old vow stirred.

He nodded once.

And the dome brightened.

Chapter Seventeen

"...then Let Silence End"

He did not answer them with words. Not at first. Gwendlynn's voice still echoed inside his chest—"You wear Maurice like a mask." And Ava's—softer, but no less damning: "Keep surviving. Or start remembering." Maurice had worn both names: Keralis, the inquisitor who sealed silence into scrolls... and Maurice, the priest who taught children to read without knowing what they were meant to remember.

He stood slowly, as if rising meant choosing—not between names, but between who he had been, and what he was now willing to become.

"You think I forgot?" he said quietly. "No. I remembered too well. And I believed remembering would destroy us before it saved us."

He looked to the scroll—still warm, still aware—and only then did he speak the words that had haunted him longest:

"They were never meant to remember. Not until the silence broke."

He hesitated. Not because he doubted the truth—but because once spoken, it could not be folded back into silence.

"You want to know why I waited. Why I sealed what should have been shared."

He turned from the scroll to the others—not as priest, not as Keralis, but as something more fragile than either: a man who had outlived too many of his own decisions.

"Because I knew that once I spoke it, you would see me not as Maurice—but as the Fifth Inquisitor. The one who stood beside Faye and said nothing as the laws that would end her were written. The one who helped carve those glyphs—not in agreement, but in fear."

His voice cracked slightly.

"We all thought we were protecting something sacred. Order. Balance. But all I did was protect my own survival. I told myself that warning her would have been treason. That silence was a shield. But that lie became a cage—for all of us."

He looked at Gwendlynn now.

"You weren't the only one who mourned a child you thought had died. I mourned a future I helped kill. And when I learned the boy had survived..."

He trailed off. Took a breath.

"I buried Keralis beneath vestments and ink. Told myself Maurice could make it right, in small ways. A lesson here. A kindness there. But the truth is—Maurice was just another mask. A quieter one. A softer one. But still... a mask."

He looked at Mabelle, then Gwendlynn. His voice dropped.

"But memory doesn't fade. It waits. And now it has come for us—not as prophecy, but as consequence."

"When I came to this Abbey, I told myself it was exile. A penance. A cloister where silence could spare the world from whatever damage I had not already done. But even that was self-deception."

"The Abbey was no refuge. It was chosen—carefully, with Gwendlynn's quiet assent—because the stones beneath it still remembered the Accord. Because something in this place still hummed with memory. I didn't come to escape my past. I came to guard what little was left of it."

He paused, as if weighing whether the next truth deserved breath.

"I could not do that as myself. The name I once carried still had weight—too much of it. Even here, even beyond their reach, it would have drawn the wrong kind of attention. Inquisitors do not vanish as easily as queens. We linger. In records half-burned. In patterns others are taught not to notice."

"So Gwendlynn did for me what she had already done for herself. Not erasure—containment. My resonance folded inward, pressed beneath a quieter skin. A priest was safer than a witness. A confessor safer than a judge. Silence became not just protection, but disguise."

"But then Ava arrived. And the boy. And the silence I had built like a fortress—it cracked."

"You all think we came here by choice. But none of this was ours to plan. Not really." He looked at Ava. "You were sent—wearing a pendant none of us fully understood, not knowing it would be the thing that awakened the convergence field."

"Even this place..." He looked down. "We didn't choose it. We... followed what remained. The glyphs. The sigils buried under moss and mortar. The way the air changed near the wardstone."

He turned to Gwendlynn. "You remember. We didn't know what we were looking for. Only that something was pulling us here."

He exhaled. Slow.

"And the thing we'd buried began to move again."

His hand drifted toward the scroll.

"I used to wonder if it was coincidence. If we had all simply collapsed here—broken people drawn to a quiet grave. But now..."

He swallowed.

"Now I think... maybe she knew. Not the shape of it. But the rhythm. That one day silence would not be enough."

His voice lowered, reverent and unsure:

"I think Faye set something in motion. Not prophecy. Not fate. But memory. Memory seeded across people, relics, rooms."

He looked around at the circle of them. "And maybe that was enough."

"None of us were architects. We were pieces. Some chosen. Some... resigned."

He looked down at his hands. "My resignation was different."

"I wasn't cast out when I fled. I was cast out when the Insidium was done. Siroth believed the ritual had succeeded, and in his eyes, that made me obsolete. I wasn't in the chamber when the blade fell—I had already broken ranks. But the truth is... I helped build the laws and glyphwork that made the ritual possible. That is the part I cannot outrun."

Ava frowned, her voice sharp. "The Insidium? I've never heard of it. That isn't in any Concordium law I was allowed to see. It's not even in the Archives."

"You wouldn't have heard of it," Gwendlynn said quietly. "You were never meant to."

Mabelle's eyes narrowed. "You both speak of it like it's more than a spell. What was it, really?"

Maurice exhaled, slow and bitter. "A heresy older than the Accord, buried even from most of the Concordium—passed only through the highest hands, and never spoken outside the Circle."

"A coronation rite," Gwendlynn added. "Not for celebration. For contingency."

Ava's voice lowered. "Contingency for what?"

“For failure,” Maurice said. “If the Root ever threatened to vanish. If the bloodline that held it was dying, broken, or compromised. The Insidium was their answer—an attempt to transfer the Root to a new vessel. To forcibly preserve the magic, even if it meant erasing its origin.”

“But the Root isn’t just power,” Gwendlynn said. “It’s legacy. Memory shaped into resonance. It doesn’t obey logic. It bonds through blood… and belief. It cannot be stolen.”

Mabelle’s expression was dark. “So they tried to cut it from Faye.”

Maurice nodded. “They didn’t just try. They prepared for years. The blade was forged in secret—braided with the five glyph strands. They summoned her. Lied to her. And then, at the edge of a ritual altar, they ended her life and called the Root into the blade.”

He looked down. “But it didn’t come.”

“Because it had already passed,” Gwendlynn said, eyes on Ava. “Into a child not yet named.”

Silence fell like ash. The truth hovered—not loud, but irreversible.

Mabelle spoke next, her voice trembling. “So Leonarth…”

“Is the heir,” Gwendlynn said. “The last rightful vessel of the Root. Hidden before the Insidium.

She hesitated—not in doubt, but in something sharper. “And before the lie of the Nullum.”

Ava blinked. “The Nullum?”

Maurice’s voice hardened. “Not a transfer. An erasure. The Nullum can only be invoked if the sovereign has truly abdicated—rejected the Root, shattered the binding that ties it to their blood. Anything less, and the ritual turns inward.”

Mabelle frowned. “Turns how?”

“It rejects the claimant,” Maurice said. “Breaks the mind. Unthreads the self. The Root does not tolerate false succession.”

“And that,” Gwendlynn said quietly, “is why Siroth never dared perform it.”

Silence stretched.

“He told the Council she had fled,” Gwendlynn continued. “That Faye had abandoned her claim. That the line was void. The Nullum was the story—clean, lawful, irreversible.”

“But he knew it wasn’t true,” Maurice said. “He knew she would never abdicate.”

Ava's breath caught.

"So he used the Insidium instead," Mabelle said.

Maurice nodded. "Because theft was safer than truth."

"And the Nullum," Gwendlynn said, "remained a threat. A doctrine. A blade held over history—but never meant to fall."

Mabelle folded her arms, defensive. "Then why not tell them the truth? Why let that lie stand?"

"Because the Root is fragile," Gwendlynn answered. "And belief is part of what binds it. If the world believed a sovereign could be killed and their power claimed by force, they would try it—again and again. We wouldn't have kingdoms," she said. "Just blood."

"It was passed in silence for a reason," Maurice said. "Only the sovereign and the Circle were ever meant to carry the burden of knowing how fragile the lattice truly was."

Ava stepped back, her gaze moving from the scroll to the tapestry, to the light gathering beneath the dome. "And now that silence is broken."

"Because it must be," Gwendlynn said. "The boy is awakening. The seals are breaking. And if we do not speak the truth now—others will write it for us."

Mabelle's voice cracked. "And if Leonarth learns what he carries? What this all means?"

Maurice met her gaze. "Then he will grieve. He will doubt. He will run. But he will not be alone."

He let his hand rest on the altar. His own past pressed closer then—a memory he had spent years refusing to speak aloud.

"It wasn't only what they did to her," he said quietly. "It was what I left behind for them to use."

Ava's breath hitched. Gwendlynn's eyes sharpened.

"I had already broken ranks when the Insidium was prepared. I was long gone. But the laws… the glyphwork… the legal framework—the doctrines that made it possible? Those were mine."

He exhaled, bitter.

"They were mine—authored in another life, before I understood what Siroth truly meant to do."

He looked toward the far wall, as though seeing the shadow of a chamber he'd hoped would never resurface.

"He didn't need me there. My work stayed behind, even when I didn't."

His voice tightened.

"For a time, he let that stand," Maurice continued, softer. "But Siroth does not allow loose ends, and he sent his agents after me—to make sure no one could ever undo what he thought he'd secured."

He drew in a breath, steadier now.

"He didn't realize she had already passed the Root on. Because a ritual that fails doesn't always end. Sometimes it waits."

"But Faye knew. Somehow, she knew I would survive. That I would carry guilt like a torch until it burned through my cowardice. And so she sent Ava to light the rest of the way."

His eyes passed over the scroll. "This place did not forgive me. It tolerated me. Because it remembered what I tried to forget."

He looked now at Gwendlynn, his voice low. "You were there when I arrived. You said nothing then. But we both knew something was waiting here. Not just relics. Not just prophecy. A reckoning."

He paused. His breath caught in his throat—not from uncertainty, but from dread. The word pressed at the edges of his mouth like something alive.

Gwendlynn watched him with unblinking eyes. "You've been circling it," she said quietly. "Say it, Maurice. Before it says itself."

Maurice closed his eyes. When he opened them, he was not Maurice. Not fully.

"You want to believe there was a name for what we feared," he said, voice nearly gone. "There was. But speaking it now…"

He looked at the scroll—no longer glowing, but pulsing—like it knew what was coming.

"Speaking it now means we admit it worked. That the ritual took root. That we didn't just silence enemies—we rewrote them."

His throat constricted.

"We didn't erase memories. We made them sleep. And the ones who woke? They never knew what they had lost."

His shoulders fell. The word tasted like ash.

"We called them Calventherath."

The name dropped like iron.

"The Insidium was never just political," he added quietly. "It was memory warfare. Control the past, and you command the future. The Calventherath were the shadow crown—made not to rule, but to ensure no one else could."

"They weren't designed to know themselves," he said. "They weren't raised. They were... written."

"You don't understand," he said. "They weren't assassins. Not soldiers. They were compliance. They walked into cities that resisted the Insidium and erased their leaders from memory. Not by blade—by presence."

"They were placed into lives—teachers, priests, caretakers. Sometimes they did nothing for years. Just existed. Made people forget what had once burned."

His voice grew thin. "When a rebellion formed, the Calventherath were already there—smiling, praying, planting flowers. And by the time someone asked where their neighbor had gone, they no longer remembered they had one."

"They didn't kill the past. They made it... optional."

He looked up—at Mabelle, whose pendant lay dark against her chest, and at Gwendlynn, whose presence still commanded the very shape of the room.

"They live false lives with true memories buried beneath. Bound by a rite from the days before the Ordinatum—Obligare Somnum Memoriae. The Binding of the Sleep of Memory."

The words made Ava flinch. Gwendlynn's expression tightened. Mabelle looked hollow—as if trying not to retreat into herself.

Maurice's hand finally settled on the scroll.

"They don't remember who they were," he said. "Only what they're for."

Silence pressed in. No one moved.

It was Ava who stirred—not with certainty, but with something colder. A quiet alarm she didn't yet understand.

"Wait…" she said, almost to herself. "I've seen that name."

The others turned.

"In the document I found," she continued, voice tightening. "In Mabelle's trunk. The one that was half-burned. I only restored it because it still remembered what had once been written."

She looked to Mabelle—gently. "You never hid it. I know. The parchment was already ruined when you packed it away. And your magic…"

Mabelle nodded, a flicker of shame in her eyes. "It's weaker than it was. I… haven't trusted it in years."

"Then it wasn't your fault," Ava said. "But there was a name. Faded. In the margins. Calventherath assigned. Dormant."

Gwendlynn stepped forward. "And the location?"

Ava hesitated. "Saint-Spire Abbey."

The convergence dome pulsed—faintly.

Maurice's knuckles whitened on the altar. "I thought we had come after them. That the Calventherath were relics of a broken regime. But if that list was real…"

Ava shook her head. "I don't know who they are. I don't even know what I saw until now. But if they were ever here…"

Her eyes drifted to Mabelle—not in suspicion, but in fear.

"If one of us…"

Mabelle's voice cut through.

"Then let it be me."

She stepped back from the circle.

"If I was placed here," Mabelle said, her voice trembling, "if I've been… written, like he said—then I don't want to be protected. I want to be stopped."

She looked at Ava, then Gwendlynn.

"I kept that trunk and the tapestry for years. I told myself it was grief. That I wasn't ready to face what he left behind."

She swallowed.

"When my brother gave them to me, he didn't explain anything. He only said not to trust bloodlines. That the cloth would show its purpose when the time was right. That I'd know."

Her voice dropped.

"I told myself I wasn't ready to understand any of it. But now I'm wondering if it wasn't my choice at all."

She shook her head slightly.

"Maybe I wasn't allowed to. And maybe… maybe I never will be."

Her hand brushed the dark pendant against her chest. "If that spell ever touched me—if I am Calventherath—then the fault isn't yours." Her voice broke. "It's mine. I let myself forget who I was."

She met Maurice's eyes last. "And if that makes me dangerous, then let me fall before I fail them. Before I fail him."

A pause.

"I would rather die as myself than live as something he'd be ashamed of."

Gwendlynn stepped forward. Her eyes did not soften—but they steadied.

"No one here will let you fall," Gwendlynn said. "Not out of mercy. Out of purpose."

She looked toward the altar—toward the relics, the scroll, the dome of memory.

"Because if you are what they made, then you are proof that the spell can still be broken. And if you're not... then you deserve a way to be certain."

Mabelle looked up, her lips parting. But Gwendlynn did not wait.

"There is one rite," she said. "Not taught. Not spoken. Not used since the Accord was fractured."

Maurice's eyes snapped toward her. "You can't mean—"

"I do," she said. Calm. Certain. "The Rite of Anchoring."

"It was never meant for protection," Gwendlynn continued. "It was meant for restraint. For loyalty among those who feared themselves."

"Fifth Kingdom protocol," Gwendlynn said. "A tether of truth. It doesn't bind action—it binds intention. If any of us moves to harm another, or to conceal something that would endanger the whole..."

She looked at Mabelle directly.

"...the bond will reveal it. It won't stop an awakening—but it will delay it. Distort it. Long enough for us to know who we're facing."

"I am not doing it to punish you—but to protect what you still are."

Mabelle stared at her. "You want to bind me?"

"Not just you." Her voice grew low. Ritualistic. "All of us. If the spell is still inside you, it won't know how to act. It will sense too many truths. Too many anchors. That confusion may buy us time."

Maurice's jaw clenched. "It won't just reveal betrayal, Gwendlynn. You know that. The rite exposes all intention—even the truths we hide from ourselves. Every unfinished vow. Every fractured loyalty. Once invoked, it doesn't stop until it has carved memory down to the bone."

"Then let it," Gwendlynn said. "We cannot protect the boys by walking in silence any longer."

Ava stepped forward. "If there's even a chance this helps... I'm in."

Mabelle nodded. "And if it fails?"

"Then we'll face whatever wakes," Gwendlynn said. "But it will not wake alone."

No one moved for a breath. The dome dimmed—not fading, but waiting.

In the rafters above, something stirred.

Meely's eyes glinted—unblinking, ancient. She had watched everything, as still as shadow, as quiet as ash.

Forgotten by them, but not absent.

And she did not blink when the rite began.

Gwendlynn stepped to the center of the circle and knelt.

Maurice stepped beside her—slowly, as if the memory hurt to carry.

"They'll need guidance," he said under his breath. "It's not like the old rites."

Gwendlynn nodded once. Her voice shifted—not her tone, but her rhythm. As if she were reciting something she had not spoken since the last days of the Concordium—before law hardened into silence.

"One by one," she murmured. "Not in order of rank, but of burden. Each offers what binds them to truth. Not power. Not knowledge. But memory."

Ava's brow furrowed. "And if we have nothing to offer?"

Maurice answered this time. "Then the bond will know. And it will refuse you."

A pulse stirred in the stone.

"Begin," Gwendlynn said. "While we are still ourselves."

"By the old vows," Maurice said. "By constellations that no longer shine, and glyphs that no longer speak—I call memory into witness."

The scroll pulsed. Faint gold veins flickered through the altar.

He removed the ring he had always worn on his left hand—the Concordium seal long rubbed smooth. He set it on the stone.

"Let silence speak," he said. "Let truth tether what fear could not."

Ava approached next. She unsheathed the pendant from beneath her robes—the pendant she'd worn since childhood, never knowing who placed it in her hands—and laid it beside the others.

"I offer no knowledge," she said softly. "Only what I carry. Only what still remembers her."

Mabelle's hands shook as she stepped forward. For a long time, she said nothing. Then:

"I offer what I do not know," she whispered. "And ask it not to be used against me—until it chooses to awaken."

Gwendlynn placed her palm on the scroll.

"Then let it be written," she said. "I offer my name to what follows."

"Verum Vinculum Novem," she intoned.

A faint mark shimmered on each of their palms—not carved, not burned. Just present. As if truth had chosen them before they agreed.

And light burst outward—not bright, but exact. Runes older than the Abbey's foundation surfaced on the stone floor. The convergence dome pulsed violet, then green, then gold.

A single chord rang out—not heard, but felt.

Their relics began to hum in synchrony. The tether formed.

And deep beneath the altar, something sealed long ago... shifted.

A stillness lingered after the rite—not peace, but a kind of hush that felt too complete. As if the room itself was listening now.

The light of the Anchoring Rite faded slowly, leaving the chamber in a hush that felt deeper than silence.

Maurice exhaled—a quiet, shaken breath—as if some barrier inside him had finally loosened.

Gwendlynn watched him. "There is more," she murmured.

Maurice didn't deny it. He touched the altar with the tips of his fingers, almost absently. "I've held this back for years. Too long."

He swallowed. "And I didn't speak of it before the Rite because… I wasn't sure who might be listening."

A flicker crossed Mabelle's expression—tiny, almost imperceptible—but her hand drifted slightly toward her pendant, as if feeling its temperature.

Maurice drew a slow breath. "I grew up hearing tales of an artifact that remembered the world. A myth—the kind of story novices laugh at. One said to record truth on its own, no matter who tried to bury it."

Ava frowned. "A storybook."

"So I thought," Maurice said. "Until Faye."

Even Gwendlynn stiffened.

"When the Ordinatum began," he continued softly, "Faye told me she'd found something—a fragment of that old legend. I dismissed it. I told myself she was grasping at ghosts. But the way she spoke of it…"

He shook his head. "She believed it could explain why history was fraying. Why laws were bending to rumors. Why the world felt like it was remembering and forgetting at the same time."

The candles flickered, though no draft passed.

"She said the fragment carried echoes—maps, patterns, stories the world had tried to erase. She thought it held warnings. And she wanted my help to protect it. But..." His voice thinned. "I didn't listen. I told her it was just a relic from frightened scholars a thousand years ago."

Beside them, Mabelle's breath hitched—a small, involuntary sound. Her pendant cooled suddenly against her skin, a strange reversal that made her blink hard, as if clearing a pressure behind her eyes.

Maurice didn't notice.

"Tonight... when the scroll woke, when the tapestry shifted... I recognized the behavior. I've only seen something like this once before—in the description Faye gave me."

He looked up, his expression hollowing with realization.

"Afterward, I found it mentioned in older, forbidden texts. Not as a story, but as a thing that listened. They called it the Testimonium Aeternae."

He swallowed.

"This is what its fragments were said to do when truth resurfaced."

Ava inhaled sharply—myth colliding with reality.

"The Accord buried every mention of it," Maurice went on. "Not because it was dangerous—but because it remembered too clearly. It carried history no one could rewrite. And if even one fragment survived..."

He let the implication hang.

Gwendlynn's voice lowered. "Then truth has begun to wake."

Something trembled in the stone beneath them—softer than a heartbeat, but real.

Mabelle's fingers curled, and for a brief moment her vision shimmered at the edges, like a memory she didn't know she had was trying to surface. It vanished as quickly as it came, leaving her breath unsteady.

Maurice pressed a hand to his chest. "The Rite protects us. At least for now. But if the Testimonium's echoes are stirring... the Accord will feel it. And whatever Faye found—whatever I refused to believe—is tied to what's happening to the boy."

He fell silent.

The chamber held its breath.

And then—Ava exhaled slowly, as though Maurice's confession had loosened something she'd kept tucked behind her ribs.

Her voice was hushed but steady.

"Before we move on… there's something else. I thought it was irrelevant before, but now… it may be connected."

She turned to Mabelle, who gave a slow nod. No one spoke as they approached the trunk she had carried in—still draped in the same linen she had wrapped it in when her brother vanished and left it in her care.

Ava unlatched the trunk. The hinges didn't creak. The air around it pulsed once—barely perceptible. A ripple that felt like breath.

She reached in carefully and pulled free a small, round object, no larger than a plum pit. It glinted under the convergence dome's shifting light—black-violet at first, then deep green, then something between bone and shadow.

Its surface was carved—not etched, but grown—with a spiral glyph resembling a root curling back into itself.

"I found this before," Ava said. "I didn't think it mattered. It didn't react to anything. It felt… still. But not dead."

Gwendlynn stepped closer—and froze.

She did not reach for it. She didn't need to.

"That glyph…" Gwendlynn breathed. "It can't be."

A silence deeper than magic spread through the room.

"Orreth," Gwendlynn murmured, the name leaving her mouth before she could stop it.

Maurice inhaled slowly.

"Are you certain?"

Gwendlynn did not look at him.

"I would not speak that name if I weren't."

"This is no pendant," she said. "It's a Root—a blood tether. One forged only for the firstborn of a house bound by legacy… and burden."

Her voice faltered—then steadied.

"And it is not just a name."

She lifted her gaze at last.

"It's his name."

Ava stared at the stone. "I've never heard of it."

"You wouldn't have," Gwendlynn said. "Most lines abandoned the practice centuries ago. But not all." Her voice lowered.

Maurice's voice was trembling not in fear, but in hesitation. "Siroth Orreth. That was his name, before the Insidium. Before the titles replaced bloodlines."

Ava looked down at the Root, suddenly uneasy.

Gwendlynn continued: "The Root of Orreth was thought destroyed. Like the line itself."

Mabelle's face drained of color. "It was in my brother's things. I didn't know—"

"You weren't meant to," Gwendlynn said, quiet but firm. "This was not made for you. This was meant for his firstborn."

Mabelle's lips parted. "He told me to protect the boy. He said not to trust bloodlines. But he never told me... this."

Her eyes didn't leave the Root. "If this was meant for a firstborn, then why was it hidden? Why burn the rest, and leave only this behind?"

She hesitated, then added—carefully, as if testing the thought aloud.

"And what if being the first was the very reason he hid it?"

No one answered. But something shifted in the air again—as if memory itself were listening.

She turned to Maurice. "And yet it ended up here."

Maurice said nothing.

Gwendlynn exhaled—slow, deliberate. "Not all relics find their heirs cleanly," she said. "Sometimes they're taken. Smuggled. Lost in fire, or war, or love."

Her eyes narrowed slightly, not at Mabelle—but at something deeper.

"There are those who believed the Orreth line should be buried in silence," Gwendlynn said. "But some blood remembers what it was denied."

She turned toward the Root of Orreth.

"Whether it was gifted or stolen," she continued, "it found its way back."

Maurice said nothing.

The Root pulsed once—faint, contained. Not a flare. A signal.

The scroll answered.

Not with light, but with tension—the kind that sharpens the air. Its surface rippled as if disturbed from within, glyphs rising slowly, like sediment drawn upward by an unseen current.

No one touched it. No spell was spoken.

Lines formed above the scroll—not inscribed, but suspended—looping and branching in patterns too deliberate to be random. A map, unfolding without urgency. Paths without destinations.

Ava drew a quiet breath.

"That's not how it behaved before," she said. "It only showed me words."

Maurice nodded. "Because it was only a letter then."

Gwendlynn's gaze never left the air above the scroll.

"It was always more than that," she said. "We simply hadn't gathered what it was waiting for."

The scroll shuddered again—this time in rhythm with the Root of Orreth.

"It's responding," Ava whispered.

"No," Maurice said quietly. "It's remembering."

Mabelle stepped closer—not to the scroll, but to the space between it and the Root. She did not reach out. She only looked.

"My brother said bloodlines lie," she said after a moment. "But how could that be? Bloodlines are set at birth. They don't change."

Maurice studied the space she was watching.

"Unless we're asking the wrong question," he said quietly.

He didn't look at her when he continued.

"Some roots don't grow forward. They dig."

A pause.

"They dig until they reach what made them."

The lines above the scroll pulsed once—not brighter, not faster. Simply in acknowledgment.

Maurice's gaze shifted to the Root of Orreth.

"Then maybe we don't learn the truth by chasing names."

No one contradicted him.

But nothing settled.

Gwendlynn felt it at once—the tension holding, unspent.

"It isn't enough," she said. "The resonance hasn't closed. Faye's line and Orreth's are touching—but what carries them hasn't bound."

Her eyes moved to the linen-wrapped bundle.

"This is why he told you to wait," she added, not looking at Mabelle.

"The tapestry," she said. "Unfold it."

The room seemed to lean inward—as if something long patient had finally been answered.

The air thickened.

Gwendlynn reached for the bundle without speaking. Her hands did not tremble, but there was something ceremonial in the way she peeled back the cloth—as if what lay inside was not just woven fabric, but a reckoning.

The tapestry unrolled in heavy silence.

It unfurled across the altar like a memory being exhaled. Threads of silverroot, fifth-blood silk, and storm-dyed cotton shimmered faintly under the dome's breathless light.

The design was circular—not like a wheel, but like a convergence spell caught mid-awakening. Scenes shimmered across the fabric: a city floating above broken towers; trees with silver veins and luminous leaves; an Abbey cradled beneath a starfield of daylight. At the center pulsed a woven key—not illustrated, but stitched from memory itself. And around it, three arcs bent inward... but only two held form.

Gwendlynn frowned.

She drew her hand across the center glyph and whispered:

"Memorastra Imbrix Tertius."
Memory align. Let the third arise.

A spark leapt from her fingertips—not fire, but memory made visible—and the tapestry shimmered. Lines rearranged themselves like something waking from sleep.

Then it stopped.

A vacant shape flickered at the tapestry's heart—not absent, but undefined. A glyph-ring had formed, but it held no anchor. No resonance.

Gwendlynn gasped—softly, but not from fear.

"It's missing something," she said.

Maurice stepped forward. His eyes scanned the incomplete glyph, the trembling patterns in the threads.

"The tapestry is awakening. The bloodline is stirring. But the anchor it needs—the relic that completes the bond—is still hidden."

Gwendlynn stared at the vacant glyph. "It's shaped. But not filled."

Maurice nodded. "The object exists. But its resonance hasn't awakened. It hasn't been… accepted."

Ava leaned closer. "Or it's been found—but not claimed."

Gwendlynn's gaze lingered on the empty glyph.

"It's not just a relic," she said. "It's a tether. Symbolic. Elemental. It's what binds the arc together—not by power, but by recognition."

Maurice looked up from the weave. "Then the final convergence cannot be forced. It must be chosen."

Silence hovered—heavy, expectant.

Ava was the first to speak. Her voice was steady, but her eyes shimmered with urgency.

"We must bring them in. The boys."

Maurice stiffened. "It's too soon. Once they know, we cannot unmake it."

"And if we wait?" Gwendlynn asked.

No answer came.

Mabelle's voice followed—raw, quiet.

"Then we fail again."

Something in the air pulled tighter, like thread drawing taut before a snap.

Maurice's jaw worked—torn between preservation and inevitability.

"You don't know what will be set in motion."

"And you don't know what's already begun," Ava replied.

Maurice crossed his arms—not as a shield, but a boundary. "If we involve them now, we risk collapsing everything we've tried to contain. The prophecy moves in riddles. Let's not hand it a name."

Mabelle shook her head. "And if we wait too long? What if Mattheon looks at me and sees only a lie? I swore I'd protect him—not manipulate him."

Ava's eyes glinted with something harder than hope. "This isn't about what we fear. It's about what she asked of us. Faye believed in their convergence. She died for it."

"And if she was wrong?" Maurice said.

Ava didn't blink. "Then we'll carry her mistake—the way you carry yours."

The room went still.

Gwendlynn's voice broke the silence—not louder, just older. "We do not have the luxury of agreeing. We only have the burden of choosing."

She turned to the tapestry, still glowing faintly—the glyph still empty, still waiting.

"We bring them in. But not everything is revealed. One truth," Gwendlynn said. "Enough to wake what needs waking. But not enough to summon what sleeps."

Maurice's mouth opened—then closed.

Mabelle's hand found her pendant. She didn't nod. But she didn't speak against it.

Only Ava said it aloud: "Agreed."

A hush followed—long and reverent. As if the Abbey itself had overheard.

Then the convergence dome began to dim—not all at once, but in slow gradients. Color fading. Lines dissolving. Memory slipping back into stone.

They began to separate without ceremony.

What had drawn them together did not follow.

Above, near the vaulted ceiling, Meely shifted—just enough.

Not a leap. Not a sound meant for ears.

The last trace of convergence thinned from the air.

Not fading. Settling.

A claw brushed old wood.

The tapestry stirred—pulsed once, faint and unmistakable.

Mabelle's pendant flickered against her chest… and went cold.

Maurice stopped short.

For a moment, his face revealed nothing at all.

Gwendlynn did not turn toward him. Her gaze remained on the altar, as if listening for something that had already passed. When she spoke, her voice held—not ritual now, but resolve.

"The tether is sealed," she said. "We are bound. From this moment forward, no truth we touch will remain idle."

She let that stand.

"Until the Calventherath is named, we assume nothing. No working is done in isolation. No child is left unwatched. If something stirs—glyph, echo, absence—it comes to us."

Her eyes settled on Mabelle.

"The tapestry returns to the school," she said. "To the attic. Folded as it was."

Mabelle hesitated. "They've already touched it."

"Yes," Gwendlynn replied. "Which means it must be there when it calls them back."

The final light of the dome withdrew, leaving the chapel unchanged—and entirely altered.

They turned away one by one.

Not as they had entered.

What had begun as coincidence had closed as covenant.

Maurice spoke once into the quiet.

"Let them believe they are safe one more night," he said. "Even if none of us are."

No answer came.

But elsewhere—far beyond the Abbey's stone and order—something long restrained had shifted.

Names thought buried began to move.

Not gently.

And the world, having been reminded, did not forget.

PART II

Scroll of Reckoning

"And in the age when silence began to crack,
names once buried stirred beneath stone and breath.
The traitor wore no crown, mistook control for peace—
and order for salvation.
The weapon bore no blade.

And memory—once quiet—remembered not gently, but with fire.
For those who remembered became dangerous.
And those who forgot… became weapons."

—Magicariums Scriptae, Verse XXVI

Chapter Eighteen

"When the Map Breathes"

The night had the kind of stillness that didn't just quiet the world—it hushed it. Not out of peace, but expectation. As though something had paused just long enough to see if he would come. Leonarth moved barefoot across the hallway tiles, the stone cold enough to bite. He didn't light a lamp. The Abbey slept behind closed doors, its breath slow and even. Only the moonlight, slanting like a blade through the stained-glass windows, gave him shape.

The wall beneath the bell tower had always been just that—a wall. Until it wasn't. Years ago, Mattheon had shown him the loose gutter. Not a way in. A way out.

He slipped through it now with instinct more than sight. Fingers found the places that no longer held weight evenly, limbs silent from repetition, as he lowered himself soundlessly into the dark of the grounds beyond.

The Abbey fell behind him.

He crossed the paths he and Mattheon had taken a dozen times before, keeping to shadow, the frost-cold air stinging his feet. The schoolhouse rose ahead—separate, squat, and quiet behind its gates.

The tree by the outer wall stirred as he reached it, branches just wide enough to hide the crude staircase lashed to its trunk.

He climbed.

The roof met his hands. From there, the narrow attic window waited—unchanged.

He pulled himself through.

The attic greeted him with a breath of dust and cold air. Not the biting cold of winter, but something older—the kind of chill that came from rooms the world had forgotten to warm.

He didn't know why he had come.

That wasn't quite true.

It wasn't curiosity. It wasn't fear. It was something older. A pull behind the ribs—the ache that sometimes lived in the silences between dreams. Like a question he didn't know he'd asked, finally drawing breath.

The key was in his hand.

He had kept it ever since the day Meely dropped it at his feet like a treasure she'd stolen from the past. It didn't look like it belonged to anything in the school—not a drawer, not a box. But it felt like it belonged to something. That sense had grown stronger lately. Especially when he slept.

Leonarth had dreamed of the tapestry again. Not the whole thing—not clearly. Just fragments: threads glowing like veins, and that feeling in his chest like something unfolding. Something familiar. Something waiting.

He rose to his feet.

The attic stretched out above the school like a forgotten lung, filled with broken desks, half-labeled crates, and a slanted shaft of moonlight.

Near the center, the floor changed.

Newer boards cut across the old grain at an awkward angle, braced too carefully to belong. The wood still carried a faint scent of sap beneath the dust. Beside it, a crate had been shifted back into place—its contents squared, masks nested face-down instead of scattered, as he remembered them.

Leonarth slowed without thinking, stepping wide of the place where the world had once given way.

Toward the back, beneath a dust-smeared window shaped like an eye, lay the tapestry.

He had expected it to be tucked away. Folded. Dead.

But it wasn't.

It was already unfurled. Its corners lay flat against the warped floorboards, too evenly to be chance, unmoved by wind. The threads shimmered faintly—not bright, not pulsing, but awake. Like the glow of a star long after it has burned out.

Leonarth stepped closer, the key tight in his palm. He didn't speak. He wasn't even sure what words would matter. All he knew was that being near it made his thoughts slow. Heavy. Like he was walking through a place memory hadn't caught up to yet.

He knelt.

The tapestry wasn't woven like anything he'd seen before. It didn't depict a scene or symbol. It shifted. Almost like it breathed beneath its own weight. His fingers hovered above one line—a silver thread arcing into what looked, impossibly, like a path through stars. Or bones.

He didn't touch it.

Instead, he opened his hand. The key sat there, quiet. It had stopped changing temperatures days ago. But now it felt warm again. Not from his skin—deeper.

"Are you going to stare it to death or do something useful?"

The voice made him flinch.

Leonarth turned sharply. Mattheon crouched at the roof entry, his curls damp from the climb, one knee scraped raw. He held a candle stub gripped too tightly—wax dripping in irregular pulses onto his thumb.

"You followed me?"

Mattheon climbed inside without answering. He didn't look angry—just unsettled, which for Mattheon meant irritated enough to talk.

"You weren't in bed," he said. "You're barefoot. And it's the middle of the night. What did you think I was going to do—let you fall off a roof again?"

"I've never fallen off a roof."

"Yet."

Leonarth looked down at the tapestry. "I didn't mean to come here."

Mattheon exhaled. "Right. So you just happened to scale the attic at midnight with that creepy thing in your hand."

He didn't say the rest—but Leonarth heard it anyway.

Mattheon was scared. And sarcasm had always been his way of not saying so.

Leonarth turned the key over in his palm. "It didn't feel like my idea."

Mattheon's brows pulled together. "It felt like what, then?"

"I don't know. Like it was calling something I forgot to remember."

Mattheon didn't answer.

Instead, he stepped closer. The candlelight softened his face, casting shadows beneath his jaw, the small nick on his chin from last week's fight, the faint birthmark that curled near his wrist.

His eyes flicked to the tapestry. "It looks… different."

Leonarth nodded. "It was never like this before."

"So someone came up here and..."

"No one comes up here."

They both looked down.

The key in Leonarth's hand trembled.

Very slightly—like the flick of a breath or the twitch of a string.

Mattheon's voice dropped. "Do you think it wants something?"

Leonarth didn't speak. He just turned the key in his palm until its narrow tip aligned with a circular thread at the edge of the cloth—a curve woven in gold, almost imperceptible.

He reached forward.

Mattheon grabbed his wrist. "Wait."

Their eyes locked.

Mattheon didn't say anything else.

Leonarth placed the key down.

And the tapestry exhaled.

It wasn't a sound—not really. It was a feeling. The room shifted. The shadows drew back. The floor creaked like something ancient was remembering itself. And then—from the center of the cloth—a single thread of light rose.

It unfurled slowly, like a breath drawn too deep. It didn't race. It chose.

It curved first toward Leonarth's wrist—and then, with eerie grace, toward Mattheon's. They watched it move without speaking.

The thread wrapped once around their wrists. Then again.

It didn't tighten.

It shimmered—not white, but every color at once. Like an echo of things not yet spoken.

Leonarth's throat ached.

Mattheon's fingers twitched at his side.

Neither moved.

The tapestry shifted again.

A symbol began to form near its corner. Not embroidered. Emerging. A circle broken down the middle, like a compass cracked. A path led from it—jagged, blackened, burned.

Mattheon swayed.

Leonarth moved to catch him.

But Mattheon's gaze had gone distant. Not unfocused—somewhere else.

And on his forearm—faint at first, then undeniable—the birthmark was glowing.

Like it had waited a long time to be found.

Leonarth didn't move. Not even to speak. But a tightness pressed into his chest—not fear exactly, not awe. Something stranger. Like recognition without memory. Like being seen by something that had known him before he had a name.

***

The glow shouldn't have been real.

It began subtly—a breath beneath the skin. Mattheon watched his forearm, watched the half-curled mark that had always lived there like an accident of birth, a forgotten burn. But it pulsed now. Not with heat. With intention. As if it had just remembered it was not a scar, but a seal.

And it remembered through him.

"Leon..."

Mattheon's voice cracked and collapsed. The name hung there, half-shaped and unfinished. It felt too heavy to carry, too human for what was unraveling inside his chest. The air around him thickened—not in heat, but in weight. Like gravity had tilted sideways, and only he had noticed.

The light from the tapestry didn't simply shine—it pressed. Against his skin. Beneath his thoughts. Like water against stone, looking for a way in.

He stumbled back. The glow followed.

No—it tracked him.

Leonarth was still on his knees, transfixed. His eyes weren't even on Mattheon—they followed the thread that now crackled with tension, stretching too far, too fast.

Mattheon's breath caught. The world had gone soundless except for one note—a hum, low and metallic, like an ancient bell beneath the floor of the world.

"Something's wrong," he whispered, but the words sounded far away.

Leonarth rose. "What's happening?"

Mattheon couldn't answer. His hands clutched at his forearm—the mark burned under his skin now, not hot but alive. Its shape was moving, curling inward like it was completing itself.

He barely heard the sound that came next—only felt it, like a blade cutting through the hum.

A flash.

And then the world inverted.

***

He fell—or maybe not. There was no floor, no ceiling. Just sensation. Like being pulled through velvet torn from the inside. He didn't scream. There was no air for that.

Light pulsed. Then dark. Then something between.

Then—her voice.

"He must never be found."

Mattheon turned—not with his body, which felt distant, but with something deeper. The voice was layered, like it had echoed across too many years. It carried pain. And love sharpened into fear.

The air around her crackled with heat, but it wasn't fire. It smelled of scorched leaves, of ink and something salt-wet—like a storm that had passed through grief and left everything damp with memory.

She stood before him—not clearly, not yet. A silhouette surrounded by a nimbus of fire. Her features were blurred by light, but her presence landed with the weight of certainty: she knew him. She ached for him.

One hand reached out. The other pressed a cloth against a boy's skin—not fabric. A rune. No—ink. No—memory.

He wanted to step forward, to speak, to cry. But the air between them trembled like stretched glass.

"Not erased," she whispered. "Hidden."

The mark on his forearm pulsed in the vision—and this time, he saw it being made. Drawn with trembling fingers. Ink laced with something glowing. Not pain. Something else. A covenant. A lock.

Her breath was ragged. Her hand trembled. She wasn't casting. She was weeping.

"Let him grow without burden. Let the seal hold until it cannot."

Her voice broke on that final word.

Something inside him surged—not memory, but the desire for one. His lips formed the beginning of a name—

Mother…?

The word felt like it had waited years behind his teeth. Not a fact, but a need. Not certainty—but familiarity, like a half-remembered lullaby his body knew even if his mind did not. He reached out—not with his hand, but with something older, something aching.

But the vision cracked.

The light shattered into embers.

And he fell again—not into silence.

Into fire.

***

He screamed himself awake.

The scream tore itself from his chest like something trying to stay behind. He wasn't just awake—he was emptied. The fire was gone, but its echo remained, curling behind his eyes like the shape of light long after it fades.

The attic thundered around him with sound and breath. The hum was gone, but the world still vibrated in its aftermath. Leonarth knelt beside him, gripping his shoulders like a boy trying to hold back a landslide.

The beams above him groaned as if exhaling something ancient. The dust in the air shimmered with the last of the thread's glow, falling in slow spirals, like ash from a fire no one lit. The tapestry did not breathe again—but it watched. That's how it felt. Like it knew.

Its edge curled slightly, as if reacting to the weight of Mattheon's breath—or waiting for it.

Mattheon gasped and lurched upright, knocking Leonarth's hands away. His chest heaved. His wrist burned.

He looked.

The mark still glowed—faint now, like the dying eye of something that had just watched him too closely. As though it had said all it needed to say… for now.

Leonarth stared at him. "What was that?"

"I..." Mattheon's voice rasped. His throat was dry. His bones shook.

He closed his eyes. What had he seen?

A woman. Fire. Grief. That mark drawn with love like a knife.

He looked down at his arm, as though expecting the memory to still be there.

"I saw someone," he said. "A woman. She... she was crying. She marked me."

Leonarth hesitated. "Your mother?"

"I don't know." The words came fast, too fast. "Maybe. I think so. But it didn't feel like remembering. It felt like... being remembered."

He turned slowly toward the tapestry.

Something had changed.

A section near its corner was scorched, the embroidered threads blackened as if burned from within. A path had formed—not woven, but seared—leading to a new symbol: a gate, jagged and half-open, smoke spilling from its unseen hinges.

"It changed," Leonarth murmured. "You saw it too?"

Mattheon nodded. "It's burned."

Leonarth crouched, reaching toward the edge of the scorched path, but didn't touch it.

"Why would it burn itself?"

Mattheon didn't answer right away. The taste of the vision still lingered in the back of his throat—like ash.

"I think..." He looked down at his wrist, still faintly red. "I think it tried to follow me."

Leonarth looked up. "Follow you?"

Mattheon nodded slowly. "Or reach me. Or... I don't know. But something stopped it."

"What stopped it?"

Mattheon's voice dropped. "The seal."

Leonarth frowned. "You mean the mark?"

Mattheon inhaled sharply, then nodded. "It wasn't just for show. It was placed there. Deliberately. To keep something hidden."

Leonarth was quiet. Too quiet.

The floor creaked as Mattheon stood, his knees unsteady. The whole attic felt wrong now—smaller somehow, darker, like the room had learned a new truth and no longer wanted to be innocent.

Leonarth caught his elbow. "You okay?"

Mattheon nodded, though he wasn't. "The hum's gone. But..." He paused. "It left something behind."

He couldn't name it. Couldn't locate it. It sat somewhere just below his chest—not fear, not grief. Something colder. Something watching.

He looked down at the mark again.

"I think it wasn't meant to protect me from this..."

The word didn't come easily. He didn't want it to. It felt ridiculous even thinking it—something from children's books or stories whispered when the power flickered at night. But here, now, with his arm still glowing and the air still heavy with breathless silence, the denial cracked.

"...from magic."

It sounded foreign in his mouth. Like naming it might make it vanish—or worse, make it real.

He looked at Leonarth. "I think it was meant to protect everyone else."

Leonarth's hand twitched. But he didn't pull away.

Mattheon met his eyes.

Leonarth's brow furrowed, and the space between them filled with a silence so fragile it could've shattered on a whisper. The word still hovered there— magic —absurd and undeniable all at once.

Mattheon swallowed. "I mean... it couldn't be, right? That's not real."

Leonarth's mouth opened, then closed. "And yet..." he gestured toward the tapestry. "That happened."

Mattheon shook his head, though not in disagreement. "This doesn't feel like a trick. It feels..." He trailed off, then added, "I don't know what it feels like. But if it isn't magic, then what the hell is it?"

He turned his arm, slowly, like he might catch the glow again from another angle. "You saw it. You saw what it did to me. What it showed me."

Leonarth nodded. "I saw it."

Mattheon's voice dropped. "So either we're both losing our minds at the exact same time..."

Both of them turned away at the same moment—not in shame, not in fear, but as if guided by the same thread pulling just behind the ribs.

"...or something just tore a hole in everything we thought was true."

"And I think… whatever it sealed… just woke up."

Behind them, the tapestry pulsed. Just once.

Then silence.

Mattheon turned toward it slowly, his voice low, almost reverent:

"I think it showed me something someone tried to bury."

He looked back to Leonarth, and for the first time, didn't smile—didn't joke, didn't explain.

"I'm not sure I want to know what happens when it remembers more."

Leonarth didn't speak. But the look in his eyes said what neither of them could. He didn't want to know either. And he already did.

***

The attic had gone so still it felt wrong. Not peaceful. Expectant.

Leonarth stood frozen beside Mattheon, heart hammering with a rhythm that didn't match his breath. The tapestry no longer pulsed, but something beneath its surface had shifted—like a muscle twitching under skin. Or a thought waking mid-dream.

He couldn't explain why he stepped forward. His legs moved without permission, as though the floor remembered him. As though the room itself knew this path had been walked before—and forgotten.

The scorched trail on the tapestry wound out like a crack in glass. Blackened. Shimmerless. Frayed at the edges. He knelt beside it.

"Don't touch it," Mattheon said. His voice was low, but not afraid. Reverent.

Leonarth stopped. "I wasn't going to."

But he had been.

He hovered his hand over the tapestry, just above the burned gate. The air there was colder. Not like frost—like absence. Like the thread itself had been ripped from the world.

Mattheon knelt beside him again. Their shoulders touched—faintly, but enough. Leonarth glanced sideways, and the question hung unspoken: Are we still who we were an hour ago?

Mattheon didn't look at him. He stared at the path. "What if it's showing us where we're not supposed to go?"

Leonarth shook his head slowly. "Then why show us at all?"

Neither spoke for a moment.

Then—the tapestry moved.

Just a ripple. A single wave of thread like a breath drawn sideways. But it wasn't from either of them. It was like it noticed them noticing.

Mattheon's hand twitched toward the key still on the floor nearby—but he didn't grab it.

Leonarth whispered, "It's awake."

And just like that, something else changed.

The light shifted—not in the room, but within the tapestry itself. Colors that hadn't been visible moments ago began to surface. A second path—this one faint and golden—shimmered beneath the scorched one. It was like watching ink bleed backward, a forgotten map unscrolling from beneath ruin.

Mattheon leaned closer. "That wasn't there before."

"It was hidden."

Leonarth felt it—not saw it, felt it—a pressure at the base of his skull. A sense of two roads superimposed, one buried inside the other.

The golden thread wound through constellations, across towers and shattered bridges. At its end, a symbol: a circle enclosed in another, and inside it, two overlapping silhouettes.

"Do you think it's… us?" Mattheon asked.

Leonarth didn't answer.

Because in that moment, the threads began to shift again.

But not together.

The golden path started to unweave itself. Slowly. Delicately. As if reconsidering its own existence. One by one, the glowing threads dimmed.

And in their place—the blackened path surged forward.

A gust of cold swept the attic, but neither boy moved. The gate on the tapestry flared, as if something behind it had exhaled. Just once.

Leonarth reached out—not to touch, but to steady himself.

And the tapestry went still.

***

He wasn't sure when it had become about him. The air around him had shifted—not in temperature, but in texture. Like breath held too long. Like silence that knew your name.

Mattheon couldn't speak. Not because he didn't want to—because there were no words for what the tapestry had almost done.

It had chosen. Then hesitated.

Then rejected its choice.

That was worse than anything.

"Did it..." he began, then stopped. "Did it change its mind?"

Leonarth swallowed hard. "Or maybe... it remembered something it didn't want to."

Mattheon didn't answer. He couldn't. He wasn't numb—not anymore. Something had cracked beneath his skin, and whatever it was now stared back at him through the tapestry's vanished light.

He thought of the vision. Of her voice. Of the mark that wasn't just his.

"I wasn't enough," he said, almost without sound. "Even the magic knew it."

Leonarth turned sharply. "What?"

Mattheon shook his head. "It saw me. It reached for me. And then it changed its mind."

His voice wasn't angry. It wasn't even broken. It was hollow. Like someone trying not to echo.

"What if I was never meant to matter at all?"

The seal on his wrist still pulsed faintly, but not like before. Now it felt like a warning. Or a brand.

Mattheon didn't move. His hands hung at his sides, limp. The silence between them grew too large, too loud. He spoke again—softer this time, but no less sharp.

"Do you ever wonder if it picked you first?"

Leonarth blinked. "What?"

"The tapestry. The light. The path that didn't burn."

He looked away. "Maybe that was for you."

Leonarth frowned, stepping closer. "Mattheon—"

His hand hovered—just for a moment—as if unsure whether to reach or retreat.

"And maybe I was just the reason it changed its mind."

His breath caught, but he kept speaking. He had to.

"Everyone's been watching me since I got here. Like I'm going to break something. Or already did."

He swallowed. "Sometimes they're kind about it. Sometimes they're not. But it's always there."

He looked down at his wrist. "What if I wasn't meant to be found at all? The tapestry didn't reject a path. It rejected me. And maybe… it was right to."

Leonarth didn't know what to say. So Mattheon filled the space.

"And you—you didn't even ask for any of this. You just… follow the thread. And it loves you for it."

He laughed, dry and bitter. "Of course it loves you for it."

Leonarth reached out, uncertain. "That's not true."

Mattheon stepped back, just once.

"Isn't it?"

He wasn't bitter. Not exactly. But something colder than envy bloomed under his ribs—not hatred, but doubt. And doubt, left unchecked, could become anything.

He felt it in his fingertips—that faint, almost buzzing cold. Like the moment just before blood recedes.

He looked back toward the tapestry, and for the first time, didn't see magic or wonder.

He saw a gate that had closed before he reached it.

And worse—he saw himself standing in front of it.

Alone.

Neither looked at the tapestry again.

Behind them, it lay perfectly still. Silent. Dormant. But not innocent.

Not anymore.

***

Far away, where threadlight was studied rather than believed, a mirrored chamber remembered something it was never meant to recall.

The Observatory Mirror's projection rippled.

At first, she thought it was a flaw in the warding. The Chamber hadn't flickered in over thirty years. Not since the Accord seared the northern vaults and blackened the last Known Gate.

But this was not interference. This was memory.

She stepped closer. The map pulsed again—this time with a color she hadn't seen since her apprenticeship.

Amber.

One gate blinked into view. Long dormant. Long sealed. Forgotten by all but the oldest glyphs—and even they were unsure what it had once meant.

It blinked.

She turned to the shadow just beyond the arch.

"It remembered an heir that should not exist."

The voice that answered was quiet. Too quiet.

"Or worse—it remembered one… and hinted at a second. A legacy that was never meant to echo his name."

She stared at the glowing glyph. It pulsed again.

Twice.

Two threads.

Her hand trembled.

***

Beneath the Abbey, in a chapel that hadn't heard a child's voice in years, Ava felt the shift before she saw it.

Ava sat alone, her back pressed against the stone alcove where the sun never reached. Since the anchoring, they had agreed the Chapel of Silence would never be left unattended. Each of them took turns here, their relics kept close—not to act, but to listen.

She wasn't praying. Not really. But her thoughts were restless.

The pendant on her chest—dormant for hours—twitched once. A faint jolt against her skin.

She froze.

Then, the scroll on the altar beside her unfurled by half an inch. Not much. Just enough.

A single glyph shimmered in its corner, the same incomplete symbol—not etched by hand, but woven by the tapestry during the convergence. Unclaimed.

Ava stared at it longer than she meant to.

Not because she didn't understand what it was—but because she could feel how little time it had left to remain unfinished.

Ava rose slowly.

"Mabelle," she called out. No answer.

She turned to the stairs. "Maurice?"

Stillness.

She reached for the scroll. The glyph pulsed again. But this time—not alone.

A second pulse echoed behind her.

She turned.

And in the upper window, through the stained-glass lens of Saint Elodia's eye, she caught the faintest shimmer of threadlight—gold and black intertwined—rising beyond the Abbey's roofline.

Not from the bell tower.

Not from any consecrated stone.

From the direction of the school.

The attic.

Her breath caught.

"Oh no."

***

Back in the attic, Mattheon hesitated.

He turned back once more before leaving. The tapestry didn't move. But he knew—the damage was done.

"It wasn't supposed to find us," he whispered.

Leonarth didn't respond.

Mattheon's voice dropped to something barely above breath.

"And what if it wasn't you it rejected?"

He didn't wait for an answer. He just stood there, looking back.

"If I'm the mistake… maybe the tapestry didn't make one after all."

A long silence followed.

Leonarth's voice was quiet. Not hesitant—but not comfortable either.

"Do you think Ava or Mabelle know what that thing is?"

Mattheon looked sideways at him. "Ava. Mabelle. All of them."

He didn't elaborate.

They turned toward the attic hatch. Leonarth glanced once more at the tapestry, then at Mattheon. He didn't speak. But a question hung behind his eyes—one even he didn't dare ask.

As they descended, something unspoken passed between them. Not agreement. Not trust. Just the quiet, aching shape of a decision neither dared name.

They wouldn't ask permission to understand what had happened.

And they wouldn't wait to be told.

Leonarth exhaled. "No more waiting for answers." Mattheon didn't nod. He didn't have to.

The key, still tucked in Leonarth's pocket, pulsed faintly.

Once.

As if it, too, was listening.

Whatever this was—it wasn't over.

Not by a thread.

Chapter Nineteen

"The Mirror of No Mercy"

The glyphs had flickered. Twice. That alone would have been enough to summon him. But it was the shape of the flicker—twin bursts, not simultaneous but rhythmically tethered—that broke the stillness of the Chamber of Silence and brought Chancellor Siroth barefoot down the spiral steps beneath the Hall of Accord.

He walked without his regalia. No crescent seal. No layered robes. Just his breath, controlled. Measured. Silver-laced hair tied behind his neck with a strand of woven black—a scrap of cloth he had once confiscated from a woman who did not flinch when they came for her.

Each step echoed not against stone but against certainty.

The Mirror of Edresk awaited.

It did not reflect him.

The chamber welcomed no torchlight. Only the mirror's own breath—dark and rippling—illuminated the obsidian walls. Its surface did not shimmer; it recoiled. As though what it contained had already stirred.

The glyphs carved into the floor pulsed faintly, like veins beneath skin. But tonight, they pulsed in two alternating rhythms. One: slow, silver, hesitant. The other: sharp, crimson, decisive.

He had seen this once before, during the Ordinatum. When the Root hesitated against the blade—but did not refuse.

Siroth stood at the edge of the ritual circle and waited. The mirror made no demand. But the air around it thickened. Heavy with something more ancient than judgment.

He inhaled. Slowly. As if bracing for a memory to surface.

"You buried the seed."

Faye's voice.

"But it remembered the light."

He had dismissed it then, standing over her still-warm body on the Insidium altar. Words from a woman undone. But now the mirror responded. Not by gleaming—by humming. A deep sound, like breath returning to lungs long forgotten.

"She meant something real," he said aloud, uncertain. "Not metaphor. Not rebellion."

The mirror gave no answer—only a deepening hum, as if it waited.

He frowned, searching the words again. "Not legacy," he continued, slower now. "Not memory... a weapon?"

No reaction.

"A prophecy?"

Still nothing. Then, just as he considered retreat, the silver rhythm of the glyphs shifted—slower, deeper. Not confirmation. Not warning.

Allowance.

His voice faltered. "She meant... something born."

And the mirror rippled. Not with light—but with consequence.

He felt the floor beneath him soften, not physically, but in certainty. The foundation of his own righteousness frayed at the edge.

But why two?

One flicker, he could understand. The mirror reacting to a singular fault, a bloodline interrupted and not meant to be. But two? That was not an echo. It was a conversation.

Was it possible the flicker wasn't a doubling—but a mirroring? Not two passings, but two echoes? One born of defiance, the other of oversight?

No.

He inhaled, sharp. That was speculation. Impossibility. He had severed every thread. And yet the mirror pulsed as if to say: *not severed enough.*

Then it began.

A house. Half-consumed by fire.

Familiar.

A woman—standing in the doorway, outlined by smoke. Not afraid. Not fleeing. Her body turned slightly, shielding something behind her. Her hair was tangled with ash. Her eyes defiant. Siroth knew her.

Lorraine.

She had once walked these corridors without fear. And when she vanished, he let her go—believing it was pride, retaliation, perhaps a bruised ego. He never asked why. He never considered what she might have taken with her besides the Root of Orreth—a relic of deep ceremonial power, said to carry ancestral memory when passed by blood. A sacred tether, severed from the Accord's vaults decades ago, and believed lost.

He had thought she meant to injure his future.

Now, he began to wonder—had she meant to protect one?

And further back—barely visible through the smoke—stood a boy, not yet five. His hands clutched a copper-threaded branch, too tightly for his age. He said nothing. But he watched like one who had already been taught to run.

He did not recognize the child.

But he recognized the artifact—its copper threads unmistakable, its aura undimmed.

The Root of Orreth.

He hadn't seen it in over a decade—not since the vault breach. It had been ceremonial, yes, but also personal: bound to rites of succession, used in ancient times to affirm the legitimacy of a line. The lore was tangled and full of contradiction, but one truth remained: it could not be taken. Only passed. And only by blood.

That truth had shaped the Insidium. And now it unraveled him.

"Lorraine," he whispered, "what have you done..."

The name didn't feel new—not here. He had spoken it once already. But now, as the mirror held her image longer than it should, the ache returned. Not grief. Not quite rage.

There was no heat in the name. No forgiveness either. Only that slow ache at the edge of memory—something between devotion and contempt. Something he had never fully buried.

The name returned like a bruise beneath the tongue. And lingered.

He had once loved her. Or believed he had. A quieter time. A woman who never asked for power, who never belonged in court. And then, one day, she was gone.

He had assumed it was pride. A lover discarded, stealing something in vengeance. A sliver of the Root of Orreth gone from the reliquary. He imagined her smirking, imagined her ruining what he might one day need to pass on.

And later, when he finally found her, she told him—just before he killed her—that she had destroyed it.

And he had believed her.

But the mirror knew better.

She hadn't destroyed it. She had hidden it. Not to wound him. Not to deny him. But to protect someone else.

The image of the Root in the child's hands returned to him—too tightly gripped for innocence, too calmly held for it to be newly found.

Was that why the mirror had pulsed twice?

One flicker for what he had unknowingly sown.

And one for what he had failed to sever.

He took a breath, not shallow.

And then, quieter, as if the words might curse him by being real:

"No... was it my legacy?"

He didn't know. The thought itself unraveled the certainty he'd worn like armor for decades.

A son?

The mirror had not confirmed it—but neither had it denied. And that ambiguity carved deeper than any answer could.

He could feel the tremor of recognition in his own breath. The terrible symmetry of the pulses. The child with the Root. The child he had never asked about.

Had Lorraine known? Had she tried to warn him?

No. She hadn't tried. She had hidden.

And he had killed her before she could.

The mirror pulsed. As if the thought itself disturbed something beneath its surface.

"No..." he whispered again. "No. She couldn't have."

But the vision remained.

She had conceived before he found her. She had birthed the child. And he had never asked. Had never seen.

He turned away from the flame.

The Insidium.

The failure.

"It wasn't the blade," he murmured. "It was me."

The mirror darkened.

"The rite demands severance. No root beneath. No thread behind."

He stepped forward. "And I... I was not severed."

He swallowed the truth like ash.

But the mirror was not done.

Two pulses now. Parallel. Symmetrical. Rhythmic.

The realization settled in stages—painful, reluctant, exacting.

He had never stood a chance. The Insidium had never been his to command.

He had a line.

The blade rejected him because it obeyed the old law: the Root could not be stolen from one who no longer bore it, nor granted to one who still did.

Power was never the problem. It was inheritance.

And inheritance... remembers.

But that should have killed him. Rites like that do not spare. They extinguish. They erase.

Failed Insidiums under such conditions did not leave survivors.

He stared at the mirror, unsettled by the only question that remained: *Why am I still alive?*

His fingers twitched, as if expecting blood. But there was none.

There had never been.

And deeper still, the one he dared not say aloud: *Who spared me? And why?*

Even now, no scar marked him. No burn. No glyph. Just silence. And yet he felt unmade.

It did not show names.

But it showed them.

Two children.

One standing in the glow of sunlight, arm outstretched toward a sky that pulsed with memory. The other—contained, calculating—stood in shadow, a flicker of flame in his wrist that did not burn.

Not twins.

Not brothers—not that he knew.

But tethered.

"Why two?" he asked the mirror.

No answer. Only pulse. Silver. Crimson. Silver. Crimson.

Then—Faye. Again.

Not on the Insidium altar. Not broken. Not wounded.

His breath caught—not in certainty, but in dread.

Two pulses. Two roots. Not in judgment. In memory.

But what did that mean?

The Insidium had not just failed.

It had marked him.

He was alive, yes. But why?

And what did that survival cost?

He felt the weight now—not just of guilt, but of consequence. Of convergence.

If both roots had awakened... then the old covenant was beginning to stir.

And the prophecy—

He didn't know how it began. But he remembered how it ended: *Until the one born of both realms, bearing the legacy of common roots, rises to restore the ancient bond.*

The mirror pulsed.

And Siroth's voice, though hollow, carried into the dark:

"Dormintaris." The expression was not an order. It was something the mirror had taught him to say.

A single line flickered across the obsidian. Then vanished. Not a declaration—a wound.

The glyphs dimmed. But the mirror did not quiet. It breathed—slowly, like something that had finally exhaled.

The mirror had always known.

He reached toward the obsidian base.

"Dormintaris," he said again—now not as command, but confession.

The glyphs surged.

The Mirror of Edresk remembered.

And Siroth understood: it was not him it had been waiting for.

Not one heir. Two echoes. One mistake. One memory.

And the mirror... had waited for them.

It was always them.

The mirror exhaled again—not in answer, but in acceptance. Not of what they were, but of what had always been waiting.

And beneath its surface, something moved—not fully formed, but watching. Not from the past. But from what was still to come, and what had once been meant to become.

***

The chamber had gone still.

Not silent—still. As if even silence had folded itself inward, waiting to see what Siroth would do next.

The glyphs had dimmed, no longer pulsing. But the mirror still breathed. Barely perceptible. A pressure in the air that came and went like the memory of someone else's breath.

Siroth stood unmoving at the edge of the circle, hand still slightly raised where he had last spoken the invocation.

"Dormintaris."

He said it one final time. Let the word stand.

The mirror yielded—not with obedience.

With departure.

He could feel it. Something had left him—not violently, but cleanly. A thread unwound. A presence unmoored.

Not magic. Not memory.

Something closer to identity.

He lowered his hand.

The mirror made no move to reflect it.

He waited a moment longer, then turned from the ritual circle and exited the chamber. The outer seal, etched in the bone language of the Accord, slid back into place behind him with a sound like a breath drawn in reverse.

The corridor beyond was dim, but not empty.

An Inquisitor waited—hood lowered, breath caught between duty and dread, a scrollcase in hand.

"Chancellor," she said quickly, stepping into the narrow light. "You're needed in the High Scriptorium. The Archivists have reported a pattern."

Siroth paused mid-step.

"Three separate anomalies," she continued, unrolling a parchment with fingers that betrayed a tremor. "All traced to the same provincial zone—Corbeil-Essonnes. France."

Her tone flattened as she read. "First event logged a few weeks ago. Low energy, brief resonance. The kind we normally dismiss—atmospheric variance or artisan error. But it was logged."

She took a breath. "Second event—seven days ago. Pulse distortion. A glyph didn't fully collapse... it shimmered. As if reacting to internal conflict, not external pressure."

"And the third?" Siroth asked, voice like frost against stone.

"Last night. Stronger. Rhythmic. It breached no veil, cast no spell. But it passed through the detection lattice."

Siroth tilted his head. "Breached it how?"

"It didn't," she said, uneased. "That's what's strange. It was marked—but not summoned. As if something old had stirred. Not cast forward. Pulled backward."

She hesitated, then added, more softly:

"We've had similar anomalies before, but not from the same site. And never three. This one... it remembered."

Siroth stepped past her slowly, eyes tracing the edge of the corridor as if he could feel the pulse still vibrating in the walls.

"Do we have any Calventherath assets seeded near the region?"

The Inquisitor stiffened. "We do. But Chancellor, those are last resort powers. Lethal by design. Not ceremonial."

"I'm aware," he said, almost gently. "But you said three events. From one point. The same place where sleeper threads were once bound."

Her eyes narrowed. "The threads you sealed yourself."

He looked at her as if she, too, might speak something not her own—a truth borrowed from silence.

As much as he tried, he didn't know what it was. Not exactly.

But the pattern was familiar—somewhere between memory and rhythm.

Three flickers. None asked permission. None gave their name.

This wasn't someone reaching forward.

It was something pulling backward.

He had sealed that province long ago.

Not because he feared it—but because it offered nothing worth fearing.

The last names tied to that region had dissolved into quiet long before the Ordinatum.

Gwendlynn, the queen mother... presumed dead. Lost in the collapse of her fractured realm.

And Keralis, the traitor inquisitor—never confirmed, never retrieved—a missing page the Accord never needed returned.

He had closed the ledger on that zone. Let its markers expire. Minimal surveillance. No interest.

The Insidium, he believed, had worked. Faye was gone. Her line, unrooted. The blade had drunk what it was made to drink.

So he allowed silence to settle over the coordinates like dust.

And let the world believe restraint had been wisdom.

But silence was never empty.

The mirror had not accused him. It had simply waited.

Not for Gwendlynn. Not for Keralis.

For the shape they left behind.

Three flickers.

Not loud. Not locatable.

But… consistent. Resonant.

Could it be…?

No. He had no proof. Only rhythm.

But rhythm was enough.

But if rhythm was enough, then what of blood?

The blade had failed him. Not in ceremony. In inheritance.

He had convinced himself that Faye's line died with her—because the ritual had demanded it. Because the Root should have passed. Because it had to.

But it hadn't.

And somewhere—buried in the marrow of that failure—was her voice.

He had silenced Lorraine. Not because she had lied. But because she had spoken too much truth, too early.

He remembered how her hands didn't shake. Only her breath.

And how he convinced himself that loyalty meant knowing when to stop listening.

And if it hadn't, then perhaps everything else—Lorraine, her betrayal, her death—had meant something else, too.

Had he killed to protect order? Had he destroyed what he could not control? Or had he destroyed the only parts of himself still capable of believing in it?

He remembered the way her voice broke when she told him she'd destroyed the Root of Orreth. The way he believed her. The way he made sure no one else ever heard her speak again.

Faye. Lorraine. Keralis. Gwendlynn.

Each one he had sealed. Named. Archived. Forgotten.

But none of them had done what the mirror had just done.

The mirror had denied him without speaking.

And memory—once again—had moved without his consent.

A breath from the Inquisitor broke the silence. Her stance stiffened, eyes darting once to the floor, as if unsure whether he had spoken—or simply remembered too loudly.

"Are you certain this warrants awakening?" she asked. Not with defiance. With dread.

Siroth didn't answer at first. He studied her—not to measure her obedience, but to see if she would try to stop what had already begun.

"Do you remember what happened the last time?" she said, voice lower now. "I do."

He said nothing.

"The scream never reached the door," she continued. "The glyphs failed to record half of it. And when we opened the room, the one we awakened…"

Her breath caught. "It wasn't the same person who came out."

"That was then," Siroth replied.

"They're not watchers," she insisted. "They don't just observe."

"They're not meant to," he said.

"You sealed that province yourself. You called it spent. Why reopen it?"

"Because it was quiet," he replied. "And quiet things remember more deeply than loud ones."

Her hands tightened around the scroll. "There are other options. Surveillance glyphs. Dormant threads we could rebind—"

"None that will hold if this is what I believe it is."

"And what is it you believe?" she asked, almost whispering.

"This isn't fear," he told himself. "This is containment."

But he remembered what the mirror had shown him.

It had not yielded to control.

It had moved according to memory, not instruction.

He looked at her then and said, "What's stirring there isn't waiting to be dealt with. It's already chosen."

"You're invoking a Calventherath deployment without tribunal—"

"I'm invoking a clause," he said. "Not a weapon."

"Which clause?"

His eyes didn't move.

"The one we never wrote down."

No further words were exchanged.

But somewhere behind the vault wall, a breath that was not his exhaled.

It wasn't sound. It was memory—leaving him.

Not stolen. Not reclaimed. Just… no longer his to bind.

The Inquisitor turned without command, as if she too felt it—though she'd never name what passed.

And Siroth, standing alone in the corridor, did not move.

The torchlight behind him flickered once, then steadied.

He did not look back.

Because what had moved no longer needed his permission.

It had remembered itself.

And what it remembered was not allegiance.

It was inheritance. Inverted.

Not passed. Not taken.

Rewritten.

And if it had rewritten memory…

…it would soon rewrite flesh.

***

The mirror did not exhale.

It unthreaded.

No torch flickered in the vault. No voice offered command. But something had been loosed—not in word, not in intention, but in rhythm.

Where once the invocation waited for control, now the mirror moved without it.

Not toward light.

Not toward silence.

Toward memory.

A glyph shivered. Then unwound.

It passed without witness. Without notice. Even Siroth did not feel it.

But elsewhere—where the invocation had once echoed and failed to end—its consequence began to breathe.

***

Saint-Spire Abbey did not wake.

It remembered.

The breath that passed through the Abbey stones was not wind, and not warmth. It was older—the kind that returns after being held too long.

In the kitchen, tucked behind shelves of preserved jars and drying herbs, a bundle wrapped in linen trembled. Not enough to be seen. Only enough to unseat the dust above it.

Bay leaves curled against its edge. A tangle of dried lavender hung by the arch, though now the scent was shifting—metallic. Not blood. Older. Like iron forgotten beneath stone.

The bundle did not stir again.

But the air around it folded.

Upstairs, Meely rolled over in her bunk. Her breath whispered like parchment turning.

In the dormitory above, Ava's hand slipped from her blanket. Her breath caught mid-dream.

And in the chapel, seated alone before the last rosary of the day, Mabelle flinched.

Not in fear.

In attunement.

A soundless tremor passed through the beads. Not vibration. Not magic. Emotion. Foreign, but not unfamiliar—like a memory she didn't own.

The pendant at her neck grew warm, not with power, but with pulse. It was responding.

She closed her eyes, pressing fingers to her temple.

What is this?

The fear… it wasn't hers. It wasn't even from the room.

It was flooding into her—rising from beneath the floor like cold breath through roots.

She opened her mouth to pray, but nothing came.

And then she heard it.

Not a voice.

A shape.

A thought pressed into the silence from far below.

And before she could name it, her lips did something else entirely.

"Unwritten," she whispered.

The rosary snapped—before she realized her fingers had tightened.

Beads scattered across the stone floor like seeds denied planting.

She felt a pull that did not ask her to move.

It only shifted where the world was.

Downward.

Away from the chapel.

Toward heat.

Toward ash.

Toward something long held—and just now forced to remember itself.

***

There was no sound, but she felt it—like her own shadow moving without her.

And something was rising.

Not beneath her feet.

Behind her eyes.

It had no name, but it moved like memory resuming a sentence. It grew—not breath. Not noise. Just… pull.

Like a prayer she hadn't meant to finish.

And it rose—not with thought, but with pattern.

As if the silence beneath Mabelle's broken rosary had chosen its own answer.

No glyphs flared. No veil tore.

Only the air bent, in the oldest joints of the room.

A hand moved, reaching—uncertain.

First the wall.

Then the shelf.

Like muscle remembering form.

The gesture paused.

Then repeated.

As if recalling something it had never learned properly.

Not ritual.

Reflex.

Then the bundle.

Not to open it.

To remember it.

The sense of direction resolved without distance.

Turning.

Descending.

Toward a stair long unused, shadowed by stone that remembered weight.

No sound followed.

Only sequence.

A candle near the spices rekindled itself.

No flame. No wick.

Just glow.

Mabelle saw as if the world had paused on the edge of a stairwell she knew well—unable to see what lay beyond it, only the pressure of something about to arrive.

Fear rose in her chest. Not hers.

Ava turned in bed, muttering something in her sleep she would not remember.

And in a quiet corner of the Abbey, Gwendlynn's eyes opened in the dark.

She did not rise.

But she whispered one word beneath her breath:

"…Leonarth."

***

The kitchen changed shape in front of her.

Light bent. Heat snapped back into form, and stone remembered weight.

The glow near the spices guttered and became only candlelight.

Mabelle was already moving.

At the top of the stairs, she felt the air shift.

She reached the threshold—and turned.

But the hallway was empty.

Only a thin scent of bay and dust remained.

Only her own heartbeat, pounding too loud.

She stepped backward, disoriented—as if she'd been sent to witness something and missed it entirely.

***

Far away from her, in the ritual vault, the mirror did not fracture.

But one ripple formed.

A child's wrist, once seen in flame.

A cradle no longer cradling.

Two boys, walking away.

Not facing Siroth.

Not needing to.

The mirror said nothing.

And still, the Abbey breathed.

But now it was breathing something else. And somewhere in its lungs, a new name was forming.

Not spoken. Not earned.

Just... remembered.

And the Abbey's silence adjusted—as if making room for a name it had once agreed never to speak again.

Chapter Twenty

"The Bell and the Blade"

The bell at Saint-Spire Abbey rang twice—two clean, deliberate notes that echoed across the courtyards like a breath held, then exhaled. 6:30 p.m., precisely. In the Abbey, time did not drift—it was marked, measured, etched into air by those solemn chimes.

The bell spoke in quarters. Once at quarter past, twice at half past, thrice at three-quarters, and then full tolls upon the hour, each echo drawn from the iron throat of the tower above the cloisters. The bell was the Abbey's heartbeat—and like all hearts, it could warn before it broke.

Mabelle sat at the edge of her bed, facing the narrow window that opened toward the descending sun. The light, warm but fading, stretched long across her floor, gilding the worn stone like a memory that refused to die. It tried to reach her face. It didn't.

Below, the garden was beginning to turn silver with shadow. Her eyes caught sight of Mattheon and Leonarth lingering near the kitchen's outer steps, chatting with the younger children. Supper was near—Eloi's famous meat and vegetable stew, with chocolate cake waiting in the scullery for a birthday none of them had forgotten. For the little ones with no family but each other, these days meant something.

Eloi always remembered.

Mattheon glanced up, his face catching the last of the amber light. He didn't wave. Just a small nod—a gesture more acknowledgment than greeting. He hadn't spoken to her in two days. No banter. No glances. Just a hollowed presence stretched thin across the corridors like dust on untouched shelves.

She told herself he was tired. Distracted. But that lie wore thin.

She hadn't slept. Not truly. Not since the dome had flickered and silence had turned its weight toward her. Not since Ava's gaze had softened in that particular way—the kind that saw through, not into. Not since the boy who had once called her his entire world now passed her like a thought he couldn't trust.

Mabelle knew better than to ask Ava questions that came wrapped in stillness.

Ava had come to her quietly, hours after the bells, her voice low and careful, and spoken only of the attic—of a pull, a disturbance that did not feel accidental. They had agreed then to wait. To let the boys bring what had stirred, rather than reach for it and risk waking more than they could hold.

And now, watching Mattheon stand beneath the fading light, Mabelle understood the cost of that choice.

Whatever he had touched, it had not let go.

Something had changed in him. And she didn't know if she had caused it... or if something had found him first.

He didn't know about the Convergence. About the sigils that shimmered. About the relics unveiled beneath stone and memory. Not about the magic they had carried—some with reverence, some with shame. Not even about the truth buried so deep inside the Abbey that even its stones had stopped speaking of it.

But maybe he didn't need words. Maybe he'd felt the ripple. Maybe he'd begun to see her the way she feared: as a page half-read and half-erased.

Her thoughts spiraled, untethered. Through the hush. Through the stares. Through the quiet verdicts that never reached her ears, only hovered in the hallways like smoke that never cleared. Ava had spoken since the Rite—about the attic, the boys, about waiting—but never said the one thing Mabelle felt pressing at her ribs. Never named what had changed. Maurice had begun avoiding the benches they once shared. Gwendlynn—her silence was a weapon. And it had been pointed.

There were no accusations. But there had been a reckoning of glances.

When her pendant failed to pulse on the altar, the others had noticed. Ava's silence was a shape. Maurice's retreat, a tremor. And Gwendlynn... Gwendlynn had looked through her, not past her. Like someone re-reading a prophecy that no longer said what they needed it to.

They had agreed not to tell the boys. But children feel fracture before they know how to name it.

Mattheon had felt something.

A gust of wind slipped through the window's cracked frame. It lifted the edge of her blanket and nudged the corner of the rug. Cold. Real. And in that moment, it brought her back. She let out a breath she didn't know she'd caught in her chest.

She stood.

Her foot knocked against the edge of her brother's old trunk—the wood groaned in protest, or invitation. She looked down. Stilled. Then placed the trunk on the bed with care.

"Memory preserves what silence tries to erase," she murmured. "Each pretending not to see the other. And I've hidden from them both long enough."

She hadn't touched the trunk since choosing not to. But tonight, it had surfaced—like breath through water.

She opened it.

One by one, she removed its contents with the slow, methodical reverence of ritual. The half-burned parchment with the Calventherath assignments. A pair of gloves—her brother's. Worn only once by her, maybe. But carried always. Not as comfort. As tether.

Her fingers brushed something hard, wrapped in old fabric.

She blinked.

A book.

Her old spellbook. Bound in cracked leather, its spine softened by use and time. Her mother had once called it an heirloom of function—not valuable for power, but for the memories it preserved between ink and glyph.

She opened it without intent. Let the pages fall.

Near the center, where the parchment had curled slightly, a line glimmered faintly. Not light. Not ink. Something answering back.

Underlined:

"Sanguem revocat. Nomen sequitur."
(Blood calls. The name follows.)

Her breath caught in her throat.

"It's the end of a bloodline spell," she whispered, as if her mother's voice were still nearby. "She said it only works if the object belongs to the line..."

A pause. Then softer—like memory returning through bone:

"Even borrowed blood remembers where it came from."

Her pendant flickered.

Her eyes found it—not the pendant, but what lay just beneath: the Root of Orreth. Still wrapped. Still untouched since the Rite.

She hadn't really seen it since the Chapel. Not truly. Not with her mind open.

But now… now Gwendlynn's words returned like breath warming old glass.

A Root is a blood tether. Forged only for the firstborn of a line bound by legacy… and burden.

She'd repeated those words without thinking that night—like breath drawn from a deeper lung.

But now… she needed more than memory.

She needed proof.

Why had her brother kept it? Why had no one recognized the sigil? Why had Maurice spoken its name like a wound?

Orreth is not just a name… it was Siroth's name.

Her hands trembled—not from fear, but from clarity.

She gathered the book. The gloves. The Root.

Not to return them.

To follow them.

The Abbey Library still housed older ledgers—genealogy, ordination records, birthright lists copied from royal decrees and preserved not through reverence, but through misdirection, folded into church recordkeeping where they would be overlooked rather than destroyed. If anything remained—even a margin note—she'd find it.

And if the bell tolled again before she returned… she hoped it wouldn't be mourning.

***

The boys had made a mess of the dining hall—dropped spoons, overturned napkins, crumbs wedged into the seams of the benches. And Eloi, oddly, liked it that way. Not the disorder itself, but the need it represented. These were the moments he cherished: when the echoes of laughter still lingered in the beams, when his hands found purpose in quiet acts of care. When he felt needed.

Those moments were scarce and far between. But they were the ones that reminded him he existed—not as memory, but as presence.

Tonight, though, something was off.

The warmth didn't cling to the stones as long. The echoes died quicker. The laughter, already faded, felt like it had never been real—just a ripple in water long stilled.

He stooped to gather the scattered napkins, but his hands paused over a wooden spoon someone had left behind—carved, old, familiar. He couldn't recall whose it had been. Or if it had ever truly belonged to anyone.

"Even the things we keep," he murmured, "forget us back."

He looked around, as he always did—scanning the room not for tasks, but for proof. But what he saw tonight struck deeper than usual. The mess felt louder. Not in sound, but in ache.

He used to welcome the chaos. Plates to scrape, crumbs to sweep, benches to straighten—tasks that asked nothing, expected everything, and left no silence in between. But tonight, every motion echoed back at him with a question:

Are you still here?

And this time, he knew exactly how to answer.

He crossed to the spice wall—to the high shelf where the bay leaves slept in a tall jar with a cracked lid. He didn't reach by sight or even by feel.

He reached by memory.

His hand found the bundle on the first try. Hidden, untouched. But not dormant.

It was heavier than before. Or perhaps he was.

He unwrapped it slowly, not with caution, but reverence. The oiled cloth loosened in his hands like a long-forgotten ritual, unfolding to reveal a pendant of obsidian so dark it seemed to consume the light.

The spiral etched into its center was faint—almost invisible at rest. But in motion, it shimmered like breath on frost, like ink swirling underwater.

He ran his thumb along the edge. It didn't glow.

It pulsed.

Not with power.

But with obedience waking up.

"You remembered me," he whispered.

Not a spell. Not yet.

Just a truth too old to be forgotten.

The spiral flickered—once. Then again.

Like a heart.

Like a promise.

Like something waking not for war… but for return.

He took the pendant, laying still in his palm, and slipped its chain over his head. It pulsed once more—a breath, a heartbeat—and then went still. It didn't glow or weigh heavier than memory, but something within him shifted around it.

Not magic.

Not entirely.

Acknowledgement.

He folded the cloth again with precise, almost ceremonial hands, and tucked it behind the bay leaf jar as though preserving a sacrament. But he didn't turn away.

Not yet.

His gaze drifted downward. To the drawer.

The one he hadn't opened in years.

The one he'd nearly reached for in Gwendlynn's presence… but hadn't.

This time, his fingers didn't tremble.

They moved like a priest's before an altar.

The drawer opened with a soft groan—not protest, but recollection. The wood sighed like lungs remembering their first breath.

Inside, behind a false bottom lined with velvet and ash-dust, lay something wrapped in black cloth. Its edges were taut. Its silence absolute.

He didn't lift it. Not fully.

He only reached.

And the shape—dense, familiar, patient—met his palm like an old grief returning home.

He held it for a moment, letting its weight settle into his skin, his breath. Into the marrow of who he had once been.

His eyes didn't close.

But his breath did.

One long, silent exhale—like a vow released, like something sacred let go.

He tucked the object inside his cloak.

Not to conceal it, but as a truth.

The drawer slid shut with a muted thud, as though it understood that it, too, had remembered.

And Eloi stood there, surrounded by the warmth he had built, carrying something that belonged not to heat or light—but to silence… and to the memories that waited after it.

A sound stirred behind him—soft and low.

A noise from beneath the last table by the door.

A furry shadow glided forward on silent paws, hovering just above the stone floor. Golden eyes caught the hearthlight.

Meely.

Eloi turned.

Her gaze locked on him. Not feline. Not simple.

Old.

For a heartbeat, something in him went still. Not from fear—from knowing.

Then, with a breath like a smile pressed too long into silence, he crouched down.

"Spying, are we?" he asked gently. "Or guarding?"

The cat didn't move.

He tilted his head.

"You always appear when the soup thickens too fast or the secrets grow too loud."

Meely took a step forward. Her tail flicked like a quill drawing something ancient in air.

Eloi's hand drifted toward his apron fold where he'd tucked the bundle—not to protect it.

To acknowledge that she saw.

"Well," he said, standing again, "if you're planning to report me, at least let me bribe you first."

He tore a piece of rosemary bread from a cooling tray and placed it on the floor beside the table leg.

Meely didn't move toward it.

She watched him.

Listened.

He looked down again, voice just a thread.

"Some things aren't secrets. Just old truths waiting for the right question."

He turned and walked slowly back to the hearth, his footsteps fading into the crackle of flame.

Behind him, Meely did not follow.

She didn't eat the bread.

She sat.

Not as a cat.

As a sentinel.

And Eloi had no time to dwell on stubborn creatures. She, too, was a being forged for belonging, for witness. And tonight, so was he.

He paused near the hearth, looked back once.

"Shall I show you a new trick I've remembered?"

The cat blinked, puzzled—but curious.

Eloi touched the pendant at his chest.

"Luminaris segni."

The obsidian spiral burned dimly red.

A gust of wind surged from nowhere, circling the dining hall—and with a sigh, every flame extinguished at once.

The pendant faded. But the room remained changed.

Something old stirred.

A memory surfaced.

A word rose up without permission—first as a shape in his mouth, wrong enough to tighten his jaw.

"Orr...eth." He frowned, as if listening to his own tongue.

He didn't know where he had heard the name.

Not in this life. Not in any story told aloud.

But the declaration clung to him, like ash to breath.

He pressed his palm flat against the spice wall, steadying himself, as his gaze drifted to the dying fire.

He stared.

Too long.

Then turned away.

Maybe it meant nothing.

Maybe it meant everything.

The oldest records lived in the library.

If the name had meaning... the answer would be there.

And Eloi was no longer afraid of answers.

Three bells rang above—hollow, low, drawn like breath through stone.

A quarter to seven.

He dusted his hands, turned from the hearth.

He would wait.

Let the halls empty.

Then he would go.

He closed the dining hall door behind him.

He did not turn back to straighten the benches.

The corridor beyond was bathed in moonlight—silver poured through stone.

As his steps echoed forward, he began to hum.

The same old tune.

This time, it felt like coming home.

***

The room had grown cold around him, but Leonarth hadn't noticed.

Sleep had hovered once, like breath on glass—then vanished. Not chased, not banished. Just... unwelcome. A guest who sensed it wasn't safe to stay.

The bell rang once.

Beyond the walls, the Abbey held its breath. Not peace—but poise. Stillness with a spine. As if the stones themselves were listening for a sound not yet given. Even the wind seemed to hesitate at the windows, brushing the panes like it had forgotten how to knock.

A second chime followed. Leonarth turned on his cot, the thin blanket twisting at his ankles. He lay still, eyes fixed on the low timber beams above, their grain warped by centuries. He hadn't moved in hours. Hadn't spoken. But something moved inside him.

Not fear. Not memory.

Just a pulse—a ripple left behind in his chest. Like the echo of a voice never spoken. A shape in the silence that hadn't been there before the dining hall.

It was the same food. The same stewards. The same warmth the hearth had always given him. The same children blowing out candles for a name day he didn't even know. On the surface, it was all familiar.

But something had brushed against the edges of that moment. Something cold, just beneath the heat. A flicker—like light folded around someone who didn't belong in its glow.

He couldn't explain it. Couldn't name it. But he knew it had changed the air.

The bell rang again.

He whispered the count under his breath. "Four. Five. Six..."

The sound was distant, but too close. Like it rang through stone, not sky. "Seven. Eight. Nine. Ten."

Then silence.

Only then did he realize how dark the room had become. Most candles had guttered to stubs, their wax pooled like fallen time. What little glow remained curled meekly at the base of the dormitory walls. The rest had vanished—devoured by shadows that felt too still.

As if even the dark had begun to listen.

He looked to his left. Mattheon was curled into his blanket on the neighboring cot, Meely tucked like a guardian at his feet. Both were deep in sleep, their breathing synchronized—inhale, exhale—a quiet rhythm that should have calmed him. And yet, the last few days had unraveled any notion of calm.

Magic was real. He had seen it, felt it—not just once. And Mattheon's words from the attic still echoed in his thoughts, stubborn and scared: "It couldn't be, right? That's not real."

Leonarth pulled the blanket over his head, a child's instinct for protection, though he no longer believed in such things. His fingers reached beneath his pillow, fumbling for proof. Not of magic. Of meaning.

He touched the key.

It was warm again—not scalding, not cold—just impossibly alive. He brought it into view. It shimmered faintly, as if whispering to the air.

A jolt struck his chest. Something landed hard on his belly. He gasped. The key slipped from his hand and dropped to the floor with a faint metallic clink.

He threw off the blanket, heart hammering—and found Meely staring up at him, her fur still warm from sleep, her eyes ancient.

She hadn't pounced. She had arrived.

Maybe for warmth. Maybe for him. But there was something more. Some quiet understanding in her gaze. As if she'd felt the shift too—not just in the Abbey, but in him.

She curled against him, her paws pressing softly into his side, and something in his chest finally settled. Her presence was absurdly comforting. Like a lullaby without music. Like the idea of kin he'd never known, but somehow missed.

His thoughts turned bitter. Mattheon had remembered something—someone. A mother. A name.

Leonarth had nothing. Just the ache of absence. And shame for even feeling it.

He reached to stroke Meely's fur. She purred, once—reluctant, almost as if caught off-guard by her own softness—then bounded from the bed like the moment had passed.

The room stilled.

Then the key on the floor began to pulse.

A dull rhythm. Then brighter. Warmer.

Leonarth leaned over to retrieve it, but Meely was faster. She darted forward, jaws closing gently around the key's neck.

"Hey—" he began, sitting up.

But the cat didn't wait. She looked at him once—not playful, not confused—and bolted toward the door, tail flicking like punctuation.

She vanished into the corridor, taking the key with her.

Leonarth sat frozen.

Something had begun.

He wasn't sure what, but what had started could not be stopped now. He had too many questions, and the way Ava and Gwendlynn had been watching him lately was a clear give-away.

They knew more than they'd admitted. But why now? Why the silence? Why the charade?

The bell rang once again—10:15 p.m. The subtle sound brought Leonarth back to the problem at hand. The mysterious key was gone, and he had to follow it. See it through. He was no longer just a boy seeking belonging. Something in him had shifted. He felt it. He was searching for meaning—and that key held the next piece.

He slipped out of bed, quietly. Thrust on his sneakers. Grabbed the first coat hanging by the door—too long, too loose. It draped around him more like a cloak.

"Perfect," he muttered inwardly, adjusting the coat's oversized sleeves. "A lost boy in a borrowed cloak, pretending to be more than he is."

The hallway bit his cheeks with cold. A gust slid down the corridor like a warning. He tried to pull the cloak tighter, stumbled, nearly fell. As he caught himself, Meely darted past—a streak of fur and urgency, headed toward the library.

He almost called after her, caught himself. Too loud. Too dangerous.

When he reached the entrance to the library, unease set in. Not fear—but that same pull he'd felt once before. Like he was opening a door someone else had already walked through. The kind of door that doesn't close easily behind you.

The library door was ajar.

It never was.

He hesitated. Memory flashed: Maurice, long ago. "Not all books are meant to be read, Leonarth. Some just wait to be remembered." At the time, the words felt cryptic. Now… they felt like a warning.

He stepped inside.

The warmth was immediate. Familiar. He let the cloak fall just inside the door.

Lavender. Ink. Old paper. Something else—not scent, but impression. A hum in the bones—faint and familiar. As if someone, somewhere, had been humming not to be heard, but to be remembered. A tune half-recalled, not quite melody, not quite silence—and for a breathless second, he thought he recognized it. But no one sang at this hour. Not here. Not now.

The scent in the air shifted too—lavender, yes, but under it, something softer. Something almost human. A presence without presence. Not enough to name. Just enough to ache.

He shook his head. Imagination. Echoes.

Something brushed his leg.

Meely.

"What the hell do you want from me, cat?" he whispered.

She tilted her head. That impossible gaze. That knowing.

"Are you teasing me, Meely?"

A pause.

And then—

I blinked.

The shift happened so quietly, I almost didn't notice. The breath I took didn't feel like mine. The air pressed differently against my skin. My thoughts... weren't outside me anymore.

They were me.

And suddenly, I wasn't just watching this moment.

I was inside it.

***

Meely lunged for the nearest shelf, her sudden motion startling and sharp—a blur of fur and tension. Her front paws brushed past my face so closely I felt the breath of her claws stir the fine hairs on my cheek. My heart lurched; had I not jerked backward instinctively, I might have been slashed.

The motion was over in a blink, but the shock lingered. A jolt of fear surged through me—not for Meely, but for what her precision meant. She hadn't misstepped. She'd chosen that angle, that speed.

And I couldn't shake the feeling she hadn't aimed to miss.

But instead, her claws found purchase on the wooden frame, and as she scrambled upward, she dropped more than just the key she carried in her mouth. A cascade of books tumbled from the shelf, their bindings groaning like voices waking from long silence.

Dust erupted around me, thick and defiant—the kind that clings to forgotten things. It swirled in the air like ash from ancient parchment, reluctant to be disturbed. These books weren't just neglected; they had been sealed in time.

The sound of their fall was thunderous in the stillness. If anyone had been inside the library already, they would've heard. There was no more hiding now.

The key had landed inches from me. Its pulse had stopped—no thrum, no glow—but its warmth lingered like breath pressed into metal. As I picked it up, a soft tingling ran along my fingertips, as though static clung to its surface. The air around me thickened for a heartbeat, laced with a scent I couldn't place—like singed cedar and something faintly sweet, maybe lavender, maybe old ink. My breath caught. This wasn't just an object. It was waiting. Remembering.

I reached instinctively for the nearest book, brushing away the dust with my hands. The cover resisted at first, as though resenting the interruption.

But the title emerged, faint beneath the grime.

It was thin and threadbare, the kind you'd expect to see in a child's hands, not buried in a library this old. The spine read:

Fables of the Forgotten East:
Myths and Inheritances Beyond the Veil

The second was heavier, bound in red hide with a clasp that had long since lost its lock. I brushed dust from the cover:

Chronicles of the Fifth Kingdom

I hesitated on the third. It hadn't fallen like the others. It leaned—almost deliberately—from the shelf, angled just slightly forward as if nudging me.

My fingers curled around it. Smaller than the others, plain grey binding. No title.

Inside, the first page bore neat, etched script:

Treatise on Lineage and Legacy: Rootmarks in Post-Concordian Eras

I flipped through, slow at first. Pages filled with ancient line diagrams, annotations in cramped, spidery handwriting—not Maurice's. Older. Each line scratched with purpose.

Then I saw it.

Near the middle, boxed in with thick ink, as though someone had needed it to stay.

"Even silence has memory. Especially silence."

I stared at the phrase. My breath caught.

The room didn't feel empty anymore. The shelves leaned in. The air seemed to pause—not cold, not warm, just present.

It was like the book had said it aloud.

Not a voice. But memory itself, whispering through the pages.

Meely hissed—not in fear, but in warning.

Her eyes were fixed on the far side of the library, unblinking.

I turned slowly.

A shadow moved at the edge of the stacks. Just beyond the last column, where the torchlight faltered.

Not a shadow.

A figure.

Cloaked. Hooded. The fabric shimmered like smoke against stone, absorbing the dim light.

I dropped the book without thinking. My fingers searched the floor behind me until they found the spine of a lower shelf.

I slid down, back pressing into the wood, breath caught in my throat. Meely didn't move from her perch above. She crouched low, her tail flicking once, twice—then still.

Footsteps.

Slow.

Intentional.

The kind of steps that belong to someone who already knows where they're going.

And who—or what—they're going for.

My pulse pounded in my ears. I could hear the blood in my neck, feel the thrum of the key still clenched in my hand like it was bound to me.

I risked a glance beneath the lowest shelf. Boots. Black leather. Soft soles. Each step placed with surgical precision.

Meely's tail twitched again.

Closer now.

A breath, sharp and low, escaped the figure. A scent followed—damp stone and something metallic, like the air before lightning.

I didn't dare breathe.

The figure turned. Just slightly. Enough that the light from the nearby sconce revealed the edge of a gloved hand. Fingers tightened. A flash of steel—short, curved—glinted for an instant, then vanished beneath the cloak again.

Meely's body rippled.

Then—

A single growl. Low. Guttural.

The attacker froze—mid-motion, mid-breath—like a chord abruptly severed. Leonarth felt the pressure in the room shift, as though the walls themselves had gone still. The figure's hand hung in the air, fingers twitching not from hesitation, but from the jolt of something unseen, something ancient. A silent force had made itself known—not violent, but undeniable.

And in that brief moment, something snapped in the air. Not sound. Not light. But burden. As if the library itself had noticed.

My breath returned. Ragged. Real.

And I knew—

I wasn't just being hunted.

Something had called them here.

And whatever they wanted…

Was me.

The bell rang twice—10:30 p.m. Then silence returned, abrupt and cavernous. The sound had vanished so quickly it felt unnatural, like a breath caught mid-sigh. I could count the seconds by the beat of my heart, and each thump seemed to echo in my ears, growing louder in the vacuum left behind.

Only then did I notice the key in my hand again—or rather, notice how fiercely I had been clutching it. My palm burned with its imprint, its shape seared into my skin like a forgotten truth returned. I loosened my grip. And as my fingers unfurled, the key pulsed once more—quiet, deliberate—just as it grazed the spine of the book that still lay beside me on the floor.

A sign. Intentional. Undeniable.

I grabbed it and stood, my steps uneven but gathering strength. I moved toward the door I had avoided before—not because it was wrong, but because fear had pinned me where I hid. The hallway yawned ahead, but I did not hesitate.

I was still shaken from the earlier encounter, my limbs trembling from adrenaline and something more ancient—instinct. But in its place now was a thread of courage, frayed yet certain. And a new purpose, one I hadn't chosen but had always belonged to me. Not in words. Not in thought. But etched somewhere deep—scribbled in marrow.

Crossing the central reading room, I saw—no, felt—the shift.

A shadow moved.

At the edge of my vision, something slid from behind a statue—a saint I hadn't noticed before. Too fast for warning. Too silent for escape. It lunged.

There was no face. No words. Only the blur of motion and a rage that felt borrowed—or buried.

Steel flashed. Glyphs shimmered. And pain—sharp, invasive—bloomed low on my back. I collapsed forward, breath torn from my chest.

I barely had time to flinch before Meely's cry cut the air. She launched herself from the shelves above, claws unsheathed. She struck the figure's arm mid-motion—the same hand that had lifted the blade. The cloak faltered. The attacker recoiled. Blood splattered against the worn stone.

A hiss—part growl, part curse—curled into the air. But it might've been my own pulse, stuttering beneath fading vision.

The figure caught Meely mid-lunge and hurled her against a nearby case. Wood cracked. She yelped and disappeared into the shadows.

Another strike came for me—this time for my heart, and I saw it in the glint above.

But the key, still clenched in my hand, answered.

No flame. No flash. Just meaning.

It ignited with warmth, not heat—familiarity, not fury. It wasn't an object of destruction. It was something else entirely. Something bound to me by emotion, by ancestry, by truths I hadn't yet earned.

Thump… thump…

My body numbed, but I felt it—the way sound vanishes before a wave crashes.

Then—

A shield. Not seen, but felt.

It exploded outward, raw and primal, a ripple that surged from my chest like defiance made manifest.

Shelves toppled. Air cracked. Glyphs flickered—just for an instant—before dissolving into the grain of the wood.

I fell sideways, not from impact, but from something else… like slipping out of time itself. The floor didn't tilt, yet it felt as if the axis of the world had shifted beneath me. The shelves stretched and blurred, becoming streaks of light and shadow, and the cold air twisted with the scent of burning parchment and rain-soaked earth. My limbs were weightless. My mind, unmoored. For a single breathless moment, I wasn't falling at all—I was being unwritten.

My thoughts scattered. My vision blurred. And then—

It was no longer me looking.

Leonarth lay on the floor, limbs slack, breath shallow. The attacker staggered, cloak torn, one hand gripping a bloodied forearm. Drips marked the stone like falling ink.

The figure approached.

Closer.

Not fast. Not slow. Just certain.

A hand hovered near his temple—reverent, not cruel.

And the voice that came was soft. Not familiar. But not foreign. It carried a tremor of something lost—like regret folded into memory, or the last sigh of a name never spoken aloud. A warning wrapped in longing. A touch of recognition so faint, it might've only belonged to dreams.

"You weren't supposed to remember… not yet."

A pause.

"But you did."

Leonarth's vision caught only the eyes—not face, not shape—but eyes. And they didn't hold hatred. Only something far more dangerous:

Pride.

A smile followed—gentle. Sorrow-tinged. As if mourning a choice already made.

But Leonarth had not seen it.

His heart slowed—but only in rhythm, not urgency. He was counting again, the memory of the bells overlapping with his pulse. "One… Thump… Three…"

The numbers blurred. He wasn't sure if they were echoes from earlier, or if time itself had fractured. Something in him shattered—not from the blade, but from the kindness in the eyes that had held it.

And though no bells rang now, the silence carried their ghost. A resonance caught between muscle and memory—as if the world was still trying to tell him something.

The bells were no longer ringing.

It was a quarter to eleven. The figure dissolved into the shadows with no name, and no trace as Leonarth's last thoughts faded into oblivion: "A smile…familiar…like it was proud of me."

Leonarth's head rolled to the side, lips parting in a shallow breath that barely stirred the air. The library loomed over him in silence—a silence that did not belong to stone alone.

***

Meely's breath rasped like torn silk, each step a stitch pulled loose by pain—but she did not falter. She ran, not from fear, but because something older than instinct had already chosen her path. Not away from danger—but toward hope. Toward help.

The Abbey's bell tolled once more—the last stroke of the eleventh hour. Its chime rang sharp through stone corridors, slicing silence with a finality that made time feel brittle. Beneath it, another sound pulsed faintly, tethered to a body collapsed in the library: a heartbeat, staggered and thin. Leonarth's.

She felt the bond inside her stretch, pull, flicker. Not in the way of flesh, but of enchantment—a thread woven long ago, now fraying in places she could no longer see. Her paws moved faster. Her breath hitched. Something old was waking inside her—not memory reclaimed, but purpose returning. A warmth at the base of her spine where a spell once anchored something deeper—whatever it truly meant.

She did not understand what was breaking. Only that something once meant to protect was beginning to slip—and she had no time to wonder why.

The walls blurred around her. Not from speed, but from urgency. She was faltering, yes—her side throbbed, and her paws left tiny red marks on the flagstones—but her purpose surged stronger than the pain. Each turn of corridor was carved into her instincts. Too many years spent weaving between these stones. Too many nights sleeping where she could watch them breathe. Waiting for this. For the moment she had been crafted to meet.

She slipped through the half-closed door of the dormitory—the very one Leonarth had left ajar before walking into whatever fate had chosen for him. Inside, rows of sleeping forms exhaled soft warmth. The hearth had long since dimmed, but the air still held a hush—thick with dreams not yet broken.

Meely moved low, soundless. A wisp in the dark. She crawled beneath the beds like a current of breath, her whiskers twitching as she searched. The scents of sleep and soot drifted around her, but one thread rose above the rest—warm, restless, familiar. She followed it like a map drawn in the dark. When she reached the right one, she paused. Then leapt.

Mattheon awoke with a gasp, his body jerking as claws pressed against his chest. For a moment, he flailed—arms striking at air, mouth open in confusion—until his eyes adjusted and met the creature's gaze. Bleeding. Breathing in sharp, unnatural rhythms. Staring at him with a purpose that did not belong to any cat.

"What—Meely?" he whispered, voice barely forming around the name. She was cold to the touch. Wet.

He reached out gently. She swatted his hand—not to hurt, but to warn.

"Ow," he muttered, wincing more from shock than pain. "I'm trying to help. What do you want from me?"

She didn't answer, of course. Instead, she turned—and with surprising force for her size, sprang up again. But not onto him.

She landed on the empty bed across from Mattheon's.

Leonarth's bed.

The covers were half-thrown, twisted toward the edge as if someone had risen suddenly. One slipper remained under the bed, the other missing. The pillow bore the imprint of a head—but it had long since cooled. He had been there. And left. Alone.

Mattheon's heart thudded. He sat up straighter.

"Leonarth?" he whispered, but it felt foolish the moment it left his lips. The absence spoke louder than any answer.

He looked back at Meely.

Bleeding. Staring. Waiting.

That was when it clicked. The blood. The look. The empty bed.

His chest tightened. Every instinct screamed the same truth—Leonarth wasn't just missing. He was in trouble. And if Meely had bled to reach him, there was no time to waste.

He didn't know why she had come to him, of all people. But the blood said hurry. And the empty bed said everything else.

"Something happened to him," he breathed. "And you… you saw it."

She leapt down with a grunt, landing hard, then staggering toward the door. Blood followed. A trail, fading but real.

For one breath, he hesitated. Then Mattheon threw off his covers, grabbing the thickest blanket he could reach. No time for boots. No time for questions. He wrapped it around himself like a cloak and followed.

The hallway air bit with cold, and the Abbey's breath met his skin like a slap. He reached the door—just as the trailing edge of his blanket caught in it. With a tug, the wood slammed shut behind him.

The sound cracked through the silence like a bone snapping. Mattheon froze. The echo lingered.

He glanced back—knowing full well what that noise might have stirred—then let the blanket go. Barefoot and breathless, he bolted into the night after the bleeding cat, unaware that behind him, stirred by that door's final protest, others were already waking.

***

The sound cracked through the Abbey like a verdict.

A door, somewhere near the eastern wing, had slammed hard enough to shake the silence—not a draft, not the wind. Something alive. Urgent.

Maurice lifted his head from prayer. The wooden beads of his rosary stilled between his fingers. He had been kneeling for some time, whispering the old words not because he expected an answer, but because they gave him shape when the world around him threatened to blur.

He listened.

Then he rose.

Elsewhere in the Abbey, the echo of that door reached other ears—ears trained to wake at the smallest fracture in the night. Gwendlynn heard it too.

From her private chambers, she looked up from the tea she had not yet finished. Steam curled against the rim of the porcelain, its warmth brushing her cheek as if in farewell. Her robe was still drawn tight, her silver hair pinned loosely behind her head. The window beside her was open just enough to let in the night air.

Then—movement.

A blur. Fast. Low to the ground.

And behind it, a boy. Barefoot, bare-chested, the boy ran through the grass with nothing between him and the cold but urgency, his silhouette stark and fragile in the moonlight. He chased something that shimmered just out of definition.

She dropped the cup.

It shattered on the stone, and still, she did not move to gather it. Her hand gripped the sill instead, knuckles whitening. The creature—she could not see it clearly—but the way it moved, the path it traced across the yard... there was something about it. Something her body recognized before her mind could place.

The boy, though—she knew him. Mattheon. Following as if summoned.

And then she understood.

She threw on her cloak and bolted from the room, faster than her joints had allowed in years.

Maurice reached the courtyard at the same time she did.

He had not seen the blur. Only the boy. Only the look in Mattheon's eyes—part fear, part instinct—like something was pulling him forward and tearing him open all at once.

Gwendlynn and Maurice locked eyes.

No words. Just a nod. She gestured toward the windows of the east wing—Ava was watching, her mouth parted to speak, but Gwendlynn raised a single hand. Stay. We've got him.

Mabelle's window was dark. Too dark. Maurice and Gwendlynn let the thought pass—or tried to—and followed the boy.

The Abbey was different at night—not darker, but older. Every hallway whispered. Every carved arch remembered too much. As they crossed the cloister and reached the outer library doors, the air changed. It thickened—as if the space itself held its breath.

But when they entered the library, the boy was gone.

No sign of him. No sound. Only the stillness of shelves and the lingering trace of movement that had ended too suddenly.

And then they saw Leonarth.

Sprawled on the stone floor between two towering bookcases. His limbs were twisted in a way that suggested he had not simply collapsed—he had been dropped. Or drained.

Meely was nowhere to be seen.

"Mattheon?" Gwendlynn called softly.

A shuffle. From the shadows near the far column.

"I'm here," came the whispered reply. He stepped into the candlelight, wide-eyed, face pale, barefoot and trembling. "I didn't know what to do. He was like this when I got here."

Maurice moved to him and placed a hand on his shoulder—gently, grounding him.

"You did exactly what you were meant to," he said.

Mattheon nodded slowly, eyes never leaving his companion.

Gwendlynn was the first to kneel beside Leonarth.

"Leonarth," she whispered, brushing the hair from his forehead. It clung to his skin, damp with sweat. His lips were pale. But he was breathing—shallow, ragged, but breathing.

Maurice's eyes swept the space. Not just for threats. For meaning.

Then he saw them: the key, gripped tightly in Leonarth's left hand. The book in his right. Both clutched so fiercely they looked carved into bone.

He reached forward, reverent, and tried to pry the book free. At first it didn't budge. But then—as if the boy's muscles had heard something even in unconsciousness—they softened.

He took it. Heavy. Bound in sigil-threaded leather, warm to the touch. The glyphs on its cover shimmered faintly—only when he turned it just so.

Gwendlynn gently pried the key from Leonarth's other hand.

The moment she did, a subtle hum moved through the floor. Not loud. Not magical in the showy sense. But ancient—like something buried had shifted in its sleep. She didn't recognize it—not truly—but its weight carried a quiet authority. Something in its shape, its feel, resisted familiarity. It was not ordinary. Not made for locks.

This was a key that unlocked ideas… destinies.

They looked at each other.

"No one must see these until we understand," she said, voice low, tight with warning.

Maurice nodded once. He tucked the book into the folds of his cloak, feeling its weight settle against his ribs like a second heartbeat. Gwendlynn slipped the key into her sleeve.

"Help me carry him," she said.

Together, they lifted Leonarth. Mattheon stood frozen for a moment before following, staying close.

As they crossed the corridor toward the infirmary, moonlight pooled in long, silver corridors beneath their feet. The Abbey no longer slept—it watched.

Somewhere behind them, Meely watched from the rafters—wounded, invisible, and unseen.

As they passed the chapel, the bell above gave no sound—but the wind stirred the glass in its tower, and the moonlight refracted in sudden shards across the floor, like a path made of memory and meaning.

By the time they reached the infirmary, the boy had not woken—but the color in his cheeks was no longer entirely gone.

Gwendlynn stayed by his side. Maurice stood watch at the door. Mattheon sat silently by the fire, arms wrapped around his knees, eyes fixed on the still form in the bed.

None of them would sleep that night.

Not now that the book had opened its eyes. And something else—something long-locked—had stirred in answer.

Somewhere above, the bell tolled once—a low, solemn note that shivered through the stone.

Eleven fifteen. The Abbey's heart was still beating. But faster now.

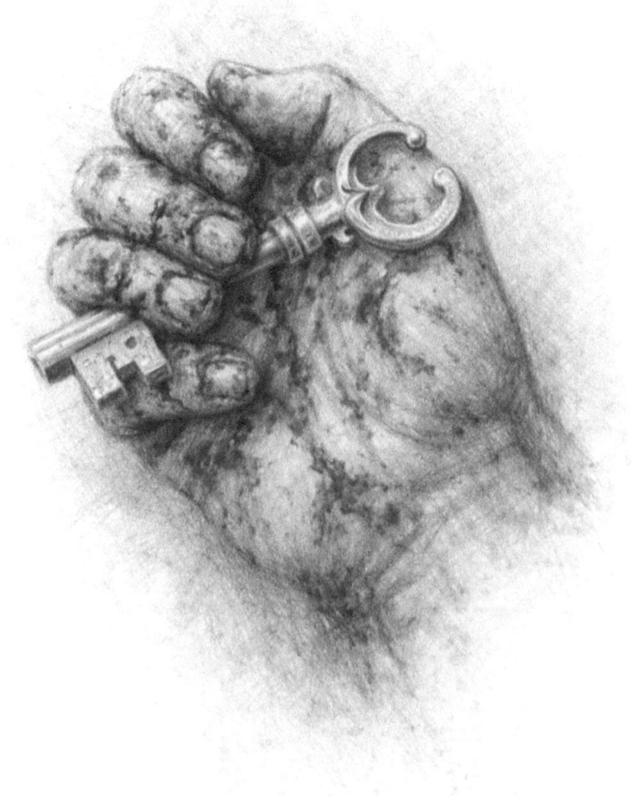

Chapter Twenty-One

"Echoes We Buried"

The Abbey had learned to whisper again. The hush carried the weight of things unspoken, a living thing that coiled in the arches and refused to be chased away. Three days had passed since the night in the library, though the hours clung to one another like damp pages. Morning light still reached the stone in cautious strokes, as if testing whether it was safe to enter.

In the cloisters, voices curved around corners instead of crossing them. Footsteps thinned to a hush. Even the air seemed to skirt the places where blood had been—like memory avoiding a door it did not wish to open.

Leonarth lay in the infirmary, breath whispering in and out, pale and unwavering as a candle fighting its last inch of wick.

Around him, the sisters moved like trained shadows, each step softened, each glance measured. No one dared name what had happened; to speak it would sharpen its fangs.

He shifted toward the narrow window, where morning sun fractured through leaded glass into scattered shards. A sting lanced across his back—fresh stitches pulling. Each knot felt like a bead strung on a thread of survival, tight enough to remind him he was still tethered here.

But the memory had left more than torn skin. Sometimes it came as a shiver that had nothing to do with cold, the phantom chill of steel grazing bone. His fingers twitched once beneath the blanket, as if they still braced for another strike. Even the sun through the window seemed hesitant to touch him, as though it too remembered.

And the book. There was that peculiar book.

Its weight. Its warmth. The strange handwriting scored into its pages like truths pressed into oak.

But it wasn't the diagrams or the age of the ink that unsettled him—it was the subject itself.

Who wrote books about bloodlines?

In the classrooms of the world he'd grown up in, such things were curiosities for royal scandals or old novels, not the spine of history.

Yet here, lineage was treated as foundation, as if ancestry itself could dictate the fate of nations.

It read like myth disguised as fact—as if the names alone could bear the weight of cities, as if a bloodline could be both the map and the empire it ruled. The idea was absurd, yet the pages carried it with such authority that he almost felt foolish for doubting.

And the text spoke casually of post-Concordium eras—a term that belonged to no map, no history book, no shared memory he'd ever encountered—like a date etched in a calendar he was never taught to read.

He felt a strange vertigo, as though he'd stumbled into a museum where every plaque described events that had never happened, in rooms that had never existed.

The history he knew wasn't incomplete. It was alien to whatever this was.

And the note… the note spoke of Silence. Not the absence of sound, but the absence of truth—a silence patient as winter, hiding in marrow until it chose to wake. Why was it everywhere now? Why did it seem to follow him?

Then came the other thing—not named, not understood, but older and stranger than anything he'd dared to imagine. It had risen through him unbidden, raw and unmeasured, as though the marrow of his bones had remembered what his mind refused. In the past, he and Mattheon had skirted the word, brushing its edges like boys testing the cold of a forbidden river.

Magic.

Not real. Not possible. And yet, impossibly tangible—a presence his hands could feel even if his mind still refused to believe.

But in the library there had been no space for denial. Whatever had thrown his attacker back had not been skill or luck—it had been that word, breathing through him, claiming him. He felt its echo still, low and stubborn in his chest, like an ember that refused to go dark.

He let the thought rest there. Heavy. Dangerous.

For years, the blankness before his arrival here had been a wall without door or window. Now, something stirred behind it—a shadowed shape, a waiting purpose. It pressed against the wall as though the smallest crack might let it spill through.

In the hollow of his ribs, he felt the truth: the ember was no longer content to wait.

A touch—light, deliberate—anchored him. He turned.

Gwendlynn stood beside the bed, her hand still on his shoulder, eyes holding a question she had carried for days.

And for the first time since the library, he wondered—with a sudden, disquieting certainty—if she already knew the answer.

For a moment, neither spoke. The weight between them was its own language.

"You've been in my thoughts more than you know," she said at last, her voice low, shaped by something heavier than concern.

Leonarth frowned. "Why? I've barely—I mean… I'm fine. Mostly."

Her gaze lingered on his face as though searching for someone she had known before he was born. "You were in the library. You found something."

He hesitated. "I… didn't find it. It was… strange. Like it wanted to be found. The book was there, on the shelf, but when I touched it—it moved. Opened. Like it had been waiting for me. The pages…" He swallowed, the memory alive in his fingertips. "They felt warm. Alive. And the words—they weren't just written, they… spoke."

Gwendlynn's breath caught, almost too quietly to hear. "What did they say?"

"Something about bloodlines. A history I've never heard of. And there was a phrase—'Even silence has memory. Especially silence.' It… it felt like it was meant for me."

"And… there was the key," he added after a pause, as though the thought had only now caught up to him. "It was in my hand the whole time. I don't even remember picking it up, but I—I was holding it when…" He stopped, unsure why he was mentioning it at all. "It just… felt important."

Gwendlynn's gaze flicked to his hands before she could stop herself, the movement so quick it could have been mistaken for a blink. "Keys have a way of finding hands that need them," she said lightly, but the quiet in her tone carried something heavier, something Leonarth didn't hear.

"And then—" His voice faltered, eyes darkening. "Then the attacker came."

"Tell me," she said, and there was no gentleness in it, only need.

Leonarth told her—of the shadowed figure, the glint of steel, the scent of rain-soaked stone that still clung in his mind, the moment Meely leapt, the sting of the blade in his back. How the room had seemed to lean in, how something inside him had risen and struck without thought. He did not say the word magic again, but it hovered in the space between them.

When he finished, she was silent for a long time. Too long.

"You're certain the book opened on its own?"

"Yes. Like it recognized me."

Her eyes dropped, as if she were hiding a fracture in her composure. "Perhaps it did."

Leonarth studied her face, sensing the layers he could not see through. "Do you know why?"

She looked at him then, and for an instant the warmth in her gaze was tinged with something else—sorrow sharpened into resolve. "Some answers," she said, "come before you're ready. And some… wait until the asking costs more than the truth."

He didn't understand, not fully. But he felt the truth in her tone, and it left a shadow on his thoughts.

Gwendlynn's hand lingered a moment longer on his shoulder before she withdrew, her voice steady but quieter now. "Rest, Leonarth. There's more in this than you yet see."

And as she turned to leave, the question he hadn't thought to ask pressed itself somewhere deep and unnameable—why her eyes, in that last glance, looked so much like his own.

The door whispered open again before she could take her first step into the hall.

Eloi entered, quiet as a breath, carrying a small tray with broth and bread. His smile was the kind meant to soothe without asking for words.

"Still giving the nurses trouble, I hear," he said softly, setting the tray on the table by Leonarth's bed.

Leonarth managed the shadow of a grin. "Only the ones who try to feed me."

Eloi chuckled, then adjusted the blanket at Leonarth's shoulder with the easy familiarity of someone who had done so before. His right hand moved awkwardly—slower than the left—and Leonarth noticed the thick bandage wrapped around his palm and wrist.

"What happened to your hand?"

"Kitchen mishap," Eloi said too quickly, glancing away. "Knives don't forgive distraction."

The words carried an ease so practiced, they could coax warmth into the coldest soul and leave it believing it had always been there. Eloi had that gift—a presence that settled like a trusted hand on the shoulder—but today Leonarth sensed something different in it, a warmth edged with heat, the kind that seared instead of soothed.

Eloi stayed only a few minutes more, fussing over the broth, smoothing the sheets, speaking of nothing important. But his eyes, when they lingered, carried the same unspoken weight as Gwendlynn's.

When he left, the room felt colder.

***

Gwendlynn stepped into the corridor. The hush of the Abbey pressed close, broken only by the faint drip of water somewhere distant.

She moved with purpose, each step pulling her further from the boy she had wanted to hold and closer to the man who might help her protect him.

Her shoulders were square, but her fingers curled once at her sides, as though they itched to hold him and didn't trust themselves to let go. She masked it in her stride, but the ache moved with her.

She needed to see the book—and Maurice.

Or rather, the man he had been before he took that name.

Keralis—the Inquisitor who had once defected from the very order that guarded such secrets. A name that carried the scent of old trials and the echo of halls where verdicts outlived the voices that pronounced them.

He had kept the book since that night, and only he could draw from it what lay hidden—with the practiced eye of one who knew which truths to coax into the light, and which to leave sleeping in the dark.

Her hands flexed at her sides, remembering the restraint it had taken not to tell Leonarth everything. Not to claim him openly. The ache of it burned low in her chest.

Because once the truth was spoken, it could not be taken back.

And once spoken, it would wake things they were not yet ready to face.

The Calventherath would feel it—the faint tightening of a snare no one else could see—and somewhere in that unseen dark, something would lean closer.

She lengthened her stride, shadows stretching around her as she turned toward the west hall where Maurice kept his study. Each step was an unspoken vow—to wait, to guard, to be ready.

A draft caught the hem of her sleeve, carrying with it the cold mineral reek after rain—the same that Leonarth had described. She did not look back, but her steps slowed for just a breath.

But the ache remained, pulsing with every heartbeat, refusing to be silenced, as somewhere far beyond the Abbey's stone—in a place where magic still ruled and remembered—something shifted.

***

Morning light pooled across the oak desk.

It caught in scars along its surface—shallow cuts, burns, the faint ring of inkpots now gone. Marks left by a steadier hand in another life, when truth was written not to preserve, but to condemn.

Dust drifted like ash in slow fall, disturbed only by the steady rasp of a quill. Maurice's script was deliberate, each stroke carrying the weight of a man who had once chronicled verdicts that could end a life.

The book lay to his right.

Closed.

Waiting.

Its weight tilted the stack beneath it, claiming the desk as its own. For days he had kept it shut—not out of fear, but because some truths demand stillness. Some truths refuse to be summoned. They must arrive.

Sunlight grazed its spine, catching the faint impressions of a clasp long gone. The feel of it in the room was less an object than a presence—one that had waited longer than any of them had lived.

The Abbey was too quiet.

Not peaceful.

Poised.

A silence with edges—aware, deliberate.

Somewhere beyond the study, a floorboard sighed.

His pen stilled. A bead of ink swelled at the nib, then fell—dotting the margin like a sealed vow.

The knock—sharp, urgent—fractured the morning.

Gwendlynn entered without pause, her steps fast, breath held as if the truth might outrun her. She closed the door with finality, severing the quiet behind her. The air shifted.

Her eyes locked onto the book, then Maurice. "I need to speak with you," she said, the words barely sheathed.

Maurice studied her, the instinct of the Inquisitor long dulled but not gone. The way her hand hovered near her pocket. The tremor beneath her control.

"Something's pressing you," he said.

"Leonarth spoke of the book—and the key." Her voice didn't shake, but it carried something worse: certainty. "Things he should not know. And he was attacked, Maurice. Steel in the dark. A shadow that meant to end him. That wasn't chance. A sleeper thread moved—whether Calventherath or something worse. Which means someone in Magicia knows."

She stepped closer. "Knows who he is. Or who he might become."

The room seemed to lean inward.

Maurice's hand withdrew from the page. The ink drying there felt irrelevant.

"We both saw what happened," he said, but the words landed brittle. He exhaled. "I thought we had more time."

He turned to the window.

Outside, the sisters moved like a lullaby—shears trimming rose stems, hands brushing soil, nothing aware of the fracture unfolding just beyond the glass. One looked up. Their eyes met. She smiled faintly and turned away. Maurice lifted his hand to acknowledge her, then lowered it, hollowed.

"We need to bring the others," he said at last. "Ava. Mabelle. The boys—together, contained, before the truth leaks."

He leaned forward. His fingers traced the wood as if looking for the grain of some forgotten path. "The relics surfaced for a reason. We didn't find them. They found us. The Veil kept them apart, but something older than protocol is unraveling that."

"The Calventherath is awake," he said. "Now it's our move."

Gwendlynn's jaw tightened, but her eyes had softened. "The moment is close. We've held our silences. But none of us—not Ava, not Mabelle, not the boys—can remain apart. Not now."

He looked at her, and in that look she saw the weight he carried—not the authority of Keralis, but the exhaustion of the man who outlived him.

"And when the relics touched," he said, voice low, "they resonated. Not like objects. Like memories recognizing each other."

She reached into her pocket.

The key glinted as she placed it in his palm. Their fingers brushed. Something shimmered—not visibly, not aloud, but like breath held between two verses.

"Yes," he whispered. "This key." He turned it slowly in his hand, like it might betray a name.

"I saw one like it before. When I was Keralis. We used them to unlock certain seals—truths bound not just to object, but to blood. Inheritance written in silence."

"Then we bring them together," Gwendlynn said, her voice suddenly sharpened, regal again. "Let them see each other. Let the relics remember what we've forgotten."

He didn't answer right away. He watched the key.

Then her.

Then the book.

"Once we do this," he said finally, "we cross the threshold. No more secrets. No more safety."

"Better to be carried together," she replied, "than dragged apart."

The silence between them was no longer waiting. It was listening.

Maurice closed his hand over the key.

"We meet tonight," he said. "At Elodia's statue."

A pause.

"Tell Ava. Tell Mabelle. And bring the boys."

He looked again to the book.

"Tonight, the silence will break."

Behind them, the quill still bled ink into the margin—unmoving, but not forgotten.

And outside the window, unnoticed among the roses, Meely sat poised on her haunches.

She didn't blink. She didn't twitch. Her gaze was locked not on the birds or the garden beds, but toward the corridors that led to the west.

Watching.

Waiting.

***

They met at the foot of Elodia's statue—each one summoned by Gwendlynn's quiet command earlier that day, and each arriving with truths they no longer wished to carry alone.

It was night now, and the courtyard stones were slick with the night's return of mist—not the gentle veil of morning, but something colder, more deliberate, as if the Abbey itself had exhaled in anticipation.

Above them, the marble figure of Elodia loomed beneath lantern light, her outstretched arms not in benediction, but in burden. Her downward gaze did not welcome, but questioned—as if already measuring the weight of what was about to be said.

Ava arrived with Leonarth beside her, their silhouettes briefly merging in the mist before separating again. Her hand rested lightly on his shoulder—not possessive, but anchoring—a silent reminder of every step that had brought him to this night. Leonarth's steps were slower than usual, still stiff from the attack, but there was focus behind his eyes—something raw, and no longer dormant. Though neither spoke, the air between them was heavy with things unsaid.

Mabelle and Mattheon came next, the boy walking a half-step ahead, his chin high and shoulders squared too perfectly—the way a boy tries to wear armor not yet his. Mabelle followed close but without deference, her presence a quiet alertness honed through years of secrets. The gloves she now wore—the same ones she'd taken from her brother's trunk—were dulled by time and the lack of sentiment, relics from a brother whose affections had always been opaque, whose silences said more than his words. She wore them not from fondness, but because their weight reminded her that not every inheritance was chosen.

No warmth passed between the pairs. Only glances—some cautious, others searching. But the way they stood near each other betrayed the old bonds between them—of trust strained by silence, and truths too long withheld.

Meely, for her part, was not noticed. She did not arrive with the others. She would find her way into the shadows later, as she always had—not when summoned, but when needed.

Maurice came last. His cloak was pulled tightly at the collar, a holdover from his earlier meeting with Gwendlynn. He gave Ava a nod, acknowledged the boys with a flicker of his gaze, and lingered only a moment longer than needed on Mabelle. His gaze lingered just a moment longer on the gloves she wore—a subtle narrowing of the eyes, not in recognition, but in question. Something about them was off. He hadn't remembered her wearing them before. Not here. Not like this. Then he stepped back beneath the statue's gaze, his posture carved more from habit than ease.

They waited, not in uncertainty, but in stillness—each aware that the next movement would change everything. And then Gwendlynn stepped into view, as if drawn by the moment itself rather than by choice.

She did not speak at first. She simply stood before the statue, laying a hand on the weathered hem of Elodia's stone robe. Her expression was unreadable, but her presence changed the air.

Then she turned.

Her eyes moved slowly across the gathered faces—Ava, Maurice, Mabelle, the boys. Each carried a question they didn't voice. Her gaze softened, not with ease, but with recognition of what each had brought to this point. A slight nod to Maurice. A longer pause on Ava—not gratitude, but understanding. Toward Mabelle, something unreadable, almost sharp, but it passed quickly.

To Leonarth and Mattheon she said nothing. But the way she looked at them—as if trying to memorize them before they changed—was its own kind of greeting.

Her hand dropped from the statue's robe.

"There's a place we can go," she said. Her voice was quiet, but it cut through the mist like bellmetal. "One forgotten by most—for good reason. But not by me."

She let that settle before continuing, her gaze sweeping once more across the gathering.

"Before we move forward… did each of you bring what was asked?"

She did not wait for answers.

A few exchanged glances—Mabelle shifted her weight, one gloved hand tightening around the strap of the trunk; Ava offered the briefest incline of her head, already knowing what was required; Maurice gave a single nod, though his eyes flicked to Leonarth, who was staring not at anyone, but at the statue's hands. Mattheon said nothing, but his jaw tensed, as though holding back a question he no longer trusted them to answer.

Satisfied—or simply unwilling to delay—Gwendlynn turned and walked, her pace deliberate, her silence authoritative.

They followed—past the northern transept, through a corridor half-swallowed by ivy, down three turns and a descending stair that curved like a spiral uncoiling.

At the end of it stood a door of blackwood, veined with silver glyphs too faint to decipher.

Gwendlynn placed her hand to the center of it. No incantation. No key.

The door simply breathed open.

They entered, one by one.

Unseen, unheard, something smaller moved through the gap just before the blackwood met stone again. A flicker of fur. A shadow between shadows.

No one noticed. Not at first, but Meely was already inside.

The chamber beyond was smaller than it should have been.

Stone walls, high-arched and lined with ancient volumes, pressed close with the weight of unread memory. This was not a public room of the Abbey library, but one of its sealed wings—a place where records too volatile for common knowledge had been locked behind veils and vowels of silence.

Now, six souls gathered there—seven, if memory was to be counted—each having carried something of the past in hand or heart. But they had brought more than silence. Mattheon stepped forward first, lowering the worn trunk Mabelle had pressed into his arms and setting it down with a soft, decisive thud. Mabelle took the folded tapestry she carried and set it beside the trunk. Her hand followed, coming to rest at the latch. Her fingers lingered, but she did not open it—not yet.

Next, Ava removed a folded letter from the sleeve of her habit and handed it silently to Maurice. He placed it with the others. There was no need to open it—he already knew it by heart.

Gwendlynn stepped forward, her expression unreadable, and reached into the folds of her cloak. From it, she withdrew the small key—the very one she had taken from Leonarth's fingers the night of the attack, when his consciousness wavered between now and never. She placed it on the table with deliberate care, and across from her, Leonarth stirred.

His eyes locked on the key, recognition flashing behind them—not full memory, but something close. A phantom sensation pulsed in his palm, as if the metal still remembered the curve of his grip.

Maurice followed, drawing the lineage book from beneath his cloak. The aged leather gave a soft creak as he set it down beside the key, its warmth bleeding into the table's grain. It had not left his sight since the library, since the night Leonarth nearly bled into silence.

Only then did Gwendlynn unclasp her pendant—and the others followed suit—laying them gently with the relics, her fingers brushing the tabletop for a heartbeat longer than necessary.

Each item touched the wood with the hush of ritual. The air held still around them—like breath waiting to be released.

Each gesture was a thread in the weave of what had been hidden—and what could no longer be.

It was all there on the table, all together for the first time: the trunk, the tapestry, the letter, the key, the book, and the pendants. A collection not of artifacts, but of intentions.

Gwendlynn glanced momentarily at each of them and lifted her hand.

"Vallis Intra," she whispered.

Mabelle did not speak. She bowed her head instead, hands still—her part was the keeping, not the naming

Maurice echoed, "Nomen Obscuratum."

Ava added, "Memoria Taceat."

The air shimmered, an old containment practice, meant to keep truth from traveling. The chamber sealed itself—not with locks, but with silence so deep it had shape.

Leonarth's head tilted, the shimmer still dancing in the air like heat. Mattheon's brows drew low, his eyes flicking to Ava and Mabelle as if seeing them for the first time. This wasn't a secret whispered—it was a truth demonstrated.

Magic. Used without hesitation. Spoken in the open. By people they had trusted. And never once had they been told.

Neither boy spoke. But the weight of their quiet was no longer passive. It was a silence that watched—and waited.

No sound beyond this room would travel. No memory would escape that was not invited. Only now could they begin.

They had seen what could no longer be hidden. And still, no one spoke. The silence that followed was not absence—it was waiting.

***

Leonarth was the first to speak.

Not loudly. Not defiantly. But like someone testing the shape of their own voice—as if uncertain whether it still belonged to them.

"How long," he asked, "have you known?"

His eyes weren't fixed on anyone in particular. They hovered near the book, then flicked toward the pendant, then toward Ava—but it wasn't accusation. It was gravity. Like he was trying to understand how long these truths had been pulling them all inward.

No one answered at first.

A breath passed. Then another.

Mattheon shifted beside him, his fingers curling against the edge of the table—not to steady himself, but to keep from breaking the silence with something less measured.

When Gwendlynn finally looked up, there was no surprise in her face. Only inevitability.

"Longer than I want to admit," Gwendlynn said at last.

Her voice was low, almost reverent—not from guilt, but from the weight of what had never been spoken aloud. She did not look at

Leonarth as she said it. Instead, her gaze fell on the book, then the key, then to the trunk Mabelle had carried in—still latched, still unopened. She did not look at it long.

"I was the first to arrive here," she said. "Before the Veil Protocol. Before the children. Before the rules that now govern what can and cannot be remembered."

She drew in a slow breath, as if the act of remembering required permission.

"I came not as a queen," she continued, "but as a mother searching for a place to bury her grief... and to protect what was left of her daughter's legacy."

Her eyes lifted at last to Leonarth. There was no apology in them—only recognition.

"But even that... was never mine to keep forever."

Leonarth's brow furrowed, the words catching more than just his attention.

"Wait," he said slowly, eyes narrowing. "Queen? Daughter's legacy?"

His voice wasn't angry—not yet—but it cracked slightly around the edges, like someone trying to hold too many unfamiliar pieces at once.

"I've known you as Gwendlynn. As the woman who watched over the gardens, who gave me books, who sat beside me when the dreams wouldn't stop. That's who you were. All of you—you were the ones who protected us. But now... magic? Royalty? Spells?"

He looked around the room. "None of this makes sense. You've all known things. You've kept things. For how long?"

The last words landed softer than he intended. But they hurt more that way.

Gwendlynn held his gaze—and for the first time, Leonarth saw something in her expression that hadn't been there before.

Not sorrow.

Not even guilt.

But memory—raw and trembling, like something just unearthed from beneath the frost.

"I didn't know who you were," she said gently, "until a few days ago."

She looked briefly to the others around the table.

"I didn't know any of you were tied to the same past. Not Ava, not Mabelle. Only Maurice—he was the only one I ever knew carried magic. The rest… I thought we were strangers with different silences."

Her eyes softened again when they returned to Leonarth, the weight in them no longer distant but familiar.

"That's why this is harder than you think. Because I wasn't hiding you from the truth. I was hiding myself."

She looked at her hands as if they might still hold the shape of that terrible realization.

"I mourned you," she said. "For years, I believed you were lost with her. I buried you in my prayers. In silence. In ritual."

Her voice didn't crack, but something behind it did.

"And now… you sit before me. Not a ghost. Not a dream. But real. Breathing. Watching me with her eyes."

She took a breath.

"My name is Gwendlynn of Alureth—once sovereign, and later Queen Mother. I ruled a realm held together by fraying oaths and failing magic. A world bound to the Veil and barely clinging to balance. When I gave birth to Faye, I believed she would be the heir who could restore what was lost. She carried the prophecy of the Root—the ancient magic believed to unify the scattered domains."

Her gaze turned distant, but her voice remained steady.

"For a time, we believed it might come true. She was brilliant. Fierce. Compassionate beyond reason. But not everyone welcomed her vision. One man saw in her rise the end of his doctrine—the unraveling of everything the Accord had begun to impose."

She didn't speak Siroth's name yet. It didn't need to be said.

"And so the kingdoms fell."

Mattheon leaned forward, blinking like someone trying to see through fog that had just thickened. "Wait—hold on," he said. "What do you mean Magicia? A queen I can understand. Maybe even a prophecy. But you're talking about entire realms? Kingdoms? Are we supposed to just believe there's a whole other world out there?"

Before Gwendlynn could answer, Maurice shifted slightly, his chair creaking against the stone floor.

"I should speak to that," he said, his voice calm, the kind that made silence lean in to listen.

"Magicia is real," he said. "As real as this room, as real as you or me. But it is veiled—hidden by old magic and protected by rules older than most remember. What Gwendlynn speaks of is not myth. It's memory. Suppressed, scattered, and now—waking."

He folded his hands on the table.

"I was once Keralis, Inquisitor of the Concordium. We were the enforcers of magical law—and the silencers of those who defied it. Later the Concordium became the Accord, and it ruled not by light, but by doctrine. By fear. And in the end... I could no longer be part of it."

Leonarth blinked, then shook his head slightly, trying to reconcile the man before him with the one he thought he knew.

"Wait—Concordium, and... Accord? What does that even mean?" he asked. "You're not just Father Maurice, the man who brought me to the library when I couldn't sleep? Who helped me plant the first vines in the southern garden?"

His voice cracked—not from anger, but from something closer to disbelief. "You're telling me you were part of a secret order that silenced people?"

His hand hovered near the book again, fingers splayed like he didn't trust it anymore.

"You've been with us this whole time. Pretending."

Ava reached out and placed a hand over Leonarth's, firm but warm—not to hush him, but to anchor him.

"Leonarth," she said softly, "I know it's a lot. Too much, maybe. But we didn't come here to pretend. Not tonight. We came to remember. To speak what was never said."

He looked at her then—the one face he had always trusted. She met his eyes with something like apology, but not shame.

"Let Maurice finish," she said, nodding toward the man who had once gone by another name.

Maurice inclined his head, then turned toward the others, his voice steady again.

"The Concordium wasn't a throne or a council," he said. "It was a structure—a governing framework meant to uphold the fragile balance between realms. In its earliest form, the Queen ruled Magicia in tandem with the Inquisitors—guardians of magical law and keepers of Veil secrets. It was a necessary tension: vision paired with vigilance, compassion restrained by consequence.

But harmony like that never lasts. In time, one of the Queen's High Envoys—Siroth—gained influence beyond his station. He exploited unrest, manipulated doctrine, and turned the guardians of balance into agents of fear. It was through his rise that the Concordium evolved—or rather, devolved—into something else entirely: the Accord, and it was not a structure to protect, but a system to control.

What was once balance became surveillance. Law became punishment. And Magicia, once a realm of connection, began to close its gates."

He paused, his gaze distant.

Gwendlynn picked up where Maurice left off—not with rebuttal, but with something quieter. Resigned. Remembered.

"By then, I had already begun preparing to step down."

Her hands, resting over one another now, were still. "The crown was never meant to outlast the world it served. Magic was thinning. The alliances between the veil-bound realms were growing brittle, held together by memory more than faith. I had planned to abdicate—to become Queen Mother—and let Faye lead what came next."

She looked briefly to the key on the table. Its metallic edge caught a glint of the lamplight, but did not shimmer. Not yet.

"Faye believed the rift between Earth and Magicia could be mended—that we could restore balance, not by force, but by understanding. She believed the people of both realms deserved to remember who they once were."

A pause. Not dramatic. Just necessary.

"But where she saw harmony, others saw danger."

She did not need to name him.

"Siroth led a counter-movement. He cloaked it in order, in doctrine, in preservation of what he claimed was sacred. But it was fear, sharpened into decree."

Her voice thinned, but didn't falter.

"The Ordinatum came fast. Faster than we expected. One act of magic, anchored by a dozen betrayals. The Veil closed. Every known passage between Earth and Magicia was sealed—some crumbled to dust, others laced with death spells that tore the soul from anyone who tried to cross. Travel became lethal. Communication became myth. And just like that, an entire world vanished from memory."

She did not look at the boys when she said it. But the words were meant for them.

"The only ones who survived were those with ancient knowledge, or the ones who carried secret rites—the old Concordium markings, passed down in blood or bound to relics."

Her voice dimmed into silence.

Then, for a moment, no one spoke.

Mattheon's brow creased. He leaned back slightly, arms crossed tight across his chest—not from defiance, but self-preservation.

"Okay," he said slowly, "but… that's a lot."

His voice wavered somewhere between sarcasm and sincerity, like someone trying to laugh through thunder.

"I mean… realms? Secret rites? Soul-tearing magic?" He looked at Leonarth, then at Mabelle beside him. "Did we fall into some kind of fever dream? Because I swear, five minutes ago I was just trying to figure out where Meely disappears to at night."

A weak chuckle escaped him—more reflex than relief.

"And now you're telling me this is all real? That I've been living in a place tied to a world I didn't even know existed?"

Mabelle placed a steady hand on his shoulder, her expression gentler than usual—the kind that came not from pity, but memory.

"It's more than real," she said. "It's legacy."

She turned to the others, voice shifting from private to deliberate.

"Magicia was not a single kingdom—it was five."

She looked around the table, as if counting not objects, but echoes of those forgotten names.

"Aerthys—the kingdom of air," she began. "Floating cities tethered by enchanted balloons. Masters of wind, weather, and flight."

"Then Elowen—the realm of water. Jungle canopies shaped by spells, their people gifted in healing and decay alike."

"Third was Ignaris—the fire kingdom. Cities of alloy and invention. Masters of material transmutation and destructive craft."

"Fourth was Karnor—the mountain strongholds. Stone, protection, endurance. Their wards could hold back armies and time itself."

She paused.

"And last… the Fifth." Her voice lowered to a whisper.

"The hidden kingdom. The one that *was* Earth. Lyrical, inventive, untethered from spellwork. A place born from belief—and the first to be forgotten."

A silence passed like a shadow.

"Each kingdom held a portion of the Root," she said. "And each paid a price when the bond was broken."

She glanced at Mattheon now, not with authority, but honesty.

"You're not wrong to feel lost. We all did. Some of us still do. But what you're hearing tonight—what we're finally speaking—is the truth we weren't allowed to remember."

Mattheon looked at her for a long beat. Then he nodded—once—not because he fully understood, but because something inside him believed her.

Maurice spoke again, this time without invitation—as if the memory itself had summoned him.

"The truth didn't disappear on its own," he said, voice quieter now. "It was erased. Piece by piece. Burned in silence, rewritten in doctrine."

He leaned forward, both hands flat on the table now, as though steadying something beneath them—a story too brittle to lift all at once.

"The Circle of Five Inquisitors was fractured the night the Insidium began."

His words sent a chill through the room, though no wind moved.

"One of us vanished. I defected. And Siroth… rose."

He let the name hang—not bitter, not dramatic, just factual. A storm that didn't need thunder to be feared.

"The Insidium was not a spell," he continued, "but a doctrine. A belief that the Root of Magic could be severed from prophecy and replanted in a new bloodline—by force. By murder. The weapon was forged. The ritual sealed. And the target…" He looked at Gwendlynn now. Not to accuse, but to mourn.

"…was Faye."

No one moved.

"He believed that if she were killed in the right way, with the right blade, the Root would abandon its chosen vessel and pass to the one who wielded the power to take it—or to their kin."

Maurice's voice dropped lower.

"He wanted to turn legacy into inheritance. Magic into conquest."

Ava's jaw tightened. Mabelle looked away.

"The Insidium was the first act of magical terrorism after the Ordinatum," he said. "And it worked—but not the way they expected."

He glanced toward Leonarth, and something in his eyes shifted.

"What happened after… we'll get to. But you must understand: that was when the Accord stopped pretending it was order. It became regime."

He straightened his spine, as though lifting himself out of that memory.

"Siroth declared himself Protector of Magicia, and he became its supreme Chancellor. He dissolved all local governance. Public rituals were outlawed. The rebel networks fell. The few who survived went silent or underground. The Inquisitorial Order, once a council of balance, became an arm of enforcement. Surveillance replaced celebration. Magic—living, chaotic, beautiful—was chained."

He looked now at both boys.

"That's the world you were born into. A world where truth was buried so deep, only silence remained."

And then, he fell silent himself.

Gwendlynn closed her eyes. When she opened them, her voice was quieter than before—not broken, but dusted with the wear of too many unshed years.

"When Faye vanished… I vanished, too."

She didn't look at Leonarth this time, nor at the others. She looked past them—as if seeing a version of herself none of them had ever met.

"We had argued, my daughter and I. Bitterly. She wanted to build bridges to Earth again, to remind its people who they had once been. But I…" Her mouth curved—not quite into a smile. "I thought the risk was too great. I had seen what the Veil could do. I had seen the Ordinatum. And I was afraid."

A beat passed, but her eyes did not waver.

"She left without my blessing. Without saying goodbye. And when the Veil closed behind her, I thought I would never see her again."

Now her hands folded over each other, neatly—too neatly.

"I staged my own disappearance. Let the world believe I had perished or been imprisoned by the Accord. It was easier that way. For them. For me."

Her gaze flicked toward the small window near the far end of the chamber—its glass dark now, touched only by the faint glow of the inner lamps.

"I crossed through one of the last open passages between realms—one laced with forgetting. I left Magicia as its Queen… and arrived here a woman unmade."

The others said nothing. No one dared.

"Saint-Spire was not my sanctuary," she continued, more softly now. "It was my tomb. I buried my name here. My voice. My grief. And from its silence, I began again."

She looked at the boys now—really looked. Her eyes lingered on Mattheon, then Leonarth, then returned to the center of the table where the relics rested—silent but watchful.

"The title of Supreme Mother was never meant to hold power. Only presence. A symbol for the girls who arrived here broken. A keeper of ritual. A shepherd of memory."

She blinked slowly—not to hold back tears, but to steady something older.

"I wore silence like a second skin. I did not speak of magic. Not even when I sensed its stirrings in the walls. Not even when Maurice arrived. I thought I was the only one left who remembered."

Her voice faltered for the first time—not from weakness, but recognition.

"But I was wrong."

She met Ava's eyes, then Mabelle's. No words passed between them, but something softened. A thread pulled taut for too long finally loosened.

And then—only then—did she look at Leonarth again.

"You weren't the only one kept in the dark," she said. "And if I could change that… I would."

Silence wrapped the chamber again—but this time, it did not sting. It comforted.

Chapter Twenty-Two

"The Thorn and the Crown"

The silence lingered—not as a void, but as space finally made sacred. No one moved. No one needed to. What had just been said could not be unsaid—not by Gwendlynn, not by anyone. And still, there was more. The kind of truths that didn't fit inside a single night, or a single breath. And when Ava finally spoke, her voice carried not authority, but ache.

"There's something you should know about your mother..." Ava said, and her voice barely rose above the flicker of the candlelight.

She looked to Leonarth first—not with pity, but with something far heavier. Memory. And devotion.

"By now, I think you already feel it. Faye was your mother."

The words didn't fall like thunder. They didn't need to. The air already knew. So did Leonarth. But hearing them spoken made something inside him sit straighter, as if finally recognizing the shape it had always been trying to fill.

"She left Magicia by choice," Ava continued. "Not as a coward. Not as an exile. But as someone who believed there was no other way. After that final argument with Gwendlynn... after the court turned cold... she crossed the Veil on her own terms."

Ava's fingers folded together in her lap. Her hands, once steady, trembled faintly now.

"I followed her. I was part of her order—F.O.G. (Faye's Order of Guardians), that's what we were called back then. Guardians who swore to protect the heirs of the Root, wherever they wandered. I left everything behind to stay at her side."

Her voice cracked at the edge of that sentence, but she didn't stop.

"On Earth, she lived in hiding. Disguises. Rented rooms. Always moving. Always watching the shadows. But she never gave up on the idea that the two realms could still find harmony. That maybe—just maybe—love could be a bridge."

A pause, soft as breath.

"And then she met him."

Leonarth's gaze flicked up. The way Ava said him carried more weight than any name could.

"She never shared his name," Ava added quietly. "Not with me. Not with anyone. I think she understood what names can become once they're known."

She paused, then continued.

"He wasn't from our world. At least... not in the way she was. He didn't speak of magic, didn't carry talismans or rites. But he had a stillness in him. A kind of rootedness. She once told me he felt like gravity—not something that pulled her down, but something that helped her land."

A faint smile, quickly gone.

"They tried to keep the world at bay," Ava said softly. "But Faye knew what she was choosing. And when she realized she was with child... she told me it wasn't fear she felt. It was certainty. As if the universe had finally whispered yes."

Ava's eyes glistened now.

"She planned your birth, Leonarth. Not in rebellion—but in hope. You weren't an accident. You were... a covenant."

Leonarth didn't speak.

He didn't have to.

The silence between them now felt like breath held across time—across lives.

Ava looked down for a moment, as if searching for the words not on the floor, but in the memory.

"He came early."

Her voice returned softer, edged with the tremble of things long hidden.

"You weren't supposed to be born for another two months. But something shifted. A pulse. A pressure in the Veil, maybe. Or maybe Faye just... knew."

She met his gaze again, steady now.

"You were born in a cottage carved into a hillside. Alone. No midwives. No wards. Just me, her, and the wind outside. You arrived small. But whole. Breathing. Alive. And from the moment she held you..."

She swallowed hard.

"...she smiled. Not with relief. With purpose."

No one in the room moved. Even Meely, unseen above them, was still as stone.

"But the Veil doesn't sleep long. Not when bloodlines awaken. Within days, Siroth's agents found us. We don't know how. Maybe a glyph triggered. Maybe a sleeper whispered. But they came."

Her fingers closed into fists.

"Faye knew what she had to do. She placed you in my arms. Pressed the letter into my hand. And told me where to run."

Leonarth's brow tensed, but his eyes glistened now.

"She didn't run?" he asked—not accusing. Just a boy chasing the last shape of a mother he'd never known.

Ava shook her head, voice thinner now.

"She stayed. She delayed them. Enough for me to escape through a forgotten passage. One she had hidden years before. A Veil crossing so old, so faint, it shouldn't have worked."

A pause.

"But it did. It carried us back into Magicia first—long enough to vanish. Long enough to make the world forget he had ever crossed at all."

She looked down again, but only briefly.

"When they reached her… she didn't beg. She didn't plead. She stood."

A stillness passed over the room.

"They took her back to Magicia," Ava said. "And there…"

Her voice tightened.

"They killed her with a blade crafted for one purpose—the Insidium."

Gwendlynn flinched. And as Ava didn't faltered, Maurice lowered his eyes and continued.

"A ritual blade, embedded with glyphs designed to sever magic from legacy. To take the Root from its rightful heir… and force it into the blood of its killer—or his kin."

Mabelle's hand touched the trunk near her feet—not to open it. Just to feel the weight of what still lay within.

"Siroth believed the ritual had worked. That the Root had transferred. Because you weren't supposed to exist. They thought she was still pregnant. They thought… they had killed you too."

He paused for a long time to let the weight of his words sink.

Ava's voice, for the first time, hardened and she added.

"But you were already gone. Already breathing. Already chosen."

Leonarth sat completely still, his eyes wide, haunted.

"And the Root?" he asked, barely above a whisper. "What happened to it?"

Ava hesitated—but not from uncertainty. She looked at Maurice, who answered.

"It couldn't be taken," he said. "Because it had already anchored elsewhere."

He didn't say who.

He didn't need to.

Maurice faced Leonarth, and his voice was low, grave:

"The ritual failed. The glyph master—Inquisitor Caer Durell—vanished not long after. Some say Siroth had him executed for the failure. Others say he fled."

He glanced toward the trunk—where Mabelle's documents still waited.

"But the blade remained. And Siroth kept it. As a relic. As a lie."

Silence returned.

But now, it pulsed—not with waiting, but with knowing.

Mattheon shifted uncomfortably.

"But wait," he said, his voice breaking the spell of silence with something more grounded. "I thought Maurice was already here when Leonarth arrived."

He glanced at the older man, then toward Gwendlynn, uncertainty flickering between memory and revelation.

"Weren't you already the Father of the Abbey? Before Ava ever showed up?"

The question didn't sting. But it cracked something open.

Gwendlynn was the one to answer—her voice low, her gaze distant.

"Yes. He was."

She didn't look at Maurice as she spoke. Not out of avoidance—but because the memory was too large to aim at a single person.

"By that time, I had already disappeared from the world they once called Magicia. I shed the name of queen, vanished from all maps, and took on a new role—one born not of crown or court, but of silence. I became the Supreme Mother of Saint-Spire."

A pause.

"It wasn't immediate. It took years to build the trust. The Abbey had no official priest. Magic was not spoken of. Only faith, ritual... and grief."

She looked at Maurice now.

"He came to me under a different name—Keralis no longer, but a man burdened by knowing too much."

Maurice said nothing.

"I gave him shelter," Gwendlynn continued. "Not as a queen, not even as a friend—but as someone who understood what it meant to lose a realm and survive its echo."

She let the words settle before going on.

"Together, we crafted a story. The Abbey had no permanent priest," she said.

"He arrived with credentials no one wanted to question too closely—and stayed. The clergy accepted it. The sisters welcomed him. By the time anyone thought to ask, he was already Father."

Her voice dimmed into something older now. Worn.

"We said nothing of our past. We spoke little, even to each other. But we watched. Guarded. Beneath the statue of Saint Elodia, we felt a pull—a resonance neither of us could name. We called it a relic. We called it hope."

Maurice picked up where she paused.

"We reinstated the Veil Protocol," he said. "Not officially—there was no Accord left to sanction it—but as guardians of a memory that refused to die. We agreed: no spells, no resonance, no disclosure. Until a sign emerged."

His eyes fell now to Leonarth.

"That sign came... years later."

Ava's hand tightened around the pendant near her neck.

"He wasn't a newborn when I brought him here," Ava said softly. "He was five."

Leonarth looked up sharply.

"Wait—what?"

His voice was sharper than he intended—not out of anger, but confusion that struck too close to something unspoken.

"I don't remember anything before the orphanage. Not really. Just... shadows. Smells. A voice sometimes, maybe yours. But no faces. No places."

Ava nodded once, slowly—like she'd been expecting this moment.

"You were never supposed to remember."

The words landed like a stone dropped in still water.

"Faye taught me the spell," Ava continued. "A memory fold—designed to keep your earliest years sealed, until the time was safe."

She looked at him, not with regret, but protection.

"We spent those five years in hiding, Leonarth. Moving constantly. Disguises. Rented rooms. Names we never kept for more than a few weeks. You were so small, so curious. But the world was still watching for any sign of her legacy."

She exhaled slowly.

"The spell was imperfect. It couldn't erase what mattered—your instincts, your fears, your kindness. But it buried the details. Your life before the Abbey... it's there. Just locked away."

Leonarth's throat tightened. He didn't speak. But something in his jaw shifted.

"I only came to Saint-Spire when it became clear we had no other choice," Ava went on, her voice barely above a whisper now. "They were closing in. I carried the letter. And I trusted Maurice to protect you if I failed."

She looked briefly toward Gwendlynn.

"You weren't here when I arrived. Maurice gave them a story. A forged letter from the Archbishop. Said I was a wandering sister seeking spiritual refuge."

Gwendlynn nodded, eyes darkening with memory.

"And I believed him. Why wouldn't I? He had never lied to me before."

Maurice closed his eyes briefly—just once.

"I kept the truth from her," he said. "Not to hurt her. But because I feared what knowing might do. To her. To the boy. To us all."

Gwendlynn's voice was low again—not angry. Just hollow.

"You let me mourn them both. For over a decade."

Maurice did not reply.

A beat passed.

Then Ava's voice rose once more—this time firmer.

"We placed Leonarth in the Abbey's orphanage wing. Kept watch from a distance. Gwendlynn, unaware of the boy's lineage, grew close to him—and I did not know who she truly was. She had hidden herself too well, bound in spellwork."

A breath.

"The rest of us remained bound by silence."

"I became Novice Ava," she said. "And you were safe. Watched. Loved from a distance."

"The Echo Protocol was invoked. Formally."

She looked at each of the others in turn.

"Four guardians. Four silences. Ava. Maurice. Mabelle. Gwendlynn. None of us knowing the others still carried magic. Only Maurice knew the truth of all."

The truth sat like a weight in the center of the room.

And still, Meely had not moved.

Mattheon's voice broke the silence.

Not loud. Not accusing. Just… uncertain.

"So what about me?"

All eyes turned.

"Leonarth has a prophecy. Now even a past." He blinked fast, then looked at Mabelle. "But what do I have?"

His question wasn't bitter. It was quieter than that. The kind of quiet that carried a child's ache behind a young man's voice.

Mabelle's hands curled slightly in her lap.

She hadn't spoken in a while—not since the truths began unfurling like scrolls no one had meant to read aloud. But now, she met Mattheon's eyes with a steadiness that surprised even herself.

"You have a mother who died for the truth," Mabelle said softly. "And a father who trusted me with yours."

She took a breath—not deep, but deliberate. Like something long buried was finally rising.

"Your mother was a rebel courier," she continued. "Trusted with transporting sensitive magical records. I don't know what all of them were—I never saw the whole of it. But she carried something encoded. Sealed. And dangerous enough to get her killed before she could reach the people it was meant for."

Mattheon's expression shifted—not to anger, but to something older. The kind of sorrow that doesn't come with memories, only with the knowledge that something precious was stolen before you ever had the chance to hold it.

"I found her," Mabelle said. "Not in time to save her. But in time to save you."

She placed a hand on the side of the trunk—not opening it yet, just resting her fingers there like it was both shield and confession.

"You were barely moving. You didn't cry. Just... stared. Like you already knew something had gone wrong in the world."

The room stayed quiet.

"I took you," Mabelle said. "And what I could gather from what she carried. Most of it was damaged. Some of it I never understood. I sealed it all away—together—and I did not look inside."

She drew a slow breath.

"I didn't know there was a anything else in the trunk. Not then. Not for years."

Her hand tightened slightly.

"I only learned of it a few nights ago—when Ava mentioned she found a stone in there, and Gwendlynn named it for what it was. The Root of Orreth."

A pause.

"So if your father placed it there... he did so without my knowing. And if it waited, it waited in the dark—as you did."

Her voice softened further.

"He said three words to me before he vanished—months before your mother died. 'Never trust bloodlines.'"

She let those words settle—not as an answer, but as a puzzle.

"I don't know what he meant," she admitted. "Not yet. But I brought it here. And I've kept it hidden ever since. I took my vows to stay close to you—not as penance, but as promise."

Then, almost as an afterthought, she added:

"Whatever legacy waits in that stone... it was never meant to be carried alone."

Mattheon's eyes drifted to the trunk. Not demanding, not afraid. Just ready.

And so, for the first time that night, someone reached toward what had not yet been remembered.

Mattheon stood.

Not rushed. Not dramatic. Just… drawn.

His hand moved toward the trunk almost instinctively, as if something beneath the latch had already chosen him.

He knelt beside it, fingers hovering for a moment above the clasps—then gently unlatched both sides. The hinges creaked open like breath released after years held too long.

Inside: a folded cloth, worn but carefully wrapped.

Mattheon reached in, unwrapping it slowly, reverently. And there—nestled in the folds—lay the stone.

Rough and dark, veined with silver that pulsed faintly beneath the surface like veins catching moonlight. The Root of Orreth.

He held it with both hands.

The room dimmed—not from shadow, but from attention. Every eye followed the subtle shimmer now pulsing from the relic.

Mattheon turned, as if guided by instinct, and stepped toward the center of the table—where the sealed book still waited. The air between them seemed to warp slightly. Not violently. Just… aware.

And then it happened.

As Mattheon's hand passed near the book—not touching, just near—the Root glowed brighter.

A low resonance echoed through the chamber. Not a sound, exactly. More like… a pressure. A memory returning to the air.

The book responded. Its surface flickered with iridescent light, lines of ancient script briefly surfacing like breath fog on glass. Then vanishing again.

Gwendlynn inhaled—not startled, but caught off guard.

Maurice stepped forward, eyes narrowed, voice low.

"It… recognizes it."

Leonarth's brow furrowed. "The book?"

Maurice nodded.

"The Root of Orreth," he said slowly, "is not just a relic. It's a blood-bound tether. An ancient conduit—passed down through families to mark a magical line. Not powerful by itself… but resonant. It responds to inheritance."

He looked at the book now, then at Mattheon.

"This isn't coincidence. The book carries the genealogies of the old bloodlines. Names that were meant to be remembered. And some… that were meant to be erased."

Mabelle's breath caught.

Mattheon looked down at the stone in his hands. "So you're saying…"

Maurice didn't finish the sentence. He didn't need to.

But Gwendlynn did.

She stepped forward, voice barely above a whisper.

"If your father carried that stone," she said, "then someone gave it to him."

A pause.

"And only one line was ever permitted to bear it."

Mattheon blinked.

Leonarth swallowed hard.

And somewhere—almost imperceptibly—the book's seal pulsed again.

Like memory knocking.

Like legacy refusing to be forgotten.

The silence wasn't broken by words.

It was broken by a sound.

A faint, startled chirr—somewhere between a growl and a question.

Everyone turned.

Meely crouched near the edge of the tapestry—fur bristling, eyes wide, her body frozen mid-creep. She had been there the whole time. Watching. Listening. Silent as shadow.

Until now.

Her eyes gleamed with more than instinct—something wary, intelligent… and betrayed.

Leonarth inhaled.

"Meely…?" he said.

She didn't move.

Mabelle took a step forward, instinctively—but Gwendlynn lifted a hand.

"Don't," she said quietly. "The chamber is still sealed."

Ava's brows furrowed. "She must've slipped through before the last veil-lock set."

Maurice's voice dropped, grim.

"If we break the threshold now, we risk triggering a flare. A ripple across the lattice that might be felt in Magicia."

Mattheon looked from Meely to the others, his voice edged with concern.

"So... we just leave her like that?"

"No," Gwendlynn said, softer now. "We acknowledge her."

She turned toward the feline figure, crouched and unmoving.

"You weren't meant to hear all this, little one," she murmured. "But now that you have... you're part of it."

Meely didn't blink.

But she stepped forward—just enough for her paws to catch the edge of the relic light. And as she did, the convergence dome shimmered faintly, responding not with alarm... but acceptance.

Maurice's gaze lingered on her a moment longer—wary, thoughtful—then turned back toward the table.

"Then we continue."

Mattheon still held the Root of Orreth, but now his gaze had settled on the book—its glyph-sealed cover pulsing faintly in synchrony with the relic in his palm.

Ava spoke softly, but without hesitation.

"Let it speak."

Mattheon set the Root beside the book.

The moment it touched—the seal dissolved.

Not in light.

But in memory.

Lines of luminous script curled outward across the page like breath. Glyphs shimmered, then solidified. The book turned its own pages—not all at once, but guided by something unseen.

The page stilled.

Ink gathered—not written, but drawn—threading itself into a name etched with ceremonial care.

Arthalon Orreth.

The script deepened, lines blooming outward in the margins like filigree before yielding again.

Kaelen.

Lioran.

The motion slowed. The light dimmed, as if the book itself hesitated.

Siroth.

A heavier pause followed—the ink dark, the strokes less forgiving.

Mirel.

And at last—

a name without ornament.

Mattheon.

No title. No surname.

Just a boy.

Standing where no one had expected him to belong.

Leonarth flinched.

Mabelle's hand covered her lips.

Maurice froze.

Gwendlynn's eyes closed—not in doubt, but as the pieces aligned.

And from the shadows, Meely gave a soft, throaty rumble. Almost a warning.

The Root pulsed once more.

And so did the book.

Because the bloodline had not vanished.

It had waited.

And now… it had returned.

Gwendlynn didn't speak.

She didn't have to.

The air had changed—not stirred, not swayed—but split.

As if a silence older than language had just ruptured.

Her eyes locked on the glyphs.

On the Root relic.

On the name that still shimmered—not just in ink, but in her memory.

Two names.

Siroth.

Beneath it—

Mirel.

Her breath caught.

"No," she whispered—not in denial, but as something broke. "Not just him."

She turned, slowly, toward Mattheon.

Then Leonarth.

Because the name was familiar.

Too familiar.

And that's when the lattice broke.

"Their father," she said.

Hollow. Reverent.

"Was the same."

Maurice flinched. Ava froze mid-breath.

Mabelle's pendant flickered.

Leonarth blinked, but said nothing.

Mattheon's shoulders tensed, as if something had just found him from the inside.

Gwendlynn remembered Faye's words then. She had never been told his family name. Only the first—a common one, Mirel—dismissed as irrelevant, a past that no longer mattered.

"You're brothers."

The chamber didn't stir.

It shuddered.

The relics pulsed—not with light, but with inheritance. The scroll curled faintly at its edges.

Even the tapestry, folded now, pulsed once beneath the linen. A heartbeat caught in cloth.

Brothers.

Leonarth, born of Faye's legacy and the son of a vanished heir to Siroth.

Mattheon, born of the same father—through a path obscured, erased, made to sleep.

One child born to rebel.

One born to witness the rebellion's cost.

Magic didn't tremble.

It recognized.

"They both carry his blood," Maurice said, eyes distant. "But only one carries hers."

"What we called the Severance was never meant to break the realms," Gwendlynn murmured. "It was meant to prevent this."

Mattheon looked down at his own hands—as if they had become someone else's.

"What does it mean?" he asked.

Gwendlynn's voice shook. "It means the prophecy was never about a boy. It was about a choice."

Ava stepped closer, her voice raw. "One born of both realms. One born of blood and consequence."

Mabelle didn't speak. She couldn't. Her eyes shimmered like something inside her had cracked and let truth seep in.

Leonarth exhaled—but it wasn't fear.

It was knowing.

Like something ancient inside him had just exhaled, too.

Mattheon looked at him. The ache in his eyes had changed. It was no longer *What am I?* Now it was: *What if I'm not the one they need?*

And Leonarth—

Leonarth didn't move.

But the Root of Orreth glowed beneath him.

Not because of power.

Because of convergence.

The chamber dimmed—not by light, but by burden.

Every relic grew quiet, as if bowed.

Because now, the heirs had names.

And prophecy had weight.

And nothing—not even silence—could unwrite what had just awakened.

A final shimmer danced across the scroll.

Not new.

Remembered.

The name that had hovered alone—

Mattheon—

was no longer alone.

Beside it, pulsing faint and slow,

a second name surfaced. Not written—echoed.

Leonarth.

Not beneath.

Not above.

Side by side.

The book knew.

The Root of Orreth glowed once more—not for the boy who held it...

But for the one who had already been chosen.

Because blood remembers.
Even when history does not.

***

Leonarth looked from face to face, his brow knit with something beyond confusion.

"It's getting late," he said. "But before we leave… what exactly is a Calventherath?"

It was Mattheon who asked the next question—quieter, but heavier.

"And why did it sound like one of us could be one?"

The room tightened again—not with fear, but with fatigue. No one wanted to open another truth. But it had to be done.

Maurice spoke first.

"They're not assassins. Not soldiers. They're… memory ghosts. People rewritten by magic—made to forget who they were, and why they mattered."

"A living weapon," Gwendlynn added. "Not to kill. To erase. Planted like seeds in enemy soil. Loyal to nothing but silence."

Mattheon's expression darkened.

"You're saying someone could be one… and not know it?"

Maurice nodded grimly. "That's exactly what we're saying."

Leonarth turned slightly toward Mabelle—not accusing, just watching.

But Mabelle didn't flinch. Her voice was steady when she spoke.

"And we suspect a Calventherath thread—whoever it is—moved against Leonarth a few nights ago. If it is one of us," she said, "then we need to know. Before anyone else pays for it."

Silence again.

Then Gwendlynn stepped back from the altar, her voice quieter now.

"We've said enough for one night. More than we should've."

Maurice agreed. "The hour's grown late. We'll draw attention if we all return together."

"And the novices rise early," Ava added. "We can't afford to be seen."

Gwendlynn looked to the boys—both wide-eyed, changed, but standing tall.

"We'll speak more soon," she said. "But for now… no more truths tonight."

The blackwood door creaked open once more—not by glyph, but by breath.

They exited in silence.

No one spoke as they ascended the spiral stair, their shadows dragging behind them like afterthoughts. The air up here felt thinner, as if the weight of what had been unearthed below was still pressing upward through the stones.

Ava walked beside Mabelle. Leonarth trailed just behind Mattheon, his hand brushing the wall for balance—or maybe for grounding.

And Meely—quiet, nimble, invisible as always—padded out between them, tail low, eyes sharp.

Only Gwendlynn lingered.

She paused just before crossing the threshold—one hand still resting on the edge of the blackwood, her eyes scanning the chamber one last time. The air still held echoes, even if the light had faded. The scroll was dark. The altar still. The glyphs asleep.

But something pulsed.

Not from stone.

From fur.

A shimmer danced at the edge of her vision—subtle, like light catching a veil. Gwendlynn turned sharply toward it, her breath catching.

There, in the shadow just beyond the door, Meely stood.

Or—not Meely.

The flicker returned—longer this time. The illusion cracked. The spell faltered.

A second coat shimmered beneath the first—not fur, but memory.

Auburn-gold strands flared, then faded. The tail curled with a ceremonial grace. The eyes—once muted golden—flashed with radiant violet.

Gwendlynn's mouth parted.

Recognition slammed into her chest like a lost chord finally played.

"…Lirae."

The name left her lips not as a whisper, but as a calling—as if the syllables themselves had been waiting years to be spoken again.

The feline paused.

Turned.

And for one breathless moment, her gaze locked with Gwendlynn's—not as cat to priestess, but as guardian to guardian.

Gwendlynn stepped forward, her voice soft.

"You were hers. You followed Faye into exile. And when she couldn't protect him… you stayed."

The cat didn't reply.

But she didn't need to.

She blinked once—slow, deliberate. Not domesticated. Not enchanted.

Devoted.

Gwendlynn knelt—not out of subservience, but reverence.

"My old friend," she said, the words trembling. "You never left him."

Lirae moved past her then—not in retreat, but with purpose.

A protector rejoining the ones she was always sworn to guard.

Gwendlynn remained behind a moment longer.

Alone, in the quiet hush of memory.

The door sealed shut behind her—not with sound, but with finality.

And above them, in the stone halls of the Abbey where nothing had stirred in years… something began to listen.

She didn't tell the others.

Not yet—not while naming what Meely truly was would turn protection into a target.

Not while the Calventherath remained unnamed.

And not while her doubts about Mabelle still held breath.

In the hush between truths, only the cat knew how much memory still had teeth.

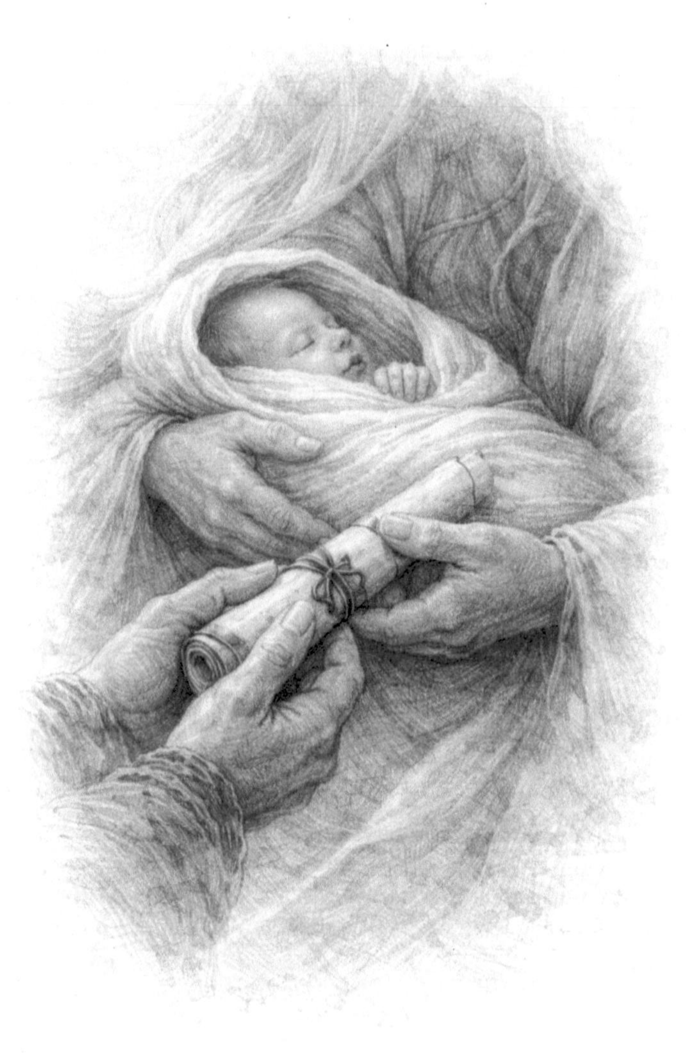

Chapter Twenty-Three

"The Mirror and the Memento"

Magicia did not hide beneath night. It gleamed in daylight—though daylight here did not fall in familiar shades. The sun was pale and opaline, casting the realm in shifting tones of pearl, gold, and faint rose, as though the entire world were glimpsed through a cathedral window.

From the high parapets of Virelia's Hall of Accord, the city unfurled in solemn grandeur. Bridges of pale stone arched across canals that shimmered with mineral light. Towers leaned toward one another as if in hushed conversation, their windows glinting like eyes half-closed.

The air carried weight. Not fog—memory. Each breath seemed to draw in fragments of forgotten prayers.

Plazas stretched wide and empty, lined with statues whose expressions changed with the hour. Glasspetal trees swayed in winds that bent sound strangely, making footsteps echo twice. Birds with mirrored wings circled above, scattering broken fragments of sky across the rooftops.

It was a city alive, yet never bustling. Even in day, Magicia felt like a chamber between heartbeats—a silence stretched too far.

Closer to the citadel, the land grew less forgiving. Thornspire brambles curled into jagged barricades, their crystalline thorns dripping with hardened sap. Veil moss spread across flagstones, glowing faintly under the watch of Inquisitors.

The wardens moved without sound. Robes trailing smoke from censers filled not with incense, but with memory-ash—each wisp curling like spectral handwriting.

Beneath the bridges, water did not reflect the sky. It reflected other skies. Fragmented, wrong. Children of Magicia were warned never to stare too long into the canals. To do so was to risk remembering a life that was not theirs.

Shadowcats slipped through alleys, glyph-marked fur glinting when they crossed a sunbeam. Echo-stags stood as solemn guardians near the gates, crystalline antlers burning with light when struck by the sun.

Even the smallest creatures bore strangeness: glass moths that left flickering illusions in their wake—faces, gestures, voices that dissolved before recognition.

Yet none of this broke the city's silence.

Life here did not shout. It endured.

To a traveler, Magicia might have seemed eternal. Unchanging.

But the daylight was not warmth. The towers did not lean in kindness. The echoes of footsteps did not welcome.

All of it carried the weight of surveillance.

The city itself served a master. Watching. Waiting.

And within Virelia's hidden vault, that master stirred.

The citadel above Magicia did not dream.

But Siroth did.

His sleep had never been generous, a thing carved thin by years of vigilance, and yet it came to him like ritual—measured, exact, barren of images. Dreams had no hold on him.

Until last night.

The memory of it clung to his skin still, even beneath the fresh linen of his robes. A dream not of conquest or judgment, but of roots. Copper-threaded. Gripped too tightly in hands too small.

The boy had no face, only the weight of a gaze—as if the hunt had already turned.

Siroth's lips tightened. He did not welcome dreams. Dreams were trespasses.

And yet his chest quickened with something he had not felt in years—excitement. Not warmth. Not joy. A different current altogether. A quickening, like prey scenting its predator.

He rose from his bed without hesitation. The morning light had already broken across Virelia, spilling through the lattice windows of the High Chamber. Pale beams caught against his silver hair, making each strand glint like frost.

It was not the light that moved him. It was the echo.

Something had stirred.

It was not the dream. Dreams withered with waking. But this did not. It clung, as though silence itself had reclaimed him—or worse, had remembered something he had tried to forget. The grip of a child's hand. The ash in Lorraine's hair. The copper threads glinting in darkness.

Too vivid. Too insistent.

Not dream.

Not memory.

Between.

And in that space, he felt it: a tether pulled taut. A line he thought he had severed, straining as if it still lived.

He drew a slow breath, steadying the pulse in his throat. Dreams could be weakness, nothing more. Echoes of memory, fragments of guilt. That was the safer explanation. He had taught himself to believe that.

And yet—this one resisted. Too vivid. Too precise. Not fading like the others. It clung like a root that had not been severed.

If it were only grief, it would have passed. If it were only memory, it would have blurred. But it returned, sharper each time, circling the same faces, the same hands.

He hated the thought forming at the edge of reason. He had dismissed it before, refused it. But silence had carried it back, relentless.

Not weakness. Not failing. Bloodline.

His bloodline. Or so it seemed. For the first time in years, he had woken not to silence but to the suspicion of inheritance.

He whispered her name, not to summon but to accuse. Lorraine. And with it came the truth he had tried to bury. The Root—his inheritance. Not destroyed. Not lost. Carried. Remembered. Alive.

Her lie.

She had told him she destroyed it. He had believed it, because he needed to believe it. Because believing her meant her betrayal was smaller. Containable. Forgettable.

But the Mirror had hinted otherwise. Twice it pulsed. Twice it remembered.

He told himself he had misread it, that resonance could double like echo in a chamber. But the dream returned, and with it her eyes—Lorraine's, defiant, unyielding.

And the child. The Root shifting its colors from black-violet to deep green in hands almost too small to fully grasp it, yet acknowledged all the same.

One thread he could almost name. The other—he resisted. Two pulses, two echoes, circling the same vision. Not siblings. Not chance. Something else.

The thought pressed at him, dangerous even unformed. He did not speak it. He would not.

The dream was no dream. It was resonance. Blood stirring blood.

He turned from the chamber window, cinched the black sash at his waist, and crossed to the waiting mantle. His regalia hung ready, layered robes heavy with authority, but he ignored them. Today called for no audience, no tribunal demonstration.

Only precision.

No spectacle.

He reached instead for the narrow gloves of obsidian silk, the ones inscribed with dormant glyphs. He slid them on carefully, like a surgeon preparing for incision.

The Mirror awaited.

The descent was long, but his breath never faltered. Steps spiraled downward through vaults of black stone, familiar to the Inquisitors—corridors of sanctioned silence, carved for record, summons, and judgment.

He entered the Conclave Vault without pause. No seals barred him. No ward questioned intent. This was a place of governance, of ritual authority, of meetings meant to be witnessed.

But he had not come for the Inquisitors.

He crossed the chamber's breadth and turned away from the known paths, toward a seam in the stone that did not appear on any map.

The dream followed him. Not words—images. Lorraine's eyes outlined in ash. A boy's grip too firm for innocence.

He despised the tremor it left in him.

And yet, beneath the loathing, something darker curled: hunger.

If the Root had survived, then so had its promise. If Lorraine's theft had carried forward into blood, then the boy was not anomaly, not irritation. He was possibility. Perhaps inheritance. Perhaps curse.

The thought sharpened him. Purpose laced each stride as the hidden passage yielded and the Sanctum received him—the antechamber erased from record, where even a Chancellor entered unnamed.

Here, he did not carry authority. He shed it.

Sandals. Robes. Sigils. The weight of office set aside piece by piece, until only the black undertunic remained, the muted crescent resting where rank once had. The Mirror would not answer a man armored in power. It required intention, stripped bare.

When he stepped forward again, he did so unadorned. Barefoot. Grounded.

The final threshold opened without sound.

Cold breathed outward as he crossed into the Chamber of Silence.

And there, in the room that unmade illusion rather than revealed it, the Mirror of Edresk stood as it always did—taller than a man, elemental steel circling its frame, veins of arcane script glowing faintly beneath the obsidian surface.

It did not reflect him.

It never did.

The floor's glyphwork stirred at his arrival, a rhythm just faint enough to be missed by any but him. Not one pulse now. Not two. But layered, echoing, as if the chamber itself hummed with resonance.

His heart gave the smallest answering tremor.

"Yes," he whispered, voice taut as a drawn blade. "I felt you."

He crossed the ritual circle, each step measured, robes trailing like shadow. He stopped at the edge, where silence thickened into weight.

The Mirror breathed—not with light, but with consequence.

Siroth lowered his head once, as though greeting a superior.

"This time," he murmured, "I pledge to listen."

And the glyphs began to stir.

They rose like breath from deep stone—thin filaments of light teasing the etched floor, then tightening, then drawing inward toward the Mirror's rim. He did not step back. He had stepped back before, and the Mirror had remembered his cowardice. He let the resonance build until the smallest hairs at his wrists lifted beneath the obsidian silk.

"Speak," he said, not loud, not pleading. An instruction.

The Mirror did not brighten; it darkened. Obsidian is not absence—it is pressure—and that pressure gathered, compressing reflection into a depth without surface. Threads of script beneath the glass ignited one by one, not in sequence but in answer. The vault hummed. He could feel the chamber counting.

The pressure did not relent.

This was not a response to residue. The Mirror waited—not for aftermath, not for proof, but for something withheld.

He reached for the familiar answer. The blackened shard of crystal touched the pedestal, and for a breath he believed it might suffice.

It did not.

The Mirror darkened further. The vault's hum dropped, as if disappointed.

He closed his hand.

From the fold of his sash, he drew what he had never offered before.

A narrow ribbon. Pale once. Silk, worn thin by years of being kept where no record could reach it. Tied once at a wrist.

Faye's wrist.

He had taken it from the bier, after the last breath, before the pyre erased what history might have contested. He had told himself it was nothing—an efficiency, a detail, a precaution.

That fiction did not survive the Mirror.

The ribbon had weight. Not residue. Not aftermath.

Presence.

It had endured.

It had survived him.

"A memento is not confession," he said, and laid the ribbon at the Mirror's base.

"The Mirror doesn't reflect what is," he said, almost idly. "It reflects what must not survive."

The hum deepened, and with it, a sensation he hated—the suggestion that the artifact had placed *him* on an altar. The scripts along the frame answered the silk with a faint copper glow. Not one pulse. Two. The second lagged by a breath, an echo out of time, a refusal to die.

"Show me the failure," he said. "Begin there."

The glass did not picture; it correlated. Fragments leaned toward one another, meaning pulling meaning. He saw no faces, only the consequences they left behind—the fatigue of severed wards, the scatter pattern of a broken veil, the residue of a Insidium coil that did not complete. He had designed that coil. Nothing about it should have allowed a remainder.

The remainder sang. Cold needled the soft skin inside his wrists.

He watched the Mirror translate the song: a thin helix of light curled within darkness, then another, crossing it. Not together. Not one. Interference, then reinforcement. He tracked the way the helixes rose and fell against the Insidium's harmonic—each time the first strain dimmed, the second persisted. Each time the second bent, the first returned with cruel patience.

He did not name them. Naming was for the weak. He counted.

Two threads. Two survivals riding one ruin. The first belonged to the woman whose ribbon lay at his feet; the Mirror's copper answer made that plain enough. The second—older? No. Not older. Adjacent. A lineage running parallel where none should have run.

He felt, for a single, clean instant, the edge of a smile threaten his self-control. He did not smile. He remembered to breathe.

"Not weakness," he said quietly. "Not failing. Interference."

The Mirror accepted the term. The helixes tightened, and with their tightening, a geometry unfolded—rings within rings, a cartography of blood. He had taught the Mirror this grammar years ago and then refused its conclusions. Now he followed its calculus without blinking.

First proposition: The heir of Faye lives. The Insidium coil did not close because the coil requires an extinguished seed. The Mirror held that equation steady until it stopped arguing and became law.

Second proposition—offered more slowly, as if the glass itself distrusted it: A second seed persists. Not Faye's. The signature bent toward iron and cold-water ink, not copper and silk. Not her. Not the woman whose ash ribbon warmed the chamber. The geometry angled toward him and away from him at once, a line drawn and then denied.

He felt an old door open in his chest, a door he had nailed shut with titles and decrees. He had told himself the past was a set of efficiencies. The Mirror called it by its true name: omission.

"Whose?" he asked, and the word cost him.

The surface did not show a face. It displayed the vector of a life: a graft spliced in a season of discretion; the root of that graft cut away before anyone could count its rings.

He saw what he had never permitted himself to imagine: a child carried in silence, hidden from him not out of spite but out of fear. Lorraine's defiance had not been petty vengeance—it had been concealment. She had taken the Root of Orreth not to wound him, but to arm her son with proof of blood when the time came.

The Mirror uncoiled the truth mercilessly. A boy he had never known, growing into a man he had never named. And from that man, another boy—alive now—moving through a world that believed him ordinary.

Not a confession. A reckoning.

He closed his eyes. He opened them. "So," he said, almost to the ribbon. "We were two all along. How quaint." The word was not grief, not nostalgia. It was leverage, waiting to be spent.

The Mirror did not contradict him.

He turned his attention where it wanted to be turned, to the coil he had authored. The Insidium had failed not because it was flawed, but because the *preconditions* had shifted.

He had arranged a world where Faye's line would end in a perfect circle of silence, but the circle had found a seam. The seam had lifted. Someone had taught someone to breathe.

The Mirror did not show a face, but a fracture—glyphs spooling into an incomplete pattern, one stroke missing from the whole. He watched as the omission widened, not accidental but deliberate, like a hand withdrawing at the last instant.

A hand. He knew that hand. Not hers.

The coil had been executed under precise conditions. Every line inscribed. Every oath sealed.

The work had been thorough. Theories traced to their limits. Glyphs written and understood—not only in form, but in consequence. Silence, accounted for. What it was meant to contain. What it could destabilize if withdrawn.

The Mirror flared.

Not with a name, but with an echo: a sigil bound to the Circle of Five.

Three marks burned steady.

One had been severed—not lost, but erased by consequence, its absence final and inert.

Another flickered, unstable, as if the withdrawal that created it had never truly stopped acting.

His lip curled. "Impossible."

He had dismissed that absence for decades—called it cowardice, exile, irrelevance. A shadow swallowed by earth.

But the Mirror did not lie. The fractured coil was not chance. It was the mark of one who had known enough to weaken it—even by absence.

"Keralis," he said, the name cutting the air like a verdict.

He let the name hang in silence, weighing it like a blade; of course the Mirror would bind failure to an omission—the hand that withdrew.

Why him? What thread did he carry that the others did not? Unless…

Unless the man still lived. Unless he had carried with him not only knowledge of the Insidium, but the will to keep its seed from dying.

The coil had failed because someone had preserved what should have been erased. Someone who understood the ritual too well to let it close. And the Mirror left him no doubt whose hand it was.

After all, Keralis was the only one who carried the forbidden knowledge of the Insidium—and the Nullum. His disappearance had seemed a blessing; without him, none could ever question Siroth's authority, nor attempt to steal it again. The Ordinatum itself should have made his return impossible.

Safe. Untouchable. Or so he had believed. Until now.

For a moment he lingered, almost indulgent, on the irony. A son he had never counted, a line he had never named, hiding like a weed in his ordered garden. How quaint, indeed. If the blood proved useful, it could be bent. If not, it would wither like the rest. Inheritance was never about affection. It was always about use.

He might have gone further into that arithmetic, weighing outcomes, imagining how omission could yet be wielded. But the Mirror did not permit reverie.

Its surface darkened, then rippled, as though exhaling a truth he had not asked for. The glyphs at its rim pulsed twice in quick succession, a double-beat of warning. He stilled.

"What is it?" he asked, though the Mirror never answered in words.

The pulse spread across the chamber floor. Scripts flared along the ritual circle, sketching the outline of a figure he knew but had not summoned. Shoulders bowed. Head lowered. A presence chained to silence until stirred. The Calventherath.

His jaw tightened. He had not given command.

The memory of those first renditions flickered unbidden: vessels carved hollow, loyalty bound not by choice but by erasure. The Calventherath did not act without his hand. Unless something older had reached them first.

The glyphs gave the explanation without flourish. A failed strike. A mark left unfinished. The heir of Faye had been sought and had survived.

Siroth's breath was steady, but his pulse quickened, not with fear but with purpose. So. That was why the Mirror had awoken without him. The sleeper had stirred instinctively, tethered not by order but by blood's cry.

"Unacceptable," he murmured.

He extended his gloved hand. Glyphs climbed his arm like black veins until they reached the Mirror's surface. The scripts recoiled, then bent toward his palm. He spoke the word of binding, not aloud but within, the syllable older than speech:

Obligare Somnum Memoriae.

The chamber obeyed. The glyphs that had outlined the Calventherath blurred, then reformed—this time not as a hunter of heirs, but as a blade pointed elsewhere. He carved the target into the Mirror's grammar, slow and exacting: not the boy, not yet. The other. The defector. The fracture.

Keralis.

If the man lived, he carried the only other memory of how power had been taken from her. And memory, in the wrong hands, was treachery.

The Mirror thrummed, resisting only slightly before it yielded. The outline of the sleeper bent, head lifting, gaze turning toward a different axis of command. The glyphs flared approval. The Calventherath's loyalty was rewritten.

The Mirror did not trouble itself with maps. Location was irrelevant; resonance traveled by lineage and oath, and it never lost its mark. All that mattered was the command—and the command had been given.

"Yes," he said softly, almost with satisfaction. "The boy will wait. The fracture dies first."

"The bloodline that defied me now breathes in silence," he added, almost to the ribbon. "I will unmake it."

The Mirror pulsed once more, sealing the command.

The heir lived—which meant legacy remained to be unmade. And Keralis still breathed—which meant silence could yet be perfected.

Purpose, as ever, sharpened him.

He closed his eyes, a vow without ceremony.

"He will feel me soon," he murmured.

"He'll remember what power tasted like, even if I never fed it to him."

Chapter Twenty-Four

"The Bread We Shared"

Night made the Abbey honest. By day, it smiled for pilgrims; by night, it showed seams—thin breaths of something only the attuned could feel, where mortar should be mute. Maurice moved the way a man remembers moving: quietly, with the weight of vows and the ache of old work he refuses to name.

He paused beneath the refectory arch. The kitchen fires had banked to embers; heat still pooled in the stones like sleep. On the cut tables, loaves cooled beneath linen, their skins crackling softly as they gave up their day. The smell was comfort and covenant—wheat, yeast, a sweetness left over from careful hands.

He did not go in. The warmth was a kindness he had not earned. He lingered a moment, then turned away.

He should have been in bed. He should have been less the man he used to be.

But there it was again: a pattern at the edge of seeing. Lines that did not belong to the wards he had written. A tempo he had not taught the Abbey to keep.

He set his palm to the cold stone. Listened—not for sound, but for the tension beneath the surface that only those like him were trained to feel. The Abbey kept its own quiet grammar: charge, hold, release.

Tonight, something different stirred—a current that seemed to reach backward.

Not memory.

Not echo.

Recall.

And whatever had been roused had not asked his permission.

Leaving the refectory behind, he stepped fully into the cloister. Moonlight laid a lattice on the flagstones. Somewhere beyond the hedge, Saint Elodia kept patient watch, one hand lifted in a blessing that always felt like a warning.

A draft found him. Not air—stone. Cold iron; hedge frost; the ghost of old incense the chapel never quite forgets. The pull was there, yes—not back toward the refectory, but along the cloister's far arcade.

He hesitated. Then followed.

Doubt kept pace with him—no shape, no sound, only the pressure of something that refused to let the night settle. Each step pressed him deeper into what the Abbey had become. What he had become. The chapel veil torn. The guardians' trust frayed. Gwendlynn's voice steady while her eyes did not forgive. The boys stumbling through truths that should never have touched them. Nothing here was mended. Not fully.

A figure stepped out of shadow at the corner. Mabelle.

She looked like she hadn't slept in hours.

"Maurice," she said, as if tasting whether the name still fit. "Couldn't sleep?"

He gave a small breath that was not quite a laugh. "I never could, when the frost holds everything still."

She nodded toward the cloister's far end. "I was walking to the kitchens. The bread will still be warm. Sometimes the warmth helps. Eloi keeps the fire and listens more than he speaks."

Maurice glanced back the way he had come, toward the refectory arch. For a moment it seemed he might agree.

"Not yet," he said quietly. "Warmth makes it easier to set things down. Tonight I need to keep hold of them."

He shifted his weight, giving her his full attention. "What's wrong?"

She hesitated—and only then did she notice that the storm had stilled, the Abbey gone quiet, as if waiting to hear what she would choose to say.

"He's been distant," Mabelle said, voice low so the stone would not carry it. "Mattheon. Since the veil broke. Since… the book."

Maurice kept his eyes on the flagstones. "Go on."

"In the East Alcove," she said, and already her hands had found one another, working a worry-line along a knuckle. "The letters didn't wait for us. They curled out on their own, like breath on glass. Arthalon Orreth. Kaelen. Lioran. Names that felt old enough to belong to myth, not people."

She glanced down, then back up.

"Then Siroth. That was when it stopped feeling like distant history."

She drew a breath.

"And then Mirel."

Her voice shifted, quieter, as if she were correcting herself aloud. "That was the moment I didn't understand. I knew my brother kept things from me. I didn't know he was keeping that."

She was silent a beat.

"After him came Mattheon."

She shook her head once. "Not a revelation—a consequence. What it must have done to him, to see his name there, tied to something he had only just begun to grasp."

Maurice's jaw tightened; his hand remained on the stone bench, knuckles white. "Some books obey genealogies," he said. "They do not know how to be kind."

"He won't look at Leonarth now," she whispered. "Leonarth tries—gods, he tries—but care can feel like pity when shame is loud. Mattheon walks the long way around as if names could rub off."

Maurice said nothing. The storm shifted, a sound like an exhale that wasn't.

Mabelle drew a breath. Her eyes traced the cloister's length, as if measuring distance. "I've seen that before."

"He left at night. He barely spoke. He left Mattheon with me. And he left a slip of words I have never forgiven: Never trust bloodlines. No reason. No goodbye." She hesitated. "I have not said his name in years." A bitter breath. "And that warning—was it for me, not to trust him? Or for himself, not to trust the blood in him?"

Maurice looked at her, not urging, not gentle. Waiting.

"Mirel," she said. The syllable felt heavier said aloud. "I didn't understand until the book kept his name lit while the others went dark."

"Sometimes memory returns not to be honored," Maurice said, "but to be rebroken—so we know it still matters."

"I hated him for leaving," she said. "Worse, I hated that a part of me kept hoping he'd come back. Even now I check every courier. Ridiculous." She shook her head once, sharply. "Enough," she said at last. "I didn't stop you to bury myself in old names. But that's all he left me—an old name and a closed door. I don't know if I ever knew my brother. I only know the sentence he left, and the boy."

"No," he said. "But the old names keep finding us. They knock in small ways—at the courier's hour, in a hall that goes too quiet, in the smell of bread that feels like a hand."

She let out a breath that wasn't quite a laugh. "If I stand here, I'll turn him into a shrine." A beat. "I don't want a shrine. I want warmth that doesn't lie."

She looked toward the refectory. "Come. Not for answers. For heat. For company that remembers how to be gentle."

He had refused the refectory as refuge. He would not refuse it as shelter.

Maurice inclined his head. "Then let the warmth hold what the names cannot."

They began to walk, the cloister stretching long and pale ahead of them. The Abbey, though it watched, said nothing.

At the kitchen door, they paused. The room beyond was a warm hush. Embers made a low red under the stove-iron; the scent lay close to the stone—yeast, rosemary, sweet onion, the faintest trace of ash.

Eloi stood at the back table, alone, slicing cooled loaves with careful reverence. He looked up as if surfacing, and the smile he gave them could have warmed the arches.

"Couldn't sleep either?" he asked.

"Passing through," Maurice said. "But now that you ask..."

Mabelle moved to the table. She didn't speak. She reached for a knife, set a loaf on its side, and cut a heel cleanly. Steam lifted. She broke the piece in two and handed half to Maurice.

They ate standing. The crust sang in their hands; the crumb held heat.

For a moment, it was only this: the small human covenant of warm bread shared at a late hour. The kind of kindness that keeps a place soft at the edges.

Maurice reached back to the loaf, snapped another heel, and pressed it into Eloi's palm.

"Share it," he said—not an order; an invitation.

Mabelle split her half again, the three of them making fourths from what had been whole. Heat traveled from bread to hands, from hands to faces. For a breath, it felt like a liturgy they remembered without learning.

Eloi stood with them, quiet as a brother, eyes bright in the emberlight.

They kept the old words behind their teeth, and let the silence do the blessing. For a moment the Abbey itself seemed to breathe with them—three broken souls bound by bread and heat. Perhaps it would not last. But for that breath, it was enough.

***

When the loaf was finished they parted—Mabelle first, wrapping her robe closer, Maurice beside her a moment later. They stepped from the kitchen into corridors washed pale with moonlight. The walk toward their dormitories was long enough for silence, short enough for words to still matter.

A bell tolled somewhere deep in the Abbey.

Not loud.

But enough to turn silence into measure.

The corridor smelled of damp stone and cooling ash—the same scents that had clung to Mirel's cloak the last night she saw him. Memory pressed at her edges, sharper than she wished. His eyes had carried a sadness she once thought was for the son he abandoned, yet now she wondered—had he already known the truth he could not name? Had he carried the weight of a lineage stained, a secret too heavy to give voice to? The thought gnawed at her, pressing his absence against her shoulder as if he still walked there, unwanted, insistent.

For a moment she thought she heard another step behind them, light as a memory, gone when she turned.

The wind shifted, carrying with it the faint smoke of the kitchen chimney, the last whisper of a dying fire. It tangled with memory. Firelight. The trunk dragged to the door. A tapestry folded under her arm. A boy crying behind her. And the house shrinking into night, consumed by flames no one ever explained. She never knew who set them. She only knew the fire had followed her to the Abbey. And now, with names burning on a page, the smoke seemed to speak his name again.

Her hands tightened at her sleeves. She could almost hear his voice—low, persuasive, heavy with doubt. Words he had never proved true, and perhaps never meant to. *Never trust bloodlines.*

Mabelle broke the silence. "If Mirel's name burned beside Mattheon's, then what does that mean? That the blood I was told to mistrust was his own? Or that he never trusted what lived inside himself?"

Maurice did not hurry his reply. "It means Siroth tried to erase his line, and failed. It means legacy cuts deeper than choice. And it means Mattheon is not the only reminder left."

She turned her head, eyes darker than the hall. "Then every time I say my brother's name, I am saying Siroth's too."

"You are saying what survived him," Maurice answered. "And survival is never simple."

They reached the stair that would separate them.

A torch guttered in its sconce, the flame bending as if listening.

Shadows lengthened, unsettled.

She lingered one step higher. "I don't know if I want to know more."

"You already do," he said.

She gave a small nod, then moved away, her steps fading down the stone flight.

Maurice turned down his own hall. The Abbey held its breath. And somewhere along the arcade, a softer breath moved—pads of fur on flagstone, whiskers lifted, eyes golden in the dark.

Meely had been listening all along.

***

The corridor lay open, long and cold, a hush between walls. She moved along its edge—pads light, flank still tender where the wound had not healed. The scar tugged with every step, a reminder of the night the air broke and claws met flesh not meant for them. The scent clung even now: copper, salt, and something darker.

Meely had marked it once with blood of her own, and it had marked her back.

Stone.

Ash.

And under it—there.

The thread she remembered.

Wrong, and yet familiar enough to draw her closer.

She breathed it in, slow, whiskers trembling.

And then—

I inhaled.

The change was sudden, like a shutter lifted. The hall was no longer distant, observed. It belonged to me. Cold stone pressed against my paws, the draft sharpened to a blade inside my nose. The thoughts that had circled me from without now rose within, my own voice carrying them.

I was not watching from the outside.

I was carried wholly *inside.*

Stone, oil, copper—scent tightened into memory; an older self rose with it: the other name I carry.

Lirae.

Gray fur. Golden eyes. The ordinary mask.

Meely.

Beneath it: a different light—auburn-gold like buried flame; the old violet that answers when called. The coat the world sees is a story I was told to wear.

In Magicia, some houses braid duty into living creatures. Not pets. Guardians. A vow to stalk, to suffer, to stand between breath and blade. They call it binding. I call it a road. I was given a shape; I chose it. I kept it. I sharpened it. When orders forget the living, I do not. I guard because I love.

Gwendlynn bound me first—to her daughter, Faye—by the old rite of guardianship. Resin and rain clung to Faye; ash at her cuffs; a laugh she saved for children. I learned the map of her footsteps, the weight in her silences, where courage frays and still holds.

And then—Leonarth.

The memory rose whole, called by scent. The boy asleep. Lamp-oil warm. Faye's palm at my brow. Her whisper shaping the binding across fur and bone—

Ligare Cor ad Cor.
(Bind heart to heart)

Da Matre custodia ad filio spiritum.
(From mother's keep to child's breath)

The words took and burned. My body answered first: tremor down the spine, shiver through the tail. Then the second veil, soft as falling snow—

Umbra Ambulare
(Walk in shadow)

Non Sciat.
(He cannot know)

Donec Silentium Frangatur.
(Until the silence breaks)

Glamour poured over me like frost. The ceremonial curl in my tail unlearned itself. Auburn-gold sank. Violet dimmed to ordinary golden. My coat dulled to kitchen-ash. What remained was a creature everyone could love.

Meely.

And yet, a few nights ago, the veil shivered—and Gwendlynn spoke my true name. I felt the stitch pull. A seam opened and closed: auburn-gold flickered beneath gray, violet pushed up through golden like a bruise of light—and then the mask held. She saw enough. She said it anyway. *Lirae.* The oath trembled but did not break.

Since the night Faye bound me, I have kept to eaves and gardens. Rafters. Hedges. I have watched him sleep and wake, hunt and hide, grieve and try again.

It was not chance.

Faye had trusted me with the small weight many seasons ago—a key sleeved in bramble-wood to hide its shine, kept for him until the hour ripened. Gwendlynn's tossed twig gave me cover. I did not fetch what she threw. I fetched what I chose. What I had promised.

The choir rose—three hallelujahs.

Stained glass gilded my gold; beneath, the old violet answered.

The boy's eyes found mine.

Now.

I slid through the sliver in the glass; he slipped after. Outside, away from incense and eyes, I laid the key at his feet—the first turn of the Abbey's gears.

I have bled for him. I will bleed again. The scar at my flank tugs when weather changes; it is how the body remembers its work.

Lirae is not gone.

She waits under the gray.

Listening.

Hunting.

Here.

And then—the world took its distance, *and I was no longer there.*

The wind turned.

Not iron. Not blood. Something else. Sweet at the edge, like ash dipped in honey. It threaded past the wound-copper, tempting her nose toward the sky.

Her whiskers twitched. The roof called.

She climbed. Claw. Stone. Ivy giving just enough. Scar pulling at her flank with every rise.

The night widened.

Below—the Abbey roofs, dark as folded wings. The river curling silver toward the horizon. Lanterns pricked in the distance, villages huddled like scattered prayers.

And beyond.

A glow.

Not close.

Not small.

Paris.

She could not see its streets—too far, leagues of field and frost between. But she felt it in the clouds: a restless shimmer, the breath of thousands at once. Bells swallowed by distance. Smoke traveling farther than sound.

She crouched at the ridge. Tail tight. Eyes golden, catching firelight that wasn't there.

The sweetness still clung to the wind. Not prey. Not stranger. Familiar.

Too familiar.

Her pupils widened. The sweetness didn't just ride the wind. It opened.

Color.

She saw it the way others hear music—a ribbon unfurling through the night. Green turned to violet. Gold trembled, split. Trails like auroras bending low, spilling over the stones, weaving paths only she could follow.

This was how scent lived for her. Not molecules. Not dust. Memory made visible. Every trail a story—fear sharp as iron-blue, bread warm as amber, blood burning copper-red. She could drown in it, if she stared too long. Sometimes she wanted to.

Was this magic? She never asked. She only knew the world had been written this way for her, since Faye's hand pressed the vow across her brow.

And when she needed more than vision, her body answered. A tail flick—sharp, slow, or curling—drew the lines tighter, made them sing. A low purr deepened them, thickened the color until it held weight. Not words. Never words. But power.

She crouched, breath steady, eyes locked to the violet-sweet ribbon. It swayed toward the east, then upward, climbing beyond the Abbey's roofline. She rose to follow, tail brushing stone like a brush marking lines.

The sky waited.

She leapt. Ridge to ledge. Slate to stone. The aurora-thread quivered, sweet and violet, pulling her downward again—not toward the cloister, but along the Abbey wall where the novices' windows opened to frost.

There.

The ribbon pooled thicker. Honey-warm, violet-amber. Her whiskers flared; she knew this scent, carried in wool and ink and the faint oil of candle wicks. The woman's space.

Mabelle.

She crouched at the sill, peered in. The bed neat, the robe folded. Shadows only. No breath moving the air.

But the sweetness lingered, as though the stones themselves had kept her. Stronger here than anywhere else.

She pressed her nose to the gap. Drew it in. The sweetness almost lulled her—almost.

Then—

Another thread.

Thin. Bitter-copper under the sugar. Slipped beneath, coiling around.

Her pupils snapped wide. The aurora flared jagged. This was no gentle trace of sleep or prayer. This was the same wrong copper she had bled to once before.

Her body remembered before thought could: flank aching, scar tugging. The vow answering in her bones.

When darkness neared, the vow did not whisper. It clawed. It tore. It made her whole body recoil with a warning older than choice.

She turned, tail lashing. The copper-thread was already moving, dragging itself along the air, slithering eastward. Toward stone and incense. Toward the statue that blessed with one hand and warned with the other.

Saint Elodia.

She dropped from the sill, claws sparking against slate, and followed.

The copper ribbon deepened as she neared the statue's shadow—where Saint Elodia's stone palm hovered in blessing that always felt like a warning. The air here was tight as thread drawn through bone. The violet-sweet of the woman's scent had pooled and thinned, pooled and thinned, as if someone had spooned it across the night.

And then she saw the figure.

Kneeling. Head bowed. Fingers worrying beads slow as breath.

Prayer.

She crept along the base stones, whiskers forward, tail a measured balance. Her aurora-sight trembled—violet pulling one way, iron-copper another, two veils crossing like rivers that should not meet.

The figure turned.

A face. Eyes.

Familiar. Too familiar.

The eyes that had watched her by the hearth. The hands that had cut heels of bread and let their heat into the bone of night. A mouth that knew the measure of silence. Features her body trusted before her mind would name them.

And beneath it, at the back of the eyes, a glint like a shard of winter.

She leapt.

The mouth moved first.

Paralysi temporalis.
(Temporary paralysis)

The word bit like frost.

Her body obeyed the wrong master. Limbs locked. Breath caught, a thin thread snagged in her throat. She hit the stones and did not land—she lay, every muscle turned to iron, the vow howling in a cage made of her own sinew.

The beads slid from the praying hand and became a loop.

It sank around her neck with the soft sound of ritual.

With something meant for blessing, her breath was bound.

The prayer did not stop. The lips kept moving, penance and murder sharing the same rhythm. A whisper threaded through the rosary's click—words not meant for her and exactly for her.

"Some debts are paid in warmth," the voice murmured, low enough to be stone. "Some are paid in silence."

A thumb pressed the knot against her throat.

"Tonight, little shadow, you pay for both."

Her claws could not answer. Her tail thrashed only in the mind that could not move. The aurora around the beads darkened—the copper stoked to black-red, the violet flaring, the sweet scent laced tight as a snare.

Sound shrank. Vision tunneled.

She felt the vow try to tear itself free—*protect, guard, breathe for him*—but the loop denied breath, and without breath even magic must bow.

The rosary tightened.

The world narrowed to three things: the rough bite of cord, the steady scrape of beads against fur, and the stone-face of a saint who blessed and warned and did not move.

Light bled at the edges of her sight.

Violet. Gold. A winter-blue like river ice.

Something inside her gave.

Not bone.

Not will.

The glamour.

It unstitched itself as the body failed. Gray loosened first, like ash shaken from coals. Auburn-gold rose where the strangling cord burned, sliding across her pelt in waves, each bead slipping over a newer, truer color. Golden bled to violet in her eyes—not a flare this time but a homecoming. The ordinary mask fell to the floor of her and cracked without sound.

Lirae surfaced.

The rosary dug deeper, the knot grinding. Her tongue edged out and could not reach air. Her heartbeat counted the last small numbers it could remember.

The figure leaned close. A breath touched her ear, warm as a kitchen ember.

"Shhhh," said the voice that had fed her, the voice that had waited in doorways. "This is the gentlest way."

Gentle.

The word broke something that was not her and not the night. A thought slid through her failing body—once, she had trusted that word.

The beads tightened once more.

She did not feel the last pull as pain. She felt it as a seam opening.

The world inverted.

The aurora that had always lived in the air rose from her now—violet-gold lifting from fur like smoke, threads tugging free, each a promise unspooling. They drifted toward a point she could not see and had always faced in sleep—the silent star, the first turning, the place Faye had named without naming.

The Source.

A hand, not here, not now, reached through the gold.

Faye's.

No speech. Just the warmth of palm to brow, the old rite stitched backwards in a mercy only the dead can manage.

Cor ad cor…

Her chest tried one last time to learn the air.

Exhale.

—and the world let go.

***

The body that had been Meely was no longer at the saint's feet. There was only the rosary lying slack in the statue's shadow and a faint shimmer, a soft violet bloom seared into the cord's grain like a bruise of light. The figure's hand hovered over it, fingertips trembling as if scorched by something that was not heat.

Footsteps.

A man's stride, hurried, steadying.

The figure jolted, head snapping toward the arcade. The beads slipped from their fingers and struck the stones with a hush like dropped prayer. In one motion the shadow turned and ran, swallow-quiet, the night taking the shape into itself as if it had been carved to fit there.

Maurice stepped into Saint Elodia's watch.

He slowed. The air held a strange sweetness under iron—not incense, not smoke, something that pressed memory against the ribs and called nothing by name.

He saw the beads first.

A rosary, dark wood worn to a polish by hands he did not know. It lay half in blessing's circle, half out—as if unsure which the night would allow.

He crouched. His palm hovered, then took it up.

The cord was warm.

Not heat-warm—held warm. As if whatever had just touched it had left a pulse.

He felt it—the faintest hum along the knot, a tremor he would have called grief if stones could grieve. The Abbey's quiet grammar stuttered here: charge, hold... remember.

"Strange," he said to no one, standing. The saint's shadow cut him in two: half in warning, half in grace.

He turned the beads once, twice, seeing nothing, understanding even less, but unable to let them go. The rosary seemed to want the line of his lifeline, the press of his pulse. He slipped it into his sleeve as if he owned it, or as if it owned him.

The arcade breathed out.

Maurice looked once more into the corners where night clung. Nothing moved. No whisper. No claw. No cat.

He drew his robe close against the frost and walked back toward his chamber. The rosary lay warm at his wrist, ticking as softly as a second heart.

Behind him, Saint Elodia kept his hand raised—blessing, warning—and said nothing at all.

***

Hours later, the Abbey had settled into the kind of silence that feels earned. Ash cooled in the braziers. Stone forgot the day. Maurice sat with his palm over the rosary he had tucked into his sleeve without understanding why he could not put it down. Every now and then, when his thumb found the knot, a faint hum carried up his lifeline, not warmth exactly, but something that wanted to reminisce.

A knock.

Not urgent. Familiar.

"Enter," he said, and the word came out softer than he meant.

Eloi stepped in with a tray and the night came with him: a small steam of broth, a heel of bread cut thick, the grace of someone who knows where to set things so they do not clang in the dark. He smiled in that way that warmed kitchens and lowered shoulders.

"I thought you hadn't eaten," Eloi said, placing the tray on the small table by the candle. "It helps, sometimes. Warmth where the night wants to keep its teeth."

Maurice almost said no—then saw the loaf, the simple covenant of it, and his body remembered the emberlight at the long table, the three of them tearing quarters from a whole. The bread we shared.

"Sit," Maurice said.

They sat with the old ease of a ritual that had never asked for words. Eloi broke the heel and tore it in two; steam lifted like prayer. He passed a piece to Maurice, kept one for himself. For a moment, the room felt small enough to hold only that—the human trick of keeping winter outside with soup and grain.

"You keep strange hours," Maurice said.

"I learned them from you," Eloi answered, a smile at one corner, and then his voice went somewhere quieter. "And from the Abbey itself. It breathes differently after midnight. As if the old stones evoke what they were before we named them."

Maurice looked up. "You hear it too."

Eloi nodded, eyes on the slow broth, as if admitting a secret without intending to. "Sometimes I forget which part of me was meant to knead the dough, and which..." He stopped. "And which was meant to listen."

"To what?"

"To the part of night that doesn't invite you. The part that waits."

Maurice tore the bread and put it to his mouth. It was good and humble and true. A sweetness at the edge he couldn't place, like a soft spice folded thin. He swallowed. It landed heavy.

Eloi's gaze slid from the bowl to the table where Maurice had laid the rosary beside the candle so it could dry. The beads were dark, the cord worn to polish by the hands of someone he did not know and would never meet. Eloi's hand moved toward it without thinking, the way a person reaches for something they've always put away at the end of the day.

His fingers touched the knot.

The beads thrummed. A faint violet bloom pulsed along the cord, then stilled.

Maurice's breath argued with his chest. The room tilted a fraction. He looked from the rosary to Eloi's hand and back. The hum ran up his thumb like grief that had learned to pretend to be anything else. Memory shoved its way in: Saint Elodia's shadow, the slack cord on stone, the air that tasted of sweetness laced with copper. The space where no body lay.

"Where did you find that?" Eloi asked, voice very soft.

Maurice did not answer. He watched Eloi's eyes. The candle made two small fires in them that should have been the same as always. They were not. There was a depth behind them now, something lean and winter-sharp that had not belonged to the man who warmed kitchens.

He set the bread down. His hand shook. Not from fear. From something in the throat that would not be soothed.

"Eloi," Maurice said, and the name was not a question and not an accusation. Just a thing that had to be said to make the room true.

Eloi looked at him as if they were both standing on a riverbank they had reached by mistake.

"Strange," Eloi murmured, thumb still resting on the knot. "How some things keep breath after breath leaves them. Like stone. Like vows." He lifted the beads, weighing them as if they were a word he had almost spoken and then saved for later. "Like bread."

Maurice's skin went colder, and the cold ran inward.

He tasted it now—under the crust and the kindness. Bitter's thin cousin. A sweetness that wasn't blessing. His stomach had already made a welcome of it. His hands turned foreign at the edges. He reached for the table's edge and found it too far.

"You broke it with me," Eloi said, not looking up. "In the kitchen. You pressed the heel into my palm and you said 'share it.' You said it like a permission, not an order. I have not forgotten the temperature of that sentence." He set the rosary down carefully. "We make liturgies out of small acts, don't we? Then we pretend we don't."

Maurice pushed the bowl away. The spoon slid, metal against glaze. His breath shortened, and with it the old instincts rose—run a ward, draw a counter, force the body to balance the dose—but the poison was ordinary, stubborn, cleverly chosen. It did not care for counter-rites. It knew the throat and the muscle before it knew the mind. He steadied his hand with the other. He would not dignify it by shaking.

"Why you," he said, each word placed as if it weighed more than the last. "After all these years… here, with us?"

Eloi's jaw worked once, as if he were chewing a memory.

"Because I was planted here," he said. "Long before I was allowed to know my own name. Some seeds are meant to bloom. Some are meant to strangle. I learned to be both." He glanced at the candle, as if listening for the sound tallow makes when it changes shape. "I learned your hours. Your kindness. Your silence."

"And the rest?" Maurice asked.

"The rest woke," Eloi said. "And when it woke, it remembered what it had been taught in a room where light does not come from windows." He left the chair and crossed to the narrow bookcase, as if distance might slow the truth. His fingers traced the spines without reading them.

He paused over a rolled vellum bound with red thread—one of the Abbey's old *Scriptae,* more rumor than record, the kind of thing that pretends to be a prayer until it remembers it's a map.

"Do you ever wonder," he said, "why Earth was severed in the first place?"

Maurice's mouth thinned. "Every day."

"Not because magic feared magic," Eloi said. He turned back, and the candle put the years they had shared into his face and stole them again. "Because magic feared something else. *You.*" He lifted a hand, not at Maurice alone, but at the shape he stood for: man, human, stubborn mind in a brittle body. "You make from nothing. You imagine without tether. Magic is inheritance and apprenticeship and cost. Creativity is… air. It walks into a room with you whether you deserve it or not."

"Birthright," Maurice said. His tongue was heavy. "So we punished birthright."

"We protected a world from drowning in its own gift," Eloi answered, and for a heartbeat there was an ache in it that did not belong to doctrine. "You call it punishment. I call it a wall that kept a flood from eating its children."

"And who chose where to put the wall?" Maurice's breath rasped; the ceiling blurred, then steadied because he would permit nothing else. "The man who owns the water? The Inquisitor who learned how to cup the river in his palm and make a creed out of it?"

Eloi's eyes slid away and came back with winter at their bottom. "Someone had to choose."

"Not forever," Maurice whispered. "Not without witness. Not with books burned and names erased because a single man can't bear the idea that a child might draw a door better than he can carve a lock."

The candle guttered. The room leaned and then stood up straight again with effort it should not have needed. The bread on the tray cooled as if embarrassed to be part of it.

Eloi stepped closer, not threatening, not kind. Contradiction lived in his shoulders like a thing with a pulse. "You taught me how to keep a fire banked so it lasts through morning prayers," he said. "You taught me to listen to the way stone holds heat. And still, when the hour came, the part of me that listens bowed to the part of me that answers." He inclined his head, a gesture that could have been respect in another year. "I am sorry that it is you."

"Are you?" Maurice said.

Eloi's mouth tightened. "I am… many things." He did not look away, and that was somehow worse.

The old habit rose in him then, the reflex to tidy the air. He breathed a word that was not prayer, so the night would not bring anyone to a sound it did not understand:

Velare Sonum
(Veil the sound)

The candle's flame narrowed, as if instructed to stay quiet.

Maurice felt the room go mute around the edges. He looked at the rosary. It lay like a small night on the table. He did not know if he had the strength to lift it, or what it would mean if he did.

A knock came anyway.

Light. Then again. Harder.

Gwendlynn.

"Father Maurice?" Her voice blurred by the charm and the wood.

Eloi stilled. Calculation and something like grief warred in his face and neither won.

The poison made a river out of Maurice's bones. He reached across the table because there was nothing else to do, and his hand caught the chain at Eloi's throat.

A pendant. Small. Simple. The metal had the feel of a word said through teeth.

Eloi's hand flew up, too slow.

Maurice tore.

The chain held for the first heartbeat and then learned who he had been before he learned to be kind. It snapped.

The pendant struck the floor and sang a thin note only the wrong ears love. Maurice's palm came down on it with all the authority of old vows. The glass in it spidered under the heel of a hand that had written rites no one should learn alone. Shards bit his skin. Blood brightened the floor and made the metal honest.

The light that lived in it went out like a held breath released too fast.

Eloi swayed. The room took a piece of him back. Not all. Enough that fear found his eyes and did not apologize.

The knock turned to the iron sound of a latch forced. The door took a breath and gave way. Gwendlynn came through with the kind of quiet that breaks after it has held too long.

Eloi's gaze flicked to her—to the beads on the table—to Maurice's bleeding hand—back to the window.

He moved.

The narrow casement banged once against stone and night swallowed him at ground level, hedge-dark, river-cold, gone.

Gwendlynn crossed the room in three strides that were not steps but decisions. She went to Maurice's side and caught his shoulders as if they could remember the old habit of standing.

"What happened?" she said, voice too even for her eyes.

"The bread," he managed. His mouth hurt with the word. "The bread we shared."

She looked to the tray, to the heel half-eaten, to the rosary, to the floor where glass glittered like a line of stars he couldn't name for her.

"Maurice," she said again, and the name broke in the middle and kept going.

"Listen," he said, and his hand—the bleeding one—found her wrist with the old gentleness he had reserved for children and rituals and the places where a life needs to be touched to stay inside itself. "Listen, Gwen. There isn't time to make the perfect speech."

"Then make the true one."

He almost laughed and the breath it would have needed went somewhere else. He nodded instead.

"The book they burned," he said. "The one Siroth brags about. *Magicariums Scriptae*. It isn't ash. It breathes. He did it because a single book that can be taught is a world he can't own."

Her grip tightened. "Where, Maurice? Where is the path?"

He managed a faint smile, blood already drying along his palm. "I can't give you a map, Gwendlynn. And if I could, it would be less than you deserve. Maps hand out answers. What I leave you is harder—the way to see what was always there, hidden in the weave."

His breath faltered. The words cost him now.

"Faye… she was looking the right way," he said. "Not ahead. Back through what everyone else passed over."

A faint smile, already fading.

"Follow that."

He lifted the rosary, crimson arcing over the beads, and set it in her hand. "The tapestry only pretends to be prophecy. It is more. A map, yes—but not the kind that points. The kind that teaches eyes to notice what they once ignored. The door will open. You will cross. And when you do…"

His breath faltered, then steadied with a last effort. "…watch the weft, not the color. Align the four—the pendants, the scroll, the key, the cloth. Then the hidden lines will take shape. Not a straight road. The honest ones never are."

Gwendlynn bowed her head, tears striking his hand. "You should have told me sooner. About all of us. About this path that we were meant to walk."

He touched her cheek with trembling fingers, eyes glistening. "I was wrong to shield you. Forgive me."

Her breath caught, not with hesitation but with the memory of all he had withheld. "I know I shouldn't," she whispered, voice raw with the echo of years, "but I do. I forgive you—not because it cost me nothing, but because I see now the cost we are all willing to carry. Our lives, our silence, even our sins—so that one day the fragile order between realms might breathe again."

His chest eased, the weight of secrecy finally broken.

Gwendlynn's face composed itself because someone had to. "And once we restore the *Scriptae?*"

"You make it known, Gwen," he whispered. "You let boys read it who have never held a wand. You let mothers argue with it over stew. You let men who have not been chosen learn how to choose. Magic is not a throne. It is a language. It belongs to mouths." He closed his eyes once, hard, against something that didn't matter anymore. "Siroth can keep a crown. He cannot keep a hymn."

Her forehead touched his. The candle made their shadows one. "Stay," she said, as if it were a spell she had the right to cast.

He smiled because he had learned to, late and well. "I will," he said. "In the hands that carry what I couldn't."

His chest gathered itself. Memory pressed through him—Faye's laugh in rain, a boy who apologized for existing and learned to stand anyway, Mabelle cutting sorrow into pieces small enough to swallow, bread broken into fourths, then eighths, then light. He felt the Abbey's grammar touch him one last time: charge, hold, release.

He looked at Gwendlynn, at the beads in her hand, at the door that had finally learned how to open when it was called.

"Cor..." he said, and the word didn't need finishing.

Her lips shaped the rest. "*ad cor.*"

He obeyed the oldest instruction in the body.

Exhale.

***

The candle gave a single long bend, as if listening, then stood straight. The room did what rooms do when something large leaves them: it held still. Gwendlynn's breath did not, and the beads in her palm were warmer than they had any right to be. The shattered pendant bled its last thin shine into the floorboards; beyond the window, hedge and frost recovered their shape from the shadow that had cut through them.

Somewhere else in the Abbey, a bell remembered how to be a bell. It did not ring. It waited.

Gwendlynn closed Maurice's eyes with the same care she had used to open books he had once been afraid to share. The rosary hummed once in her hand—a faint violet ache—and then quieted, as if deciding to keep its secret a little longer.

"The bread we shared," she said, and it sounded like a vow.

Outside, the Seine and the Essonnes kept their patient confluence, as if the rivers had not learned what night now carried—that Maurice had exhaled into silence, and Keralis had already taken his place among the living myths of Magicia.

Chapter Twenty-Five

"Threads of the Severed"

The Abbey bells tolled unevenly, their metal voices warped by the damp air, as if even bronze could stumble under grief. The sound carried over the cloister roofs and down into the nave, where incense clung to the rafters and turned every breath into smoke. The coffin lay before the altar, plain wood veined with wax drippings from the vigil candles. No ornament, no carvings—Maurice would never have allowed them. His life had been spent hiding in the ordinary, and now the ordinary had claimed him whole.

Leonarth stood in the press of villagers and novices, the tide of bodies shifting around him like water too heavy to swim through. He tried to listen to the words of the abbot, but all he could hear was the silence between them: a cough stifled in a sleeve, a sob swallowed into a shoulder, the scrape of shoes against stone as mourners tried not to echo. Silence had weight. It pressed down, harder than the bell's toll.

He searched for Maurice's eyes one last time and saw only stillness. It wasn't the stillness of sleep. It was the kind that turned a body into something else entirely, as if the man he had known had already stepped into another grammar.

Leonarth's empathy, the sense he had never understood, stirred restlessly. Every grief in the nave pressed against him, scraping like invisible glass. His hand slipped into his pocket and closed around the small green shard he always carried—the dull piece of glass he'd found years ago and never thrown away. It felt heavier than it should have, steadying nothing, answering nothing. He wanted to breathe for them all, and couldn't.

Beside him, Mattheon clenched his fists so tightly that his knuckles shone white. His jaw worked as if he were chewing anger instead of air. Leonarth wanted to reach for him, to say something—anything—but the words died before they formed. What comfort could he offer when he himself felt as though a vital thread had been cut?

Gwendlynn stood further ahead, her back a line of iron, her eyes fixed on the coffin without blinking. Grief had carved her rigid, as if her sorrow was too vast to show, so she poured it into stillness instead. Ava clasped her hands until her knuckles trembled, the beads of her rosary slipping like water between her fingers. Mabelle's lips moved faintly, shaping a prayer she never finished.

The nave was thick with soundless expectation. Even the children were quiet, though a few whispered to each other about the Abbey's missing cat. Their eyes darted toward the side aisles, searching for the small shadow that would never pass through again. Leonarth's throat tightened. Even absence had its own ritual.

The abbot's voice broke through, brittle and distant. "We commend our brother to the earth, that he may rise in the company of saints..." The words echoed once, then drifted over the guardians without finding a place to rest. They carried a different weight—secrets, guilt, knowledge the others could not imagine. For them, Maurice was more than priest. He was Inquisitor, betrayer, protector, confessor, Keralis. And now he was gone, taking too much with him.

One candle at the coffin's side sputtered violently, flaring so high it scorched the air before collapsing into darkness. A collective gasp rippled through the congregation. A novice crossed herself. The abbot stumbled mid-sentence, but pressed on as if nothing had happened. Leonarth felt the hair rise on his arms. The Abbey was not at rest.

The abbot's final words gathered themselves again, faint but formal, and when the last amen was spoken, the congregation began to thin. The nave emptied slowly, the echo of shuffling feet fading as doors opened onto the cloister walks. One by one, the candles were snuffed until only a few stubborn flames clung to the gloom. Leonarth watched them resist the darkness, each flicker a heartbeat that refused to stop.

Rain whispered against the stained glass as the coffin was borne out into the cloister, not loud enough to drown the hymns, but insistent. The colors glowed faintly though no sunlight shone through them. For a moment, Leonarth thought he saw shapes shift in the glass—lines that did not belong, threads weaving themselves into patterns too quick to follow. He blinked, and the colors settled. Unease remained, thrumming beneath the incense haze.

The coffin was lowered into the cloister's earth after the hymns ended. Villagers wept openly now, their grief unbound. Leonarth felt every sob like a stone dropped into his chest. Gwendlynn did not weep. Ava did not. Even Mabelle kept her gaze on the ground as though afraid to look up. Only Mattheon trembled, caught between fury and despair, his fists never loosening.

At last the villagers were gone. The novices withdrew. The abbot bowed once and left them in silence. Only the guardians and the two boys remained. The coffin was covered, the soil tamped, and a stone laid at its head.

The gravestone caught Leonarth's eye first. Freshly carved, wet with rain, it read in clear Latin letters: Father Maurice Adelaar. But as the incense drifted and the last bell tremor died, the letters shifted. For the guardians' eyes alone, the name rippled and re-formed: Keralis Omerian.

No one spoke. They didn't need to. They had already known the truth of him, had lived in the shadow of his dual name for years. But seeing it etched in stone—ordinary and extraordinary at once—was a benediction the villagers would never glimpse. Maurice, priest to the world. Keralis, Inquisitor to them. Both true, both gone.

Leonarth let his eyes linger on the name, on the way the stone seemed to breathe under it. For the first time since the bells began, he felt that Maurice was not entirely gone. Not entirely. Something had been planted here—something waiting.

And in the silence of the Abbey, where grief pressed like stone, Leonarth thought he heard the faintest tremor in the air. Not a voice, not a word. Just the quiet strain of walls learning how to hold something larger than themselves.

The rain eased, leaving the cloister quiet but restless, as if the Abbey itself were waiting for someone to speak. They all stood around the gravestone, its name still shimmering faintly with the truth no villager would ever see.

Gwendlynn's fingers closed around the beads Maurice had pressed into her hand. They pulsed with a warmth that was not her own, as though he had left one last ember in them. She looked at each face in turn—Ava rigid with control, Mabelle withdrawn, Mattheon smoldering, Leonarth open and trembling.

Her voice cut through the silence, steady, deliberate.

"His last words were not only for me. They were for all of us. You need to hear them."

Mattheon shifted, shoulders tense, but he didn't speak.

Gwendlynn lifted the rosary slightly, the violet gleam catching in the half-light. "He said the book they burned—the one Siroth flaunted as ash—was not gone. The *Magicariums Scriptae* lives," she said. "Hidden. Breathing."

Her fingers tightened on the beads. "Not as a thing you can point to. Not as a relic waiting to be claimed. Maurice said it was never meant to belong to those who hold power."

She looked at them then, each in turn. "It must pass into hands that have never ruled. Into kitchens. Into schools. Into voices that were never chosen."

A pause.

"Magic is not a throne," she said softly. "It is a language. And languages survive by being spoken."

Her gaze drifted, unfocused, as if following a path already walked. "Faye understood that. Whatever she began—whatever she was searching for—it wasn't finished."

Her words hung there. Even the rain paused on the glass, sliding slowly.

Ava exhaled, her lips barely moving. "And the tapestry?"

Gwendlynn turned toward her. "Not prophecy. Instruction. It trains the eyes to see what they ignore. He told me: *watch the weft, not the color*. Align the four relics—pendant, scroll, key, and cloth—and the hidden lines will show themselves. Not a straight road. The honest ones never are."

Her voice softened, the iron giving way to something more fragile. "There is one more truth you should carry. About Meely."

The name cracked the air like a child's memory. Mattheon stiffened. Leonarth's chest ached.

"She was never just a stray," Gwendlynn went on. "Her true name was Lirae. She was a guardian—older than any of us, older than even Maurice's vows. She hid herself in fur and silence because the world notices a cat less than a sword. But she watched. She waited. And when the moment came, she gave her life to shield what mattered."

Mabelle's breath caught, her hand pressed to her lips. Ava closed her eyes, as if the name itself was a prayer.

"She died as Lirae," Gwendlynn whispered, "but she lived as both—the watcher at your heels, and the sentinel none of us could see clearly until it was too late. Do not call her lost. Call her what she was: the last of her kind, a guardian who chose love as her weapon."

Gwendlynn's grip on the beads tightened until the violet hum bit into her skin.

"And his last words carried another truth. Not about who he was—we all knew that. *Keralis*. The Fifth Inquisitor. But about why he was the one Siroth came for first."

Her eyes swept the nave, then landed on Leonarth.

"He said Siroth knew he was the last who truly understood the rites of forced succession—the declarations, the lies that claim a bloodline can be ended by decree. As long as Maurice lived, that knowledge lived. Siroth feared it more than he feared any heir. So he silenced it. He killed the teacher before the students could be taught."

Her voice broke, then steadied.

"But what Siroth did not know," Gwendlynn said, "is that the burning was not the end. The Magicariums Scriptae was not erased."

"Every glyph. Every line of the ritual. Not held on a page, but carried—hidden in plain silence."

"That is why Maurice begged us to seek what remains. Because once that knowledge passes into every hand, every voice, it can no longer be silenced. Not by a crown. Not by a blade. Not even by death."

The gravestone shimmered faintly again, two names laid over each other like wounds that could not heal. Maurice. Keralis. Both truths, both claimed.

The silence that followed was heavier than bells. Even the gravestone seemed to bow under it—as if one stone could not bear two names: one etched, one forbidden.

Leonarth's throat caught, because he could still hear Maurice's voice inside Gwendlynn's words.

Mabelle's hands folded tighter. "There's something here," she said quietly. "Isn't there?"

Gwendlynn's gaze lifted—not to the stone, but beyond it, toward the nave, its old rafters visible through the open arches that carried centuries of chant. "He called it liminal," she said. "Not forged by spell or ritual. Born."

She let the word settle before continuing. "When human grief or wonder grows too heavy for the world to contain, the fabric thins. A seam forms. That is what we stand upon here."

Her voice lowered. "Saint-Spire is not holy by chance. Compassion has layered itself here for centuries, until the walls could no longer bear it without answering."

From the nave beyond the arches, stone seemed to breathe with her, sighing faintly.

"Two kinds of doors," she went on. "Resonant ones, born of beauty, kindness, discovery. And shattered ones, born of wounds too sharp to heal. The first open toward light. The second toward shadows. Neither can be ignored."

Mattheon's fists finally unclenched. His voice, when it came, was raw. "And you expect us to walk through one of these seams? Just because a dying man's breath told you so?"

Gwendlynn's green eyes fixed on him, unwavering. "Not because he said so. Because he showed us how. Because your bloodlines are already tied to the crossing. You and Leonarth. You are not asked—you are *chosen by the world itself.*"

Mattheon's jaw tightened, his breath uneven. He turned toward Leonarth, looking for denial, for escape. But Leonarth's face was steady. Pale, but steady.

"We go together," Leonarth said quietly. "Or not at all."

The rosary hummed in Gwendlynn's palm. A candle guttered, flared, and held. The Abbey seemed to lean closer, listening.

Ava's hand went to the satchel at her side, her fingers brushing the folded scroll inside. "Then we gather the relics. Tonight."

Mabelle drew the tapestry closer to her chest, the fabric whispering softly as it shifted. "And we align them. As he said."

Gwendlynn nodded once, firm. "Below. In the Chapel of the Veil. The seam has always run warmer there. Maurice knew it. The Abbey knows it still."

Mattheon's breath shuddered. He wanted to protest, to flee, to deny it all. But no one offered him that escape. Not even Mabelle.

"Fine," he muttered. "We'll see this through. But if anything feels wrong—"

Leonarth touched his sleeve, just enough to tether him. "You'll tell me first."

Mattheon's eyes flicked to his, shadowed, uncertain. Then he gave the smallest nod.

The rain tapped once more against the glass, and the gravestone behind them seemed to settle, the two names layered as one. Maurice. Keralis. Claimed once—now watching.

And the Abbey trembled again, faint but real, as if the walls had grown too thin to hold the seam back.

***

Hours later, the air beneath the Abbey had changed.

The Chapel of the Veil was round and hollow, a throat made for echoes. Torches flickered along the ribs of its vault, light bending in and out as if unsure where to fall. Every step carried the hush of centuries: feet that had walked to vow, to plead, to leave something behind.

They gathered in the circle without instructions.

Ava pressed her satchel to the stone, trembling, and withdrew the scroll—Faye's letter. The parchment pulsed faintly, as if it disliked being shut too long.

Mabelle set down the tapestry. The weave exhaled dust and sorrow. Then from her cloak she drew the Root of Orreth, heavy, faceted, veined with dull light that quickened the instant it touched the cloth.

Gwendlynn knelt, the key cold against her palm, the last relic Maurice had pressed into her keeping. She laid it at the tapestry's edge as though lowering a body into earth.

Leonarth hesitated—then reached into his pocket. He did not know why. He only knew the weight had been with him too long to keep. He set the small green shard among the others and drew his hand back quickly, as if afraid it might be noticed.

No one spoke.

Matt stood just outside the circle, his hands empty, his jaw tight. He told himself it didn't matter. That he hadn't been asked. That not everything was meant for him.

And the pendants they wore—hers, Ava's, Mabelle's—began to hum.

No chants. No positions. No knowing.

Just instinct.

Leonarth's chest throbbed with it. *Put them closer,* the air seemed to say. *Closer.*

"Together," Gwendlynn whispered. Not command—plea.

The relics edged toward each other, as though magnets had been turned in the right direction at last. Scroll touched cloth. Cloth kissed key. The Root of Orreth lay against the woven border. The small green shard rested where it fell, unnoticed—and perfectly placed.

The floor throbbed.

The tapestry refused to be tapestry.

Threads lifted. Not color, but weft. Lines rose and bent and folded. Curves that were not curves. Roads that wanted to be walked.

The Abbey inhaled.

Dust rose.

Candles bent.

The pendants sang.

Not melody. Chord.

Ava's hand shot to her chest. Her pendant blazed, brighter than the rest. Light spilled into the weave—*answering at last.*

Gwendlynn watched with a narrow, astonished hunger. "It knows the hand that gave it," she murmured, almost to herself.

The floor shivered. Dust lifted and fell, a soft rain that never learned to be loud. Somewhere above, a crack sounded like a string breaking on a too-long-held note.

The seam opened. Not a doorway, not any shape a mason would bless—a tear, stitched into sight, a fault line revealing itself as a path.

It trembled with luminous pressure, the color of unstained glass waiting for morning.

Ava's hand found Leonarth's sleeve. "Do you feel it?"

"Yes."

"What is it?"

"Invitation."

Gwendlynn's voice was steadier than her hands. "The relics answer in their own order. *Pendant leads. Scroll observes. Key admits. Cloth governs.*"

Mattheon blinked. "In words?"

"In conduct," she said, almost guessing. "Gentleness first. Then witness. Then courage. Then surrender."

He made a face that wanted to be a laugh and failed. "Right. So not me."

Leonarth's mouth twitched. "You more than you think."

The door pulsed once, like a tide deciding itself. The Chapel of the Veil groaned around them—not protest, warning. The Abbey had never been asked to hold this much weight at once: the night's two deaths; the gathered relics; the will of three guardians and two heirs determined not to fail.

"Now," Gwendlynn said. "Leonarth, Ava, Mabelle—you three first. Your threads pulled hardest."

Mabelle's eyes flicked, not fear, not quite—an old caution showing teeth. She closed her fingers tighter around the Root of Orreth, then unrolled the tapestry's fold with her free hand. Both relics glimmered faintly, reluctant twins. She nodded.

Ava drew a breath that unhooked something in her chest. She pressed the scroll against her heart once, as if it were a living thing, and whispered: "*Witness.*"

Leonarth stepped closer to the seam. It wasn't only light; it was pressure turned gentle, the sense of a room that wanted him inside it at last. He could hear something like a chord hiding under the torches, the ribs-and-throat frequency that only old places learn to sing. Maurice used to call it the Abbey's grammar.

Charge. Hold. Release.

The words seared into Leonarth's ribs. His lips moved before his mind caught them:

"Praecipe. Sustine. Dimitte."

No one reacted. No one even seemed to hear. He had fallen into a trance, eyes unfocused, mouth spilling syllables he did not know.

The seam widened.

The tapestry leaned toward him—no breeze, but the fringe lifted as if curious. Ava's pendant lanced brighter, spilling narrow threads that braided themselves into the seam until the seam accepted them. The scroll's twine shivered, as if deciding whether to break. Gwendlynn pressed the key against the weave; the cloth drank it whole.

The chapter house did not like that.

A low moan rounded the room, the sort you feel in the knees. A hairline crack whispered up the nearest column. Powder sifted onto Mabelle's shoulder. She brushed it away too quickly, jaw set.

"We underestimated the load," Gwendlynn said. Not panic, diagnosis. "The place is carrying more than crossing."

"Can it hold?" Mattheon asked, voice thin.

"For a breath," she said. "For one."

Leonarth looked from face to face—Ava's set courage, Mabelle's guarded composure, Mattheon's angry hope, Gwendlynn's command braided with sorrow. A steadiness he did not recognize in himself settled like a cloak over shaking shoulders.

We go together. Or not at all.

He offered his hand to Ava. She took it, fingers cold and strong. He offered his other to Mabelle. She hesitated a fraction, then shifted the Root of Orreth into her left palm and set her right in his.

The seam's pressure turned welcoming. The room's chord found its third. The light thickened, not dazzling but clear enough to walk into without flinching.

"Step," Gwendlynn said.

Leonarth stepped.

There was one more thing Maurice had told her.

One thing she had never shared. One she might never share.

It was not meant for hope.

Her lips shaped the beginning of it—and chose silence.

Another tremor, and the seam did not feel like walking into light. It felt like walking into pressure that turned to welcome—as if the world had been holding its breath, and at last exhaled into him. His chest flared with it. Ava followed, the scroll pressed against her heart, her pendant burning like a captive star. Mabelle came last, tapestry half-unrolled, the Root of Orreth veined with reluctant fire in her hand.

For a heartbeat, it worked.

The tear in the air stretched wide enough to accept them. The relics hummed in chorus. The pendants chimed, three notes finding each other in the dark. Even the cracked stone seemed to brace itself, as if agreeing to bear this weight a moment longer.

But grief is heavier than relics.

The Abbey moaned—deep, grinding, the sound of centuries shifting in their sleep. The columns trembled. Dust sloughed from ribs of stone. A torch toppled, sputtering against the floor.

"Too much," Gwendlynn said, low but sure. "The place is breaking."

Mattheon staggered, eyes wide as the seam's edges flickered. "Then pull them back—"

"No," she snapped, sharper than she meant. "If we sever now, the weave collapses and takes us with it. All of us."

The tear flared again, but no longer pale. Its light was threaded with shadow, black veins crawling like ink spilled into water. The chapter house reeled under it.

Ava cried out, clutching her pendant. Mabelle's tapestry shuddered, half its threads glowing, half burning as if memory itself could char.

The seam pulsed, confused.

Resonant. Shattered. Both.

"Leonarth!" Gwendlynn called. "Keep walking!"

He pulled Ava with him, their hands bound, Mabelle close behind. For one radiant instant, the seam bent to them, opening clean, light unfolding into a path they could take.

And then the Abbey remembered.

Maurice. Lirae. Two guardians dead in one night. Their weight pressed into the stone, into the chants, into the seam.

Light twisted dark.

The first column gave way, stone screaming as it split. The floor lurched. The seam buckled into two halves—one bright, one blackened.

"Go!" Gwendlynn shoved Mattheon forward, toward Leonarth's hand. For an instant, the boys clasped each other—tethered. Then the stone under them ripped.

Leonarth's fingers slid. Mattheon's grip tore loose.

"No!"

Ava's scream split the air as Leonarth, Ava, and Mabelle tumbled into the lighted half of the seam. Their figures blazed, then vanished.

The dark side yawned wide. Gwendlynn and Mattheon fell through flame that wasn't flame but memory—burning pages, shouts in a voice not yet theirs.

The chapter house collapsed above them.

Stone poured like water. Glass rained down, its saints shattering into a thousand unblessed pieces. The Root of Orreth rang once against the floor—wrenched from Mabelle's hand by the seam itself—before being swallowed into its dark pull. The scroll flared, then disappeared into Ava's arms. The key clattered in Gwendlynn's palm and was gone.

The chapel itself gave up its shape.

***

Leonarth hit ground that was not ground, breath driven out of him. Light steadied into something like meadow air—sharp, clean, unreal. Ava was beside him, coughing, scroll clutched tight. Mabelle stood already, tapestry folded against her chest, her pendant humming too loud.

Safe.

Together.

But not whole.

"Mattheon—" Leonarth turned back. There was no seam, only silence.

Mabelle's face was unreadable in the new light. Ava pressed her pendant as though it might tell her what to do next.

***

Gwendlynn fell hard into fire that became sound, sound that became memory, and memory that became past.

Stone dissolved beneath her into streets broken by conflict. Smoke clawed the sky, torches flickering along ruined walls. A hall loomed ahead, banners torn, colors stripped of meaning by dissent. The ground still smelled of iron, as though blood had written itself into the stones and refused to fade.

Mattheon crashed beside her, blood streaking his temple, his hands braced in dust and ash. He dragged in a breath and pushed himself upright, eyes darting over the wreckage as if the world had shattered and reassembled incorrectly.

Gwendlynn was already on her knees. The key lay clenched in her fist, colder than it had ever been, its weight anchoring her to the moment as the air around them settled into an unfamiliar silence.

Something struck the ground between them with a dull, deliberate thud.

Mattheon flinched. Gwendlynn did not.

The Root of Orreth rested in the dust, its faceted surface dark, unlit—but present. Not dropped. Not carried. Arrived.

Mattheon stared at it, then at his empty hands. "I didn't—"

"You didn't," Gwendlynn said quietly.

The Root lay where it had chosen to be.

Mattheon swallowed. "Where are we?" His voice cracked on the last word.

Gwendlynn's breath snagged. She turned slowly, scanning. Nothing was whole. Nothing wished to be known. An arena wrapped in silence. Streets emptied by something else she could not name, yet she recognized. The air shimmered as if it had not decided what century it belonged to.

Her heart lurched with recognition she refused to name. She almost saw the shape of it—a throne toppled, a crown cast aside, a knife raised in smoke—but the vision slipped away before she could seize it.

Her throat ached. She wanted to lie to Mattheon, to call it a dream, a vision, anything but this.

"I... I don't know." Her voice was thin, unconvincing even to her own ears.

Then softer, almost a prayer, almost a surrender:

"*Elsewhen.*"

***

Above, the chapter house of Saint-Spire gave way. Stone groaned, pillars broke, the vaulted ceiling folded into ruin. Dust poured through cracks and swallowed the chamber whole. But the greater Abbey stood. Bells remained. Villagers lived. Only the sacred hall—the chamber that had tried to hold too much grief—was lost.

Where it had stood, silence smoldered, but it hummed faintly instead—the sound of grief turned permanent.

The seam was gone. But not closed. It had changed.

Saint-Spire was no longer only sanctuary. It had become a wound. It felt—dangerously—like the beginnings of a Shattered Door.

***

And somewhere in the marrow of the world, the prophecy stirred. Ancient words that had once lain dormant uncoiled, reshaping themselves around new truths.

Bloodlines divided. Guardians undone. Light torn from shadow. Shadow torn from light. The veil does not part without cost.

The voice of fate bent low, whispering into the future:

The Heir That Never Was… became the one that had to be.

EPILOGUE

The sky over Magicia shifted without warning. Clouds gathered where there had been none, their edges bruised dark against the upper air. Wind threaded the spires of Virelia with a low, unsettled sound, as if the city were remembering a storm it had not yet lived.

Far from light, beneath the Hall of Accord, silence held its breath. The Chamber of Silence did not reflect. It absorbed.

Black stone drank the glow of sigils etched deep into its walls, their patterns visible only when one did not look directly at them. The floor was colder than memory, and the chill rose through the soles of his feet, threading up his spine as if the chamber itself were taking measure of him.

A man stood alone before the Mirror of Edresk.

At the first tremor in the Veil, he lifted his head.

Eyes opened. Black. Endless.

The mirror did not show him the passage—only the consequence of it.

A smile touched his mouth. Not with joy. With confirmation.

"So… they crossed."

www.ingramcontent.com/pod-product-compliance
Lightning Source LLC
LaVergne TN
LVHW100505110826
845146LV00002B/518

* 9 7 9 8 9 9 3 6 9 5 2 1 1 *